A Bloody Summer

By
John C Chislett

To my mother,

without whose endless,
but welcome, criticism and encouragement,
this would never have been written.

Love and appreciation to my wife, Teresa,
for her constant patience and inspiration.

Thanks to Steve Jones for the cover
and technical help.

English Patented Collier Revolver
Circa 1819
(Photo taken by the author, with kind permission of
The Victoria and Albert Museum, London)

PROLOGUE

A wet winter, a dry spring,
A bloody summer and no king.

Irish Prophecy for 1798

"Zero, Echo, come in, *please.*"

Sarah's 'please' unnerved Pete. She was feeling the pressure too and he needed her to be strong. She was carrying him.

Covert operations in Northern Ireland could change from the mundane to the deadly in seconds. Unlike other war zones, it was all too much like home. A cosy country pub, an inner city housing estate, both seemed innocent enough, but for the IRA sniper on the roof or the bomb in the pram.

For Pete, it was one tour too many. SAS, Paras', he'd done it all. Now his nerve had gone and he knew it. The blackouts, the flashbacks, only his partner Sarah knew the truth. He just needed to finish this one last tour, just hold it together a bit longer.

Squashed together in the little old Chevette, watching an arms dump, the two operators needed a decision. A vehicle containing two men had passed down the country lane towards it. Go in and risk their cover or hold off and miss a pick up?

"Echo, Zero, read you. Remain two up complete," the radio crackled. Stay put and do nothing.

The sweat was running down Pete's back, he put his hand to the window handle.

Sarah shook her head. "Too risky, they'll hear the radio."

She was trying to make contact and it was likely the Section Head was off site. The Operations Officer wouldn't make a decision.

"It's always the bloody same. We sweat our arses off waiting for some action and when it finally comes, we can't move because some Rupert's on the sodding golf course."

Pete had no time for officers and had felt that by joining 14 Intelligence Company he would be able to operate with more independence. Usually it was true, but this was becoming complicated.

A local farmer, at huge personal risk, had made them aware of an arms dump on his land and an Observation Point had been set up, about half a mile away. A four man IRA Active Service Unit was known to be operational in this area and they hoped to catch them red handed. But it wasn't that simple. It could be a set up. That would render them useless for undercover operations in the Province.

To make it worse, they had been ordered to be extra cautious. Recently, in a similar situation, a farmer's son had been shot dead in error. Nonetheless Pete and Sarah were under considerable pressure to ensure that the weapons did not fall into enemy hands.

"Let me have a go," said Pete and leaned into the microphone, concealed in the sun visor over the driver's side of the car. "Zero this is Oscar." Pete's frustration made him break procedure. "If we don't make a move soon, they'll be away across the fields. Give us the go ahead or we'll go in anyway!"

"Negative Oscar. Await authority. Is that clear?"

Reluctantly Pete double clicked the mike to acknowledge his acquiescence.

His hand was shaking. This was supposed to be a routine operation, but then nothing ever was in Northern Ireland. Sarah was not her name and Pete wasn't his. She did not know his background nor he, hers. A woman partner! They were best behind desks or, better, over them, but this one was different. Cool and a good driver, he knew she had saved his life when she'd caught him blacking out, in an alley just off the Falls Road. Unable to stand up and draw his weapon, she'd dragged him away, until he came round. She had other uses too. On surveillance, in the Catholic estates, a couple necking was much less conspicuous than two hairy ex paras' reading the paper and farting.

Precious minutes passed. His shirt was soaked. For the first time in his life Pete started thinking about a 'normal' job, a home with a wife and kids.

Still the radio remained silent.

Sarah searched patiently through the windscreen for any sign of activity. Her hand resolute on the steering wheel, his constantly moving between the tick in his eye and the concealed weapons.

"Echo, Zero. OP possible …" The Observation Point had sighted another car approaching their position.

"This is crap. Why can't we talk direct?" moaned Pete.

The radio link was only with the centre. Provisional IRA receivers could easily pick up uncontrolled radio. This system was more secure, but information was relayed via a middleman. It caused delays and made dialogue difficult.

"Affirmative Echo. Charlie 2 mobile …" The new vehicle was turning into the lane, where they were waiting.

"The bastards. We've been set up." Pete pulled the Browning pistol out of his shoulder holster and slid it under his right thigh, just the butt protruding. A hand movement to his leg was less obvious than reaching inside his jacket. He eased the MP5K, the Heckler & Koch sub-machine gun, from under his seat so that he could grab it faster, whilst still concealing it with his legs. The weapons reassured the old soldier, plenty of stopping power, both took the same 9mm ammunition.

"Echo, Charlie 2 Green 800 …" 800 yards away the car had stopped, four suspects exited and they were heading in their direction. This was serious.

"Pete, this car could be the real pick up and the other car here by chance," suggested Sarah, voice still steady.

"Or the other way round. Whichever way we go we could blow it or get ourselves killed," Pete's voice was cracking. He needed to *do* something. "We need better information. Come on let's take a look. See if you can sight the car in front from the hedge and I'll take a look behind."

They both slid out of the car, leaving the doors open for protection and a faster escape. Crouching low, they ran to their viewing positions.

The radio crackled into life. "Zero, Echo..."

Sarah, who was nearest, heard 'dickers,' kids working for the IRA, but missed the rest of the message.

Shit, I should have activated my personnel radio, she thought, as she ducked back into the car and leaned in to the set.

"Say again Zero, this is Echo"

"Echo, two incoming o nine hundred, fast. Wait." Clearly more information coming in.

"Echo, they're armed,.."

Portadown, County Armagh
The previous day

"Do you want to play a secret game?" Patrick, eyes sparkling with mischief, enquired of his kid brother, 'Little Mick.' Michael was his middle name, his father being Michael too.

The younger boy nodded eagerly. He was the youngest of six, four boys and two girls. He idolised Patrick, the oldest and the only one who ever treated him like an equal. His other brothers bullied him. His sisters treated him like a doll to be mothered and dressed up.

It was easy to admire Patrick. Confident, strong and exceptionally tall for his fourteen years, all his brothers envied and emulated him. Kevin, the next oldest copied all his actions and mannerisms, but Seamus, at twelve, knew it all. He could do anything better than Patrick, but he still measured himself against his older sibling. If Patrick was a little headstrong, Seamus was wild and had a mean streak. When the mood took him, he'd torment Little Mick till he cried out in pain. It was a fine art, for he'd practise on Little Mick before tormenting the other kids in the street.

Today was different. It was Patrick who was interested in *him* and little Mick nodded with all the enthusiasm that only an eight year old can muster. Patrick was too often busy, running errands for his Dad. Today he wanted Little Mick to play a game and share a secret.

"What do I have to do, Pat?" He was pushing his luck now. Only the grown ups called him Pat. Now he was feeling both lucky and excited, affected as he was by the atmosphere of tension pervading the house and the whole street. It was always the same in early July, during the build up to the 12th, when the Orange Day Marches took place. One of these ran very close to the terraced street where Little Mick and his family lived.

The same bizarre ritual was repeated each year. Besashed Orangemen, many in bowler hats, would march twice through the streets, once on the way to their gathering point and again on their return. Despite protests, the Royal Ulster Constabulary put up barriers and kept the local Catholics behind them for hours.

The area known as 'The Tunnel' acted like a magnet for the young lads. Last year, Patrick and Kevin had joined forces with some of the other kids and pelted the parade with coins and ring-pulls. Violence had erupted from the melee and several kids had been arrested. Kevin returned home sporting a broken nose, blood drenching his white school shirt. Little Mick couldn't grow up fast enough to join in.

"First of all, you have to promise not to tell, especially to those sisters of yours. They'll only tell our Mother." Patrick knelt down and drew him in until their eyes were only inches apart. "Do yer promise? Not a word or the wee men'll come and cut yer tongue out!" Patrick pulled a face and twisted his tongue.

Little Mick, eyes like saucers, crossed his heart and gasped, "I promise."

"Right. Yer've to get bottles and bring them to me in the shed." Patrick spun him around and propelled him towards the yard gate with a final pat on his behind to speed him on his way.

Little Mick's face fell, mouth drawn down in disappointment. He hesitated. This wasn't a secret; it was Patrick having him run errands. He turned to protest. "But Patrick, what'll I want bottles for? I don't want to get bottles. What sort of bottles? Where'll I get them? Why do I...?"

Patrick cut him short and pulled him back. "We'll be wanting bottles to make a secret and I'll let you help. You've not to tell anyone this, Mickey boy. Any kind of bottles will do as long as they're glass and tell yer Mother, if she catches yer, that you've ter do it for a school project. Now off yer go and mind yer come in the back way, not through the house."

Little Mick, now convinced of his mission's importance, shot off, creeping back an hour later. Trying to muffle the clanking of his stolen booty, he placed the bottles carefully amongst the litter in the narrow alleyway, which backed their yard. Frowning with concentration he scrambled to the top of the gate to check the coast was clear. Gripping the gate with one hand and the toes of his trainers, Little Mick reached over with his spare hand and released the catch. There was nobody about.

"Heh Patrick!" he whispered at the shed door, "I'm back. Is that you?"

The door to the shed opened and Patrick's head appeared. "Have yer got them?"

"I've got loads, Patrick" and he scampered back into the lane to retrieve his collection.

"Bring them in here." Little Mick staggered in, his arms full, and put his haul down on the shed floor. Patrick seized Mick by he arms and lifted him on to the bench. Eyeballing him, Patrick rasped, "Now listen carefully Mickey boy. If you breathe a word of this, I'll come up to yer room in the middle of the night and I'll slit yer treacherous throat."

"Yer could slit me throat a hundred times Patrick and I'd never tell on you. Never!"

Patrick laughed. "I know I can trust yer, little brother. Now grab that funnel and help me."

While Little Mick held a funnel over the bottles, Patrick poured petrol into them from an old rusty can. When the bottles were about three quarters full, he took some lengths of old rag and tore them into strips. Each full bottle had its own strip of rag stuffed into the neck to prevent the petrol evaporating.

"What are they for?" asked Little Mick, when they were finished.

"I'll show yer, but not now," replied the older boy. "They've to be a secret until next week. Now help me hide them behind all this old crap in the yard." Patrick moved some old pieces of timber and broken pallets in the corner, while Little Mick crept into the gap and hid their secret weapons.

That night a row erupted in the house.

Had Mum discovered the bottles?

Although Little Mick was in bed he could hear it all clearly, as the kitchen door was ajar. He feared it was about the bottles in the yard, but nobody came up for him, so he listened in trepidation. He could hear Patrick's voice raised.

"I'm not bloody going. That's it. Yer can't make me!" Other voices were raised in support. Then his Mother's voice drowned all the other sounds.

"Yer going whether you like it or not and that's final! Come on Michael, support me on this."

"Yer Mother's right. It's for the best. Now I don't want to hear any more about it." Little Mick's Dad didn't seem so sure, but he held the line. With a slamming of doors and a crash of falling furniture, the row eventually subsided and Little Mick drifted off to sleep.

The following morning, he discovered the cause of the uproar. They were all to be packed off to relatives until after the 12th of July and soon he found himself, with Patrick, in the back of his Uncle's car, heading off to his farm in the south of the county. His other brothers and sisters were going to Donegal to another branch of the family. Unlike his older brothers, who were sulking, Little Mick didn't mind at all. It was great! Away from his parents and his other siblings, he had his beloved Patrick all to himself. Just as good, his Aunt would spoil them rotten and let them run wild over the whole farm.

Sure enough there was a huge lunch waiting for them, at the big old farmhouse. Home made sausages and piles of mash and Auntie had remembered that boys like baked beans with all that good farm food. Strawberries and fresh cream followed and by then even Patrick didn't seem so ill tempered. By the time they left the long wooden table, Mickey's world could not have been more perfect.

His brother whispered, "Come on Mickey boy, let's go and explore."

The two boys slipped out from the cool low-ceilinged kitchen and into the yard. The heat bounced off the cobbles and the bright afternoon sun hurt their eyes. They squinted at the vast blue sky and headed for the refuge of the barn. It was dark inside. Narrow shafts of sunlight pierced the gloom from the cracks in the old wooden door. The air was heavy with the smell of straw and manure. Little particles of dust danced for their brief moment of glory under these spotlights, before drifting into dark animal recesses.

Intoxicated by the smells and sights, Little Mick felt his throat tighten with the dust in his lungs. He fought the urge to cough, afraid to disturb the silence. Gradually his ears tuned to the faint rodent rustles, sounds too soft to notice in any urban environment. They were vaguely aware of the distant sound of their uncle's cattle in the top meadow. It was a different planet from the streets of Portadown they'd left behind.

Patrick lay out full length on the straw, hands behind his head, long legs draped over two bales. Little Mick mimicked him, except his shorter legs, not reaching the second bale, dangled aimlessly. He wanted these moments to last forever and his young mind sought desperately for anything to engage his brother in conversation. He wriggled around until he was more comfortable, gave a little sigh and, looking up at the roof said, "Heh, Patrick."

"What Mickey?"

"Patrick, when is it alright to kill someone?"

"Heh where did that come from little mate?"

"Well Seamus was saying how he'd like to kill them Orangemen on the march," admitted Little Mick.

"You just stick with me and I'll see yers right." The older boy reassured his brother.

The conversation continued and Little Mick, seemingly content with this response, drifted off to sleep as the effects of the disturbed night, the warmth and his Aunt's lunch overwhelmed him. He dreamed of heroic deeds in a great war, which he knew to be important, but was not quite sure why. He was at Patrick's side as they fought an unseen enemy. All the time Patrick's face smiled down upon him.

Something disturbed this image and he woke to find Patrick shaking him. "Come on Mickey. Come and see what I've found. We'll have our own little party after all." He led him around the back of the barn to an ancient stone building, with a rusty corrugated iron roof.

"Patrick," Little Mick tugged at his brother's arm, "we're not meant to go in here." It was the building where the tractors and machinery were stored.

"Don't worry little broth," Patrick reassured him. "We're only going in for a moment. I've found some bottles and some petrol and this old shirt will do the job."

"We can't Patrick. If we get caught they'll kill us."

Still protesting Little Mick followed the older boy into the forbidden building and together they found and filled an old beer bottle. It smelt of something disgusting, but the petrol soon killed that. Patrick laughed at him, as he tried to rip the shirt into strips. The material was too much for him and although he used all his strength, it wouldn't give. Patrick took his pocketknife to it, despite Mick's cries of 'cheat'.

The two boys scurried up the field at the back of the farm, taking care to keep the barn between them and the farmhouse. Climbing the wall at the head of the field, they continued up through the pasture. Their uncle's Friesianschewed the rich grass and gazing disdainfullt as the the two apprentice rebels scurried past. These old ladies had seen it all before.

"We'd better go to the other side of the woods Mickey. Come on now. Keep up."

Mick's little legs were going as fast as they could.

When they entered the woods, not much more than a copse, Patrick sat down on a fallen tree, in a bit of a dip and let the younger boy catch his breath.

Armed men approaching fast. Even Sarah's heart was pumping now, but it took her only milliseconds to digest the information. The primary threat, now that she knew they were armed, was this new element coming in over the field. The others could wait and they would need backup. She acted swiftly.

There was enough time to call in the Headquarters Mobile Support Unit, before pulling out her own weapon. Hissing a warning to Pete, who had his back to the imminent danger, she indicated with her left hand the number and the direction of the expected attack.

The boys were standing now. The trees of the little coppice screened them from view. A few yards in front was a bank, which marked the road and the boundary of their Uncle's land.

"Have you got a light, Mick?" Patrick asked his brother, grinning. Little Mick looked horrified. How could he have forgotten that and let his brother down? "I, I didn't think Patrick to..."

"I'm only kidding you Mickey. Here, I've got a lighter." Relief spread over Little Mick's face.

Patrick thought he'd been a touch hard on his brother. "Heh Mickey, you have a go," and he handed him the bottle and the lighter.

The younger boy hesitated, the weapon in one hand, the flame in the other.

"Come on now, it won't hurt you. Not so long as you don't tip it or drop it," said Patrick.

Mickey's hands trembled.

"Oh give it here. I'll show yer how it's done."

With that, Patrick seized the bottle from his brother, lit the top and, eyes and bottle ablaze, raced out of the trees and towards the bank at the top of the field. The younger boy gave chase but his shorter legs could not keep up.

In situations like this the training kicked in. Pete moved like a programmed machine. In one movement the Browning came up, as he spun around. He assumed the Weaver firing position, prescribed by the Special Forces. Steady breath, both eyes open, primary target - man moving at speed over bank. The 9mm pistol came to bear.

A voice in Pete's head issued the orders. Wait. Arm rising, hand holding petrol bomb, immediate threat. Tap, tap. Two shots to the upper body. Target down. Next target appearing. Small boy, unarmed. No immediate threat. No other persons in view. Any other activity? Sweep length of bank. Check Sarah, covering. Sarah shouting.

"You've shot a kid. Pete. You've shot a bloody kid!"

Pete looked. The downed target was a teenage boy, nearly six feet tall, but young, not shaving yet. A much younger child accompanied him.

Sarah again. "Echo to Zero, we have a downed Bravo - a child. No other enemy activity. Shall we offer assistance?"

"Christ Echo! Are you sure?"

Sarah double clicked her radio in affirmation.

"Any witnesses Echo?"

"Only a small child."

"Anyone else? What about the four Bravos?"

Sarah checked in the direction of the second car. They were still out of sight. "Negative, Zero."

"Then get the fuck out of there. We'll let the RUC clear this mess up."

Double click.

Pete stared at the smaller kid, who stood motionless over the body.

"Pete, we've got to go. Those Bravos can't be more than six hundred yards away. They'll have heard the shots."

Pete didn't move. He'd seen death before, killed before, but this little boy just stood, no reaction, staring at the downed youth.

"For Chrissake Pete!" Sarah was beside him now, tugging his sleeve. She steered him into the passenger seat, ran around the vehicle and jumped in. Slamming the car into reverse, she hit the accelerator hard, then, when the car gained enough speed, spun the wheel and performed a perfect J turn. The Chevette whipped around, wheels spinning, before the tyres gripped and it shot back up the lane and, accelerating fast, disappeared from view.

Patrick reached the bank ten yards ahead of his younger brother. Mickey watched Patrick's arm come up and his mouth open to yell the battle cry. No sound escaped. There was a 'crack, crack' and Patrick stopped as though he'd hit a wall. He turned slowly towards his younger brother. A dark red patch crept across his T-shirt and a little dribble of sticky dark red juice appeared at the side of his mouth. Mickey remembered the blackberry juice, the day they'd been scrumping, stains on their faces and clothes, Mother's angry shouts in their ears. He wondered vaguely if they'd be in trouble now.

For a moment nothing happened, then the lit bottle fell from Patrick's hand. The bright green glass didn't break, even on the hard dry earth. It spilled its contents and the small boy smelt the petrol vapour, as, with a whoosh, it ignited. The flames didn't spread far, nothing to sustain their fury.

Patrick hit the ground. His hair smouldered, charring his skull. It didn't matter now. Nothing mattered any more. Somehow Mickey knew it was all too late.

The child stood and stared… for hours.

As the skylarks sang in the blue summer skies over South Armagh and the sun beat down on his neck, Little Mickey waited. He was alone and while his mind slowly fell apart, in some hidden recess of his developing brain, he knew that his world would never be the same.

PART ONE

His memory is still fresh in the hearts of those who knew him. Forty winters have passed over it, and the green has not gone from it.

Words of James Hope, United Irishman, of Henry Joy McCracken

Chapter 1

Boston, Massachusetts
Friday 1st March 2002

The last of the pale winter sunshine straining through the clouds was little comfort to the men in smart dark suits and expensive black overcoats. They loitered, ill at ease and incongruous in this run down district of Boston. Kicking their feet for warmth, they tried to keep their concentration up, suspicious eyes probing the advancing dusk, the distant bark of a dog the only other living soul to be heard.

Anyone straying into this drab, deserted area of lockups and derelict warehouses wouldn't need telling twice to steer clear of this company. The scrupulously polished black limousines looked threatening in this environment and the bulges under the jackets were a further warning. The suits stood guard by one building, similar to the rest, but for the heavy steel doors, which stood ajar. Inside the meeting was in progress. No windows, pools of light fell on a hastily erected trestle table. A green baize cloth offered some illusion of respectability.

There was no illusion about who was in charge. Discussion had turned to dissent and a large man, his neck straining at his collar, banged the table, with the flat of his huge hand.

"Enough," he boomed. Then, in a quieter and more measured tone, "I will not tolerate this. It's been agreed already. The time for debate is passed. We *will* proceed. We are only here to ensure that the parts are in place." He turned to a silver haired man at his right hand. "Are the funds available?"

The Senator nodded. "It was passed this week by my committee. $3 million - enough to give us influence and the respectability of US Government support, without attracting too much attention."

The large man grunted his approval. His whole presence was intimidating. In his fifties, he was tall and powerfully built, but years of self -indulgence had pushed his frame to grotesque proportions. He turned to the end of the table. "And how has the," he paused for effect, no warmth in his smile, "fund-raising been going?" His question was directed at a slight man, bespectacled, brown brogues and a light green suit. The man felt uncomfortable amongst these senators and businessmen in their Armani suits. The pale hue of his attire seemed to indicate a lack of strength and commitment. He glanced uneasily from side to side.

"We have a further $2 million to transfer immediately."

"Is it clean?"

"Nobody will be able to trace it," said green suit.

The response was a little too eager. Seizing on the pause that followed, a new voice interjected. It belonged to an elderly man, with hints of his Irish origins still discernible in his accent. "I have to protest. Throwing this amount at such a crazy scheme is nothing short of madness. It would be better..."

The large man turned to him, shifting his bulk to hint that he might rise from his seat, and the elderly man fell silent. "We *will* continue, with or without you, but I need to be sure of your support." The words were simple, but the threat unmistakable. The older man twitched and then nodded his acquiescence. Acknowledging his acceptance with a slight movement of his eyebrows, the large man continued. "In that case, tell me, is our man in place?" He turned to the youngest man in the room, whose accent clearly revealed him to be a Dubliner.

"He is and he's perfect. Impeccable academic record, fluent French speaker and yet he can still handle himself." A low rumble of approval went around the table. "His pedigree is good too. Great-grandfather killed in the Easter Uprising of 1916 and subsequent generations, shall we say," he coughed theatrically, "very active."

"That's all very well, but has he proved himself?" The elderly voice again.

Before the young man could respond, the large man stamped his authority on the proceedings again. "We have been down that road as well. Even if we could find someone suitable from the active list, it's too risky. This is a British Government project and he will be vetted. We cannot take that chance. We have done our homework and he has every reason to be committed to this, every reason." Another silence, this time uninterrupted. Then he continued, having gained the centre stage. "In any case you'll have the chance to judge for yourself in a minute. It seems he's on the way from the airport."

A murmur of surprise rose from the group.

"Before that we have other matters to clear. Have you found a stooge yet? He will need help, someone with a detailed understanding of the situation, but we cannot risk putting two of our men in."

The young man smiled with confidence. "I believe we have."

The aircraft was on finals, Runway 27, Logan International. Boston was within reach. A headwind all the way from London, the flight was delayed slightly. That had not bothered Sean O'Grady, relaxing comfortably up front in Business Class. The trays and Champagne glasses had been cleared away, seats were in the upright position and the seat belt lights were illuminated.

A flutter of anticipation niggled in his stomach now that the lights of Boston were rushing up towards him.

It had not been a difficult journey. At Heathrow he had free run of the Executive Club bar, prior to boarding the business class flight across the pond. It was amazing how different it all seemed up front away from the cramped seats, cardboard meals and screaming kids in Tourist Class. His six foot four inch frame appreciated the extra legroom and Sean had slept off the food and drink and felt refreshed. He enjoyed the hint of deference and surprise that he received from the flight crew. He liked to think of them glancing at each other and wondering what this young man did to travel trans-Atlantic in style.

Sean, at twenty-four, was not just an academic. Entering university nearly two years younger than his peers, he had been awarded his BA, a First in Psychology, by Trinity College, Dublin and stayed on to take his doctorate. That achieved, he was now lecturing and helping the Professor with some research work. It left him plenty of time to indulge in his main passions, drinking, women and horses. There was only one problem. These passions cost money and, as a bright lad, he was certainly smart enough to know he'd little chance of making serious money in his current role.

That's why he had listened hard, when his Professor had invited him up to his rooms for a chat. It was all hints, but the gist of it was that there was a multi-national project, partly funded by the British Government. The project was to be based at one of the City Universities, recently sprung up in the English Midlands. The location hadn't thrilled him. He felt part of Trinity, with its history and traditions, but that wasn't going to give him the lifestyle he wanted. He feared the day, twenty years hence, when he would wake up, still in Trinity, still no home of his own, and still no money.

It was clear that this project was well funded. They'd also asked for him personally to play a leading role. Certainly that was flattering, but in Sean's mind it meant only one thing. If, for some reason they wanted him that badly, he would be available, at a price. He had developed some expensive tastes and they were catching up with him. There was the loan on the BMW. It had been so easy to be economical with the truth about his income. Why didn't they run proper checks? There was the excessive interest he had taken lately in the horses. He had met a bookmaker at the track, who had been very sympathetic to his credit problems. Unfortunately Sean had experienced a bad run of luck, nothing more, and now the friendly bookie was not so friendly. He was becoming very impatient and Sean had an urgent need for an increase in his income or, better still, a quick injection of cash.

He'd flown from Dublin to Birmingham. That had been Business Class too, although the short haul aircraft was not so luxurious as this 747. A uniformed chauffeur collected him from the airport, but instead of going to the University Campus at Boroughbridge on the outskirts of Birmingham, he'd been whisked off down the M5. A few minutes after leaving the motorway they entered a private road, which lead to a beautiful Elizabethan manor house, now a very select country hotel in rural Warwickshire.

Sean's feet crunched the gravel. As he approached the ornately carved porch the oak door opened and three men introduced themselves. The first was Dr. Peter Jones. Tall, thin and balding, he was the Head of Research at Boroughbridge and clearly the brains leading the project.

"Welcome to Boroughbridge Dr.O'Grady. We've heard a great deal about you," beamed Jones proffering his hand.

It was typical of the academic, recognition of his title, but absurd, since they plainly weren't at Boroughbridge.

"We'll be going to the campus in the morning, will we?" enquired Sean, returning the handshake.

Dr. Jones coughed. "I think its best if we don't on this occasion Dr. O'Grady, due to the, er, nature of the programme. Besides the building is undergoing some improvements and is not quite ready for us and I'd hate for you to see us, without our makeup on, so to speak."

Shorter, broader, almost threatening in his sharp suit, was an American, Desmond Waugh, who represented the US backers, the moneyman. Thickset neck, he looked like a man who was more comfortable in a vest than a stiff collar and tie. Sean thought he'd be useful with a baseball bat, breaking kneecaps. The American was profuse in his welcome.

"Yes, it sure is grand to meet you Doc. How are things in the Emerald Isle? I'm from Irish stock myself and I've always been meaning to visit. You'll have to tell me all about Dublin."

The accent was unmistakably from New Jersey. He pronounced 'Isle' like 'oil'. Sean didn't trust him an inch.

The third was even more unlikely and a surprise. Tall, thin and grey, he was traditionally suited in navy blue pin stripes. From MI5, Simon Smithson was the man from the ministry.

"I hope you don't mind, Dr. O'Grady. Its purely a formality my being here."

It could have been a comedy sketch, except these three took themselves and their project very seriously. For Sean, that made it the more ridiculous, so he was pleased to take the offer of a shower and a chance to change to cover his amusement.

By the end of the evening he was less amused. They had given him a hard time. It was not that the style was aggressive, just that the interrogation was incessant. The questions kept coming all through dinner, which was a pity as the food was excellent and he'd had no time to enjoy it. They hadn't stopped there. They had retired to a private lounge, once the library. Good brandy followed and so had more questions. When at last he had found a chance to ask his own questions, the answers were evasive. Dr. Jones was the most forthcoming. A commercially sponsored drug research programme to treat depression had produced some interesting psychological side effects. Before he could continue Pinstripe had interrupted him. More than this would only be revealed, if and when Dr. O'Grady joined the programme.

The American was no more informative. All Sean could establish was that the money came from some jointly funded federal-private source. Millions of dollars would be made available, provided they could meet certain requirements and one of those seemed to be his acceptance of the proposed role. It was very gratifying to be described as fundamental to the project, but Sean was too good a master of the art of flattery himself to be taken in.

By just after midnight Sean felt his guard was beginning to slip and feigned exhaustion to head up to bed. He had kept his defences up well. He had not managed to penetrate theirs. As he lay in his room wide-awake, mind working overtime, he fancied he saw a chink in their armour. It was difficult to put a finger on it exactly. What was it? Somehow they did not seem united, a marriage of convenience, no a marriage of necessity, not one born of love. If he could separate them, it might be easier to learn something, at least from the Doctor, without the protective screen of the ministry man.

He'd woken early and opted for a run rather than the pool. After a shower, he headed for the breakfast room ready for the fray and to his delight, discovered Dr. Jones alone, remains of bacon and egg in front of him and The Guardian spread across the table. Sean smiled at the stereotypical image.

Dr. Jones looked up and returned the smile. "Good morning Dr. O'Grady or may we dispense with formality now Sean? Sit yourself down and order the sausages, pork and leek, excellent." He folded the paper away and leant forward towards Sean. "We have agreed. Well we're pretty much agreed." Dr. Jones coughed and composed himself again. "That is to say we uh..."

He did not seem to be able to get to the point, which irritated Sean, who let him run on nonetheless.

"Oh, for goodness sake," continued Dr. Jones, who seemed irritated with himself. "We want you on the programme Sean. We discussed this into the small hours of this morning and whilst, I'll admit there were some reservations, we agreed to offer you the post. Oh dear me, that doesn't sound very appropriate." He spoke as though being appropriate was the most important thing in his world.

Sean felt it was best to busy himself with pouring coffee and let the man ramble on. If he could mask his surprise at being selected he might learn who held the reservations about him.

"We all felt that you were supremely well qualified for the role and Mr. Waugh, in particular, seemed very keen on your background and personality profile." Again he stopped and coughed to cover up his embarrassment, but could not prevent his ears from colouring. "I am frightfully sorry, but we have accessed your profiles and records at Trinity. Normally this would not be permitted, but the University authorities gave permission to MI5, given the nature of our project."

Sean tried hard to suppress his anger. Not normally quick to lose his temper, his humour and sense of the ridiculous usually came to the fore. Who the hell were these people to access his personal files? And for some half soaked research project? The absurdity of it all struck Sean and helped him control his temper. It would certainly explain why they had accepted him without any form of psychometric testing or psychological profiling.

For the first time since the whole charade had started, Sean began to feel that there was more to this than he was being led to believe. He decided it was time to take it more seriously, as more than a quick fix for his financial problems. He needed to find out much more and so he kept a tight reign on his temper and let Jones continue.

"Mr. Smithson did, in truth, hold a few reservations about you Sean. He has nonetheless agreed to recommend you to the London end of the project. Effectively that means that you are accepted, given Mr. Waugh's views and, of course, my own endorsement. That is always assuming that you still wanted to join us," he added anxiously.

For a moment Sean was lost for words and then snapped his brain into gear.

"I think that you'd better tell me just a little bit more about all this, before I come to a decision Dr. Jones." Sean put the emphasis on the 'Dr.' as he held eye contact.

"Of course, of course, but not here and we do need you to make certain undertakings, before we can explain much more." Jones muttered nervously glancing around for prying ears.

For Sean it had gone too far and he was bored with the games. It was time to negotiate and felt that the American was holding the purse strings.

"Where are the other two?"

Jones looked blank.

"Smithson and the American; where are they now?"

"Oh you mean Mr Smithson and Mr. Waugh? They've both gone and left me to brief you, oh, and to offer you the post," added Jones. He hesitated and then leant forward. "Mind you I don't see any reason that we can't talk about the financial package now." He made it sound like some kind of embarrassing skin complaint, not the sort of thing to be discussed in the restaurant of a good hotel.

"I am authorised to offer you £50,000 a year." Sean swallowed slightly, but Jones, too preoccupied to notice, continued, "We can also make you an immediate one off payment of £10,000 to cover any expenses, removals etc."

Smart move, thought Sean. Leave the guy, without authority to negotiate, to make the offer. That leaves no opening to haggle. It looked like a take it or leave it situation. What the hell! That was more than twice what he was earning now. The ten grand would get that damn bookie off his back and leave him some cash to play with.

Sean smiled the smile that had charmed more than a few girls into his bed, and threw out his hand.

"We have a deal Dr. Jones."

They shook hands and Jones, too hastily, reached for his briefcase by his feet to pull out a contract. His elbow caught his coffee cup and soaked the thick white linen cloth with its murky contents.

Dr. Jones, more flustered than ever, blustered, "Oh dear, how clumsy of me." He tried to mop up with his napkin. "I do need to get you to sign these and then we can pop over to the campus."

He produced a fairly standard looking contract of employment, running to several pages. The name of the company, in a blue stylised script, 'Histo-Search Ltd.,' headed every page. Under this it read 'Making History.' The bottom of each page showed the logo of Falte Pharmaceuticals and the crest of Boroughbridge University, the two organisations behind the project.

Although instinct told Sean to have it checked, it all looked pretty straightforward. Histo-Search could fire him at any time, but if they did, he would keep the £10,000 expenses and they would pay him to the end of the contract, a full year's salary. He couldn't go wrong, could he? He pondered briefly how he could get himself fired in the first week. He, in turn, would have to offer six months notice to leave and would have to repay his expenses. The contract was for a year, renewable a year at a time. Sean was not keen on the six months notice, but figured that it only applied for the first six months. After that he would have six months and reducing left on each year's contract anyway.

He scanned the document again.

"Take your time," said Jones pouring himself more coffee to replace the spilled cup.

Sean knew that he really should take advice, but that £10,000 was burning a hole in his pocket, before he'd even received it. It wouldn't solve all his financial worries, but it would give him some breathing space.

He signed.

"Excellent, excellent," said Jones snatching up the papers and thrusting them into his briefcase. "I'm frightfully sorry. We were in such a rush yesterday, I didn't have a copy run off for you, but we'll get that organised in no time. Now there's just this one to sign," he added pulling out a manila file. "If we can sort this out I can let you have your expense cheque right now. I have it with me," he said and patted his jacket pocket.

The second set of documents looked very different and Sean noticed how Jones did not make eye contact, as he presented them. The papers were heavily water marked and HM Government, printed boldly in black at the top. Sean scanned them and let out a low whistle.

"For God's sake, is this the Official Secrets Act? What on earth do I need to sign this for?"

"Well not exactly. Its something a bit like it though," explained Jones. "Don't worry, it's all quite normal. This is a project funded with a lot of Government money. They don't want you to run off and sell information to another country, say somewhere in the Middle East. I signed it too," he added lamely.

Sean looked at him. He was a middle aged academic, probably never stepped out of educational establishments all his life. He looked out of his depth with all this contractual stuff, but Sean didn't think he was dishonest. That was more the territory of the other two, certainly the American. What had he got to lose? It was only for a year and if they also paid for his accommodation, which seemed to be part of the deal, he could really get some money together and live the good life. He glanced at his mobile sitting on the table, as if it might ring at any moment. He could hear the bookmaker's threatening tones and wondered why he was hesitating.

"What the hell, who am I going to tell anyway?" he exclaimed, with a shrug of the shoulders. He took up the pen offered by Jones and signed.

Dr. Jones looked relieved. "Come on then, let's check out and go and look at our little facility. Oh, and of course this is for you." Jones handed Sean an envelope containing the cheque for £10,000.

"Perhaps we could pop by the bank on the way," suggested Sean as they left.

The visit to the University had been a formality. It was a typical modern University campus, lots of concrete and glass and not much character. The facility was adjacent to a Medical School that had been closed, when it had amalgamated with another Midlands based university. There was accommodation on site for them. It had been built for the senior undergraduates to be close to the nearby teaching hospital.

The building itself had been used for live animal experiments. It was very secure. Such was the level of objection to this work and the chance of sabotage it needed to be. With windows on the top floors only and high security gates, it was ideal for a government project. It would be a couple of months until the equipment would be on site and the teams were brought together, so there was not much to see except the building.

It certainly wasn't Trinity and it made Sean anxious. His need to know more grew stronger. Despite further questions Jones told him only the basics. Falte Pharmaceuticals had discovered, in their development of drugs for treating depression, that there were some interesting side effects. Subjects with the right background and programming would have what Jones described as out of body experiences. These gave them insight into certain historical events. There must be more. It all seemed so pointless to Sean, who had no interest in history, but he kept returning to the same thing. It was easy money.

He could ask more questions of Waugh, who was now expecting him to make a trip to Boston to meet some sponsors. He was on the payroll right away and the appropriate arrangements had been made with his Professor.

Bump. The aircraft's wheels hit the tarmac, bounced and then settled to take the strain, as the aircraft's engines were thrust into reverse. Sean was thrown forward slightly in his seat and it brought him back to the present in an instant.

With a mixture of misgivings and excitement Sean walked out into Arrivals, all the formalities of Immigration

Control completed. There was a uniformed chauffeur standing with a board, with 'Dr. O'Grady' written on it. He announced himself and the chauffeur greeted him with a "Welcome to Boston. Kindly follow me Sir." He took Sean's bag and led him to a parking lot and an immaculate black stretch limousine.

Sean tried to see the sights as he peered out of the tinted windows, but the light was fading fast and it was soon too dark to see much. He did notice that they had left the city centre and were heading into a rather drab area on the outskirts of the city. It wasn't what he had expected and his palms started to sweat. What's the matter with you? he chided himself. They're hardly going to bring you all this way just to murder you. They could have done that at home and saved the airfare.

The car stopped and the chauffeur came round to open the door for him. It was completely dark now and Sean found himself in a dimly lit street, containing a row of warehouses. From out of the gloom stepped Mr. Waugh, looking even more sinister than ever in his double-breasted suit.

"Sean, Sean it's great to see you pal. How was the trip?" Before Sean could answer Waugh was pumping his hand vigorously in a vice like grip and continuing. "I'm sorry about all this," he said waving his hand in the direction of the street. Putting his arm around Sean he explained. "We've had to use this place, to give ourselves a bit of privacy. We don't want no prying eyes do we? We've got senators and all sorts dying to meet you. Come in, come in."

He ushered Sean inside, where the party was gathered. It was a strange sight. Ten of them were grouped under the umbrella of light thrown from a metal warehouse-ceiling lamp, lowered over a table. They all looked overdressed for the venue and Sean felt a little self-conscious in casual trousers and open neck shirt, under a ski jacket. He had, after all, just fallen off a trans-Atlantic flight and had expected to go to a hotel first to clean up and change.

The largest man, and clearly the leader, grabbed his arm away from Waugh and dragged him in to meet the others. He announced himself only as Jimmy and introduced the others so fast that Sean could barely grasp their names. Some references to Senators, Harvard and various corporations were made and then Jimmy said, "Hell, where are my manners now? Come, sit down and have a drink."

A couple of bottles of Bushmills were produced, in his honour he was assured, and glasses were filled. They toasted him and then Ireland. The whisky hit his stomach like liquid fire. Sean had drunk plenty on the flight and now he was tired and the time difference was beginning to affect him.

"We won't keep you long Sean," continued Jimmy. "The guys just want to see what they're getting for their money and to get to know you a bit better. Tell me how are things, back in the old country and how are things in the North?"

The conversation was kept to small talk and another two bottles of Bushmills appeared. They all joined in and although it was casually done, the conversation always turned back to the question of Ireland. The University project was given only passing mention.

What did Sean think about attacks on the mainland? Should the Orange Day parades be re-routed away from Republican areas or, should they be banned altogether? What chances were there for a peace settlement in his opinion? Should the whole thing be left to run? After all, in a few years, the population would be predominantly Catholic and a referendum would swing in favour of a United Ireland.

What on earth would his father say if he could see him now? The thought passed through his nervous mind. He hadn't seen his father in more than five years, which didn't cause him any loss of sleep. His father's views on the Irish question were well known to everyone, including the British authorities. Sean came from the same stable but, had he not, he would not have dared confront the old man.

Forcing himself back to the present Sean was careful to express his views in as dispassionate a way as possible. Ireland should not be divided and sooner or later it would be united. It was a matter of when, not if. They were pushing him now. Whether it was the drink or his instinct to give them what they wanted, but his views became more outspoken. Ireland for the Irish, kick out the bloody English and if a few people got hurt in the meantime, what the hell! They loved him and the more they loved him the more outspoken he became. The room was spinning when the songs started.

"O Paddy dear and did you hear the news that's going round?
The Shamrock is forbid by law to grow on Irish ground...
...How's poor old Ireland and how does she stand?"

At this point they all looked to Sean, who had no trouble continuing the song with a pained expression on his face.

"She's the most distressful country that ever yet was seen..."

The singing continued, topped up frequently with more Bushmills. They ran through a range of the traditional songs that Sean had grown up with and then there was a hush. A middle-aged man in a grey suit stepped forward. He looked very serious, amongst all the ribaldry. He raised his glass and they all followed. "The men of the '98."

They all joined in. "The '98."

He started to sing, raising his glass to reinforce the words of the song.

"Oh let glasses clink and hearty drink to those of long ago
Who roamed the land with pike in hand to fell the heathen
foe
'Twas father John who spurred them on to save their holy
faith
They heard his call to fight or fall, the men of Ninety Eight."

There was a silence to follow this and then, with knowing glances, the men all cheered. Even in his drunken state, Sean had the feeling he was missing something. He suddenly felt exhausted and was quite relieved that the proceedings seemed to be concluding. Finally Jimmy leant across to him and said, "Sean you're alright," and slapped him vigorously on the cheek.

Drunk and tired though he was, Sean did not like it. There was something intrusive, even menacing about it. He noticed a very distinctive silver ring on the little finger of Jimmy's right hand. It had an Irish harp on it, but the device above the harp was peculiar. It was formed by a sort of crossed sticks over the harp, coming together under a thing that looked like a nightcap. He knew that he'd seen it before, but the alcohol would not let him recall it.

The others roared their approval and soon Sean was swept up in the backslapping and hand shaking. The next minute he was in the back of a limousine and off to the hotel. It was not the car, which had brought him and he wondered whether his bag had been transferred. He vaguely remembered an envelope being thrust in his pocket before he fell asleep in the spacious luxury of the soft leather seats. The check in at the hotel was a dream and he barely took off his clothes before passing out in the king size bed in his enormous suite.

The bottles were rapidly swept away after Sean's departure and Jimmy transformed from convivial host to strong leader.

The group was dismissed, except for Desmond Waugh and the elderly man, who had objected to Sean's selection.

Jimmy turned to the elderly man. "Do you feel any happier now that you've met him?"

"He's a right enough lad, but I've still got reservations."

"Of course you have, of course you have." Jimmy put a comforting arm around him. "I respect your views and I'll keep an eye on him personally. No hard feelings eh?"

"No Jimmy you're the boss."

"That's right. I get to do the worrying, so don't you do it for me."

"Sure Jimmy."

Jimmy steered the older man towards the door. "I've used your driver to take the lad to the hotel. Don't worry you can take my car and I'll go back with Des. We've a couple of things to talk about."

The old man frowned. "Are you sure Jimmy? I could wait for my man to come back."

"No don't be crazy. It's no trouble," and with that Jimmy summoned his driver and another huge man, who held the door of the car open. "Take care of him Norm," he murmured to the giant, who nodded and with a "Yes boss" climbed in beside the old man and was lost from sight behind the tinted glass.

The car pulled away smoothly, proceeding at a steady pace out of the industrial zone, towards the freeway and the city centre beyond. After a couple of miles the car took an unmarked exit. The road swept around under the main carriageway and then came to a halt. It was clearly intended to access a development, not yet built. As the car pulled up the old man shouted, "What the hell are you playing at? Can't you goddamn monkeys do anything right? You've taken the wrong exit."

The glass partition between the passengers and the driving compartment slid down. The chauffeur looked over his shoulder, "Sorry boss, the car is overheating." Norm just grinned and shrugged his shoulders. "Do yer wanna get some fresh air?" He opened the door for him.

"No I don't want some fresh air! And I don't give a damn about the car. Just get me the hell outta here." The old man was shaking with rage. Norm stared at him, weighing up his body mass. The driver came round from the front and climbed into the back. From his jacket pocket he produced a sheet of paper, neatly folded. His thick clumsy fingers opened it carefully, revealing the cocaine.

He looked up and caught the old man's eye.

"We got something for yer."

"Quit messing around and take me back," the old man snapped, but the authority had gone from his voice. "I sure ain't gonna use that shit."

The two heavies looked at each other and, without exchanging a word, one pushed the door open, while the other tossed the old man out, like a feather cushion.

"You bastards, if you..." the old man stopped as Norm hit him very hard, a couple of inches below the rib cage. It was a measured blow; just enough to take all the wind out of the man, without damaging any of his internal organs. The other heavy caught him and Norm reached into the car and pulled out a roll of duck tape. He casually cut a short length with his pocketknife and slapped it over his victim's mouth, while the old man clawed at the air and tried desperately to draw some breath into his lungs.

Norm pinched his nose. The old man started to convulse. Norm leant him backwards and released his nose as the other gorilla tipped the contents of the folded paper towards his nostrils. With a sharp intake of air he sucked the powder up with a whoosh. He shook, choked and tried to cough. Norm replaced the pressure on his nose. The old man vomited behind the duck tape, shook with violent spasms and finally fell still, cradled in Norm's arms.

Norm carefully turned him to face away, before removing the tape. He took the wallet out of the old man's pocket and removed the Rolex from his lifeless wrist. Then without a backward glance he dropped him to the gravel, the corpse's head flopping into an oily puddle. Strolling back to the car, he slid in beside the driver, who coaxed the limo back onto the freeway and they sped away towards the bright lights of Boston.

Chapter 2

Boston, City Centre
Saturday 2nd March 2002

It was, for Sean, a weekend of two very distinct halves. Saturday was possibly the best day of his life. Sunday, most definitely, was not.

He woke late, sunlight already streaming through the windows of his penthouse suite. Considering his journey and the excesses of the previous evening, he felt remarkably good. A glass of freshly squeezed orange juice, maybe a little Champagne, as a hair of the dog, would set him up for the day. Having rung for room service, he headed for the bathroom. On returning he noticed the envelope, still protruding from the pocket of his jacket, discarded on the floor. He bent down, picked up the letter and sat down in one of the expansive armchairs.

Jimmy's hand written note brought a smile to his face. It apologised that Jimmy and his colleagues would not be able to join him until Sunday morning. As compensation Jimmy's secretary would show him the sights of Boston and enclosed was $1,000 to cover any expenses. He was sure that Sean would find his secretary's company most convivial. She would meet him in the lobby at 10.30am. Sean glanced at his watch. It was 10.05am already! He just had time to open the door to the orange juice, champagne and rolls, before leaping in the shower.

At 10.45am she had still not entered the large marble floored, glass fronted lobby and Sean was scrutinising every new arrival. Then she appeared and she was worth waiting for. It just had to be her. Please good Lord, let it be her. A brunette in tight jeans and even tighter top arrived at the desk and looked around. No wonder she was late. It must have taken her an hour to get into those jeans! She had a jacket and bag hanging casually over her shoulder. Despite the sunshine it had to be cold outside and she had no doubt slipped the jacket off, just before entering to enhance the effect. She turned her head and flicked loose shoulder length curls, in the way that women do, when they want to be noticed. As she surveyed the lobby, Sean rose from his chair and advanced towards her. He caught her eye and held it. One and two and, he launched the smile at her with everything he'd got. It landed and she revealed the sort of dental work that only high earners afford.

"You must be Sean," she said.' "Ooops, or should I call you Doctor?" she giggled.

Sean was certain she was wearing nothing under the top. "I'm sure we can manage with Sean," he said with a little wink, "Miss er?"

"Oh it's Stephanie, but everybody calls me Steph." She emphasised the 'ever' of 'everybody,' and flapped both hands towards Sean.

He caught and kissed them, whilst looking straight into her eyes.

"You're such a charmer," she purred. "I can see I'll enjoy working today. What do you want to do? I'm all yours!"

Sean's first thought was to take her straight back to his room. That might be pushing his luck. Besides he had an image of a tearful Steph telling Jimmy how he'd raped her and Jimmy did not look like the sort of guy to upset. He settled for hiring a cab and touring the sights.

It was a bright day in Boston and the weather, combined with the company, lifted Sean's spirits. He was in sparkling form and Steph giggled gratifyingly at all his jokes and acts of mock chivalry. He made sure that she saw the $1000, when he paid the first cab. She seized his arm and squeezed it. Catching his eye she said, "I like a guy, who has plenty to entertain a girl with!" and paused long enough to let the double entendre land before adding provocatively, "I bet you've never disappointed a gal."

Sean needed no encouragement to flirt and felt a drink might move things on.

They drank coffee and a couple of large Irish whiskeys in a bar nearby. Steph was gripping his arm constantly now. They caught another cab to see the ship, where the Boston Tea Party threw the tea overboard. Sean was enjoying his Boston experience, but by now Steph's hand had found its way to his thigh and he was contemplating an altogether different Boston experience. Before he could broach the subject, Steph had exchanged the hand for the tip of her beautifully manicured fingernail, which had now worked its way up to the very top of his thigh.

Gazing into his eyes she whispered dreamily, "You don't have to worry, it's all included in the package."

Unusually, Sean faltered. "You mean that you're a..." He couldn't quite bring himself to say the word 'hooker.'

"You didn't really think I was a secretary or something did you?" Her face fell slightly. "Oh you're not offended now. I really like you. If I wasn't working, I'd sure want to date you anyways." She leant close and kissed him very gently on the mouth, the forefinger still working.

Sean regained his composure quickly, a grin spreading across his face. "Does that mean that we could...?"

She nodded smiling broadly and then ran her tongue across her lips.

Sean leant forward conspiratorially, "Does that mean that anything goes?"

A concerned look flickered across Steph's beautiful face, "You don't want any rough stuff do you?"

"Oh, in God's name no." Sean exclaimed. "I'd like to think that I'm always a gentleman whatever the commercial arrangements."

Instantly Steph's smile returned and, patting him on the thigh, she leant forward to the cab driver and redirected him to the hotel. As the cab pulled out, Steph reached into her bag and pulled out a sachet of cocaine. She held it up to Sean and said, "A little aperitif?"

Sean winced and Steph quickly changed tack. "Oh I'm sorry. You don't do you? Look, I don't need this stuff with you. Sometimes, well you know it helps..." She trailed off and went to put the stuff away.

Sean caught her hand. "I don't want to make an issue, you know. It's just I don't think it would help my trip, if we got stopped with that stuff." Sean imagined an arrest, a Boston police cell and a call to bring Desmond Waugh, or worse Jimmy, to pull him out.

Steph hit the electric window button, opened the sachet and, with a carefree shrug, flapped it out of the window. The contents flew away in the slipstream. Every sniffer dog in the city will follow us, Sean thought, conjuring up images of 101 Dalmatians. What the hell! There were better things to concentrate on, now that Steph's finger had returned to its important work.

Lunch, with more Champagne came from room service. It was long after dusk had descended that Sean and Steph thought that they might go out for dinner. They showered together, which delayed their departure further. Finally they headed for the Irish Quarter, so that Steph could show off her new assignment to the locals. He was the genuine article and well received. Sean drank plenty, but never forgot that Steph was expecting breakfast and he didn't want to spoil his appetite. The night was much like the afternoon and Sean thought how gratifying it was to meet someone who was so good at her job. He was not sure if he had caught a couple of hours sleep, just before dawn, as Saturday slipped into Sunday.

Sunday 3rd March 2002

Finally he dropped off, awaking to a knock on the door of the suite. Steph was asleep beside him. He smelt her hair as he rose onto one elbow. There was another knock. Steph stirred slightly, but showed no other signs of waking, so he slipped out of bed grabbed a thick robe, the hotel logo embroidered on its pocket, and headed for the door. It must be room service. A glass of OJ and Champagne would start the day nicely.

He opened the door and was brushed aside as Jimmy, accompanied by Waugh and a step behind, Dr. Jones, burst in. Waugh marched through the bedroom and pulled the cover off the naked Steph. She let out a yell, but was quick to see the picture. Jimmy threw her clothes at her and Waugh pulled something out of his pocket, together with a fat envelope, tucked both in her bag and tossed it to her. She headed for the bathroom. "Not that way," snarled Jimmy, holding the door to the hall open with one hand and grabbing her with the other. Without a second glance Jimmy tossed her out of the room, naked, to dress in the corridor.

Before Sean could say anything, Jimmy pre-empted him. "Don't get hung up on her. She's fine and gets well paid for her trouble. Now we've more important things to discuss. Get cleaned up. We'll see you in the lobby in ten minutes." He opened the door, ushered the others out of the room and was gone.

Sean suddenly felt tired and hung over, but he had to snap out of it quickly, if he was going to impress these guys. In fact he had exactly ten minutes.

By the time he appeared in the lobby, twelve minutes later, he was in overdrive. The smile was in place, the pleasures of Steph forgotten and his mind was focused on the job in hand.

A limo, like the one the night before, swept away from the hotel and soon brought them to the Irish Quarter. To Sean it looked very different in the cold light of day. Jimmy sat beside him in the back. Desmond Waugh sat opposite with the doctor at his side. The limo's interior was so palatial that they were not cramped and Sean started to relax. Waugh leant across and seized his knee in a fearsome grip.

"What do you see out there? " Waugh pointed at the passing streets and stared into Sean's eyes.

Struggling to retain his composure, Sean responded. "It's like Ireland out there – the whole community."

Waugh released his grip and slapped him on the thigh. "Good boy. It's not *like* Ireland. It *is* Ireland – only moved across the seas, as the people did all those years ago." He gazed out of the window. "They still feel their roots. They still feel they're Irish. That's what it's all about."

For a moment Sean thought that this head case was planning for Boston to secede from the Union. Waugh continued. "It should never have been like this. These people only came because they had to. Fear, religious persecution and famine all played their part. If those same people, who built this great city, had stayed and done that back home, who knows what a great world power, Ireland would have been today."

Sean thought the American was romanticising the Boston image with its Irish connections. He was about to point out the economic prosperity, which Ireland enjoyed, since joining the EEC. They weren't still sitting around in thatched hovels, trying to make a bucket of potatoes last all week. He caught a hint of a tear in Waugh's eye and decided that this was not the response required. Instead he said, "Who knows what might have been? But you can't rewrite history."

Waugh's grip returned with such a force, it made Sean wince. Waugh swung round. Their faces were only inches apart. Sean could smell the staleness of the other man's breath.

"That's where you're wrong Sean my boy. I," and he stabbed himself, with a finger in the chest, "can't. You," the same finger pounded into Sean's ribcage, "have the chance to…" He paused and opened his eyes wide, revealing all their blood shot detail, "… change the world!"

Sean thought that Waugh had lost the plot completely. His heart sank as, forgetting the money that had already changed hands, he realised that he was mixed up with a bunch of lunatics. There was no job here for him.

Waugh's expression changed again and he eased back into his seat, releasing Sean's knee to his great relief.

"Yer think I'm barmy don't you?" He held Sean's gaze for a moment. Then as if he'd suddenly made up his mind he turned, wrapped on the glass panel to the driver and barked a place name, which Sean did not quite catch. The driver grunted his acquiescence and accelerated.

They drove for about an hour. Nobody spoke. Sean found this more disconcerting than Waugh's hand on his knee. Jimmy and Waugh had no trouble with the silence, but the doctor squirmed uncomfortably and gazed with a forced intensity out of the window. Sean too stared out of the car and noticed the city centre turn first into suburbs and then into more open country. Finally they slipped into a land of wooded hillsides. Little piles of sludgy snow lay on the sides of the road, like dirty ashtrays, left from last night's party.

They eventually turned off the highway onto an unsurfaced road, which climbed up into the woods. The limo, not suited to this kind of road, slid on the muddy surface. The snow was still thick amongst the trees despite the constant dripping from their sad wintry branches. Spring had not yet come to Massachusetts. He looked at the heavy, wrestling with the steering wheel. As his thoughts drifted to the driver, Sean tried to convince himself once more that there would have been no point in bringing him all this way just to kill him. Somehow it seemed more difficult to find the reasons not to shoot him and leave him in the woods. After all he knew all about it now.

Hell, he didn't know a damn thing. He had seen a university building and heard about some loony project, which sounded about as likely as a catapult moon shot. They wanted to pay him good money to loan his credibility to the work and if his nationality together with his academic background made him fit the bill, that was fine. It was obvious these guys were not the sort he'd invite for dinner, but there was only one question. Was he prepared to get involved with these people to set himself up financially? After all he hadn't actually seen them do anything worse than pay for Steph's services and *he* hadn't exactly fought her off!

Thinking through this process made Sean feel more comfortable. As long as he learnt nothing confidential about these people and their work, he was fairly safe. The vehicle's tyres crunched to a halt outside a typical white, wooden clapperboard, New England house. It was small and had a homely feel to it, like visiting Grandma's.

They climbed the wooden steps to the front porch. Jimmy held the fly screen door and beckoned him in. The front door opened onto a small entrance hall, where an old-fashioned hall stand for coats and umbrellas stood on one side and a beautiful oak grandfather clock on the other. There was a choice of two doors. Sean paused for a moment, to let the others join him and was directed into a kitchen to his right. He had to duck to avoid the low beams and as the door opened his nose was greeted with a delicious smell of wood smoke and fresh coffee. An elderly lady poured the aromatic brown liquid from a metal pot on the hearth and without a word left by a door at the back.

"Cosy ain't it?" exclaimed Waugh, as he leant back in the old wooden chair and relaxed. "I'd like to tell yer that I used to play here in the yard, as a boy. I didn't. We picked it up last year as part of a real estate deal. I like to pretend it's home."

He shrugged and, with a nod from Jimmy, said, "I think its time we spilled the beans."

Sean stiffened. Before he could stall Waugh, the American continued. "You ain't been told a lot, 'cause I didn't want you to know too much. Not yet, anyway, not 'til

I'd made up my mind about you. I didn't want you thinking that we're a bunch of crackpots neither."

Waugh took a pull on his coffee, as if giving himself one last moment to change his mind. "You can't decide about all this, unless you understand it and you can't get involved, neither, unless you believe in it."

Sean swallowed some coffee too, his throat suddenly dry.

Waugh held centre stage now and went on. "I brought you out here, because it's out of the way and we won't get disturbed. I want you to feel free to ask any questions you like. We'll do our best to answer them."

Sean drank more coffee and wondered whether he should empty his bladder, before he heard any more.

"And don't worry," said Waugh, as if sensing Sean's anxiety, "if you do decide that it's not for you, that's fine. They'll be no hard feelings."

Sean was not convinced. Too late now, the £10,000 cheque had been cashed and he was in no position to pay it back. "Go on." He croaked to Waugh across the wooden kitchen table.

"We haven't been exactly straight with you." Waugh caught his eye and held it. "We have done it you know. We have actually put a man back in time and brought him back again."

Sean's head reeled. These guys really were crazy. Maybe he could raise the money on his credit card to pay them back.

To his surprise it was Dr. Jones who interrupted Desmond Waugh and spoke next. "Sean I know what you're thinking. This seems like madness, but it has been done. I have seen it myself, really I have."

Jones leant forward and Waugh eased back in his chair to give him the floor. "This did not start like this. Falte Pharmaceuticals involved Boroughbridge University in monitoring trials on a new anti-depressant. The new drug seemed to be a success, until one or two people claimed that they had recurring dreams. All those interviewed reckoned they had experienced the most vivid images of historical events and were able to recall the most extraordinary minutiae. Second year undergraduates under my supervision conducted the interviews. At first I thought that the results were coincidental. Then, when a pattern emerged, I wondered if they must have been exposed to some common influence. Perhaps they had all seen the same historical film. That didn't explain the variety of their experiences."

Jones, becoming animated, took off his glasses and pointed at Sean. "It just wasn't possible. The experiences were too detailed and varied. So I involved the Department of Modern History, who were amazed at the insight that many people, with no knowledge or training, had shown into the most complex historical situations. We even thought we'd cracked the identity of Jack the Ripper, when a van driver from West Bromwich described, down to the last detail, an incident in Whitechapel, previously unrecorded. Unfortunately he talked to the tabloids, who had a field day with it. "Ripper Tripper solves the case!" Jones grimaced. "Falte pulled the plug in days and the University lost its funding."

It was Jones turn for coffee. The mug rose to his mouth and came down, before he had swallowed, as the memory suddenly returned. "I thought I was going to be fired and then the Government Agencies were all over us. Somebody in Whitehall had taken it seriously. I was instructed to pull certain interviewees in again."

Jones gave a stilted laugh. "The irony of it all was that the Ripper man turned out to be a hoax. Many others were much more plausible, but still it was all a psychological experiment. Then something changed it all and it came from the most unlikely source."

He paused again to collect his thoughts. The others seemed pleased that he'd taken the initiative. Now it had been decided to tell the full story, nobody was inclined to restrain him.

Jones continued. "We had run through all those involved in the trials, who had related convincing stories. Nothing new came to light." He paused at the dubious look on Sean's face.

Sean enquired, "What were you looking for or that's to say why was the Government so interested? Surely not because of some murders committed over a hundred years ago."

"No, no, of course not" responded Jones. "It was the Ripper story that attracted their attention. It took more than that to make Falte pull out as well." He glanced at Waugh, who nodded. "There were problems. Some of those, who had described the best experiences, started to deteriorate."

Sean, impatient at the Doctor's ponderous style asked, "Deteriorate? What do you mean by deterioration? You were treating them for depression right? Did the depression deepen or were their other side effects? Paranoia, schizophrenia?" Jones was shaking his head. "What then?"

Jones composed himself. "There was a whole range of side effects. Yes, yes, all of those, but all of them quickly shut down; no speech, no reaction to sound or light, not even pain. Nothing – just a state of trance and in one case death."

"Holy Christ! How many were there? Where are they now?" Sean was out of his seat and pacing the kitchen. Jones rose with him, but the others remained seated and watched Sean's reaction, as the story unfolded. Sean nodded, "So that's why Falte pulled out. All this going on and then the press taking interest, just because some prat wants to pretend he's solved one of the all time whodunits. No wonder Falte walked. Did the press get wind of this?"

"No, they sniffed around, made a lot of fun about universities funding looney projects, wasting the taxpayers money and that sort of thing. As usual they got it all wrong and in an instant it was yesterday's news and some soap star's love life was back on the front page." Jones frowned. "All the cases ended up in secure psychiatric units. The Government hushed it all up, too much at risk. The pharmaceutical industry is making billions in the UK and still funding research in a big way. The men from the ministry covered our tracks, but we paid the price. Boy, we really paid the price. From that moment on, there was no doubt who was running the show."

Jones gazed out of the kitchen window. He seemed to be talking to himself now, re-living the experiences. To Sean he had simply lost his way and he wanted to pull him back on track.

"Yeah, yeah, we get the picture," he interrupted, "you sectioned half the West Midlands, but that still doesn't explain the time travel bit. What evidence did you have for that?" Sean could not believe that he had actually asked the question. It seemed to lend credibility to what was clearly some elaborate stunt. Having said that, it must have been a hell of a stunt to have people like this dig deep into their pockets. He glanced at Waugh. He didn't look like a man to be conned easily.

Jones apologised. "I'm sorry. We went to the house of one of our least likely candidates. He hadn't responded to phone calls and letters. By coincidence my colleague is a keen photographer, who has completed some excellent work on the history of photography. On a desk in the house, he noticed some fine examples of the early work of Fox Talbot, you know, the pioneer of the photographic process. Without a word to me he stole one of them. I was appalled until he explained what it was. A well documented early picture, which was destroyed in the fire of 1977 at Margam Castle, a home of the Talbot family. This photograph does not exist, not any more! If it wasn't a fake, where did it come from?"

"We ran tests on the photo and all the evidence pointed to it being genuine. Of course we started to doubt that we'd got our facts right, but the evidence was clear. So we brought the man in and questioned him. He made up some ridiculous story at first. He was worried he'd be in trouble for theft or locked up as a lunatic. It certainly was madness. What was that compared to the truth? And the truth, which emerged, was far more difficult to handle. We had not monitored the participants constantly. We didn't see the need. There were nurses and scientists in attendance. We filmed a few but not all of them. This chap claimed that he had not just seen places and events as if they were real; he claimed that he had made contact with other people in the past."

Jones paused to see Sean's reaction to this statement. Sean grinned at him. "And you believed him Dr. Jones?"

"I really couldn't be sure." He smiled back at Sean. "What I do know is that we couldn't explain the photograph." He snorted a humourless laugh. "I wanted to carry out further drug trials on him, but they wouldn't let me. You see we believe that we have resolved these terrible side effects now. We never had the chance to prove it, following these revelations. We were shut down so fast, that I hardly had time to clear my desk. That was it, no office, no project, and no job. It made no sense until later."

"Look. All this is fascinating, but why the hell have you brought me all the way over here, at considerable expense, to tell me about some drug trial that screwed up and got shut down?" Sean's impatience had overtaken his apprehension. Sean spread his arms. "For the love of God, just tell me what you're doing and what you want me to do." He hesitated. "And for that matter what on earth has it got to do with Ireland and the Irish?"

Jones was about to respond, when Waugh held up a hand to stop him. Jones fell silent. Waugh pulled his chair closer and leaned forward towards Sean. "It's quite simple Dr. O'Grady. The project has been re-opened under British Government supervision. Dr. Jones is in charge. Items have been brought back. We are convinced that it is possible to interact with people in the past. If we can interact in the past we can alter history, or specifically Irish history. We want to send people back."

Sean really did need the bathroom now. What a great party to join! he thought. They're all barking mad and they want to stuff me full of experimental drugs to fuel their fantasies.

Waugh saw the look on Sean's face. "Oh Sean, don't worry, we only want you to supervise and monitor the guys we're treating. You didn't think we were going to make you take the stuff, did you? You're not depressed are you?" he chuckled.

"Depressed? No, not until now!" Sean forced a weak smile. He needed time to think his way out of this. A flat refusal did not seem like a smart move. He probably wouldn't leave the kitchen alive. If he agreed, he was just getting in deeper. If he prevaricated, it would be obvious.

"This is a lot to take on board," Sean opened his response.

"Sure, sure," nodded Jimmy, moving closer to Sean and looking deep into his eyes.

Sean managed to keep a straight face "Can you give me a little time to think it over?" Not very original, but it was all he could come up with. They'll never buy that, he thought.

To his surprise Jimmy just smiled and clapped him on the arms. "Sure thing Sean, you take your time. Go home, get some sleep and someone'll pay you a visit at the end of the week. Meantime, why don't you take a little stroll in the woods? Get a little fresh air to clear your head. I think you had a helluva night last night, eh?"

Jimmy stood up, put his arm around him and gave him a squeeze. "Des, the Doc and I need to catch a couple of words together. One of the boys will show you around."

The driver was summoned and, with a rifle slung over his shoulder, led Sean out of the house.

Chapter 3

Business Class Atlantic Airlines Flight 173
Monday 4th March 2002

Only when Sean was sitting back in the luxury of Business Class and the wheels of the aircraft had left the deck did he start to relax. It was like a shell hole on a battlefield, a place to rest and regroup ready for the next encounter.

He had to concentrate. There must be a solution to this mess. There always was.

All the way back to the airport he had fought the panic threatening to paralyse him. He tried to convince himself that they were just a bunch of harmless lunatics. Somehow he couldn't. When Jimmy had suggested a walk with the driver, he had to admit he was scared. Sean was big, had grown up able to look after himself, but there was something about the look of the driver, not just his powerful frame it was his demeanour. He was a robot. Took his orders, said nothing and showed no emotion, the kind to kill and not even think about it. He wouldn't get a kick out of it, just a job to be done.

Rifle slung over his shoulder, he had walked about three metres ahead of Sean. They had climbed a track, through the woods, behind the old house. In summer you might drive it, but now, a four-wheel drive would have struggled. Sean panted in the damp air, as he struggled to keep pace with his companion. The robot unperturbed by the incline, plodded on, no attempt at conversation. They had reached the top of the ridge and the heavy had stopped and simply pointed. By the time Sean had reached the spot, the trees framing a lake below them, the man had walked on.

As Sean's fears of his companion started to subside, his imagination took over. Was the man keeping his distance for someone in the woods to shoot him? Or was his shadow there to protect him? Was it just part of some interview process – to see how he reacted to pressure? Sean did not know. Oh what the hell, you only die once. He decided to step it out and enjoy the views. It was pretty here; if it were to be his last walk on earth.

The bullet from the woods did not come and Sean made it back to the airport. Believing you were about to die is the best excuse for not facing up to the future. Still alive and on his way home, Sean had no excuses for ignoring his problems.

He could be cool and logical, when he needed to be, pragmatic too. If there was a problem, how best to avoid it? If unavoidable, there had to be a solution. If no solution, then better learn to live with it, or could you run away? Sean was not one to agonise over moral dilemmas or to bemoan his lot. He did not waste his time worrying about the what-might-have-beens.

Now he had time to think. He had chosen a light salmon dish from the Business Class menu, a decent Chardonnay and some cheese to follow. He refused the drinks trolley before the meal and again afterwards and settled for coffee. Time enough to sleep later. He had made a mistake at the house in the hills. He had let his imagination run riot. He had missed the chance to ask questions, which would help him make his decision.

What *exactly* did they want him to do? He could only surmise. At least they'd said he didn't have to take their damn drugs. Thank God he was not to become part of the experiment. Besides he was the wrong personality profile to be suitable, he reassured himself. They just wanted him to analyse it all.

Had they really overcome the side effects? Was he happy to put his name to this? Ever the pragmatist, that might depend on the alternatives. Sean put that question into the section of his mind marked, 'to consider later.'

He moved on to evaluating the threat to himself from this bizarre group. Each mile of deep Atlantic Ocean that the aircraft thrust behind him diminished the threat in his mind.

In contrast, with every minute that Dublin came closer, the reality of his financial situation loomed larger. The cheque had kept his ship afloat. He was not home and dry yet and still had significant debts to clear. There was more to it than that. Sean could not contemplate a life of abstinence for years until he had his affairs straight again. He smiled to himself. If he were that kind of character he would not have found himself in this mess in the first place. Sean needed a boost in his income and this was his best offer. Come to think of it, his only offer.

There was the small matter of the contract he had signed. He now had a copy with him in his hand luggage, but he saw no point in poring over the small print. He was no lawyer and he had a feeling that any good contract lawyer would only tell him what his gut advised. His signature meant he was hooked.

He could disappear. That was always a good way out of a financial crisis. Just leave your clothes on the beach. He gave it some passing thought and came to the same conclusion that he always did. That was fine if you had a couple of million in an offshore account. It certainly wasn't worth it for a few grand. No, this was not a problem to run away from.

What about all the save Ireland stuff? This was not new territory to Sean. He had grown up on it and considered himself lucky enough to escape, when, as a child, he had moved to live with his aunt and uncle in Dublin. Suddenly, plucked from near poverty, he became part of a successful family of lawyers; Sean's opportunities had changed overnight. Without distractions and sibling pressures he had taken to study with vigour and a sharp mind. Summer holidays saw him shipped off to more distant relatives in France. Sean, far from traumatised by the experience, had loved it. Long hot summers in Pontonx-sur-l'Adour, in the South West of France had been idyllic. He had learnt to surf at Biarritz and return trips during the Christmas and Easter holidays had introduced him to skiing in the Pyrenees. When had his brain made that magic transition? No longer translating from English, he could think in French.

What did it matter? It didn't matter a damn, unless they really could go back in time and that was crap. Complete and utter crap. Someone was pulling a stunt. He could neither figure out how or why. There had to be an explanation for the photo. It must have survived the fire. And the other experiences? It did arouse his curiosity. It had to be a conjuring trick, an elaborate one perhaps, but soon the masked magician would move some mirrors and all would be revealed.

That left one last question. Who was doing it? The doorway to that answer lay in the 'why?' Why was anyone doing all this? It was usually money. Perhaps somebody was siphoning off the funds. Maybe somebody was up for a Nobel Prize or a Knighthood or something. Sean had seen enough of the world of academia to know that recognition was a major motivator. Plenty had been sacrificed on that altar.

Sean became calmer as he considered his conclusions. He had boarded the plane determined to find a way out of this project. Now that he had weighed it all up; sure he was concerned about these Americans, but... He smiled to himself. It was concern now, not fear. The catatonic reactions Jones reckoned they'd resolved, Sean convinced himself. That just left the time travel bit. That had to be a fiction and so he need not worry about the liberation of Ireland and one or two minor issues, like changing history. What the hell? Play the game, take the money and who knows, he might even learn something from the drug trials. That was a point. He'd almost forgotten about the first batch of patients, the secure units full of paranoid schizophrenics. Too late! By now Sean's mind was made up.

He settled back, drank a brandy and was soon asleep. The plane pushed on towards an encounter Sean did not expect.

Heathrow and the delays with the connection to Dublin were tedious. By the time Sean arrived at Dublin Airport, it was evening and all he wanted to do was head home, take a shower and put his head on a pillow. His bag took forever to appear on the conveyor. Exhausted and irritable he cleared immigration and stepped out into the arrivals hall. As usual the barriers supported excited relatives, bored men holding up signs welcoming Mr. Smith of ABC Electronics …and his father…

Oh Christ, what the hell was he doing here? He was the last person in the world he'd expected and the one he least wanted to meet right now.

His father greeted him with a curt "Hello son," as if they had last met for the game at Lansdowne Road, a week ago, not years before. The older man was tall, but still shorter than Sean. Once sporting a mane of jet-black hair, he was grey and receding now, giving him the distinguished look of an elder statesman. He held his broad shoulders erect. In his presence Sean immediately felt resentful and fearful. There was *always* a reason for a visit from his father.

Sean pulled himself together quickly. "Hello Dad, to what do I owe the pleasure?"

"Does a man need a reason to visit his son?"

"You usually do!" Damn, Sean did not mean to be so confrontational. The sudden appearance of this shadow over his life had unbalanced him. He attempted to put things on a sounder footing. He extended an arm around his father. "I'm sorry Dad. I've just got off a long flight and I didn't expect to see you. How are you? It's been ages."

"Ah I'm just fine, fine and you look grand yourself. No you're right. I'm sorry to turn up on you unannounced. It's just I need to have a word with you. Can we go and get something to eat? It's on me. I'll treat you. It's the least that your old dad can do after all this time."

Any onlooker would have seen a loving father in a happy reunion with a long lost son. Sean saw it too. This was the father that worried him most. He knew where he was with the overbearing, domineering father. Only his mother could handle that character. At least Sean knew the danger zones and how to avoid them. This smiling, affectionate dad was manipulative and dangerous. What was he up to? Sean was going to find out whether he wanted to or not. He might just as well put a brave face on it.

"Sure Dad. Let's get off the airport. Why don't we go into the city?" suggested Sean. "We could go straight to a restaurant," he said, having no desire to take his father back to his room at Trinity.

They took a cab to the city centre and Sean directed the driver to a turning behind Grafton Street. It was only a short walk from Trinity and they soon found a bar with a restaurant upstairs. A bit formal for Sean's taste, it was quiet and Sean knew that sooner or later they were going to have to talk.

They ordered whisky with the menus and Sean checked that his father was paying, before ordering. When the old man confirmed it, Sean knew that he was in for a hard time. That was all the justification he needed to order the most expensive items on the menu. They made small talk, while they waited for their starters. His mother was fine. His brothers and sisters were fine. Yes Sean was fine as well. There was no special woman in Sean's life. Work was fine, but a little dull.

The starters arrived, big domes, big plates, small servings. There was a pause, while they both arranged their napkins and tried the first mouthful.

"If work is dull, why don't you make a change, son. You're a very bright fella and you can't be earning too much at the University. By the way you never told me where you'd been."

"And you never told me how you knew to meet me at the airport."

"Oh, er, no mystery there. I rang your department and they gave me the details, when they realised who I was."

"Who did you talk to Dad? They're not supposed to give out that kind of information."

"Oh I don't want to get anyone into trouble. So you were in the USA. Was that on Uni' business? Heh, eat up son. Don't you like it? It's costing me enough."

Sean had lost his appetite and tiredness was washing over him again, as the jolt from meeting his father wore off. He had no intention of telling his father what he was doing. It wasn't the Official Secrets Act, nor was it the nature of the Americans. He just did not want his father meddling, nor did he want to discuss his thoughts about it.

His father was relentless. "So if it wasn't work, were you taking a holiday? Are you allowed to do that in term time?"

Sean felt that he had better feed his father something, just to shut him up. "Look Dad, it was an interview. You're right it's time I considered something else. It's in an, er, industrial sponsored project and all commercially sensitive. I can't tell you much."

"So are you going to go for it and get yourself a proper job instead of all that fooling around at the University?"

Sean bristled. "I haven't quite decided yet, but I'm thinking I probably will. The money is pretty good too." He cursed himself. Why did he have to add that? Was it just to impress his father? He hated the way that his father made him feel so inadequate.

"More money! So what's to decide?"

The first course was cleared away and there was a brief interlude, when they returned to small talk, the Rugby Six Nations Tournament, and Ireland's performance. After the domes had been lifted from the main courses, Sean's father seemed to concentrate on the food and little conversation passed between them. Through all this outward normality Sean could feel the tension rising. Thank goodness his father had let the subject of his USA trip drop. The real reason for this surprise visit had still not emerged.

Sean was damned if he was going to give his father the satisfaction of knowing how it was gnawing at him. He let the conversation drift on.

They skipped desert and ordered coffee and 12 year old Jameson. With a glass of the 1780 Reserve in his hand, Sean's father pulled his chair a little closer to the starched tablecloth and leant forward. Involuntarily Sean found himself doing the same.

"I need to warn you son. No, no, that sounds worse than it is. I need to make you aware that you might be approached in the next wee while." He paused to ensure that he had his son's full attention.

He had; Sean felt his full gut tighten uncomfortably and a little stream of sweat began to form at the top of his neck.

His father continued in lower tones. "I had a visit from, er well you don't need to know. What you do know, although you often pretend not to, is the sort of work I'm involved in, up North." He looked hard at Sean, who was only too aware of his father's, indeed the whole family's republican activities. The gut grumbled and Sean wished that he'd skipped the starter. The stream at the top of his neck was building into a torrent.

"Well son, I don't know much of course. They simply asked me what you were doing these days and that they might need your help on a wee project. Nothing too heavy you know; not handling guns or anything like that. They've got plenty of boys without your brains and pretty looks for that kind of thing."

Both men drank together. Sean was now sweating profusely. A gentle request from this quarter was not to be refused. The only option on offer, if you did, was whether you wanted your left or your right kneecap reconstructed. The Belfast hospitals had become world leaders in this kind of work.

"Don't look so worried son. These boys are not going to want you to get your hands dirty. They really do have people better suited. Christ they'd be after your brothers, before they talked to you!"

Sean was scared and more than that, he was angry. The moment he'd latched on to a new job with a good payoff, his bloody father turned up and dumped all this on him. Whatever it was it could screw up the whole deal. His father's continual use of the word 'boys' infuriated him. These weren't mates, who came around to take you up the pub to watch the game. Once they had their claws into you, that was it, for life.

"Dad I'm not sure about this. It's not a good time just now."

Sean's father leaned in closer drawing Sean with him until their faces were inches apart. "You don't get it do you? You might be happy to play games with these boys, but for once in your bloody life son, this is not just about you. Your family is involved. Think about your mother and your sister, who's just had a baby."

"Oh that's just bloody great Dad! Play the family card, why don't you? Like you're bloody interested. How many times, when I lived with Aunt Margaret, did you bother to pay me a visit, unless you had to?"

"Come on now Sean that was not my doing. It was your Mother. If I had...."

Sean cut him off, his voice rising in volume and in pitch. "Don't you bloody dare blame Mum for this..."

He stopped as his father stood up, threw a pile of notes on the table to cover the bill and grabbed Sean roughly by the arm. "Get a grip on yourself man. This is not the place. Let's take a walk. You need some air."

Sean's father was still a strong man despite his years. Although Sean was bigger than him, his father manhandled him out of the restaurant and onto the street. Before Sean could speak his father spun him around until they were facing.

"I don't want to hear all your old bollocks. You've had it easy, not like the rest of your family. Holidays, a good education, it's all been put on a plate for you Sean, my lad. You weren't too worried about letting the family pay for your schooling now were you? It's pay back time. You're not going to be asked to run guns or smuggle drugs or do a bit of knee surgery. So when the call comes you mind that you answer it. I don't want to be ringing you to say that your sister's been involved in a car crash, now do I?"

Sean could have wept. As ever his father had him in a corner with nowhere to go. He felt like a little boy, forced to do the family chores, unable to go out and play. Lamely he replied, "No, no of course not Dad. Look, I'll do my best."

Sean's father put a consoling arm around him. "Of course you will son, of course you will."

They walked for a while and had a pint in another bar, but few words were exchanged. It was a relief to both men when the father turned to the son and said, "Look. I'd best be making tracks. I've an early start in the morning."

They embraced on the street without much feeling and Sean watched his father stride off, turn the corner and disappear from view. He sighed. He hadn't bothered to ask where he was staying. Even with a bag to carry, Sean walked back to Trinity. He really did need the air.

Sean's father checked his pocket for change. He walked far enough to put a safe distance between himself and the bar, where he had left his son. Not wishing to use his mobile, he found a call box. It wasn't in a main street or a station, where there might be cameras. He dialled a long number from memory. The phone rang once and a voice answered, "yes?"

"I have a message that's expected."

"One moment please" a well-spoken female New England accent responded.

Next came a deeper voice, "You have news?"

"The meeting took place, as discussed."

"Will he do it?"

"Yes he will, I'm sure of it."

"That's good. Can we rely on him to follow the whole agenda?"

This time Sean's father hesitated. After a further moment he found himself saying, "No, I don't think that we can."

"In that case you know what to do."

There was silence. The voice at the other end of the line repeated in a stronger tone, "You know what you have to do, don't you?"

"Yes I do, but for the love of God how many more sacrifices do you want me to make?"

There was no response. The voice at the other end had hung up.

Chapter 4

University College, Oxford
Tuesday February 26th 2002

"Those bloody bells! Why do they have to ring them on a Sunday?" moaned Will Peters, as he was jolted from his dreams. For a bright young postgraduate it was not his most intelligent thought. Alone in his college room, chapels and churches surrounded him. Christ Church Cathedral or Magdalen College? He didn't know and cared less.

Try as he might to recapture his dreams, he couldn't. The harder he tried the more he awoke. His dream, like the night had slipped away. So real, it had been frightening yet glorious. How could he have forgotten it? Was it something in the past, a great battle? Terrified, he had overcome his fears and vanquished his enemies to achieve something important. Was it a purpose to his life, noticeably missing in his dull Oxford world? Was it a sign of some historic event, a harbinger of his destruction? Or just a stupid alcohol induced dream? As wakefulness took over, so did reality.

Reality Will was not too good at facing. He was on a downward spiral of lethargy and drink. To any who cared to notice, the signs of depression were obvious, except of course to Will himself.

Sunday was the dullest of days in Oxford and unlikely to be enlivened by listening to his lecture to the Historical Society that evening. Reluctantly he had agreed to give a short series of talks entitled 'The Two-and-a-Half Great Revolutions of the Eighteenth Century.' The title referred to the American, French and Irish revolutions. Every schoolboy remembered the first two. The Irish Rebellion of 1798 was often forgotten, except naturally in Ireland. This brutally suppressed uprising could so easily have changed the world as dramatically as had the other two.

His doctorate research investigated the causes of the Irish Revolution. It seemed a long time since his school days when the continued impact of Irish issues on British history had fascinated him, from the Middle Ages, through Cromwell to the Brighton Bombing and beyond.

"You might be able to use the Sheldonian," his Professor had said to enthuse him for the project. For a moment Will had allowed himself to be flattered. The Sheldonian Theatre, the great venue of traditional ceremonies, could house a small army.

Two lectures later he realised how narrowly he had avoided embarrassment. Only a dozen or so had attended his talk on the French Revolution. At least the American one had been livelier. Some American undergraduates had got up a party, arriving drunk, they waved flags and bottles, cheering every mention of Washington, booing Cornwallis. Pity, one had thrown up on the floor. Thoughtfully they had used the fliers for his third lecture to mop up.

Tonight was Ireland, his pet topic. Why it should attract others, he couldn't imagine. Perhaps the continued news coverage of Ireland might fire some interest. He sighed and rolled out of bed. Grabbing his bathrobe from the back of the door, he headed for the bathroom next door which he shared with a German post-grad, Inge, in the adjacent room. Inge was all that a German beauty could be, tall, blonde and fit in every sense of the word.

Will had thought that heaven had landed on his doorstep the day she arrived, all braided hair and rucksack. Unfortunately, tall and athletic though he was, she did not take to Will from the start. What made it worse was that she had entertained the entire rowing club over the last few months and the noises had made their way through the intermediate bathroom to his room. It had become his habit to turn in drunk, except on the rare occasions when he too had shared his bed.

He was ashamed to admit that on one occasion he had made every possible noise solely for Inge's benefit. He had made such a meal of it that Suki, a young Chemistry undergraduate, he had hit on, had leapt out of bed, convinced that he was having some kind of fit. She'd burst into tears; seized most of her clothes and left. He still had her shirt in his room and couldn't bring himself to return it.

The relationship with Inge, such as it was, now fluctuated between grumpy indifference in the mornings to something close to guerrilla warfare by night.

He tried the bathroom door. It was locked. He rattled the handle.

"Go to hell! I'm washing my hair," shouted a voice.

It sounded odd, almost like a man. Maybe it was one of Inge's long stream of conquests. Before he could consider it further, there was a tap on his shoulder. Startled, he turned around to face a young man of about his own age.

"You dropped your key, mate," he said, handing Will his room key and was gone as quickly as he had appeared.

Will looked at the key, certain he'd put it in his robe pocket. He shrugged. It was a bad start to another bad day. He needed caffeine and returned to his room to dress. He found clean socks and the only remaining pair of clean underpants. Pink with roses, they'd been given to him as a practical joke. What the hell, nobody was going to see them. Dirty jeans, t-shirt and his old leather jacket would have to do. Careless about his unkempt appearance, he dragged himself to the little room opposite the Porter's Lodge, where the pigeonholes were located. He'd pick up his mail, then coffee.

His post kept going astray. He was convinced that someone was intercepting it. Or was that just paranoia? Who would be interested enough in him to steal his mail?

Strange for a Sunday, Will found a pile of post, mostly junk mail except for one official looking letter. He was about to open it, when he noticed Inge.

"Hey Inge, I thought... Can't you let your men take a shower, before you're out hunting the next?"

"Piss off Will!" Inge's English was excellent.

So who was that in the bathroom? Will gave it no more thought and he turned his attention to his letters. It *was* strange to receive so many on a Sunday. It was as if someone had stopped the mail for a few days and then let it flood through in a torrent. Maybe the letters had been posted in the wrong box and redirected that morning. One caught his eye.

"Will don't tell me that someone has actually written to you. Or is it from one of those dirty book clubs?" she giggled and turned her back on him.

"Go to hell, Inge!" he growled after her.

She turned. "Will, why don't you like me?" pouted Inge, leaning around the end of the rack of mailboxes. "I have been thinking that we should be friends. What are you thinking of this idea?"

Will stuffed the letters grumpily into the back pocket of his jeans and looked at Inge. She was very pretty, he had to admit and if she'd slept with half the Rowing Club, why not him?

"Let's get a coffee and talk about it," suggested Will.

They ducked through the opening in the huge old wooden doors that guarded the college entrance and crossed High Street. Like much of Oxford, the road allowed only bikes, buses and cabs. Nonetheless Will had learnt from experience to keep a wary eye open for cyclists. It was fortunate that he did, because a red-haired boy of about twelve shot towards them. Head down, legs pumping, he powered straight for Will and Inge. Glancing up, he caught Will's eye and laughed. Christ, thought Will, he's trying to hit us, and leapt for the pavement, pushing Inge in front of him.

"Will, what are you doing?"

"Didn't you see that maniac, Inge?"

"What maniac? I think you are seeing things, Will! You are crazy, but you are fun. I will buy the coffees."

His attention taken by Inge again, Will did not notice that the boy had braked sharply enough to spill off his bike onto the pavement several yards away. The young lad picked himself up and stared at Will, as if undecided about something.

Inge pulled Will towards her by the front of his jacket and opened her big blue eyes so wide that Will instantly forgot about kids on bikes. She released him, turned and entered the café. Will admired her figure from behind and wondered what had caused this sudden thawing of the ice-capped Jungfrau. What the hell did it matter? he thought, perhaps… Thwack! Something hit the back of his head. Turning he saw the boy, once more astride his bike, dodging between two cabs in the direction of Magdalen Bridge.

Will's foot kicked a small object on the ground. He bent down and picked up a small plastic wallet. Realising that the boy must have thrown it at him, he opened it up to see if it contained any evidence of the kid's identity. There was nothing save a photo of a small ruined country church. It looked vaguely familiar. The roof had long gone and only the walls were standing. In the foreground were rows of gravestones. Trees surrounded the churchyard. The scene was sunny and wild flowers filled the vista. It must have been taken in late spring or early summer. Will turned the photo over and sure enough there was a date, 20th June. That would be about right. Then something struck him as very odd. The year written after the month was 2003. Most people write the date when the photo was taken. 2003 was next year!

"Come on Will, are you tired of me already?" Inge reappeared, hands on hips in impatience. "I am wanting to give you something special."

That was enough for Will. He slid the photo back into the wallet and placed it on the windowsill. If the boy came back he'd see it. He followed Inge into the café.

The initial signs were very encouraging. Coffee had turned into a walk down to Magdalen Bridge and back via the Botanic Garden and Merton Field, behind the college, which gave it its name. The sun was bright, but the chill wind caused Inge to shiver and seize Will's arm for warmth. She had a prearranged lunch date with a friend. Will had unsubtly established she was meeting a girlfriend and they parted promising to meet in the college's basement bar, after his lecture. Will felt slightly disappointed that she had not offered to come. Perhaps it was for the best; he did not want her to see how few attended.

The lecture. Will reluctantly dragged his thoughts back to the more mundane, but pressing requirement to complete his presentation on the Irish Rebellion of 1798. His audience might only comprise a couple of penniless nerds, too broke to go to the pub. Nonetheless he still had sufficient pride not to risk embarrassing himself through lack of preparation. He ambled back to his room. Pulling the letters from his pocket he tossed them onto the cabinet beside his bed. He decided to shower later and, folder and laptop in hand, headed for the history section of the college library, upstairs at the back of Fellow's Garden.

At just after seven that evening, Will made his way towards the small meeting room on the first floor of the college building, which fronted onto High Street. For the first time since taking on these lectures he was confident and enthusiastic. Was his newfound energy due to his knowledge of his subject or more likely the prospect of meeting Inge afterwards? The lecture was due to start at 7.30 p.m. and he wanted to ensure that everything was ready. The room would hold twenty-five, maybe thirty at a pinch. A dozen chairs would suffice, he felt.

Outside students filled the corridor. Incredulous, Will pushed his way into the crowded room. He must have double booked the venue with some more exciting event. Then he recognised a couple of familiar faces and his confidence returned. Most of the group were undergraduates. There were a couple of members of staff, including his professor. A couple of middle aged, suited men were sitting in the centre of the second row. Will did not recognise them as staff and could not put them into any category.

Will smiled and nodded to the audience, as he booted up his laptop and connected it to the projector. He caught the eye of his professor, who gave him a thumbs-up in encouragement.

Shame you didn't attend the previous two, Will thought uncharitably. He didn't let it spoil his mood and perhaps the Prof. would think that they had all been this well attended.

For an introduction he had loaded some traditional tunes, which played while showing reproductions of drawings and paintings from the '98. It seemed to go down well.

"Good evening Professor, ladies and gentlemen and welcome to the third of my lectures on "The Two and a Half Great Revolutions of the Eighteenth Century." This is the one that everyone forgets, although clearly not tonight!" An appreciative ripple of laughter followed and Will, more relaxed now, started to enjoy himself.

His lecture, whilst he hoped the academics would treat it seriously, was meant to be an entertainment as well. So he had taken some simple themes; unlike in North America and in France, this was the revolution that failed. The old order was not overthrown, the Ascendancy, the privileged Protestant minority, held sway and it culminated with the dissolution of the Irish Parliament and the Act of Union.

Later sectarian divisions became greater and England exercised that, oh so successful foreign policy, divide and rule. Will suggested that it was a turning point, one of those critical moments in history, when the world was changing dramatically. Thomas Paine had declared the Rights of Man and everyone had listened. The United Irishmen, mainly Protestant, had joined forces with elements of the Catholic community, in a dream of a new nation, modelled on the French and American Republics.

It failed and the tumultuous history of Ireland over the last two hundred years was the result. Famine, emigration, the Easter Uprising of 1916, the divided state, the IRA and 'the troubles' had all followed. Only in recent years had the Irish Republic become the miracle child of the EU, bringing in widespread prosperity for the first time in Ireland's trouble history. In the North there was finally hope of a lasting peace.

It had been so close. The French had only been prevented from invading by the weather in Bantry Bay in December 1796. They had been lead by General Hoche, the equal of Napoleon himself. Ireland lay open and defenceless. England's Irish colony had been saved by 'a Protestant wind' that blew the invasion fleet back out to sea. By the time the French did get ashore in Killala in 1798, it was too late. Napoleon had committed France to a war in Egypt and the Middle East and the uprisings in Wexford and elsewhere had been largely suppressed.

Will unashamedly played the 'what if?' game. What if the French had landed in 1796, with Wolf Tone, the Leader of the United Irishmen, at Hoche's side? What if the uprising had come in 1797 and not been delayed until 1798, when so many key players like Lord Fitzgerald had been eliminated and the uprising lacked leadership? The Rebellion of 1798 was critically weakened too, by the army's purges of both rebels and weapons under the brutal control of General Lake. It was a good way to finish and Will played to the gallery, with a thumbnail sketch of an independent Irish state, liberated by the French, with Wolf Tone presiding over a non sectarian Dublin Parliament. He did not explain how he imagined the Irish would evict the French. There was no need for such practicalities.

The applause at the end was enthusiastic and he even received a few whistles from the Irish members of the audience.

Will blushed. "Any questions?" he looked around the room.

One of the older men in the second row raised his hand. He spoke with an accent, which Will could not quite place. It was certainly American, but with a hint of Irish. "So are you saying that the whole bloody mess is the fault of the English?"

Several laughed at that missile. Will noted the twinkle in the questioner's eye and was not foolish enough to walk into that trap.

"How long have you got?" he enquired and returned the smile. "I blame it all on the Irish weather and French naval incompetence. The French should have landed in 1796!"

The man responded immediately. "You're not getting off that lightly. That's the last recourse of the English. Blame the French!" There was a cheer from a couple of French students and more laughter.

Will attempted to regain control of the discussion. "It is important to put it into the context of the time, to understand the actions of the British Government. Ireland was considered to be a colony. Britain had not long lost its North American colonies. Initially many in Britain welcomed the revolution in France, but by 1798 the situation had changed. France had shown the world the horrors of the Terror, executed its royal family and declared itself willing to help any nation follow suit. Certainly Pitt's government was repressive, but you have to remember that there were well founded fears of invasion and revolution."

Will felt he was going overboard. Friends told him that he took himself too seriously and so he tried to lighten it. "Chaps just shouldn't do that kind of thing."

He was rewarded with another ripple of laughter.

Before his questioner could interject again and, with renewed confidence, Will continued, "Of course you can blame the English! The suppression of the rebellion of 1798 was one of the most brutal and callous acts of any government of the time. 30,000 died! That's more than during the whole of the Terror in Paris. Come to think of it, it's more than died in the American War of Independence."

Will paused to ensure his statement had sunk in with his audience. "It's incredible really. How many books, films, musicals and more have there been about Paris and the guillotine? And yet nobody outside of Ireland remembers the Irish Revolution. But I'm digressing. You could also blame the French for losing interest, until it was too late. After the failed landing of '96, they refused to invade until they could see a revolt in motion. Why don't we blame the Ascendancy too? The upper classes in Dublin were quite happy to sell out their countrymen, to keep their power and position. They had most to lose from rebellion. Finally we can blame the United Irishmen themselves for being in disarray and letting 1797 drift away, while the authorities infiltrated their ranks and the British army in Ireland organised itself.

If you want someone to blame, there is no shortage of candidates, but where does that get you? – Right back to square one and all the troubles of the last two hundred years. It is more helpful to understand why it all happened and to learn from it. What interests me out of all the 'what ifs', is the fact that, more than any other time in five hundred years, the Irish had a chance to unite and create something better."

"That's all very laudable Mr. Peters," the other middle aged man picked up the discussion, "but it needed a successful revolution for this. You say that would have inspired the French to return. What would it have taken, in your opinion, to make it happen?"

The man seemed in earnest, the question was born out of something more than mere academic interest. Will was impressed that this stranger was so keen to hear *his* opinion. Until tonight, the only questions he'd fielded were about the opening hours of the bar.

"Historians will always argue, but in my view?" Will looked for encouragement and the man nodded.

"It needed an uprising at least a year earlier, followed swiftly by a French landing. The spring of 1797 would have been ideal. At the end of '96 the British were hopelessly unprepared, but the failed landing at Bantry Bay served as a wake up call. After that the clock was ticking. With every month that went by they clawed back control. The army, under General Lake, was given Pitt's blessing to carry out the most appalling cruelty and violence in order to break down the infrastructure of the rebels and confiscate their weapons."

Will paused to note that they were all hanging on his every word. Don't take yourself too seriously, he warned himself again.

"Mind you there was always the problem of getting past the Royal Navy. The same weather, which beat the landing in December '96, was also a good cover for the French to escape the blockade of Brest. In better weather, it would not have been so easy." His audience looked convinced and Will added with a laugh.

"There were also the small matters of a lack of arms, dearth of experienced military leadership and major religious and economic differences. If that wasn't enough, most of the rebel factions were riddled with spies leaking their plans to Dublin Castle. And then of course... Look, I could go on. You've called my bluff on the 'what if' game. If they'd got on with it, had French support and perhaps some arms ahead of that, it just might not have turned out so different from what happened in France and North America.

Would that have made a peaceful, prosperous Ireland, where they all lived happily ever after? I doubt it would've been that simple. It never is, but you can make up your own answers to that one."

There were no more questions and another round of applause.

The Prof. was good enough to come over and congratulate Will, as he shut down his laptop. "Can I buy you a drink, young man?"

Will was about to accept, when he remembered, with a little smile, that he was meeting Inge in the college bar. He wished that they'd agreed to meet somewhere more private. As he checked that he had all his possessions, he noticed that most of his audience had dispersed. To his surprise the two middle-aged men had hung back.

One of them approached him.

"We enjoyed your little talk. If ever you get tired of all this," he waved his arms around to indicate the old college building, "give me a ring."

He slipped Will a card, with his name and the address of some Boston Research Association on it and the two of them were gone.

Will pocketed the card and decided that he could not wait to see Inge any longer. Instead of taking his laptop back to the room he decided to go directly to the bar. As he rushed along the corridor and down the old spiral stairs to the corner of the Front Quadrangle, he started to doubt that Inge would be there. The Quad was deserted and the darkened windows of the first floor rooms gave the place an eerie atmosphere. He descended the stairs to the basement bar and looked around, trying not to appear too anxious.

"How did it go Will?"

Inge was sitting alone at a table with a paperback and the remains of a lager.

Will smiled, hoping he was showing pleasure and not relief. "Actually, it went very well. It was a full house."

"You are so funny with your 'actually' and I thought a full house was for poker or something."

Will's confidence evaporated immediately, the euphoria of the lecture's success, disappearing fast. His face must have given him away.

"Hey, I'm sorry Will, I just mean that I don't think I will ever master English. Look! Here I am in Oxford and I'm reading some crappy German paperback." She waved the book at him.

"Any chance of buying a poor foreign girl a drink?" She raised her almost empty glass and opened her big blue eyes.

They only had the one drink, before Inge suggested that Will might prefer coffee in her room. Will lead the way past the Shelley Memorial, hesitating only to operate the keypad that unlocked the door to the student rooms. Outside her room Will suddenly remembered the pink underpants. She'd probably tell the entire college. Maybe this was just a ruse to lead him on and then turn him down.

"Um, I just need to pop into my room and get something," he murmured.

"You don't have to worry. I have something in my room," Inge replied, with a wink.

Will could feel his face reddening.

"No, no it's something else. I won't be a moment," he stammered.

"That's ok. I will make the coffee or I would if I had any!" Inge giggled.

Will could feel things happening, but decided to pursue his original plan. Inge entered her room and left Will to fumble frantically with his key, which he dropped in his excitement. Finally, after putting his laptop on the floor, he managed to undo the lock. He picked up the machine and shouldered the door.

There, on his bed lay Suki, the Chemistry first year. She was wearing jeans and a pale blue T-shirt. Her legs were twisted at an odd angle to the rest of her body. There was something wet on the pillow by her mouth.

"Suki, what the hell are you doing in my room?" Will could only think how she would ruin his plans with Inge. "Are you ok? How did you …?"

Something was wrong. He touched her hand and shrank back. It was cold.

Suki was dead.

Chapter 5

Oxford
Late March 2002

Will had thought his life deadly dull. It was nothing compared to the hell it became after Suki's death. He was taken into police custody. Lonely hours dragged by in a cell smelling of urine and vomit, fear gnawing away constantly.

Then they came for him.

How long had he known her? What was the nature of their relationship? Did he hate Japanese people? Did he have any sexual perversions? Was she not willing to play his depraved sexual games? What had he drugged her with? Where did he get the stuff? Was he a user? Was he her dealer?

The nightmare deepened by the hour.

Like the frightened fool that he was, he had said far too much before the police-appointed solicitor arrived. He kept telling himself that it didn't matter. He hadn't done anything wrong. He'd only slept with her and she had been willing enough, at first anyway. They had it all out of him in no time. Why did she run out of his room screaming? What had he done to her? Even with these horrors unfolding, the penny never dropped, that he could be charged.

Until he was refused bail. Then he was terrified.

Next his parents arrived from Harrow; mother all embarrassed and indignant, father concerned about what his perverted little son had done now. Will was forced to explain all the gruesome details and it all kicked off.

His mother clucked around him, "Are they feeding you properly? You need to keep up your strength."

His father took a very different line, "For pity's sake Cath, he could be charged with murder. Don't you realise how serious this is? Look William, all I want to know is did you do it? It was an accident wasn't it? You didn't mean to do it."

"Ronald how can you even think such a thing? This is our son we are talking about here. William would never hurt anyone."

"I know, I know, but we need to clear this up as soon as possible and with the minimum fuss."

"You mean the minimum scandal. All you're concerned about is whether this will get back to your damn Tory party." His mother was screaming now.

It was to no avail. If it hadn't been Oxford, it might not have made the tabloids. They loved it and published an old college picture that made him look like a junkie. By the time the post mortem came in the damage to his reputation was done. They decided that he could not have administered the fatal cocktail of drugs. Thank God he was presenting his lecture, at the time the coroner decided the drugs must have been taken. He had a room full of witnesses. The verdict was suicide.

Relief washed over Will like a tidal wave. He went back to his old room and tried to put the tragedy behind him. He just wanted his boring old life back. He craved normality. What he found was guilt. Somehow it really was his fault. If only he had treated her with respect. If only he had talked to her instead of just trying to lure her into bed. If only, if only... No matter how hard he tried his old life would not come back. Within days he was wallowing again in the trough of depression.

And there was something else. Will could not delete the image of Suki's corpse from his mind. The way she had been lying. It wasn't right. Why hadn't the police noticed that? Did he move her when he had found her? He couldn't remember. That wasn't all. Some of his things had been scattered on the floor, as if there had been a struggle or maybe someone carrying her body had clumsily knocked them over. It wasn't suicide, he was sure. It petrified him. He wanted to tell the police and yet when they discharged him, he said nothing. He was too much of a coward. It was easier to accept it. After all, if it were murder, someone had to have committed it. Someone still out there who'd had access to his room. Who?

The nightmare would begin all over again. The police would want to question him all over again. And all the time he would be wondering if whoever did it would come back. Will's mind spun in ever decreasing circles. It was so much easier to believe in suicide.

His post started to come in once more. The letters remained unopened. He had messages on his mobile. He couldn't bring himself to answer them.

To make matters worse he was famous, well infamous. There was nowhere to hide. He was like the monster in a Victorian melodrama, a figure of both fear and fascination. The undergraduates kept pestering him about it. Thankfully the Easter vacation came and most of them were gone. Still life did not improve. The college staff shunned him. He wanted to scream at them that he was innocent. Strangely the papers never ran *that* story. It was no good. He had committed the cardinal sin. He had brought scandal to this venerable establishment.

If he could have consoled himself with Inge it might have been easier. She had disappeared before the police released him. She had shot back to Germany without a word or even a note. It was hardly surprising. Who would want to hang out with a guy whose ex came round to top herself in his bed? It didn't look good on your sexual CV.

He avoided his usual haunts around High Street, Broad Street and St.Giles, drifting listlessly to the outskirts of town, to the housing estate pubs. These were the ugly bits of Oxford never mentioned in the tourist guides. He was unlikely to run into any students and the academic staff would not be seen dead there. He kept his own company and drank.

On Good Friday he had a visitor from another University. Will spent the day cruising the pubs and when he returned the visitor had gone. He had left a note with a phone number on a compliments slip from Boroughbridge University. Will put it in his wallet to phone later, when he felt more like it.

Easter Sunday fell on 31st of March and Will typically had spent it alone. His mother had wanted him to come home to Harrow. He couldn't face it. The police had finally released the last of his confiscated possessions. Although cleared of the murder charge, it took them until Easter to release his laptop and papers. They hadn't even had the decency to bring them to him in person. A package had been left at the gatehouse and the porter had put a note in his pigeonhole.

He knew the end was coming and, when it did, it was almost a relief. He sat on his own, in his room, on Easter Monday and looked at the note, where he had tossed it on the bed together with an unopened letter from the Department. He pulled himself together and opened the letter. It was polite, simply enquiring if he would like to meet the Professor in his rooms on Wednesday at 10 a.m., to discuss his position at the college. So that was it. Well no point in whingeing, he had moaned enough about how boring it all was. It looked like he was in for a change. He looked at the note again. He just could not be bothered to go down to the Porter's Lodge. It had waited this long. It could wait another day.

Wednesday came and so did the news he'd expected. The Prof. assured him that there was no rush and no pressure. His contribution was well respected. He had a bright future and a great potential, which he would undoubtedly fulfil at *some other academic institution*. The Prof. had good contacts at Southampton University or perhaps Will might consider a move to New England. The Prof. knew someone. It wasn't Ivy League of course…. Will wasn't listening. He thanked the Prof., although for what he couldn't imagine, said he would think about it and come back to him. Yes, yes, by the end of the week, if that was what the Prof. wanted.

He stepped out of the Prof's rooms onto Radcliffe Quadrangle. In a dream he stopped and gawped at the fan vaulting over the gateway, the pride of University College. He wandered through the little passage, passed the spiral stairs and into the Front Quadrangle. The beds around the central lawns were resplendent with their spring flowers. Passing the Porter's Lodge, for no reason he could recall, he went in and enquired about his parcel from the police. The reception he received was polite but frosty. He was accustomed to that now.

Unable to face his lonely room, he stepped through the wooden door and down the steps onto High Street. For a moment he stood surveying the scene, undecided. Then he crossed diagonally towards the café, where he and Inge had drunk coffee so long ago.

From across the street, by the gates to Logic Lane, a young boy with red hair watched him and smiled.

Will ordered coffee at the counter and took it to a seat in the rear corner of the café. He sat at a breakfast bar facing the wall. Used to making himself inconspicuous, nobody noticed him opening a large envelope. It contained letters, which had already been opened, presumably by the police, and the business card from The Boston Research Group, which he tossed back into the envelope.

Will sifted through the junk mail and his memory flickered. One letter had a Boroughbridge postmark. The envelope had been hand written. The police had taken little care in opening it and the envelope had been taped up. The contents seemed intact. It looked like an invitation.

Dear Mr. Peters

Congratulations! You have been shortlisted to be a guest at our conference. We have researched your background and feel that your contribution to the discussion groups...

Junk mail after all, thought Will and was at the point of binning it, when he noticed the venue.

You will enjoy seeing the sights of the Cathedral ....whilst staying in historic University College...

University College, Durham, same name, different city and it was where he had spent his undergraduate years. Right now any bolthole would be welcome. His old college would be great, even if it were only for a couple of nights. He read on.

Dreams have revealed interesting insights into certain historic events and new interpretations can be made. We will welcome your participation...

A research team will be set up and Boroughbridge University will be offering a one-year research post to certain candidates. Given the generosity of the sponsors, the remuneration package will be significantly higher than is normally associated with this sort of position.

Good grief, thought Will, they're offering jobs. A few weeks ago he would have turned his nose up at the thought of a modern university. Now a high paid job at a low profile academic institution was a dream come true. Reading the whole letter again from beginning to end, he suddenly noticed the dates. The letter was over a month old! They were using the University during the Easter vacation and the event was to take place in five days time.

There was a form to complete and mail back. The closing date had passed. Draining his cup, Will gathered up his papers and rushed out of the café in search of a quiet corner to use his mobile.

How stupid I am, thought Will. He had pinned all his hopes on securing a place on this conference. It was absurd and out of proportion, reflecting his fragile state of mind. The conference had become an escape for him. For the first time, since Suki's death, he could see a shaft of light.

They had been positive enough on the phone, but would they take him? Doubts began to plague him. He might have been sought after before. What if they'd heard about the Suki business? This letter had been written before all that took place. Ridiculously this conference had become the only thing in his life that mattered.

After two interminable days, he went down to the mailroom. The porters were still sorting the post. A large stiffened manila letter sat in his pigeonhole. Surely they would not need an envelope that size for a refusal? He tore it open and read the first few lines of the letter. Thank God, he was accepted!

He examined the other contents of the envelope. There was a glossy brochure about Durham City and the University. Will tossed it to one side. He knew all that after three years as an undergraduate. What caught his eye next was a folder about Boroughbridge. It contained the normal stuff, bits about the various departments, sports facilities and halls of residence. There was the usual selection of photographs of happy multi-national undergraduates, looking studious in lab coats or playing football. He tossed that aside too.

Finally he found a small leaflet promoting the conference. It was by invitation only and would include some of the top minds in their field. They were a real mixed bag, chemists, psychologists, medical doctors and of course historians. There were senior people from various multi-nationals and the big drug companies. He stuffed it all back into the envelope and, for a change, headed for one of the cafes in the indoor market, to study it all in more detail.

The market was busy and he struggled to find a seat. Appetite returned, he sat down with a cappuccino and two toasted sandwiches. He read the letter properly. They wanted his bank details to pay him for attending. This wasn't just a freebie it was a paybie and only three days to go.

Finally Will felt that life was worth living.

Chapter 6

Durham
Monday 8th April 2002

Will's old MG didn't like the journey. It drank oil and the faults in the suspension found every bump in the roads north to Durham. Will didn't care. It felt great to be free of Oxford and its oppressive atmosphere. With the top down and the cold sunshine dancing on his woolly hat, he sang loudly, through his old college scarf, and didn't care who heard him. The scene of his undergraduate years beckoned and who knew what opportunities.

Oh Durham! Home of the finest cathedral in the world. Will had been captivated, when, as a seventeen-year-old schoolboy, he gazed up at its magnificent facade, nervously awaiting his college interview. It had been love at first sight. Will could see it in his mind's eye, as he drove north. Nearly a thousand years old, it still imposed its presence over the River Wear, the city and the surrounding country. Will was not a religious man and yet still it inspired him. The centuries passed, the world moved on, but Durham Cathedral still stood aloof, defying time itself.

The reality turned out to be a little disappointing. It was fine at first. University College in its Norman Castle; he sighed with content, as he swept into the familiar Palace Green, with its well-tended grass and parked in the area, normally reserved for staff. He felt very privileged. Only gradually did it dawn on him. It was just not the same now all his old mates and many of the staff had moved on. He knew it is always the people that make a place. The Cathedral, the River Wear, the College, his favourite old pubs; all these places were still there, but where were the familiar faces, which had made it such a happy place for him?

He went through the check-in procedures in a dream, left his bags in the room allocated and strolled down Saddler Street and into the Market Place to seek solace in a familiar pub. Even the bar staff have changed, thought Will, as he drank his pint in one of the old stained armchairs. In an alcove at the back of the bar, next to the log fire, it was a favourite spot. Will and his close circle of friends had always met there. It had been their corner and he had felt stupidly resentful when somebody else had occupied it. In this very seat he had asked Alice to go with him to the gig in Newcastle, when that had all started. It was only a couple of years back and yet it seemed a lifetime ago. Oh for Christ's sake what's the matter with you man? You've got to snap out of this, Will chided himself.

Quiet though it was, the fire had been lit and the crackling logs offered Will some comfort, the beer beginning to work its magic. He eased himself back in the chair and looked around the bar. Business really was slow. Although a student haunt, it used to attract a good mix of locals, sustaining the pub, after the students had gone down. This was part of the charm of the place.

The double doors opened to let in a chill draught and a tall man of about his own age. He strode up to the bar and ordered Guinness. As he lifted the black glass with its creamy head to his lips, he made some comment and the barman laughed. The stranger leant on the bar and looked around. He appeared to Will to be at ease with the world, confident in any environment. How absurd thought Will, I have no idea who you are and yet I both envy and resent you. The man moved away from the bar and headed towards Will.

"Is there anyone sitting there?" he asked, indicating the armchair next to Will. "Why does everyone say that? I can see there's nobody there. If I was really honest I'd say something like, I'm on my own and wouldn't mind a blather. Could you use some company?" He extended a hand towards Will. "Sean O'Grady, would be psychologist flown over from Dublin for some hare-brained History type Psychology Conference." He withdrew the hand and put it to his forehead. "Oh, now don't tell me you're the fella in charge."

It struck the right chord with Will. "Will Peters, not sure why I came to Durham for some crazy Historio sort of Psychology do, main attraction all expenses paid. Great to meet you; I was just sitting here, thinking I'd made a huge mistake."

"Well, like me you're here now. Perhaps we can have a laugh. So tell me Will, what do you make of all this stuff? It didn't say much in the letter. Where have you come from? How did you hear about it?"

Will ran over the details of the letter he'd received. He explained how it had been delayed in the post, omitting the reasons why. He'd had to make a quick decision. Perhaps it was the wrong one. He hadn't really much idea about the research, but his curiosity had got the better of him. Oxford could be a bit of an ivory tower.

"Oxford eh?" Sean looked suitably impressed. "So you're one of England's top history men are you?" Sean had eased back in his chair and stretched out his tall frame to warm his feet. "They said they were trawling for the very best people in their fields. Seems it wasn't bullshit. And how is a bright fella like yourself going to make his mark in the world?"

It was such an innocent question, just showing an interest in a new acquaintance. Although it was flattering, it touched a nerve. Will's academic achievements were not in dispute. Now he had to leave Oxford and his comfort zone. It was a little daunting. He considered inventing some grandiose plan, but something in those twinkling blue eyes told him that the Irishman would not be easily taken in. The truth was depressing, a poorly paid research post at a lesser academic institution, if he was lucky. His father was hardly going to fund him any longer. Or he could opt for the dreaded teaching. He admitted to reviewing a few possibilities, which sounded lame and gave Sean the opening he wanted.

"To be honest with you Will, I'm in a bit of a dead end job. I've done my doctorate and I'm kicking my heels at Trinity. The truth of it is, I don't think they know what to do with me. To cap it all, the pay's crap an' all. I was kinda hoping there might be a job at the end of this." He shrugged, "I'm not sure I wanted to admit to that. Ah, a fella like you would probably laugh at me. After all who's ever heard of Boroughbridge? I'll tell you what, if you promise not to take the piss, I'll tell you what I found out. First things first; another pint?"

Sean didn't tell, not for a while. The beer flowed and Will heard the joke about the two Irish psychiatrists, who kept getting drunk, because they both thought that they were treating each other. It wasn't very funny and Will wasn't sure why he laughed. There was a little bit of his inbred politeness and something about the way Sean told it. You couldn't help but laugh and besides, by then, Sean was in a shocking state. How much had they had?

Sean leaned towards Will with a conspiratorial smile. "I was going to tell you what I found out." He paused to belch. "I rang them up and got hold of this guy… what was his name? Jones. Doesn't sound very likely does it? His real name's probably Smith." Sean giggled. "Anyway, he said that the whole thing is really a glorified recruitment operation." He lowered his voice and leant in a little closer. "I'm probably being very naïve, yer know, but he reckoned I was short listed."

Sean took a vigorous swig from his pint and spilt most of it down his shirt. "Look I really shouldn't tell you this. They've pulled in all sorts from industry and the academic world. They'll be some interviews and maybe some games – you know the kind of stuff – team building and so on. It should be a breeze." He leaned forward until his mouth was a hands width form Will's ear. "Have you any idea what there're paying?"

Sean's face was drifting in and out of Will's focus. "Nope!" He slapped Sean's thigh. "But you're going to tell me."

"To be sure, to be sure," Sean played the caricature Irishman. "These guys are offering up to fifty grand for a one year residential contract. You're giving your life up, but what the hell for that kind of money. Would that be enough to slum it at Boroughbridge?" He swayed and put his finger to his lips. "Shhhh."

"You're bloody joking. How much?" He leant back and tried to concentrate. "I think I'd go to Fenland Polytechnic for that money."

"Fenland what?" queried Sean, puzzled.

Like a couple of drunken swans in a bizarre mating ritual, they swayed back and forth.

"Cambridge to you," advised Will.

Sean leant heavily on the table, missed and slipped to the floor. "Heh Will, I think I'm wasted. Where are you staying?"

"University College. S'not far. Wha' about you?"

"The shame. Show me the way to go home."

Arm in arm the two men staggered up the hill to the college. With drunken goodnights, Will headed off to his room.

Sean held back and wandered back outdoors. He ambled out to the street, taking in huge gulps of cold night air. He looked up and down the street. There was not a soul in sight.

"The bloody things I do for Ireland!" he sighed and he too went off to bed.

The conference did not start until 11 a.m. to allow those delegates arriving that day, time to travel. At 6.30 Sean woke to the insistent buzz of his alarm. He dragged himself out of bed, splashed water on his face and tottered downstairs and onto the street. He bought three newspapers and took them back to the Great Hall, where breakfast was served. A coffee in hand he sat at a table from where he could admire the stained glass, the portraits and the entrance. He read the first paper. No sign of Will. He tossed it onto an adjacent table and bought another coffee. By the time Will emerged, head down and unshaven, it was 9 a.m. Everyone else had eaten breakfast and Sean was on the sports page of newspaper three.

"You look like I feel," quipped Sean looking up from the paper.

"Coffee the best you can do? I think I need some grease if I'm going to live till lunchtime," murmured Will

"Ah go on with you, I'll go after the eggs if you can."

The two ordered a full English breakfast each and more coffee and sat down. The hangovers and the food prevented much conversation at first. Gradually the clouds lifted and they turned to the events in front of them.

Will started in hushed tones. "Please tell me I didn't dream what you told me last night, you know, about the pay. Of course I'm only here out of academic interest – like hell. You know, they weren't even paying me at Oxford. It's all gowns and no cash, old chap!"

"It's the bloody same the world over. They tell you how great you are, but when it comes down to it they pinch your best research and pay you nothing. Look, don't take what I said last night as gospel."

Will's face fell.

"No, Will I wasn't lying to you. It's just that, well, what I told you was based on one phone call with some guy I've never met. He might have been saying that just to make me keen." Sean laughed. "It certainly worked. I'll be on me best behaviour and trying hard to impress." He looked across the table at Will. "Look here, I'm not being funny, but don't you think a shave might help? What time's the kick off? Do you know how we get there?"

"No, no you're right. I'd better go and clean up. We've still got nearly an hour. There's a coach picking us up at 10.30. The conference is in some new hotel, just outside the town. It seems a bit odd. I'd assumed that it was happening here at the college."

"Don't ask me. They're probably double booked. With any luck the food's better."

They parted to prepare for the day. When the coach arrived a group of about thirty-to-forty had congregated. Sean recognised most of them from his vigil in the refectory, while to Will they were all new faces. One very pretty face caught Will's eye. She was in her early twenties, he reckoned, with cute blonde hair. It was a style that his mother would have described as a bob. She was very animated, waving her arms around and talking loudly, in an odd American accent, to an older woman.

You'd hardly miss her in a crowd, thought Will, even if she weren't so pretty. He tried to figure out her accent, possibly Canadian. A name formed itself in his mind, 'Canadian Bob!' He wouldn't mind if she got through!

For the rest of them it was odd. Will found himself eyeing up the competition, for that was how he saw them, not as colleagues or chance associates at a conference. His desire to escape Oxford and earn some money re-ignited within him.

Will and Sean sat together at the back of the coach, which wound its way out of the old part of the city. As Will looked out of the window, the shoppers on the streets looked like inhabitants from another world. Will had spent all his life in the academic world and had always felt a little apart from the mainstream. He smiled. It was a kind of snobbery he supposed. Most of the people out there were not as bright or well educated as he was, but many probably earned a lot more than he would. Today he felt more estranged than ever.

Sean nudged Will back to the present. "I think we're here. Welcome to historic Durham!"

They had arrived at a modern Enterprise Park on the outskirts of the city. Like so many all over the country, it had been intended for small industrial units. Instead it was mostly occupied by retail outlets and discount warehouses. The bus paused outside a modern hotel, waiting for a gap in the traffic. They were directly opposite a kitchen and bathroom centre. Will looked at a five metre high, inflated caricature of a crazy man with big glasses and cross-eyes. Underneath it said, 'You'd be mad to drive by!'

Sean caught his gaze. "There's been a mix up. It should be outside our hotel!"

Will laughed. "I can see the family resemblance."

The contents of the coach spilled into the hotel reception and signs directed them towards the Castle Suite. Will noticed what a cross section they were. Mostly his age, they were dressed so differently. Some were in suits, others in jackets with ties and a few in jeans and sweaters. Sean and Will had agreed over breakfast on the centre ground of jackets and open neck shirts. At least the two of them looked similarly attired, if dress code was an issue.

Access to the main conference room was gained through a smaller room, where coffees and biscuits were laid out, beneath murals portraying images of the castle and the cathedral. Little groups of twos and threes formed, drinking coffee and a buzz of conversation filled the air. Before Sean and Will could even grab a coffee, a tall, thin, balding man in a bottle green cord jacket and matching tie detached himself from a group and came over to greet them. "Welcome to the conference gentlemen. My name is Dr. Jones." He pointed to a badge on his lapel. "I am heading up the project. Pleased to meet you. We'll have to get you badged up. You are...?" He extended a large thin hand towards Sean.

"Sean O'Grady. It's a pleasure to meet," he double checked the badge, "Dr. Jones."

Jones turned to Will.

"Will Peters, likewise Dr. Jones. I'm intrigued about the conference. Can you tell us what's in store for us today."

"Of course, of course." Jones glanced over and nodded to a suited man across the room, "I will be explaining all that shortly in my opening address. Tomorrow we will be selecting the lucky ones, who will be offered places on our team. We may not be able to fill all the places as we can only take the really top candidates."

All Will's competitive instincts came to the fore. He glanced at Sean, who winked.

At that moment the gentleman in the grey suit joined them. His fat hand clamped Will's and pumped it. "Waugh's the name. Desmond Waugh. I'm from the U.S. end of the project. It's not that we don't trust you Brits, we just like to see what you're doing with our money!" He laughed and, to Will's relief, released his hand and seized Sean's. "Pleased to meet you."

He looked at Jones who stammered, "Dr. O'Grady and er, er, Will Peters."

Waugh glared at Jones for a moment and then continued enthusiastically, "Great, great. Welcome aboard. You've got a fascinating day in front of you and," he leant in towards them, "for the top guys, there's a great reward. Heh, if we're all here, you'd better get this show on the road Dr. Jones. Don't worry, guys. You've got time for coffee. It'll take a few minutes to start. Bring your cups with you."

Will and Sean helped themselves to coffees and followed the rest of the throng through into the adjacent room. A heavily patterned red and cream carpet clashed with a similar colour scheme on the walls. Full-length drapes were tied back at the windows and the scent of the floral displays filled the room. It was laid out formally with rows of chairs facing a raised platform with a lectern on it. A screen had been set up beside the platform and at either side of the room at the front were printed signs, with the name and coat of arms for Boroughbridge University and the title of the conference. 'Historical Insight – Art or Science?' The coat of arms was very elaborate for a new university. Up yours Oxbridge, thought Will.

Will picked up a conference pack and sat next to Sean near the front of the room. As usual everyone had filled the seats at the back of the room first, leaving the late arrivals only the front rows.

Dr. Jones approached the lectern and the murmur of voices around the room subsided. "Welcome to our conference. Thank you all for coming. I appreciate that some of you have travelled considerable distances to be here. We also appreciate that many of you do not have a clear idea of the objectives of the next two days and probably only came for the generous remuneration package, for which we thank our sponsors." He nodded towards Desmond Waugh, who was sitting on the platform with several others.

Jones let the wave of embarrassed laughter around the room subside. "This morning, I and my colleagues, would like to outline the research we have been carrying out over the last few years. We will then lead into the plans for the next twelve months, the new project, which we wish to set up and the team we are seeking to make it happen. This will take us through to around 4 p.m. You will then have a couple of hours to have a look around Durham."

"We meet for dinner tonight in the Great Hall in the college at 8 p.m. Your dinner will be prepared in the fifteenth century kitchen." He paused to receive a gratifying intake of breath from his audience. "But don't worry," he continued, "most of the food was procured in the last one hundred years!

You will see that you will be seated along tables with bench seats. Spaces have been left for my colleagues and I to circulate amongst you during dinner and acquaint ourselves better with you all. So I will be grateful if you will adhere to the seating plan. By the end of the evening some of you may have had enough of us lot," he gestured towards his colleagues on the platform. "If the thought of spending the next twelve months with us, fills you with dread," he paused for a murmur of laughter, "that's fine. We won't take a suicide pact, but we will appreciate it if you let us know.

The reason is that tomorrow morning we will be conducting interviews for a limited number of places on our research team.

If you are not interested, we will be wasting each other's time, so you may leave with a token of our appreciation and our best wishes. From the rest, we will select a group of between six and twelve, depending on their qualifications, suitability and academic discipline. This will be demanding work and we may not fill our quota. On the other hand, we have the funding to take on more, if we feel you have something unique to bring to the party. It all depends on you. Any questions?"

He paused for a moment. Nobody responded. "O.K. enough of me for the moment. We have a short film presentation for you, by way of introduction and then we will start on the programme of presentations, which is outlined in your packs."

Sean leaned across to Will. "If we both make notes during the day, we can compare them later, when all the other jokers are gawping at the cathedral."

"Good plan," acknowledged Will.

"I'll tell yer what. We could split up over lunch and suss out the competition too. That'd be useful. What do you think?" added Sean.

"Better still," agreed Will.

By 4.45 p.m. they were sitting in Will's room, back at the college, talking it through.

"What do you think about it all Sean? Are they all barking or am I? What was the phrase that Dr. Jones used? '…so fixed in our preconceived notions of time and history that our minds won't let us lift our heads to see over the next hill'?"

"That's a helluva question, Will and I'm not sure that I know the answer. When you cut through all the blarney what are you left with?" Sean answered his own question. "Some guys have taken some cool dope and come up with some interesting historical stories. They chucked this at a bunch of you history guys, who reckon there could be something in it. The chemists have mixed up a new batch of stuff and they want to do it again. It might be crazy, but nobody gets hurt and we can earn some serious money. My only worry, Will, is that I'm not sure why they want someone like me. Historians, yes, medics, yes, clinical psychiatrists, yes, but psychologists, I'm not sure."

"I thought you said that they'd hinted you were in," replied Will.

"Well I did think so, but now I'm not so sure."

"Do you really think nobody gets hurt Sean? In spite of what you say, that's more your area than mine. I've got no idea about drugs. Are these things they've been giving out harmful? It sounded a bit like one or two of them might have had a bad trip, don't you reckon?"

Sean hesitated for a moment. "I know they said that some of this stuff was experimental. Let's face it, that's what its all about. Just the same I'm sure it's all been through the usual trials." He pulled his head into his shoulders and drew his hands up in front of his face. "Somewhere a guinea-pig has witnessed the Battle of Hastings. Squeeeek!"

"O.k. I guess I'm being a bit paranoid here," Will laughed, "but I'm a bit uncomfortable with drugs. I've seen a few people, you know, take the wrong stuff, that sort of thing." Will flushed as an image of Suki's twisted body appeared in his mind. This was getting a bit deep for comfort. "Look I've smoked the odd joint, but I don't want to be part of some horrendous drugs trial. That's all I'm saying."

"No, I'm with you on that Will. I think we're jumping the gun here, though. Don't you reckon that we ought to focus on getting selected? If, at the end of the day they do pick us, we can always say no. Shall we look at who we're up against?"

Will agreed and they pooled their knowledge on the other candidates with whom they'd chatted during the day.

He pulled out the delegate list from the conference pack. "I think my chances are good against these two. I've met them and I don't rate them at all. What about this guy – have you spoken to him?" Will indicated a Cambridge post-graduate, an historian, David Smethwick. "It's always the same," he moaned, "it's like the bloody boat race, Oxford versus Cambridge."

"I hate to be the bearer of bad news," said Sean. "I talked to him over lunch. He seems pretty switched on and keen too. We could always poison him at dinner, I suppose," he added with a laugh.

They continued through the list and then chewed over the conference presentations, anticipating interview questions until they decided it was time to get ready for the dinner.

Will and Sean entered the Great Hall together. Many of the overseas visitors were clearly impressed. To Will it was pure nostalgia and he tried to put his memories to the back of his mind. The organisers had put Will and Sean on the same table and the team moved amongst them as promised. Will found it reassuring to have Sean there. Despite his fears and doubts, Sean seemed confident in conversation with the other candidates and the project team. Knowing that he was the only one who understood Sean's doubts made Will feel an affinity for him, more than he had felt for anyone in a long time.

When they boarded the coach the following morning, Will was both shocked and then delighted to see how at least half of the contenders had dropped out. He did some quick mental arithmetic. If there were around twenty left and they took six to twelve, he had a better than fifty percent chance of selection. On the coach he counted again. There were twenty-four including him and Sean, who was doing the same sums.

"I've put money on horses at longer odds than that," said Sean. "We'll breeze it," and he gave Will a reassuring pat on the arm.

"Shame our mate from Cambridge is still with us," moaned Will.

They arrived at the hotel and were ushered into the same room, where coffee and biscuits were laid out as before. This time however, they were forced to sit and wait their turn to be ushered into the main conference room. Sean took a quick look, as one of the other candidates entered for his interview. All the chairs had been cleared to leave a long table in the middle of the room. On one side was a row of chairs for the project team, Jones at the centre. On the other side was a single chair for the interviewee.

It was nerve-wracking and it was embarrassing. Will found himself making small talk and wishing good luck to the very person he wanted to fail, David Smethwick, from Cambridge. To Will's irritation David had homed in on him, as a soul mate; the two historians left in the game. It felt worse that there seemed no logic to the order in which they were called. At any moment the door could open and your name could be called. The numbers gradually dwindled. One by one they were called in and later emerged, jubilant or crestfallen.

The door opened again and out shot 'Canadian Bob,' screaming with delight. "I'm in! I'm in!" and threw her arms around the neck of the woman from the bus stop, who was still waiting her turn. "Don't worry. You'll be fine. You'll see. Just be yourself. I'll wait for you in the bar."

Without a glance at Sean or Will, she released her friend, turned and headed for the bar. As Will watched her cute little tail disappear from view, he wanted to make it more than ever.

"This is like some kind of torture," moaned Sean eventually. "I've drunk so much coffee, I need to shed a few tears for Ireland. If I miss me slot, tell them that I did it for me country."

Will laughed and it broke the tension. He doubted the others understood. They certainly weren't amused. It was beginning to look as though he and Sean might be the last.

David Smethwick was called and again Will heard himself wishing him well. After what seemed like an age, Smethwick returned jubilant. He shook Will's hand waved to the others and was gone. Will's heart sank and it was written all over his face. Sean smiled and shrugged.

Then there were two, just Sean and Will. Sean was called. They slapped each other on the back and Will found himself alone. He couldn't face more coffee, decided to go to the toilet, changed his mind for fear of missing his interview, then changed it again and rushed to the toilet by the reception. He washed his hands hastily and didn't bother to dry them properly. When he returned, there was still no sign of Sean and he felt stupid for rushing. He flapped his hands around to dry them and hoped that nobody could see him.

The door opened and out strode Sean, big smile and double thumbs up. "I'm in and you won't believe the package." He noted Will's expression. "Don't panic, I told them I'll only do it, if they take you as well. No, no I didn't really, but I did say that you were the best qualified to do the job." He looked a bit embarrassed. "You'd better go in, you'll be fine."

They all sat across the table from Will, with Jones at the centre. "We're sorry to keep you waiting so long," he said. "We'll try to make this as brief as possible. Needless to say we've been looking at your files and you seem eminently suitable. We just have a few questions to clear up if you can bear with us a bit longer."

The questions seemed a little bizarre to Will, not inquisitive or investigative. They were easy to answer, which was a huge relief. With each one, it seemed he was taking one step nearer to the exit door that led away from the horrors of his Oxford existence.

"Do you realise that the project may be considerably more practical than the academic work you are used to currently?"

"That may present me with new challenges, which I'd enjoy."

"Are you prepared to move to a room on campus at Boroughbridge?"

"Well of course, it'll probably be more modern than the room I'm in just now."

"The work is sponsored by the Her Majesty's Government. It is confidential. Are you prepared to sign the Official Secret's Act?"

Will paused. "I didn't realise that the project would be confidential in that sense, but I can't see a problem with that."

"Welcome aboard Will Peters."

They all shook hands and a contract was handed over for him to read. When Will left the room, Sean was waiting for him. " Well?"

"I'm in!"

"I never doubted it for a minute," said Sean, with far too much sincerity, as they went for a pint to celebrate.

END OF PART ONE

PART TWO

Let George or William only send his troops to burn and
shoot,
We'll meet them here on equal ground, and fight them foot
to foot.

Extract from 'The Outlaw Reparee' (Traditional Irish Song)

Chapter 7

Boroughbridge University, English Midlands
Tuesday June 4th 2002

"Forget everything that you've heard about time travel. It's a state of mind, not of being. You might need a tardis to take your body back, not your mind," said Al Davidson.

Al was a brash middle-aged American, from Yale. Will had met him only briefly at the induction at Durham, more than long enough to take a dislike to him. Al had also spoken at the presentations made in the main lecture hall the day before, when they had all arrived. At the time Will could not place him. Now he remembered. Al had written a number of papers on probability and theories linking mathematics and historical analysis. Simplistic, popularist rubbish thought Will.

The talks so far had seemed pretty simple, even dull. After the domestic stuff about accommodation and meals, the background to the project was explained, which was already clear. The trials had been explained, which Will understood in part. The drugs were described, which Will did not understand at all.

The only issue, which really grabbed his attention, was that they were not allowed off the campus. They were imprisoned, at least for the duration of the first module of the programme. And how long was that? Nobody seemed too sure. The staff had made light of it all and quipped that they were to be electronically tagged like criminals. All the participants had laughed and Will looked around to judge the reaction of his colleagues. He seemed to be the only one to show any concern, but he went along with the process.

Sure enough they were each fitted with a narrow metal strip, containing a miniature transmitter on their right wrists, so as not to interfere with their wristwatches. Unobtrusive and dull in colour, to some it might appeal, as a piece of modern jewellery. It provided a constant reminder of their loss of liberty to Will and he fiddled with his.

The speaker continued, "I am going to explain a theory, which has evolved from research carried out by the team here at Boroughbridge. It attempts to apply simple logic to the *practice* of time travel and from this we draw up our code of conduct, when *engaged* in time travel, which will be covered in this afternoon's session."

Will was still not sure whether he was the victim of some elaborate hoax. He looked at Sean, who was sitting next to him. Sean raised his eyebrows and grinned.

"Are they serious?" whispered Will. "This has to be some kind of a windup."

"Don't you worry your pretty little head about a thing," joked Sean. "Keep smiling, think of the money and let's just see what develops."

Will's mind wandered and he glanced around the small lecture theatre. It could hardly be described as such, more like a theatre on a luxury cruise liner. If the content of the lecture seemed a bit light, those behind the project hadn't stinted on the facilities. There was no disguising the building itself. It was a concrete monstrosity, a cross between a hospital and the high security wing of a prison; not that he'd ever seen one, Will admitted to himself. The inside was a different story. He was sitting in the middle of three rows of ten seats, which were banked to give each row a perfect view of the platform in front. There the likeness to any lecture theatre, that he had known, ended.

Each huge leather bound seat resembled the most luxurious airline sleepers. Infinitely adjustable at the touch of a button, they had control panels in the armrests and tables, which swung in front electronically. These in turn were wired to take a range of electronic equipment, including the occupants' laptops. Wifi pick-ups in the tables connected the laptops to the theatre's computer, permitting the downloading of lectures and all data automatically.

Thick carpets and polished hardwood trims added to the feeling of opulence.

Will drifted back to the lecture. A complicated historical chart appeared on the screen behind the speaker and simultaneously on his laptop. It showed a timeline over a period starting in 1760,when George III ascended the British throne, and passing through 1960 to the present. The timeline passed through the centre of the graph and formed the x axis. Along its path were marked a number of key dates, the American Declaration of Independence in 1776, the French Revolution in 1789, the Battle of Waterloo in 1815, the First and Second World Wars through to the Fall of Saigon and beyond. With a click of his remote mouse the lecturer scrolled the chart from left to right. He paused with the vertical axis over 1940. A further click revealed a whole network of lines, which cascaded across the screens, each leading to notes and dates.

"This is an interactive programme, developed by the team, but I am humble enough to suggest that it is only a prototype. With the help of you guys we hope to upgrade this over the next twelve months." He looked at his audience. "O.K. I need the help of an historian now."

Will focused again.

"Let me see, do we have David Smethwick here? Forgive me, but we're only on the first day of the first semester. We'll all get to know each other real soon."

Will felt an absurd twinge of jealousy as the Cambridge man identified himself.

Al Davidson continued, "O.K. David, I'd like you to right click over the 1940 date symbol and pick 'options' from the menu." A short list of events appeared. "David, pick any one of these." 'Battle of Britain' was highlighted. "Hold on there David, I want to ask a question… no not to you. Let's have some fun. Why don't I ask one of the scientists? How about you?" He indicated 'Canadian Bob' in the front row.

That gave Will all the excuse he needed to look at the young blonde more intently. Her attraction to Will had not diminished in the period since Durham. She was wearing a low cut blouse and a very short skirt and from his position, just behind her and to her left, Will commanded a good view of her legs.

"And you are…?"

"Valerie Duschenel. Pharmacologist from Quebec."

Ah so that's the accent, thought Will. Very nice, French Canadian.

Al came forward and fawned over the pretty blonde. "May I call you Val?" She didn't look too pleased. He ploughed on.

"Right Val, my question to you is about the Battle of Britain. The British R.A.F. was on the last line of defence and stretched to its limits. Goering's Luftwaffe outnumbered them and was bombing the hell out of their airbases. We've highlighted the period in red on our programme to show that it was a critical point in history. Don't look so puzzled Val. This was the time of one of Churchill's most famous speeches."

He picked up a thick marker pen and held it to his mouth like a cigar and continued in gruff Churchillian tones. "Never in the field of human conflict has so much been owed by so many to so few."

Al really had his audience in the palm of his hand now and they rewarded him with an appreciative round of applause.

The American bowed, gave the V for victory sign and puffed on the marker pen. "Drama classes start at 6 p.m."

They loved him and everyone laughed at Al's command performance.

"O.K. Val, you'll be thrilled to know that I haven't forgotten you. The question is back to you. What do you think would have happened, if the R.A.F. had lost the Battle of Britain?"

Valerie started to fidget in her seat. "Er, well er, I'm not too strong on British history. Maybe the Americans would have flown in?" She reddened up as the theatre erupted into laughter.

"I'm not too sure that we could or even wanted to pop over to Kent at that stage Val. You know how it is, mid season, the Yankees were playing at home..." He shrugged and was gratified with more laughter. "No. I'm being very unkind to you Val...er...ie." He exaggerated her name in a poor French accent. "Have another go."

By now she was bright red and the centre of attention.

Will seized his moment and leaned forward to whisper in her ear. "Hitler would have launched operation Sea Lion and invaded Britain." He caught a whiff of her scent and a closer look at her pink lips.

"O.K. O.K.," Valerie pulled her hands through her hair.

Will noticed her slender, white fingers.

"Hitler would have launched his sea lion and captured England," she blustered.

More laughter followed at the young Canadian's expense until Al held up his hand for silence. "You're on the right track now young lady, thanks to your knight in shining armour. And who are you sir?"

"Will Peters."

"Ah, our other historian, specialising in marine mammals, by the sound of it," Al responded, glancing down at his list. "Well perhaps you'd like to run with this ball for a while." He glanced back at Valerie. "Heh, I didn't mean to embarrass you. If we want a real laugh, we'll have Will dispense the drugs later, eh?" he chuckled, rolling his eyes. "Weeeee."

With his audience firmly under his spell, Al continued. "Now Will, can we be sure that Britain would have fallen to the Nazi hordes had the R.A.F. let the Luftwaffe gain control of the skies in the late summer of 1940?"

Will thought for a moment. "No, we can't say that with certainty, but so soon after the Fall of France, most of the British army's weapons left on the beaches at Dunkirk and Britain's defences in disarray, I can't see how an invasion would have been stopped."

"Excellent Will. Good old British reserve, we can't say that with certainty." He mimicked Will's London accent to more acclaim. "Yeh, but Will's right. It's likely but not certain. What would you say Will, percentage wise?"

"Oh I don't know," Will was feeling self conscious now about everything including his accent, "say ninety percent?"

"Not bad Will. Better than your chances with the lovely Val...er...ie? No. Only kidding, only kidding. Our system rates the odds at around seventy-two percent probability of success. There are all kinds of factors to consider. Could the Royal Navy have stopped an invasion fleet? Hitler's invasion fleet was not very sophisticated, nor were his troops well trained for this kind of warfare etc. etc. Nonetheless he probably would have done it. It doesn't matter right now. That's not the point of this demonstration."

Al looked up. "Now David are you still with us? Haven't nodded off? Good. Now Val thinks the Yanks are coming and I've got Will on a ninety percent chance of an invasion and with your help... See it's just like a game show!"

He pointed dramatically at David Smethwick. "Left click the 'Battle Lost' option, David."

David did as he was bid and the whole screen lit up like a fruit machine. Lines of lights made flashing arrows to the boxes, which in turn flashed amber.

"Oh my God David! I think you've broken it!"

David's face fell.

"It's a joke. Don't panic. David has just changed history. Britain has fallen to the Nazi invasion and Hitler is having Christmas dinner with the King of England in

Buckingham Palace!" he paused to pour himself a drink of water. It seemed to Will, that even this casual act was part of his stage show.

Al took a sip and put down the drink. "Now before we look at all those exciting boxes, let's have a good look at the big picture. David, click the 'view' box on the toolbar." A menu dropped down, with date options in annual increments up to five years. "Now click on '5 years,' David." The screen whizzed around and a series of dates and events appeared, together with more flashing lines and boxes.

"O.K. everybody, 'fingers on buzzers.' What's missing in 1945?"

A forest of hands went up.

"Fine and dandy. You've all got it. There's no end to the Second World War. One change to one critical battle and the world's a different place. We can play the same game with any major battle. Let Nelson lose at Trafalgar and we've got one of the Bonaparte clan stuck on a pillar in the 'Place de la Republique' instead of Nelson's column in what used to be Trafalgar Square. No Nobel prizes for this. The trickier question is what would it take to swing these battles the wrong way? In our example here, the Battle of Britain, not a great deal, and there are plenty more examples where that came from. How about Wellington's 'damn close run thing' at Waterloo? I could go on, but let me get to the point."

About time too, thought Will, who was far from impressed with Al's brand of pseudo-scientific history. He leant across to Sean and whispered, "And if nobody had invented the atom bomb, there'd have been fewer town planners in Hiroshima. This is crap."

Sean just shrugged, though Will felt that the Irishman was not exuding his normal cool charm.

Will tried to give the lecturer the benefit of the doubt. He did not take to Al at all. He glanced at the folder they had received at the introduction. Al's credentials were impressive. Will tried to pay attention. The next stage was more interesting. Al presented some data, which showed that by altering the dates of one of the First World War battles by just a week, a different battalion was involved. The men who died were not the same. The consequences were extraordinary and Will conceded that Al did it well. The fathers of several key Battle of Britain pilots would almost certainly have been killed. The effect on the Great War of a week's delay amidst all that slaughter? – Negligible. The effect on the Second World War? Al referred them back to the initial demonstration, and like some nightclub magician, received his final round of applause and that took them into lunch.

Lunch for this elite group at Boroughbridge, was like everything else related to 'the Project.' There was no expense spared and everything was planned with considerable thought. In a modern wood panelled dining room, the tables were laid out in fours, sixes and eights. A mixture of different size groups naturally congregated at the different tables. A menu of half a dozen dishes was offered, excellent cuisine and yet not too heavy. Good wines were served at the table, permitting the staff to control the intake; enough to encourage lively debate, not sufficient to let anybody become hammered or have them sleep it off during the two o'clock, graveyard shift.

Will and Sean gravitated to a table for six. To Will's irritation, David Smethwick and a pleasant lady in her early thirties from one of the drug multi-nationals joined them. Will could not answer his own question as to why his antipathy to David persisted, now they were no longer in competition. Maybe he wanted Sean to himself to let off steam about the morning. His mood lifted rapidly as Valerie and her friend took the other two seats.

She threw a hand out to Will. "Valerie Duschenel. Thanks to my knight in shining armour. Do you make a habit of rescuing damsels in distress?"

Will accepted her hand. It felt very soft. "Will Peters. I don't like to let my broadsword get too rusty."

She caught his eye. "I bet you don't." She turned to Sean. "And you are?"

Sean took her hand and kissed it. "Sean O'Grady. Enchante de vous rencontrer, Valerie."

She squealed with delight. "Ah, vous parlez francais, Sean. Mais vous n'etes pas francais. Qu'est ce que c'est que ca, comme accent?"

Sean continued in French explaining how he grew up in Dublin, but passed many a school holiday with the French side of the family, in the South West of France. He happened to let slip that he was as at home on skis as he was on a surfboard. He was happy to chat in French or English, whichever she preferred.

Will glared at him and felt even more depressed than he had, when they had emerged from Al's game show. His rescue came from an unexpected source, David Smethwick. He pointed out rather stuffily, that as nobody else at the table spoke French and the pair of them spoke perfectly good English, maybe it would be helpful, if they all communicated in the Queen's own tongue.

Even the excellent lunch did not lift Will's mood. Sean and Valerie only had eyes and conversation for each other. It was only Day One, thought Will, and already it felt like he had lost his only mate and had all his dreams of a relationship with the pretty Canadian shattered. He remembered Al's embarrassing quip in the morning session about his chances with Valerie.

He hated them all.

Unable to moan freely to Sean over lunch, he entered the afternoon session, already convinced that he had made the biggest mistake of his life, by coming to Boroughbridge. This deteriorated, as the afternoon unfolded. It did not start well. Unscheduled in their timetable, they were subjected to another forty-five minutes of 'Game Show Al,' as he was now being called.

He opened with an apology for the schedule change. "Somebody's got to keep you lot awake after that lunch," he drawled and he was up and running with more gags at the expense of his young audience.

Will sat glowering, especially when Valerie turned around to ensure that Sean had caught every little part of the performance. Everybody else was finding Al highly entertaining. Couldn't they see what a jerk this guy was? Lost in his own thoughts, he paid little attention to the content of Al's presentation. He caught something about not changing history, if you went back in time. This guy has got to be on drugs thought Will.

"Will. WILL! Earth to Will Peters."

Will suddenly realised, with a shock, that all eyes were on him.

"Well, Will, well Will. You'll have many well-wishers wishing you well Will, so I won't embarrass you with questions on the last ten minutes. Let's cut to the chase, Will." Al was standing immediately in front of him. "And you can help us. Come on out to the front with me."

They all cheered as Will reluctantly climbed out of his seat, negotiated a route past the others in his row and stepped up onto the platform. Al put his arm around Will's shoulders. It was a nightmare.

"Will, I hope you don't mind. We're going to talk about the most basic human emotions now. You're not embarrassed are you Will? We're all friends here aren't we?"

Will was forced to nod, realised that he should be shaking his head and then wasn't certain. He managed to escape Al's grip and was aware of Valerie giggling in the front row.

"Don't be confused Will. This is very simple. What would you like to do to me right now?"

Will's face answered that question before he could open his mouth. They all roared with laughter.

Al's arm was back around his shoulders. "You'd like to kill me right now wouldn't you Will? It's O.K. I can take it. You wouldn't be the first."

At last Will had an opening. "Or probably the last."

It was predictable but they enjoyed it and cheered *him* this time, which made him feel better immediately.

"Ah, so you've woken up Will. O.K., I guess I had that one coming," admitted Al. "Hang on though. Just think of the consequences. Will might spend the rest of his life in jail, instead of becoming the world's greatest…" He looked at Will expectantly. "What are you good at Will?" Will hesitated. "Come on Will. You must be good at something. Everybody is good at something."

They were all laughing at him again. "Fencing," he blurted out.

"I bet you can be very offensive Will. No, that's good. If Will goes to jail, he may never be Britain's next Olympic gold medallist at fencing. Do I care? Not much. I care about me. I'm dead! Who knows? I might be the next President of the USA and if Will has killed me, that ain't never gonna happen."

Al paused to let his point sink in. "Now Will I'm tempted to keep you up here for the next point, but even I'm not that cruel. We're going to talk about S.E.X." The rowdy audience whistled. "Go and sit down. A big hand for Will. He's been a great sport."

Greatly relieved, Will returned to his seat, accompanied by a round of applause.

"Sex, the procreation of the species; it's our most basic instinct. Boy meets girl. Adam and Eve. It's the oldest story in the world. If killing someone is going to change history, then so is getting someone pregnant. Now I'm hoping that I don't need to go into details here. Just remember, even if you're not, no sex please we're British!"

While the laughter subsided, Al picked up a chair from the back of the platform and placed it right at the front so as to be as close as possible to his audience. He sat down and looked at them until the auditorium fell silent.

In a much more serious tone he said, "We've had some fun today. That was the plan. It's your first day. I hope you're really relaxed and at home. What I'm going to tell you now isn't fun; its serious and its for real. Then you're going to have a break and listen to people who are very serious indeed about what has happened to them. Let me start by asking a question." He paused to ensure that he had everyone's attention. "Why do you think that I've put together this little presentation today?"

For the first time in the day, there was complete silence around the room.

"Come on now. You're all bright people or, if you're not, the selection team has really screwed up. You know what the Project is about, at least in outline. Come on, anybody? Someone just have a stab. For once I won't take the piss, I promise."

Will could feel the weight of the silence on his shoulders. He wanted to say that it was just for entertainment, but he'd been the butt of enough of Al's humour for one day. Eventually a hand went up behind him.

"Go ahead, Andrew, isn't it?" invited Al.

"I suppose it was intended as some kind of light hearted session to get us all together and er um..." The speaker tailed off as Al shook his head.

Valerie's friend was next. "Just to get those of us who haven't studied history to realise that certain key events have a major impact on history..."

"You're getting warmer, but why all the stuff about Will murdering me?"

The same woman responded. "I guess that was just because he wasn't paying attention. I'm certainly not going to do that."

There was a ripple of laughter, which died quickly when they saw the expression on Al's face.

Al stood up and spoke very quietly. "You're going to meet people very shortly, who believe that they have travelled in time. I like a little gamble occasionally and I bet that, there is not one of you here today, who believes that it's possible. Am I right?"

He looked around the three rows of young faces. They nodded and murmured.

"So why are you here? Are your minds so closed that you cannot conceive that it is possible? Everything that your short lives has taught you, every fibre in your being tells you not to believe it. You've grown up on Star Trek and Doctor Who. It's all nonsense isn't it?"

There was no response this time to his question.

"Lock me up, if you want to. I can't believe any longer that it isn't possible. I've spoken to these people. I've seen the evidence. I've studied the test results. Maybe I'm missing something and somebody's having a laugh at daft old Al's expensive. If they are, they're damn good at it."

Al walked over to the table and took a drink. "I'll level with you. They're paying me big bucks to be here. I don't give a shit. I want to find out what's going on and I need your help." He paused, "Now some of you will be selected to experience first hand this time travel phenomenon."

The room was silent as he paused again and looked at his audience. "Oh yeah I've got your attention now. If this is for real, the chosen ones will have to follow the rules. We have a little thing called the SCAR Theory and it goes like this.

Go back in time, have a little look and you might leave a little scar; something that is visible under close scrutiny, but doesn't change your life. Go back and mess with a critical point in history, like your Battle of Britain, and that's serious stuff. It might end lives… it might even change history. It's major surgery.

So, until we know that this is just a psychedelic experience, we all follow, what I call Rule Two. No killing, no sex – just watching. Clear?"

There was a murmur of agreement and a little snigger, from somewhere behind Will and to his left.

Al looked up to find the culprit. "Something funny?"

He stood right at the front of the platform again and studied all of them. "So if that's Rule Two, what's Rule One? Well let's see. You are some of the smartest people on the planet. You're the best in your respective fields. If I'm going to find the truth, I need your help and I'm not going to get the best out of you, if you treat this as a joke. So I'm going to give you Al's Rule One. If you haven't listened to anything else here so far today, listen up now." He caught Will's eye, causing Will to blush.

"Al's Rule One says; Take it seriously and believe in all this, until we *all* agree that it ain't true. Anyone got a problem with that?"

They all shook their heads.

"Has anyone got a problem with that? If you have, we'll thrash it out now."

Silence.

"So I'll ask you again. Has anyone got a problem with that?"

"No Al," they all chanted and Will's wrist started to itch under his security bracelet.

Chapter 8

Boroughbridge University
Thursday 6th June 2002

It was Day Three and Sean was having a ball. Certainly he'd had misgivings about this venture. In the event it had turned out far better than he had expected. As he looked in the shaving mirror, he considered his situation. The restrictions to his liberty he could live with in the short term, given the rewards.

The so-called lectures were a joke. He couldn't wait for the one entitled, 'Targeting your Time Destination – Dosage or Historic Detail?' Why worry? The workload was far from onerous, the catering fabulous and, all the time he was locked up in Boroughbridge, the bookies couldn't get at him, he couldn't spend his money and his bank account was quietly filling up.

He had to admit that Al's little session on Day One had been a bit of a showstopper. There were a lot of nervous gags that evening about being 'the chosen one' and Will, in particular, was practically having convulsions. Fortunately the session, which followed the so-called time travellers, had proved something of a farce. They had been rolled out to relate their experiences and, to a man, had been totally unconvincing. The supposed star case was the one, which Jones had related to Sean, in the white house in Massachusetts. The traveller had claimed to steal a photograph and bring it back. To the chagrin of the team at Boroughbridge, the man had resolutely refused to appear and discuss it, even under threat of imprisonment. The session had left Sean far from convinced about it all and he was not alone. By the evening of Day Two most of the group had gathered in the bar and were merrily breaking Al's Rule One.

There were other positives as well. The company was congenial, very congenial in the form of Valerie Duschenel. If he was honest with himself, she was the main reason for his high spirits that morning. He quietly bet himself that if he hadn't lured her into his bed by the end of the month, he'd take religious orders and go into a monastery. Normally substantially quicker than that, he was in no hurry, while they were locked up together. She wasn't going anywhere and the wait would wet his appetite. Anticipated pleasures and all that, he told himself. Let's face it, there wasn't much competition, he flattered himself. Only Will, he laughed through the shaving foam, and *he* had no chance.

Ironically the only cloud on his horizon was Will. The guy had become a pain. Sean just couldn't shake him off in the confines of their restricted environment. Thank God, they didn't have to share a room! He realised that he only had himself to blame. Will was the only one of their group, whom he had actively enticed there. It wasn't that the guy was so bad; they had hit it off well enough at Durham. It was just that he seemed to have taken a bit of a downer right from the moment they'd arrived.

That was worrying Sean too. He still wasn't entirely sure what they had in mind for either of them, but already Sean couldn't see Will going the distance. If Will jumped overboard, Sean wondered how that would reflect on him. It was too early, in these first few days to be too concerned about what they might expect of him, whether Will stayed or not. It could be months before it came to that, so why worry?

Sean strolled down to the Breakfast Room, a glass-enclosed patio, high up on a south-facing wall of the building. On glorious days like this, it was a pleasant place to start the day. Sunlight poured through the glass roof and onto the starched cinnamon table clothes and chessboard-tiled floor. Vines grew up the walls and caged birds chattered in the background, mimicking the students. The early arrivals had sought shelter in the shade of the potted palms. He scanned the few faces in the room. There was nobody he wanted to join. He helped himself to fresh orange juice and sat alone at one of the bamboo tables, in a position where he could watch the door.

He smiled to himself. Why do you do this? Do people notice? He didn't care if they did. His target of course was Valerie. Whilst he was confident, it was always useful to see if she would be foolish enough to come down to breakfast with anyone. He didn't have to wait long. He had only just ordered his breakfast, when the door opened and Valerie entered, alone! Either she's smart or the way is still clear, thought Sean.

She knows how to dress too. Nothing outrageous, skirt to below the knee, where it met her boots. The shirt was long sleeved, but tight around her slim waist and the skirt was oh so tight around her hips. Nobody could criticise her for dressing inappropriately, but it was so sexy. She looked his way and Sean launched the smile. She returned it. Never fails, Sean said beneath his breath, as she approached his table.

"Mind if I join you?" she enquired. "Be warned, I'm not very good in the morning."

"Oh now, I don't believe a bit of it," responded Sean. Good God I'm flirting over breakfast. It's early even for me, he thought.

She smiled again and added, with a flash of her perfect teeth, "Where's your Siamese this morning? He doesn't sleep with you, does he?"

Sean laughed. "Ah, he's a pretty boy for sure, but I'm not of that persuasion." With a wicked twinkle in his eye, he added, "My religion might encourage it, but my inclinations won't allow it." He gazed into her blue eyes. "You never know. If we're locked up in here long enough, even he might start to look attractive. I'll bet he's still curled up with his teddy."

She laughed again and Sean noticed how the movement of her breasts made the tight shirt gape slightly, revealing a hint of her white bra. He decided that waking up and seeing that face beside him in the morning would be something special. Perhaps he wouldn't wait too long after all.

Before Sean could say anything more, she put her hand on his forearm and leant towards him. "Look, I'm not usually this forward. It's just, well, this place, you know. It's so claustrophobic and you're never on your own and, well for that matter, neither am I. So, well before anyone comes down, why don't you grab a bottle of something sparkling from the bar tonight, about ten and bring it to my room. Sixth floor, 606."

Sean couldn't help himself from grinning. "There's nothing on God's earth that I'd rather do," he breathed through his teeth.

She released his arm and leant back slightly. "Heh, steady tiger, I ain't that easy. It's the only place we can be alone together. Let's have a drink and a chat and just see how it goes from there."

"Of course, of course," added Sean quickly. "There's no rush. We're not going anywhere."

It was lucky for Sean that she had seized the moment, for immediately they had agreed to meet, Will entered the room and, spotting the two of them together, rushed towards them so quickly that he knocked over a chair. Valerie looked at Sean and crossed her eyes. Then she turned to Will, smiled, and chirruped, "Hi, Will. Do you want to join us?"

Each morning they were to gather in the Library at nine o'clock. It was an impressive reproduction of an old fashioned library, the sort you would find in a country house. Deep maroon carpet, big soft armchairs and sofas and wall-to-wall leather bound books; you could easily forget that you were cased in concrete. Dr. Jones entered at five past nine promptly and explained the details behind their programme for the day. It was very relaxed and informal and a chance to put questions to Jones or other members of the staff who might attend.

"You're going to have to work this morning, I'm afraid," opened Jones.

Loud groans and comments followed this bombshell. They were becoming easy in each other's company.

"After lunch however we have a little light relief and you will see that we have two visiting speakers," continued Jones.

They all rustled their programmes to check.

"Graham Brown and Susan Shepherd from the Royal, Military and Civil Museum, in London, will be here. Graham is responsible for the weapons collection at the R.M. & C. He is the world's leading expert in his field and will be demonstrating some of the seventeenth, eighteenth and early nineteenth century firearms. For those of you interested, there will be an opportunity to fire some replicas, which he will bring with him.

I know I should not be sexist or presumptuous, but perhaps of more interest to the ladies, will be Susan's presentation on fashions and development of dress styles, in that same period. In fact I have met Susan on several occasions and you will all find her work fascinating. She is also a leader in her field and an advisor for many of our best known TV period dramas."

"Will we have the opportunity to try the dresses on too?" Sean piped up and was greeted with howls of laughter.

"Dr. O'Grady, it seems that there are things about you which were not revealed by our rigorous screening!" responded Jones, unperturbed. It seemed there was a lighter side to the dry academic. He stroked his chin. "I can see you in a blue regency ball gown, from her collection. That would look very fetching, if she let the hem down by about a yard – very Pride and Prejudice."

They all joined in the joke. Wolfgang, chemistry graduate from Heidelberg, added, "Oh Liebchen, please save a space in your dance card for me."

Jones took out his pen and his folder, "O'Grady – disruptive cross dresser." In an attempt to regain control of the proceedings, he put down the folder and clapped his hands. "I can see we're going to have a lot of fun this afternoon. However, before that we want to start the first of what will be a series of group exercises. The objectives for these are to increase your knowledge across disciplines and to carry out team building exercises. To begin with, I want to make the first exercise brief and to keep the groups small, either twos or threes. I will read out the names and the topics, which I want you to work on. The idea is for the first team member to brief the second member on a given topic in the first's discipline, so that he or she in turn can make a presentation to us all. You will have three mornings to work on this."

Sean groaned to himself when Jones read out Will's name, the topic of the 1798 Revolution, followed by 'Sean O'Grady.' The thought of three mornings locked away with Will droning on about Irish history was almost more than he could bear. I guess it was hardly going to be 'recreational drugs with Valerie Duschenel,' he told himself. At some stage, he knew that something like this was coming, just not so soon. Valerie, he noted with a hint of bitterness had been paired with one of the better looking young guys, a sociologist, to give a talk about characteristics of leadership and dynamics of small groups, or some such nonsense.

After thirty minutes in a small meeting room with Will, Sean was ashamed to admit that he hadn't listened to a word. It was so blatant that even the introspective Will had noticed.

"Come on Sean, get with it. I know it's the English preaching to the Irish about their own history, but you're going to have to do a presentation on this lot in a couple of days."

Sean had been so lost in his own thoughts that the irony of the situation had not occurred to him. Added to that, he was the one being pulled up by Will for being introspective! It snapped him out of it.

"Sorry old son. I think this place has sent my brain to sleep. Can we start again and I'll give you my undivided?"

Will had retrieved his laptop from his room and ran over the presentation, which he had used that evening in Oxford, a lifetime ago.

"Look, before we go any further, is this all new to you or is it something that you've been into, since you were a kid?" Will enquired.

Sean could see that Will was trying to be helpful nonetheless it felt patronising. He tried to suppress his irritation. "Of course this is stuff I've grown up with, but you know what it's like, the legends and the facts get a mite mixed up. I stopped studying history, when I was about fourteen; so apart from a The Battle of the Boyne and the wives of Henry VIII, I'm pretty thin on the history front. Take it from the top and I'll tell you if you're boring me." Sean laughed and added, "Well, boring me more than usual."

Will was big enough to smile at that and they made a fresh start. The two young men sat adjacent to each other across the corner of a small table, Will with a dog-eared folder of notes and Sean with a notepad.

"Whatever you do, don't for a moment imagine that this is all about peasant versus aristocrat, Irish versus English or even Protestant versus Catholic," Will began. "It's not that simple. It's not even close to being that simple. It very rarely is. Although we historians like to make things complicated, just to show how clever we are, this period was a real melting pot in Irish history, even by your standards!"

"Well you've got a point there," admitted Sean. "We Irish never like to make it simple. What about this invasion that never happened in 1796? Would it really have made the difference, if the French had got ashore?"

Will grimaced and parodied himself. "You can't say that with certainty. There were about 14,000 of them. It was certainly enough and better than the 2,000, which were originally promised, I suppose. On the other hand I think it was the wrong place. Bantry Bay, way down in the South West, beyond Cork, was well away from the action. It really needed to be near Dublin or even Belfast. The only problem was that it was not so easy to sail a fleet from France all the way up the Irish Sea to Belfast. What with financial crises followed by The French Revolution, most of the half decent French sea captains had emigrated. Many of the crews had also deserted and so the French Fleet was pretty crap. Britannia most definitely ruled the waves."

Will scratched his head. "It was a bit of a Catch 22 really. The same storms, which helped them slip past the British coastal patrols, stopped the landing in Ireland. The French General Hoche, who was put in charge of the expedition, and Admiral Morard de Galles managed to get separated from the rest of the fleet. There's quite a lot of evidence that the captain of their frigate, Fraternite, was in the pay of the English to take them on a little cruise. To top it all, one of their ships sank in the channels leaving Brest. So it was a real fiasco. On the other hand if the weather had been better for the landing, they could easily have been sunk off the French coast by British naval guns."

"That's not the way you make it seem in your little talk. You give the impression that it was easy and that if they'd got ashore, they'd all have been drinking Guinness in Dublin Castle by teatime," responded Sean.

Will blushed. "Alright I did make it sound easy, but bear in mind that this was my little History Show for the uninitiated and Tone and his men were extraordinarily unlucky. It was so close, which is why I find it so fascinating." Will pulled a touring map of Ireland from his bag and folded it on the table to show the counties of Kerry, Limerick and Cork in the southwest of Eire. "Have a look at Bantry Bay. It's about eighteen miles long and around four miles wide. It runs from southwest to northeast. On those fateful days in December 1796 the wind was howling a gale from the northeast. For the Atlantic coast of Ireland, that's very unusual. It's no wonder that it's been described as a Protestant wind. Any other direction would have been fine, but for those big square-rigged ships, a strong northeasterly was the one thing they couldn't handle. In the confines of the bay, they couldn't sail directly into it and there wasn't much room to manoeuvre, especially if your crew wasn't really up to it. So they couldn't all get up the bay and land.

Had they got even half of their men ashore quickly and got up the road to Cork a bit sharpish, yeah, I think they would have taken the town and then it would have been game on. But they didn't. They were messing about in Bantry Bay for days, until every Loyalist in the land knew they were there."

He paused to see if Sean was still with him. Sean nodded, "Go on."

Will continued his theme. "The truth is of course more complicated and also a bit more boring. Wolf Tone told the Directory, effectively the government, in Paris what he needed, 20,000 men and a landing on the East Coast. You do know who Wolf Tone was don't you Sean?"

"Now you're taking the piss. I'm a Trinity College man, for God's sake. Tone studied law there before he got himself mixed up in all this United Irishman stuff. His death mask is in the college. Wasn't he Head of the Catholic Committee for Dublin or something? That's the bit that gets me, 'cause he was a Protestant."

"O.K. I didn't mean to insult your intelligence. Wolf Tone was the Secretary of the Catholic Committee in Dublin and, yes he was a Protestant. That's my point about all this. You had a group of Protestants, who could see the injustice of the Catholics' position and recognised that the real problem in dividing Irish society was the English. It was the English government, for example, that insisted that Ireland trade only with England. This was preventing trade directly with the new American Republic and that hurt the interests of both Protestant traders, predominantly in the North, as well as the prospering Catholic middle classes in the Dublin area. You've only got to look at the leadership of the United Irishmen, most of them were linen merchants."

"I thought that you said that this wasn't between the English and the Irish, Will."

"No. I said that it wasn't that simple. There was an elite group of Irish, who didn't want any change, the Ascendancy. That's just the name given to the ones with the titles, the money and the power. By some strange freak chance of history they all happened to be Protestant!"

"So it *was* about Catholic versus Protestant."

"Of course it was, but… how can I put this? You had a growing group of middle class Catholics. They had no political power and were second-class citizens compared to the Ascendancy, but they still had a lot to lose. They were doing all right, by the standards of the time, at any rate. On the other hand you had a bunch of rural Catholics, who weren't hung up about constitutional rights, they just wanted to know where the next meal was coming from. They were more concerned about whether it would be one or two of their kids, who would starve to death by the weekend."

"So these guys were both suffering at the hands of the English Protestants. Surely they were natural allies?"

"Up to a point, but this where it gets really complicated and experts are still arguing about it all today. Was this a plebeian revolution or a bourgeois uprising?"

Sean rolled his eyes. "Does it matter?"

"Well maybe only to the academics, except that it does explain why there was so much division and indecision. Throughout this period they were constantly divided as to whether they should wait for the French or rise up without them. For the poor rural Catholics they had reached the point of having little to lose. So why not get on with it? For the richer middle classes they feared that an uncontrolled revolution, without French military discipline, would lead to them losing everything.

Think about what had just happened in France. Picture it. 1789, overthrow the monarchy and aristocracy and everyone is better off – middle classes, working classes and rural poor, all united together in one happy revolution. It's a great theory, but then, in 1793, along came a little thing called the Terror. It was open season on the middle classes and heads were rolling by the dozen. The middle class Catholics could see themselves waving the English off at the harbour, to the sound of guillotines being built on Castle Green."

Sean grinned. "Well, like I say, we don't like to make it simple. No wonder the English played the, what did you call it, divide and rule card. When you put it like that, I can't see any way that a revolution could have succeeded. One thing I do know is that they bloody slaughtered us in 1798. For the love of Christ, there was no need for that."

"Is there ever any need for that? The English Government had two options, placate the Catholics and get them on board or crush the life out of them and eliminate the threat. They too had been divided. Grattan had achieved much to win rights for the Catholics over the previous few years. Should they grant more rights to keep the peace or clamp down on them? A Catholic Relief Act in 1793 gave many Catholics the vote, yet not to stand in Parliament. They could vote for any Protestant MP they liked! Not surprisingly the Catholics didn't think it was enough.

You may not agree with it, but if you want to understand it, you have to try and see it from the point of view of a frightened English Government. Can you imagine how it must have looked to a young guy, in his thirties, not that much older than us, who was running the show, William Pitt? Britain was on the verge of bankruptcy. It's not surprising that his health was suspect. Pitt was drinking like it was going out of fashion. Can you just imagine the pressure he was under?"

Will paused and tried to find the words, which would relate it to the present day. "I can't think of a comparison today. I guess the nearest thing would be to go back to Al's talk and think what it would have been like to become Prime Minister in 1940, like Churchill, when it looked as though the Germans would invade. Pitt was experienced, but not like Churchill was and nothing like as old. Imagine it. Suddenly the future of the whole country is in your hands. Everybody's life in Britain depends on you. It would be bloody terrifying. Thank God it couldn't happen to us!"

Added to all of that, think about the effect of losing the American colonies? For the king and the old guard it was like having a leg amputated. Then along came the Revolution in France. It was cataclysmic! Only twenty miles away and they were slaughtering the ruling classes in the streets. It would be like, like…" Will thrashed about for an analogy. "…Like aliens landing in Cornwall and murdering everyone, who paid higher rate income tax; like a scene from War of the Worlds. It was something that nobody could have possibly imagined a few years earlier."

Will paused for breath. "The whole country was falling apart at the seams and Ireland rebelling was one problem too many. If Ireland fell to the French, then England would be next. Everyone was screaming at Pitt to sort it out. What should he do? Charles James Fox and his followers supported the principles of the revolution in France, but hadn't got a clue how they'd stop it getting out of hand. Many felt that the Catholics in Ireland deserved some kind of emancipation and yet they all disagreed on exactly how much. The king and Pitt's supporters wanted all the trouble stamped out in Ireland. In the face of that, what else could he do?"

"Oh, come on Will, you bloody English you haven't got a fuckin' clue. This might just be a wee bit o' history to you, but to us Irish it's not a bloody game. It was… it *is* our country. Real people are still paying the price for all this crap today. We're still dying over this. That's the bloody trouble, no bugger understands outside of Ireland, because you've never experienced it."

Sean stood up from the table and walked to the window. Who was this middle class English college boy, with no idea about the real world, spouted on like it was a school lesson? He stared out over the campus for a few moments and composed himself. Turning to Will he seemed to have made his mind up about something.

Sitting down again, he said more quietly, "I'm sorry. Let's get back to this business of whether it would have succeeded if they'd got ashore. You never really finished that. Why was it that Wolf Tone wanted a landing in Dublin or Belfast? If he'd had his 20,000 men and landed in the East of Ireland, would he have thrown the English out?"

"Heh, er, look I'm sorry," murmured Will, unsettled by Sean's reaction. "I didn't realise that you were so wound up about all this stuff. Perhaps you're right and I don't really understand. Look, I know that you think I'm just some English prat and always trying to take the sensible middle ground. Heh, but you've got to face up to the facts. If the Irish had been that bloody determined, they would probably have done it. You might not like it, but the truth is that they weren't. Half of them didn't want it to happen and the other half were squabbling with each other. Their organisation and security was a joke and they couldn't agree on anything."

"Oh for Christ's sake. I've had just about enough of this bollocks." Sean was out of his chair again, the veins on his forehead, standing out dark and menacing. "We've been trying to trying to kick you bastards out for bloody centuries. Don't you try and tell *me* that we haven't!"

Sean leant across the table towards Will, his face ablaze and Will involuntarily shrank back. Something in Will's expression stopped Sean in his tracks. It was the mixture of fear and surprise. This man, for all his studying, really did not understand. It created in Sean a mixture of emotions. Frustration to the point of despair and yet with it arrived a germ of determination. It had been too easy for him to run away from all this. His father was right. Perhaps he should seize any opportunity, no matter how fanciful to put this enormous injustice right.

He leapt up from his seat causing Will to flinch. Sean distanced himself from Will and opening his arms wide, bowed slightly to Will. He forced himself to smile. "I'm so, so sorry Will. I don't know what came over me." He forced a little laugh. "I think you must be a much better historian, than I gave you credit for. It all seems so real. Can you forgive me?"

Staggered at Sean's change of heart, Will reluctantly conceded, "Well I guess it's better than falling asleep in one of my talks."

"That's the spirit! What's worse than getting a reaction? – getting no reaction! Or something like that according to Oscar Wilde. Heh, let's take a little break."

Will seized on Sean's idea with alacrity. "Coffee?" He stood up and reached for a pot on a side table.

"No, no thanks I think I'm a bit overdosed on caffeine. That might be me problem. Give us some of that sparkling water."

They both sat and drank for a few moments, until Sean broke the silence. "Right, I think I've got me brain back into gear. Shall we continue? What about all these factions, who were all arguing with each other?" He added with a wink, "Just don't make it quite so exciting."

Will gathered his notes and his thoughts and, with a deep breath, picked up his tale. "Look, I know it's not what you want to hear." He looked for encouragement from Sean, who just nodded. "Ireland is divided today, because some of the Irish want it that way."

Sean opened his mouth to speak and Will held up his hand. "I know, I know Sean, that's the fault of the English. We followed a policy for years of planting people, in the North especially, who were either sympathetic to the Crown, or were not Catholic, Scottish Presbyterians and so forth. It was…it was…"

"Beyond the pale?" added Sean.

They both smiled at this, a little warmth between them rekindled.

"Exactly," added Will. "The Brits were pretty damn good at infiltration too. Do you have any idea? The various revolutionary groups were riddled with spies. When the revolution did come in 1798, the most successful bit was near Wexford. The English had pretty much overlooked this area and had few spies down there."

Will paused to think for a second and to gauge Sean's reaction. Sean frowned in silence, so Will continued, "Getting back to the landing location, I think that there were several reasons that he wanted to land in the East. Firstly it would have put them right at the heart of things, near the centres of population and power. A secure landing near Dublin, for example, could have taken out the Government, before they had a chance to organise the army and defend themselves. I think the real reason was that he reckoned there would have been more support on the ground for an invasion in these areas. Dublin and Belfast were the centres of the revolutionary groups. From that point of view Belfast would have been better, as the United Irishmen were stronger and better organised in the North."

"So what the hell was the matter with them? Why didn't they do that?" asked Sean.

"We're back to the navy again. It was a lot easier to nip over to Bantry from Brest in a storm, than to set sail up the Irish Sea and run the gauntlet of the Royal Navy. Besides the west coast offered some remote locations to land with nobody defending the shoreline. Remember these were the days of sail and horses. It wasn't like D-Day. Landing an army under fire would have been pretty near impossible and the French were reluctant to risk that. If you think about it, Hitler couldn't manage it one hundred and fifty years later. What chance was there in those days?"

"That's fair enough I suppose, but why didn't the French have another go, when the weather improved?" asked Sean.

"Well that's my point really. If they'd had another go in the spring, I reckon that it would have worked. In my view, it really was one of history's greatest missed opportunities. Poor old Wolf Tone tried, but France was in a hell of a mess politically, until Napoleon emerged and started to seize control and then, of course, he had the brainstorm to invade Egypt. That pretty much put paid to a major invasion of Ireland. It wasn't one of Napoleon's brightest ideas and yet again Britain's jolly jack tars beat the crap out of his fleet at the Battle of the Nile, which stopped his supply lines. To use the old cliché, the rest is just history.

As you know Tone did persuade them to have another go, but not until 1798 and it was too piecemeal and too late. Tone was captured, before he even got ashore."

"The bloody navy again eh? We really could have done with neutralising them somehow." Sean considered this, then, collecting his thought added, "Anyway I get the too little, but why was it too late?"

Will thought about it for a moment. "If the French had thrown enough numbers at it, instead of running around Europe and the Middle East, I'm sure they could have succeeded, but as we know they didn't." He shrugged, "Ireland just wasn't high enough up their agenda. For the Irish, yet again it was Catch 22. The French wouldn't invade without a civil uprising and the Irish wouldn't rise up without French support. 1797 passed like that and all the time the English picked off their leaders, confiscated their arms and got the army organised to suppress an uprising."

Will stood up and held his hands open, as if he had just performed a conjuring trick, "And that is why 1798 was too late. It must be time for lunch now and then we get to play with the guns. Do you know I'm actually beginning to enjoy this?" He put his arm around Sean's broad shoulders. "I think you've been locked in here too long. You need to chill out a bit."

"Yeah, Yeah, sure," replied Sean and followed him out. Sean's thoughts were elsewhere. His sharp mind was grappling with just one problem, how to land 10,000 troops on the east coast of Ireland in 1797. "Yer're right. It must be this place. I'm going as barmy as the rest of them," he muttered to himself.

Chapter 9

Boroughbridge University
Friday 7th June 2002

Lunch was a sober affair. They had all been warned that there was to be no drink, if they wanted to fire the weapons that afternoon. That did not stop the lighthearted conversation or the ongoing jokes about Sean and the dresses. Nobody seemed to be taking it very seriously, as far as Sean could see. Even Will seemed to be a little calmer, now that he was in his element, sounding off about his favourite subject. Sean wondered how calm Will would be, if he knew about the planned meeting in Room 606 tonight. He shrugged. What he doesn't know won't bother him, he thought, although he knew he was kidding himself. He'd never keep that quiet for long in this place.

"Hello, so deep in thought? Can't you decide which lipstick to wear with that blue dress this afternoon?" The German had started again and soon they were all joining in.

"I don't want to sound ungrateful," Sean played along, "I don't think blue's my colour!"

"Alright you rowdy bunch, Mr Brown is ready for us downstairs." Jones was struggling to keep control. "It'll probably be easier to ask if there is anyone, who does not want to take part in the shooting."

"I only want to do it, if we can try on the men's clothes" piped up a young brunette woman, in her best deep voice. Once again the young people collapsed in a group hysteria, which had taken over, in the greenhouse atmosphere of this closed environment. They clattered along behind Jones to the basement.

A concrete staircase led from the back of the building's main foyer down to the bowels of the building. The cream walls of the staircase showed the group to a grey corridor below. Dull wire caged emergency lights guided their way until they were facing a steel door with a keypad on the wall.

Jones led the way and, shielding his actions from prying eyes, hit several numbers into the pad. The door swung open to reveal another flight of stairs, narrower this time, which took them down to a corridor with a low ceiling. "Watch your heads the tall ones," he shouted in warning, but it was lost amongst the giggling and gossip, which echoed off the cold walls.

"Watch out for the low beams in here too," called out Jones, as they finally entered a surprisingly large room through a further steel door. He waited as they all filed in and their eyes adjusted to the low light. "This was used in a former life for animal research. There are plenty of groups out there who disapprove of that sort of thing, hence the security. We have now converted it into a facility with a soundproof firing range."

Sean pictured the laboratory, cages of animals covered in electrodes and pumped full of drugs. Could these guys do that to him?

With a flick of a switch, Jones illuminated some targets at the other end of the room. They looked like the traditional army targets of charging soldiers, except they had been overprinted to look like Napoleonic period infantry, with coats, cross straps and shakos.

"Now settle down you lot, take a seat and let me introduce you to Graham Brown from the Royal, Military & Civil Museum in London." Jones directed them towards some loosely arranged seats facing a long table, which looked like it had once been a laboratory bench. It was covered with a huge array of swords, pistols and, what looked to Sean like old-fashioned rifles. "As I said before, he is one of the world's leading experts in firearms, the history of militia and the development of modern warfare. He has brought with him some priceless pieces from the R. M. & C. as well as items on loan from other collections. We are very lucky to have him with us today. Graham Brown."

They all applauded politely as a man in his fifties stood up. His long grey hair was tied back and hung in a short ponytail over a blue suit, which did not sit well with his T-shirt.

"You're too kind Dr. Jones. Well good afternoon everyone. I am told that you are a mixed bunch; that is to say, you come from a range of disciplines. I know that there are a couple of historians here, but I suspect for most of you, this may be the first time that you have examined weapons like these at close range.

We have a range of swords, illustrating some of the most common types of blade and a selection of firearms, which show the development of the modern, breech loading automatic weapons. You may handle these shortly, but keep them over the bench and do not operate the mechanisms. Two hundred year old springs have a habit of breaking. Oh and please, no swords fights, fresh blood can be very corrosive on some of the more valuable pieces. I cannot let you fire these either," he said, pointing to the collection on the workbench. "They are too valuable and some are certainly not safe."

This announcement was followed by a groan from his audience.

Brown held up his hands. "Don't worry we will satisfy your primeval urges to kill something, but not with these. I have two facsimiles, which I have had made myself. These will illustrate all the principles and pitfalls of early nineteenth century side arms, without you losing too many fingers!" He put his hand up to the side of his mouth, as though divulging a great secret. "In fact they're a bit of a cheat really, because I've adapted an early patent with a few improvements of my own. All will be revealed shortly."

"Gather round the bench to have a good look. You won't be able to see from there." He beckoned the group from their chairs. "Let me start by explaining the development of firearms over the last few centuries. We can divide them between breech loading and muzzle loading. In other words loading via some mechanism from the top or side as opposed to loading down the barrel. Whilst both systems have been around for hundreds of years, muzzle loading was much more commonplace until the nineteenth century, when metallic cartridges were mass-produced cheaply. The Industrial Revolution also brought engineering to a state, where breech loading systems were more reliable and less likely to cause harm to the man firing, rather than his enemy."

He had the weapons set out in chronological order, moving down the bench. Using beautiful examples from the collection, the arms expert ran through the different systems used, from early matchlock sporting guns to military issue flintlocks. He explained the difficulties of igniting the charge in the barrel in wet conditions until the nineteenth century, when the sealed percussion cap system was invented. Most of the group were more interested in the more modern weapons, which included Colt revolvers and a Winchester Model 1873.

Sean had not noticed the time rush past, so absorbed had he been in Brown's explanations. The rest of the group had moved on leaving just him and Will behind, as they studied the weapons from the Napoleonic period.

"What's so special about this Collier revolver?" Sean asked Will. "You know something about these things don't yer? Brown said he'd come back to the Collier flintlock later. I've got to be honest; I thought revolvers only came along with Colts and the Wild West. Were there many like this?"

"It's an early five shot revolver. Elisha Collier patented this one in 1818. It had a ratchet operated priming magazine."

Sean tried hard not to let out a sarcastic 'ooh.'

Will continued, "And it's based on one patented in the same year by a guy called Artemus Wheeler, from Massachusetts. The Americans, notably in the northern states, developed their arms industry rapidly during this period. Ultimately it was this more than anything, which led to a Northern victory in the American Civil War, in 1865. Effectively they won the arms race."

"How do you know all this stuff? You need to get out more, Will."

"Well you did ask." Will wished that he hadn't sounded quite so irritated. He continued more casually. "I don't know what he's going to say about this. Having a multi-shot weapon, at this time, was a huge advantage. Most were single shot and took ages to reload, but there weren't many flintlock revolvers made. These were some of the first, yet by the mid 1830's, Colt was making percussion revolvers, which were much more effective. Hang on he's coming back to us now."

"I see you've taken a shine to the Collier," said Brown, as the group moved back to the middle of the bench. "It's one of my favourites." He held up the revolver. It was not ornate, by the standards of some of the exhibits and quite small. The barrel seemed short, at about three inches; the revolver mechanism about two inches and the butt and firing mechanism was around six inches long. The wooden butt was carved with a simple cross pattern, more for grip than decoration and on the metal plate above the trigger was engraved 'E H Collier Patent No. 23.'

"I like it," continued Brown, "because it represents the zenith of the flintlock firearm. Soon after this was made, the percussion weapons came in and this little beauty was relegated to the history books."

Sean caught Will's eye to acknowledge that the expert had endorsed his explanation.

"I have returned to this, as it is replicas of this revolver, which you will be firing today. We have two weapons, both the same and based on this. There are some significant differences. Firstly they are made from stronger alloys. We don't want you to blow your fingers off. Secondly the original is a single action mechanism, that is to say that it has to be revolved and cocked, after each shot is fired. This has a double action."

He noticed some blank expressions amongst his audience. "It revolves and cocks itself, so you only need one hand to operate it. That leaves a hand free for another weapon or to hold on to something. We have also made some minor mods to the system for opening and closing the pan, when the cock falls on the steel to make a spark. Again this is for safety reasons."

"You all look a bit bemused! Who wants to have a go?"

Sean pushed his large frame to the front. "I do."

"And you are?"

"Sean O'Grady."

"Well now Sean, good for you. Come around here with me and take a look at this." He removed, from a metal case, two revolvers, which, to Sean, looked no different from the original Collier weapon. Handing one to Sean and keeping the other, he said, "Don't worry, it's not loaded. Nonetheless we still preserve the basic etiquette, so do not point it at anyone."

There was a nervous laugh from the group, as Sean inadvertently waved it at them, before pointing it at the ground.

Brown picked up on the reaction. "You're right to be wary of these things. Never forget, they were designed with one purpose in mind and one purpose only, killing people. Some of them may have been invented a few hundred years ago, but they're still more than capable of doing just that! Now let me explain how these little beauties work. Follow me Sean."

He took a couple of paces back from the bench so that he could point the revolver at the floor in front of him. Sean mimicked him and from here the rest of the group could still see what was happening. "Now Sean, gently squeeze the trigger."

For all his concentration, Sean could not help but notice that Valerie had put both hands over her ears. Oh God, he could not wait for ten o'clock to come around.

The mechanism revolved and a small amount of powder was dispensed from a box above the pan. A split second later the cock, which gripped the small piece of flint, came down on the steel with a satisfying click and a little spark was given off, causing the powder to ignite. Startled, Sean could not prevent himself from flinching, but still noticed that a little steel plate slid open and shut on the side of the revolving mechanism.

"Bloody brilliant," Sean heard Will say.

"Ah, we have someone here, who appreciates my little improvement," said Brown looking up with a smile. "Perhaps you would like to explain what is going on here."

"Will Peters," answered Will excitedly, before he could be asked his name. "The problem with all these weapons was that they were useless in the rain. In wet weather it was always the side, which could keep their powder dry, which won the day. There was a cover but you've improved it and found some means of automatically opening the powder pan, for a split second as the spark is created."

"Bravo Mr. Peters! You've won the chance to fire this weapon," Brown brandished the one in his hand, "along with Sean here. Come around here." As Will joined the arms expert and Sean at the other side of the bench, Brown continued, "I bet you can also explain to your colleagues, what else is happening here." He handed his revolver to Will. "Squeeze the trigger twice."

The two men squeezed again and this time Sean noticed how light and easy it was to operate. He had expected the old style pistol to be clumsy and heavy. To his delight, it was well balanced, the trigger light and the mechanism rolled smoothly. He discovered that each time he pulled the trigger and the mechanism revolved, the cock arm, holding the flint, automatically came back up, held and was released as further pressure was applied to the trigger.

"Wow," exclaimed Will, "you've turned it into a double action piece, like a modern revolver."

Sean was not slow to appreciate what he had in his hand. He squeezed the trigger again to make sure he had grasped the significance of it.

"You're spot on, once again Mr. Peters. By the look on your face, I think that you're the man to appreciate another little improvement I've made. To do that, we're going to have to move to the range behind you. I don't want to be responsible for staff cuts here at Boroughbridge" he chuckled. "Follow me."

He took the guns from the two men, picked up a shabby leather shoulder bag and led them the few metres to the firing range. "Grab a set of ear defenders," he called out indicating a rack of them next to the firing point.

When they had all put them on and settled down around him, he put both guns on the table and opened the leather bag. "This is another cheat. The purists will chastise me for this. That's fine, but you chaps and ladies, of course, will find this a lot easier. Will, since you obviously know your stuff, explain to your colleagues how you would normally load a muzzle loading weapon like this."

Will picked up the revolver again and removed a little ramrod, which was clipped under the barrel. "You would have to pour a powder charge down the barrel and then ram a ball and some wadding of some description with it, to stop it all falling out. Then you would have to put a smaller powder charge in the pan here at the side to catch the spark and that in turn ignited the main powder charge in the chamber. Although in this case Collier had already come up with a ratchet mechanism to dispense the powder."

Will peered at the pan mechanism. "I'm not sure how this opens."

"It just flicks back. See." Brown flicked open the little plate. "And you'd have to do that for every chamber of the revolver, right? How long would that take?"

Will fumbled with the mechanism and squinted down the barrel. "Oh my God, it would take ages, probably about five minutes, maybe quicker." He chuckled. "You'd have to be pretty damn careful with the last chamber, not to shoot yourself too!"

The group joined Will and laughed at his expression, squinting down the barrel of a pistol that might already have four chambers loaded.

"You're bang on, if you'll pardon the expression! With practice, you might be able to do it in a couple of minutes, but a lot can happen in a battle in two or three minutes. Now watch."

Brown pulled a tin from his bag and opened it to reveal little tube shaped paper bags. With a loud click, he twisted the cock to one side to disengage it and then pushed a tube down the barrel with the ramrod. He twisted the revolving mechanism and repeated the process five times. Clearly experienced, it took him seconds to complete the whole process.

"These packages are prepared earlier and contain a lead shot and sufficient powder. This wax paper around it serves to protect it from damp and wedge the shot and charge in place."

From his bag he produced a powder horn and filled the little box above the firing pan. "There's no need to waste time measuring this, it dispenses the correct amount automatically. Our friend Elisha Collier invented that and I claim no credit for it."

Then with a speed, which amazed his audience, he whirled around and hit a button, which caused the target, suspended on steel cables, at the far end of the range to rush towards them.

Crack, crack, crack, crack, pause, crack. Brown unloaded the weapon, before the target came to a stop, just in front of them.

Even wearing ear defenders, the sudden noise of the gun made them all start and squeal. Only Sean was looking at the target.

"You've hardly hit it," exclaimed Sean. Then realising that his comment may have caused offence. "Sorry I didn't mean it to sound like that. It's just that you blasted five shots at it."

"Well done! That is the last point about this. I held my last shot back and even then, I only just caught the edge of the target. I have created what is probably the best flintlock revolver ever, but, sad to say, you still can't hit a barn door, unless it's falling on top of you. These weapons, without rifling were very inaccurate. All these films, with the hero shooting the bad guy across a crowded bar, are just Hollywood. You'd probably kill everyone else in the room, except your intended victim."

He let his words sink in. "On the other hand, in close combat, boarding a ship or bursting into a crowded room, full of enemies, a pair of these," and he brandished both guns, "would make you a very formidable foe indeed."

The group broke into a spontaneous round of applause, which seemed to surprise and delight Graham Brown. Will looked excited at the prospect of firing the weapons. Sean made sure that he was first.

Time ran out in the firing range and Graham agreed to leave the facsimiles and return in a couple of days for another session. The weapons from the museum's collection were far too valuable and would have to be returned. Sean played along with the high spirits and jokes, whilst the fashions were demonstrated and the practicalities of different styles explained. His mind was on the note in his pocket.

Bizarrely Jones had slipped a note in his hand, as the group had thronged out of the basement. 'Meet me in the basement at 9 p.m.;' that was all it said, except for a number, which Sean assumed to be the door code. Christ, it was like something from a bloody Agatha Christie! thought Sean. I hope this doesn't take too long. I've got better things to do, come ten o'clock.

As the afternoon turned into evening, he started to worry about it. Was it something to do with Will? Was he not making the grade and now they were both being chucked out? Oh this was ridiculous and it was spoiling his anticipation of the night with Valerie.

He and Valerie made a point of keeping apart after dinner. At eight fifty, Sean excused himself, with a nod to the barman took a bottle of Champagne, from behind the bar and headed to the main foyer. He slipped the bottle behind a pot plant and, with a glance over his shoulder, took the stairs to the basement. He was conscious of the noise of his shoes on the concrete steps and paused at the foot of the stairs to ensure that nobody was following him.

The door at the other end of the corridor beckoned, but if the code was wrong, well… This was ridiculous. Sean hastened down the corridor and tapped in the code. The door swung open and he descended the stairs. All the lights were on and the door at the end was ajar, revealing the lights illuminating the shooting gallery. He entered.

"Ah, good, good, I'm sorry about all this cloak and dagger stuff, Sean."

It occurred to Sean that this was much more like the stuffy, formal and uncomfortable Jones, whom he had first met. Over the last few days at Boroughbridge, Jones had seemed much more confident.

"I needed to speak to you and this is the only part of the building, which isn't wired."

"Christ, you're kidding me."

"No, no, not at all. We have cameras and sound equipment in all the public rooms. Look never mind all that," he added, as if it was of no consequence, "we need to talk about Will."

I knew it, thought Sean and gathered his wits quickly. "I thought he seemed to be fitting in well now and he's been brilliant with the Revolution stuff."

"That's great. That's really important Sean. I was worried about him to begin with and I could have killed Al for picking on him on the first day. I need your honest opinion on Will, because we have a problem." He hesitated. "We need to advance the programme a little." Jones looked down at his feet.

It seemed to Sean as if he was trying to decide how much to reveal to him. "Perhaps you could give me an idea of what's going on and then we could come back to Will," answered Sean evasively.

"Yes, yes, of course, Sean. Take a seat." He ran his fingers through his hair, as the two men sat on a couple of chairs in front of the bench, where the presentation had been made earlier that afternoon. "We have a problem. How can I put this? We are concerned that your selection has come to the attention of certain parties."

"Is that it? Is that the explanation? For Christ's sake you're gonna have to do better than that. What's going on?"

"Alright Sean. You're not stupid, you know who the parties are, behind your selection. We believe that they are under scrutiny by both U.S. and H.M.G. agencies. It is only a matter of time before they look more closely at what we are doing here. More especially they will want to look more closely at you and your involvement. We need to advance the programme, like I said."

"By how much?"

"Er, well quite significantly."

"How much?"

"We need to have Will travel in less than a week's time. It depends a bit on how he reacts."

"How he reacts? Jesus H Christ. You're out of your tiny mind! You'll never get Will to go along with this. He's twitchy enough as it is. If he gets one whiff of this he'll be gone in a flash."

Jones had been looking at his feet. He caught Sean's eye. "It's not just Will is it?"

"Oh now, here we go. I was wondering when we'd get around to that."

"Look, look I wanted to talk about that…" interrupted Jones.

"No," countered Sean, "I've given that some thought and here's the deal." Jones tried to interrupt, but Sean talked him down. "No, I'll tell you the deal. I'll do this."

Jones looked more stunned than relieved.

"I'll do it. I'll go on this time trip, but only after I've seen Will come back safe and with most of his marbles in place."

Jones smiled. "That's the view of a Doctor in Psychology is it?"

It was Sean's turn to smile this time. "Yeah, that's about the size of it. If you can persuade Will to go on some little jaunt and you get him back in one piece *and* I get to talk to him *and* I'm happy with him, then I'll give it a go." Sean felt relieved and shocked to have come out with this. Then, as if he had suddenly remembered Jones' initial comments, "But a few days! You'll never do it! Not a snowball's chance in hell!"

Jones looked worried again. "What do you think would help with Will?"

"I can't think of anything, which will persuade him to be one of your guinea pigs. I suppose you might risk him doing a runner, but I reckon it would relieve the tension, if you let him out for a bit. Can't you adapt the security tags to track him offsite. Even with that, he won't do it yer know."

Jones simply shrugged. "That's my problem. Just leave that to me." He added glancing at his watch. "We'd better break this up, before anyone notices we've gone, but before we do, I think that we should be a little clearer on what is expected of you, since you have raised it."

Sean suddenly felt cold and isolated in this concrete cavern. He imagined that he knew how some of the laboratory animals had felt, sitting just where he was. "Go on," was all he said.

For once Jones went straight to the point. "We don't just want you and Will to go back and observe. We really do believe that you can, how shall I put it interface..."

"Interfere, you mean," interrupted Sean.

"Well yes, more than interfere. We want you to make the revolution that didn't happen, well, er, happen. We want you to organise the Irish and the French to create a successful revolution. We believe that you can do it, at least you can with Will's support." Jones stopped and looked at Sean, not knowing what else to say.

"Whew, you don't want much do yer? And do yer want me to get the little people to rise up as well? Yer know that yers all barking mad."

"That might well be the case, but if it is, we're all mad together," responded Jones and looked at Sean.

"Well there's not much more to say is there? We'll see what happens with Will," replied Sean, trying to reassure himself with the idea that Will would never go through with this, which meant that neither would he.

The two men looked at each other for a moment before Jones added, "I'd like you to meet me here every night now at the same time."

"O.K." Sean nodded. "That's alright by me." He glanced at his watch, remembering that he had another appointment shortly. He stood up and headed for the door. He considered his commitment. There's no way it'll come to that, he told himself. He'll never get Will to participate.

Jones called after him. "Oh by the way, I don't think you should become too involved with Miss Duschenel, Sean. She's one of us."

Chapter 10

Boroughbridge University
Sunday 9th June 2002

Day Six started early for Will, when he was awoken by a tap on his door. He glanced at the alarm clock by his bedside. It was only six-thirty. It must be Sean, wanting an early start. They had worked hard on Sean's studies and today was the day of the presentation. He hoped that Sean would not let his feelings spoil it. He could still feel the tension between them and the situation with Valerie didn't make it any easier. He smiled to himself, as he thought how, over the last couple of days, she had sought Will's company and not Sean's.

Will didn't feel much like leaving the warmth of his bed. There was a further tap on the door. He rose and opened it to find Valerie, dressed in tracksuit top, tight shorts and trainers, smiling at him. Her blonde hair was held either side of her head in little schoolgirl bunches.

"Hi, Will. Fancy a jog before breakfast?"

"Er, yeah, great, er, give me a moment."

"Did I wake you up?"

"No, I was awake, well just about."

Will pushed the door shut and rushed into the bathroom to slosh cold water hastily onto his sleepy face. He rushed around his room pulling open drawers and cupboards in a hasty search for something to wear. In what seemed an eternity to him, he found a T-shirt, shorts and trainers and fell out of his door.

"I've done three laps already," she teased him.

They descended through the foyer into the grounds and out into the early morning sunshine. Will inhaled the damp freshness of the day. It felt so good to Will to be escape the claustrophobia of the concrete monster. Nobody was about and, as they jogged, Valerie chatted away about her life in Canada and all Will had to do was listen and smile in the appropriate places. What a glorious start to the day!

"I'll get a shower and see you downstairs for breakfast in twenty minutes, O.K. Will?"

Will nodded and admired the vision that was Valerie Duschenel, as she slid along the corridor, the lift doors finally shutting off his view.

They met just outside the Breakfast Room and entered together. Sean was sitting at a table, facing them, on the far side of the room. Valerie gave him a little wave, as he smiled at her. It had been so easy to lead him on the night before and then leave him, without so much as a kiss.

"Let's sit here Will," she indicated a table, by the window. "You don't need to be joined at the hip, do you?" She nodded in Sean's direction. She placed her handbag on the table and slipped something into her hand. "Oh my God, do I need caffeine. It's terrible. Do you get like that in the morning Will?"

"Oh yes, especially, if I've had a couple of drinks the night before." Will was eager to agree.

"Go get some juice and I'll get the coffees? You do want coffee or do you English always have tea?"

"No coffee's fine," said Will and trotted off obediently.

As Valerie turned towards the coffee counter, she glanced over in Sean's direction. He was staring at her. She winked and turned away. Smiling to herself, she glanced at Will, who, had his back to her, and swayed her hips as she strode towards her destination. It was easy to keep her back to them both, as she poured the drinks.

Will drifted into the morning briefing on a high. They gathered, as usual in the library and waited for Jones to make his announcements for the morning.

"As you know," Jones started, "this morning you will be making your presentations on your chosen subjects. This will take place in the lecture theatre. To add a little more excitement to the proceedings, we have decided to award a prize to the winning presenter. He or she will be allowed to pick one of you from the non-presenters of another team to share the prize. And the prize is…" he looked across at Al, who had accompanied him to the library this morning.

"A dinner for two at one of the best restaurants in the county! Yes guys and gals, two of you get a late pass!"

The group chorused an appreciative 'oooh,' in the routine farce that quickly broke into laughter and speculation as to who would invite whom.

"There's no way I'm inviting you Sean," chimed up the German. "Well, maybe if you put the dress on!"

They laughed again as usual, but Jones, by now a little tired of the joke, pointed out, pedantically, that Sean could not be invited, as he was a presenter. They all groaned and drifted into the lecture theatre.

For Will the morning passed in something of a dream. To his satisfaction, Valerie sat next to him in the lecture theatre. He watched, with detached pleasure, as Sean went first and made a superb presentation on the '98. He had grasped all the key elements and presented it with a passion and vigour, way beyond anything Will felt he could have done. The rage seemed to have gone from Sean's voice and he entertained them with a range of regional Irish accents. Sean was the star of the show and Will was delighted for him.

Most of the other presenters were good, but did not have that star quality Will thought to himself. Then finally it was Valerie.

She had slipped out, changed and reappeared wearing a raincoat and trilby hat. Wolf whistles greeted her entrance on the platform. It was obvious to the entire group that she had little on underneath. All the men were on the edge of their seats. Will just sat back and watched the show, both on and off the platform. Valerie made her presentation about groups and played the roles of different characters. The climax was, of course, the removal of the coat, which revealed less than she had shown Will in her shorts that morning. Nonetheless the reaction from the men was loud and predictable.

Eventually the noise subsided and Valerie, after a brief absence to change, returned to her seat by Will. Jones stepped up from one of the end seats in the front row. "Alright, settle down now. You're all going to take a fifteen-minute break, while Al and I consider our verdict. When you return Al and I will have made a decision. In the unlikely event of a split decision, we will ask you to vote. So make your minds up, during the break."

When they returned to the lecture theatre, Jones had handed over to Al. "O.K. ladies and gentlemen, the nominations for the least lousy presentation are; Simon Jones for The New Generation of Drugs in the Treatment of Depression…" They all booed and jeered. "Sean O'Grady for The Revolution of 1798…" There was much cheering and clapping. "And last, but not least, unless you consider her scanty attire…" all the men whistled and cheered, "the very lovely…" more cheering and Valerie, without a shred of embarrassment, stood up and took a bow, "Valerie Duschenel for The Dynamics of Small Groups…"

"And the winner is…" Al played a mock drum roll, with his hands on the lectern, "Valerie Duschenel for the Dynamics of Small Groups."

The lecture theatre erupted with a cacophony of yells and catcalls. The men were whistling, whilst the women were all shouting, "fix," "rigged" and "we want a female judge."

Al turned to Jones and said in a loud voice, that they could all hear, "Wow, just think what it's gonna be like, next week, when we give away the car!" Then facing the excited throng, he held up his hands, "O.K. you lot calm down. We'll do it again shortly, so you'll all get a chance to win. Now Valerie, come up here. You've got an even more difficult job. Who's the lucky guy, or gal, if you prefer, who's gonna get a free dinner with you, doll? Remember it can't be one of the other presenters."

Valerie stepped up beside Al and Jones and looked about, as if making up her mind whom to pick. "Gee this is hard, I don't want to upset anybody." She put her hand on her lips and then, with a little shrug, pointed, "Will."

The cacophony started again. "Don't drink too much Will… I'd like to see the dynamics of that small group," the men yelled out. One or two of the women, who were still sulking about the result, were mimicking Valerie's Marilyn Monroe style selection, "Ooh, I'll pick you Will."

Despite Al's experience in organising groups of young people, feelings were running high and he was losing control. "Time out, time out. I think we should give you guys some time off. That's it for the day. Take the afternoon off."

Will was very relaxed about the whole business. He couldn't see why everyone was so excited. He sat back in his seat, in the theatre and watched it all going on around him. Sure she'd picked him for the dinner date and that made him feel good. If she hadn't, he was sure that there'd be another time.

"Well done old son!" Sean slapped him on the shoulder. "Yer got me into the final *and* won the prize. I reckon that's like choosing the top two nags in the race. I gotta say yer seem pretty cool about being picked by the top filly."

"Thanks. Yeah, it's odd really. If you'd asked me a couple of nights ago, I'd have given my right arm for a night out of here alone, never mind a night out with Valerie." Will grinned, "Still I'm not complaining."

They were due to be collected by limousine at seven o'clock. Will had not seen Valerie, since the middle of the afternoon. "She'll be getting ready," said Sean, with much waggling of his eyebrows.

By six o'clock, Will was in his room and panicking. What the hell am I going to wear? Christ I've cut myself shaving! Oh my God, I am actually getting a date with Valerie. She's gorgeous. She chose me. Is she going to invite me back to her room?

As elation momentarily swept over him, it suddenly occurred to him that everyone in the building would be looking for them, when they returned. I've got no chance of getting her on her own later. The thought calmed him down temporarily and he selected his only decent suit and a light shirt. It looked a bit formal, so he ditched any ideas he might have had of taking a tie. He looked in the mirror, changed his mind again and put on the tie.

Somewhere in the back of his mind a germ of an idea appeared. At first it was a tiny worry. Something wasn't right about all this, tonight. The idea grew as he dressed. Supposing they wanted to get him out of here and this was a good way to do it, without him making a scene. Why had she hit on him and dropped Sean so suddenly? He was starting to sweat. He didn't want to sweat, not with a clean shirt on.

It was five minutes before seven. He opened his shirt and applied some more deodorant, took a swig of water, to loosen his tight throat, and rushed to the lift, fiddling with his shirt buttons.

The lift doors opened after a couple of floors and Valerie appeared in front of him. She looked great, as she smiled at him. The doors shut and Will noticed immediately, in the close confines of the lift, that she smelt great too.

"Hi Will. Wow you sure scrub up well. Ooh I like a man in a tie." She reached up and adjusted his tie a fraction.

Her perfume was intoxicating. Will had the overwhelming urge to kiss her there and then.

The doors opened and most of the members of their group were in the lobby. As they rushed for the limo, Will guessed this was how it must be for film stars or pop idols. Their colleagues were all jostling and whistling. Through the throng Jones appeared.

"You two aren't going anywhere!" he exclaimed. "Not with those things on your wrists." He produced a tool from his pocket and released them. "Don't stay out all night."

At last they were in the back of the limousine and alone together. They looked at each other and Will, all dry mouth, could think of nothing to say.

"Are you O.K. Will? You look a little pale. Heh, give me your hand." She took his hand and stroked it. "You're really hot. Let me check your pulse." She felt his wrist. "Nurse Valerie prescribes a stiff drink, followed by the best dinner Boroughbridge can afford."

She opened the cocktail bar. "What do you fancy? They got just about everything, gin, brandy, ooh, that's cool, champagne. Will, you open it and I'll hold the glasses."

To a loud pop, Will opened the bottle and poured. With a couple of glasses of champagne inside him, Will felt more relaxed and they sat back together, on the limousine's huge sofa-seat to examine the menus, which had been thoughtfully supplied.

His head light with expensive champagne, the evening passed like a dream for Will. Valerie was in sparkling form, attentive, captivated by his stories and laughing at all his jokes. By the time their car arrived, Will felt as though he was swimming in those big blue eyes. All too soon they were on their way home. Valerie had removed his tie and undone his shirt; her head was resting on his chest. She was mumbling something, which Will could not quite make out.

She managed to sit upright and say to him, "Willy, Willy, what about some more champagne? I don't think we've drunk enough of Doc. Jones' money. Or is he a prof.? I can't remember. Never mind." She lurched forward to the cocktail cabinet.

Will wasn't sure whether it was the movement or the thought of more champagne, but he suddenly felt sure that he was going to be sick. With difficulty he controlled it.

"I think I've had enough, actually."

Valerie twisted around to look at him. "Actually. Act-u-a-lly. Ha, ha, actually so have I!"

Fleetingly Will remembered Inge.

She lay back on his chest again and they passed the rest of the journey in silence.

When they arrived back at Boroughbridge, Will was not entirely sure how he returned to his room. He vaguely remembered feeling relieved that there was no welcoming party. He did remember kissing Valerie goodnight. Was it outside his door or hers? He was not sure. No it was in his room. She had come back with him. Did they make love? God what a waste, if they had and he couldn't remember. He sat up on his bed and looked around. She was not there. With a great effort he removed his jacket. The shoes were too far away. He slept.

Sean heard a gentle tap on his bedroom door. He glanced at his wristwatch, 12.45 a.m. Who the hell was that? For once he'd ducked out of it all early. He needed a night off from the whole business. He was sick of the socialising, the watching what he said and the basement meetings. Especially the basement meetings! He hadn't enjoyed Will and Valerie's sending off party. He had gone to bed, but could not sleep. He sat on the bed, with a bottle from the mini-bar. He didn't need this.

Too much trouble to dress, he went naked to the door. "What do yer want?"

"It's Valerie. I need to talk to you."

Sean opened the door a crack and walked back to bed. Valerie entered and shut the door behind her.

"Nice meal?" enquired Sean.

"Very," responded Valerie. "We had lobster. You know, cut down the middle for two. It was delicious." She touched her lips with her finger and looked at Sean.

Sean lay back beneath the duvet, his hands behind his head. "Well now. You seem to be having a good influence on him," he said with a vain attempt to keep the jealousy out of his voice. "He seems a lot more relaxed. Where is he now? What have you done with him?"

She laughed. "You have a very high opinion of me. He's sleeping like a baby. I got the dose just right. A little top up in the champagne and he made it through dessert and back to base." She opened both hands and shrugged. "Mind you, I wasn't sure we could manage coffee, so we skipped it," she conceded.

Sean sat bolt upright as realisation hit him. "Shit! You're drugging him."

"Well done!" she said in a patronising tone, "And a bonus point for the man with no kit on." She bent down and slipped off her shoes. "Now for the big prize," she fiddled with the clasp on the belt of her skirt. "What am I using to control him for such long periods, without the little darling even having a clue?" Her skirt fell to the floor.

Sean was having trouble concentrating beyond the thong she was wearing. "Um, uh, how about Ritalin?"

"Tut, tut *Doctor* O'Grady. You can do better than that." Her arms were folded now, the undressing process suspended. "Even you must know that, whilst Ritalin works to control hyper-active kids, it has the opposite effect on adults. He'd be climbing the walls by now on that stuff. Try again."

"Rohypnol?"

" Roofies, Wolfies, La rocha, chemical name Flunitrazepam, one of the benzodiazepine family, a depressant of the central nervous system, known to most of us as…" she fluttered her eyelashes, "…the date rape drug." She smiled sweetly and held his gaze for an eternity.

Sean could feel the sexual tension crackle in the air between them. "Nice try young man, but no cigar." Her arms remained folded and Sean's pulse raced. "Do you really think I'd need to rape him? Surely I'm not that unattractive?" She pouted. "I'm not gonna need that for you, am I?" She put one hand on her cheek and the other on her hip and wiggled provocatively. "There is also the tiny, tiny problem that you can't getta hold of it, well not legally anyways, without a blue dye added. I don't know whether you've noticed, but our friend's favourite drink is not a pint of Blue Bols." She raised her voice and her tone became more aggressive. "Now come on bright boy, get yer ass in gear or I'm gonna freeze my butt off, standing here."

Sean's mouth was dry and he took a swig at the bottle from the mini-bar, beside the bed. As an afterthought he added, "Drink?"

"Stop pissing about!" she snapped. Then more gently, "I think Valerie is going to have to get cross with you."

Sean drew his knees up to his chest to cover his embarrassment.

She sucked the tip of her finger again, as if in deep thought. "O.K. I'll give you some clues. I needed something easily soluble in drinks, or a syrup, with no taste. Nothing too strong, I didn't want him passing out or fitting. And, of course, you need him awake enough to brief you on the Irish situation. One last guess."

"Valium, er, doesn't stimulate adults especially when mixed with alcohol."

Valerie shook her head.

"An amphetamine?"

"You're getting warmer, but not right." She bent down and picked up her skirt and then looked into Sean's eyes. "Ah mon pauvre Sean, look at your sad little face now…soooo disappointed." She dropped the skirt again and pulled her top over her head. "Perhaps I'll tell you in the morning." She slipped easily out of her bra and thong.

"For Christ's sake remind me not to get the wrong side of *you*," grinned Sean. "You're good. You're very good."

The naked blonde lifted the duvet and climbed astride Sean. She leaned forward so their lips were almost touching. "Believe me baby, you have *no* idea how good I can be."

Chapter 11

Boroughbridge University
Mid June 2002

The days passed slowly for Sean. So did the nights, except for the brief hour, between around eleven and twelve, when Valerie came to his room. He was spending most of his day, on his own with a selection of books on Irish history. What Will was doing, he wasn't entirely sure. Had he agreed to 'go'? Sean had been so sure that he would not do it, when he had made his agreement with Jones. Now he knew that they were drugging Will, anything was possible.

Over meals he learnt little, except that Will was involved in some new project and, of course, that he was seeing a lot of Valerie. At night she was very tight lipped about him and he couldn't get any news from her. It worried Sean that she would not talk about Will, but not that much, when there were better things to do.

It was nine at night and he was back in the basement. He didn't like these meetings. Jones always had some surprise in store for him and it was never a pleasant one. Sean was also becoming increasingly worried about what would happen if Jones discovered the true nature of his relationship with the blonde Canadian.

To make things worse he was feeling increasingly isolated. It wasn't just the amount of time, which he was spending in solitary study; it was that he had nobody, who could share his burden. To his surprise he realised that he wished he could talk it over with Will. Was he mad? He could hardly explain that while Will was drugged up, he, Sean, was sleeping with the woman, who Will probably reckoned was his girlfriend.

It was a mess and it was about to become worse.

"Sean, thanks for coming again. I have some news for you." Jones was always so polite.

"Oh, that's O.K. You have news? Is this about Will's trip?"

"Precisely. It'll be tomorrow evening, after dinner and I want you to tell him that you're going along too."

Sean turned cold. "I thought that we had an agreement about all that?"

"Yes, yes, I don't want you to be concerned about all this, Sean. I know that you feel uncomfortable. To be honest, so do I. We just need you to go through the motions. When he comes back, we can explain how there was a problem with the dosage, in your case, and you didn't make it."

"So you haven't changed your mind? If Will comes back O.K., then we'll talk again?" Sean relaxed a little.

"Yes, that's what we agreed and nothing has changed. We just want you to play along a bit. We don't want him stressed out and I don't want a scene in front of all the others. You've come a long way Sean, and it's not a lot to ask now is it?"

Sean was chiding himself for overreacting. "No, of course not. What exactly do you want me to do?"

"Well, not very much really. We are still not entirely sure about this whole business of whether you can be seen or not. It is at the heart of the whole project. What is the interface between these people, who claim to have gone back and had all these extraordinary experiences?" Jones continued absentmindedly. "I'm sorry. I always get carried away with my enthusiasm for this. It's so fascinating." He shrugged.

"So what exactly is it that yer want me to do?"

"Like I said, not very much really. Just pretend that you've agreed to go with him on a very simple exercise. Go through the motions in front of your colleagues here and, as I said, when it comes to the moment, it'll work for Will, but not for you."

Jones hesitated for a moment, "As a matter of fact Sean, one of the most obvious reasons for it failing to work, for you, would be the difference in your academic backgrounds."

"I don't follow yer," interrupted Sean.

"Well again you see this is another area that we don't fully understand yet. You see," he leant towards Sean, as if to share a confidence, "I have a theory that the most successful cases are those, where the participants have a very detailed knowledge of the target place and time. It is not just about preparing the right dosage, to hit the target. It's obvious to me that the clearer the view of the target time and place, that the person has, the more likely he is to hit it. In Will's case, he's a brilliant historian. He's lived this stuff, since he was a child. With you, we can say that it was too much to expect you to cram it all, in such a short space of time. Come to think of it," he looked a little worried, "that might be true."

Jones paused for a minute as he turned it all over in his mind. Suddenly he added, "And you don't mind dressing up?"

"For God's sakes man, what are yer talking about? What dressing up?"

"Don't look so concerned." Jones laughed, "we're not going to make you put on the dress! No, it's just that er, sorry didn't I say? If we're not sure whether you can be seen, well then it makes sense to dress you in the costume of the period. You'd be less conspicuous, if you see what I mean."

Sean conceded the logic of this. It did not mean that he liked it. To go through this whole charade and dupe Will, in front of an audience, was bad enough. He was not at all keen to turn it into some sort of period fancy dress party. Reluctantly he agreed. "Where are you getting all the gear from?"

"Oh, that's all been arranged," said Jones casually, as if he had just hired Sean a dinner jacket. "We have Susan and Graham, from the R.M.& C., back again tomorrow. Susan will be ready to kit you out and Graham will be here in the firing range for those of you, who missed out last time. Frankly I'm sure that you and Will can have another go, if you want to."

"Will? Won't he be, er, elsewhere?"

Jones guffawed, as if Sean had made the funniest joke he had ever heard. "That's the most amazing bit about the whole business. He may well have travelled thousands of miles and hundreds of years. He might be there for years, but he'll be back in moments, well minutes anyway."

Sean's head was spinning. Another great basement meeting, he thought. "Can we sit down for a moment?"

"Of course, of course." Jones grabbed a couple of chairs, which were still lying around, after their last shooting session. "It is a bit much to come to terms with."

Sean gathered his thoughts. "Where exactly is Will going? And when, I mean what date is he going to? Is that the way to express it? Christ! Does he know? Has he agreed?"

"It couldn't be better." Jones rubbed his hands with enthusiasm. "I have to confess, we have kept this from you both until now. We had a bit of luck, but before I start on that, let's go back a bit." Jones was clearly trying to keep himself in check.

He cleared his throat and explained. "When we restarted all this programme, as you know, there were more questions than answers. We wanted to find links with places and times, which were familiar to our subjects. We also did not want to throw people into difficult or dangerous situations, bearing in mind our friend and the photograph story. I have to admit, he may be a hoaxer, but if he is telling the truth... Well that's a different story altogether."

"What do you mean, dangerous?" asked Sean.

"Whoa, don't panic. All we're saying is it is better to drop back into a quiet country situation and not the middle of a city. It's also much better to avoid dropping someone into something too heavy. What I mean is, much as we all might like to take a peek, we wouldn't drop you in at The

Crucifixion. It might be a bit of a shock too, if you discovered that you'd just landed on the front rider-less horse at The Charge of the Light Brigade.

No we wanted to find something at the right time and place and then it turned up. We couldn't believe our luck. A package of documents turned up at an antiques fayre in Cork recently. They included an item, which, it is claimed, is a Declaration of Independence for the New Irish Republic of 1796, which never happened. Supposedly it was brought ashore in December 1796, when the ships were in Bantry Bay. When the landing failed, according to local legend, this document was hidden away, in the hope that the French would return.

Now, whilst they had opportunities to land some small numbers, the document tale seems unlikely. So it must be a fake, but is it? The intriguing bit about it, was that it was accompanied by some very authentic looking documents in Portuguese."

"Wait a minute that is quite possible." Sean interrupted him and surprised himself with his enthusiasm for Jones implausible stories. "I've read about this. When they sailed for Ireland, they were dead worried about one of the ships, being intercepted by the Royal Navy. So they planted a load of phoney documents in Portuguese on board to fool the Brits that they were heading for Portugal." Sean paused to think. "Mind you, if I've read about it, then so could anyone else."

"Well there is that of course," conceded Jones, "but that's the point of it all. We believe that we can send someone back to Bantry Bay to take a look. That someone is Will."

"And where am I supposed to fit into all this?" enquired Sean.

"You're just meant to be going along to keep him company. Well that's what we've told Will."

"You've told him already?"

"Well yes, he's very excited at the prospect."

I bet he is, thought Sean, if the blonde with the hypodermic has got his dosage right. Only just in time did he remember that he was not meant to know this and that he had learnt it from Valerie's pillow talk.

"Great, great," said Sean instead and before he had to think of anything else to say, they were interrupted by Jones' mobile ringing.

I'm surprised he can get a signal down here, thought Sean. He stood up and wandered towards the firing range, ostensibly to give Jones some privacy. In fact he wanted some time to collect his thoughts. To his surprise, he found the replica guns, sitting on the table, ready for use, together with the tins of cartridges. He glanced over his shoulder. Jones had his back to him and was engaged in conversation. Sean picked up one of the guns and was about to fire it, when it occurred to him that it might be loaded. He was familiar enough with them to check. They were. Christ that's a bit bloody dangerous, he thought to himself. He was surprised. Graham Brown didn't seem like the sort of guy to leave loaded guns around. There again, he considered, nobody can get access to here except Jones. And me as well, I suppose! Jones was clearly finishing his conversation and Sean returned to the seating area in front of the bench.

There was little more to say and Sean left and went straight to his room. For once he was looking forward to Valerie's tap on the door, not for the sex, but to talk this over. That night she did not appear. Sean wondered if he had nodded off and missed her, but he doubted it. He kept thrashing over in his mind, whether he should do anything or if he should say anything to Will. He did not sleep well that night.

At breakfast, Sean looked for Will and steered him onto a table on their own. He tried to remain calm and control the edge in his voice. "So I gather we're off on a little trip tonight."

"Ah, so they've told you, have they? I wondered when they'd let you in on it." Will replied with wide eyes, like the two of them were on some boarding school treat.

"You're not, er, worried at all?"

"No, not for something as straight forward as this. It'll be fascinating to see if they can arrange the temporal-geographic co-ordinates accurately, won't it? Will we be able to communicate with each other?"

"Christ Will, you sound like you've just stepped out of the tardis. Just listen to yerself man."

"Oh I think you're getting it out of all proportion Sean. Come on now, I'm supposed to be the conservative one. Just imagine, if it all works and we can go back and see all these things."

Sean was about to remind Will that all this work was experimental, including, in fact especially, the drugs, when Valerie came over and joined them. She squeezed Will's hand, as she sat down.

"All set? It's sooo exciting," she said. To Sean, she too was treating it like a holiday to some exotic location.

Sean looked at the pair of them and knew he was wasting his time. Short of blowing the whistle on the whole thing, he realised that this train was rolling out of the station and he couldn't stop it now.

After breakfast, he and Will were taken to one of the smaller meeting rooms to be kitted out by Susan from her collection of facsimile clothing. Valerie came with them, as she was to join them in the briefing session, which was to follow. The others were all back in the basement on the firing range. Sean felt detached from the proceedings, while Will was absorbed in the detail and Valerie played along with the fancy dress game.

After a couple of hours and some nimble alterations, Will and Sean were similarly clad in calf length boots, coarse linen trousers and shirts and long coats with an enormous number of buttons. Large leather shoulder bags and soft hats completed the outfits. Appropriately inconspicuous was the conclusion.

Then came the briefing and an introduction to another rule of time travel. The trio went into the lecture theatre. The auditorium lighting was dimmed, two chairs on the stage fully illuminated. The atmosphere seemed very different with just the three of them there. It was like entering a sacrosanct building, without permission. As if to complete the image, Jones and Al entered together from the back of the stage and took their places on the chairs.

"Congratulations guys," beamed Al. "It's like N.A.S.A. and the moon shot programme. You two have been selected for the next flight. Arguably this is more exciting and of greater scientific importance than the space programme." He gave them his dramatic pause to let his words sink in.

"There is one further rule, which we need to share with you. We believe that there are grounds to support a theory that one of the former staff, here at Boroughbridge, has put forward. Like all this work, it *is only a theory.* Nonetheless, you need to hear this.

I won't bore you with the arguments behind all this. That can come later. I don't mind saying that they're very complex. I'm not entirely sure that I follow it all myself." He turned to Jones, who nodded in sympathy.

"The bottom line, guys, is this. If you travel back in time, wherever you get off, on that journey, that's it. It's the end of the line. *You cannot go back any further.* If you go back to 1900, that's the whole package guys. You cannot go back next time to 1850. You can go back to 1950, but not earlier than 1900, not a day."

It was Sean's turn to look on in amazement. This was crazy. "How on earth can you say that?" he heard himself saying.

Al responded, "Like I said Sean, I don't wanna go into the theories. We have a whole series of lectures on this later. If you want to get a handle on it, I guess there are ways to explain it."

Before he could continue, Jones chipped in. "Sean, we are entering into some of the most complex areas of temporal theory here. The simplest way to explain this is to give you an example. If you were to go back to the first of January 1900, it just would not work, if you could then go back to New Year's Eve in 1899. It's this whole business of not bumping into yourself." He leant back into his chair, as if it was all perfectly obvious.

Sean looked even more puzzled. "O.K. I can buy that. It's enough of a shock for *you lot* to meet me. I'm not sure *I* could handle it meeting meself. It doesn't work though does it now? The theory, I mean."

"What do you mean Sean?" asked Jones.

"Well, think about it. If I go back on the second of January, you could bump into yerself, from the other direction, so to speak."

"Ah, I take your point, Sean. There is another set of rules that apply to that. I'll make it simple for you. You can't do that either! We should have explained. You can only go back to the second of January, if you came back to the future from the first."

Sean was not comfortable with this, but for the time being he could not find a fault in this logic, so they moved on.

"The reason for telling you this is simple," Al continued. "We're sending you back to 1796. If you have an uncontrollable desire to see the Spanish Armada and our theory is right, you won't get there. Not now, not ever!"

Al continued with more examples, while Sean's mind relaxed. This is complete crap, he told himself. What the hell am I worried about; this is not going to happen. One small cloud crept over his horizon; supposing the drugs had some appalling side effect on Will. That was only a small risk he tried to tell himself.

Then it hit him. He shivered. Oh my God, why hadn't he thought about this before? "Er, excuse me interuptin' yer now. Isn't there something yer've forgotten?"

Al stopped in mid-flow. "Sure Sean, what's your point?"

"How the hell is Will, I mean, how are we getting back? What are yer givin us to get back?"

Al smiled smugly. "You've got it already. You've already got your ticket back. It's sitting on your wrist."

Sean, puzzled, looked down at the metal band on his wrist.

"That's right Sean. Once you've travelled, that thing is activated. Do you see? There is a thinner band running around the middle of it. If you grip that with your other hand and twist, it will send an electric charge through your arm and re-activate the drug, which we will put in your system. It'll bring you back, just like the other guys, who've done this already."

Sean and Will twisted the centre section. It moved easily and made a little click, as it found its new location. Nothing happened and they both looked up, with anxious expressions.

"Don't look so worried guys," exclaimed Al. "Nothing ain't gonna happen, when you're still in the here and now. Besides we ain't given you yer magic potion, have we?"

The two men looked only slightly reassured by this. Will seemed more satisfied than Sean, with the explanation.

Sean wanted more time to think it through. He desperately wanted some time to himself and yet the day roared on relentlessly. Soon everyone knew what was happening that evening. The evening timetable was planned around the arrival of some cabinet minister from London, to witness it all. This just cranked up the level of anticipation.

At 7.30 the group were having dinner. Sean and Will were not allowed to eat. It was as well that they did not hear the conversation over the evening meal. It varied from

Wolfgang's jokes about the chosen ones to unkind comments about it being the only way to get them away from the Canadian bitch. While the rest of the group were dining and chatting with excitement, the two were dressing and receiving their last briefing from Al. Of Jones and Valerie, there was no sign. At 9 p.m. the lecture theatre was full and two chairs, with special restraining straps were placed on the platform. Sean wanted to be sick, only there was nothing in his stomach.

Wolfgang appeared and rushed up to Sean. "Sean, Sean, I have a message for you from Dr. Jones. You must meet with him immediately."

"Christ, what now? And dressed in all this? Where?"

"I don't know, he just said that you must meet him quickly and you would know where."

The cabinet minister had arrived and everyone was waiting. Sean glanced at his wrist. How stupid, no watch, just a patch, smeared with fake tan to cover the pale mark, left, where the watch had been. God, he'd better go. It could only be the basement. Ignoring the questions and comments, he rushed out and headed down the stairs. Miraculously nobody was about. I guess they're all in the lecture theatre, Sean thought. He hit the keypad by the door and descended the next flight. The lights at the bottom were switched off. It was black, with a crack of light leaking out from the door at the end. This did not feel right. He glanced at his wrist again and cursed his stupidity.

No time to think, he rushed towards the further door and burst into the room at the end. "Jones. Dr. Jones are you here?" There was no reply. Sean looked around. There was no one there, just a faint electric hum from the range lights. He whirled around to look at the door. Nobody. He was about to rush out when the light in the firing range caught his attention. He crept towards the firing point.

On the table lay the two revolvers, the ammunition and a leather bag. Was this some trap? He opened the bag cautiously and peered in. It contained coins. They looked very old, like nothing he'd ever seen before. Sean hesitated and then his mind was made up. He had to catch Will on his own. My God, how was he going to do that, with this circus going on? He stuffed one revolver into the back of his trousers and put ammunition and charges into his pockets. He put the other gun, together with about half the ammunition into his bag, along with some coins. He tried to put the bag, containing the rest of the coins in his pockets. They were full. In desperation, he tipped the remaining contents of the bag into his boots and rushed back upstairs, wincing as he walked on the coins.

Nearly overcome with guilt and fear, he fell into the lecture theatre, where everyone was waiting for him. Oh Christ, he was too late! Will was already strapped to the chair.

"We thought you'd done a runner Sean," boomed Al.

"Sorry folks," shouted Sean, pretending to fiddle with his trousers. "Last minute nerves."

They all laughed and clapped.

Sean rushed onto the platform. He went over to Will and stumbled into Will's chair, dropping his bag and knocking Will's from his lap. His excited audience giggled and Sean managed to swap the bags.

Jones had reappeared from nowhere and started to talk. Sean could not focus on what he was saying, as they strapped him in.

Sean looked across at Will and gave him a reassuring wink. Like Will, by now, he was strapped into his seat. The clamps holding his head permitted some lateral head movement, but not the full range. This did not feel right. Sean did not like this one bit and kept asking himself why he felt so nervous? Was it guilt at deceiving Will or apprehension that he was going to be sucked in too? Had he been set up too? Was he so sure that he wasn't a victim of the same deception?

Deception? What in hell's name was he talking about? This was not deception, not a little white lie. He had conspired against an innocent man, a man whose friendship he had sought. He was party to a massive conspiracy; with people he hardly knew and for reasons he hardly understood. Will's sanity or even his life could be at risk here.

He glanced over. Will looked very pale now, but still managed a smile.

For reasons he hardly understood? More self-deception. He knew why he was doing this. His father's face appeared in his mind. 'Lie to any one son, but only a fool lies to himself.' Sean knew in a flash of painful reality both how and why he had trodden the path, which had led him here. It wasn't idealism. It wasn't for a free Ireland, nor was it down to family loyalty. A wave of shame washed over him. C'mon Sean this is not like you, he chided himself. It must be the stress. It does funny things to a man.

An icy clarity settled on him. Like so many before him, when finally facing reality, he knew how he'd arrived here. Greed, laziness and lack of moral courage, he told himself. Here he was sitting in this chair, while they had pumped God knows what shit into Will. How many times could he have turned back? By the time his father had met him, that night, he'd returned from Boston, it was already too late. He had never had the strength to stand up to his father and was far too scared of those figures, which hid in the shadows behind the man. In his little world at Trinity, it was easy to pretend to himself that he had moved on. In truth he'd run away. Was that his choice?

"Sean, Sean sweetie," Valerie's words brought him back to the present. She was looking very professional in her lab coat.

"Heh, you look hot in that kit, baby." Sean's mouth was on autopilot.

"Down tiger, we don't want your blood pressure rising. Now just relax." She leant forward and whispered in his ear. "Will's been dosed and it will take a few minutes to take effect. He's watching you and I want him relaxed. I am just going to inject you with a placebo."

Sean looked up at the bright, multi-faceted lights in the roof of the lecture theatre. Just like the dentist. He could feel himself sweating. Bloody ridiculous this, dressed in eighteenth century garb, complete with boots full of sovereigns. The pistol was sticking into his back. It would probably go off and leave him a paraplegic. He consoled himself with the thought that the torrent of sweat running down his back would soak the powder, even with Brown's clever mechanism, and it would just be a flash in the pan.

With a start he felt the needle penetrate the vein in his forearm. Valerie smiled down at him. God she was pretty. He had done a lot in his short life, yet this was a first. Heh, this is quite a turn on! His thoughts seemed to accelerate away ahead of him, like a dream with something elusive, just out of reach. Tied down at the mercy of a pretty woman, maybe they could play some new games tonight?

Or perhaps he should take her more seriously? She was one of the few women, who he felt was his equal. My God, perhaps she was *the one*. He'd never thought of any woman like that before! When would they get out of here? It might be ages before he could catch Valerie on her own, without eavesdroppers and cameras. Oh sweet Lord, were there cameras in his bedroom? Why the hell hadn't he thought of that? Why meet in the basement, if his room was secure?

A movement in his peripheral vision distracted Sean. Will seemed to be convulsing. Sean couldn't watch. Bit bloody late for the guilt trip now, he thought.

He concentrated on Valerie. God, he was dripping. It was stupid wearing these stupid outfits. Stupid, stupid. What a stupid word stupid was. Valerie was gone! He tried to twist his head against the clamps, restraining him. Panic was beginning to take its destructive hold on him. If only Will would 'go' and he would get out of here. He forced himself to look at Will again.

Oh my living God. What the hell had happened to Will? Where *had* he gone? The restraining straps holding him were still fastened, but Will had disappeared. That wasn't meant to happen. Sean looked for Valerie; looked for his own legs. They were still there. Valerie was back. She was looking at her watch.

A blast of fire roared through Sean's arm. He tried to see where the needle had gone in. Hell it was burning. He looked back at Valerie. How strange! She was smiling at him. She was blowing him a kiss and waving! The flames in his arm were spreading, like a bush-fire. His whole body, like some giant steam engine, was pounding now. The noise in his head was deafening. Some power was blasting through every part of his being. He couldn't stop himself. He was shaking, fitting, out of control. Oh sweet Mother of Christ, it hurt!

With a superhuman effort Sean twisted his convulsing torso to catch a last view of Valerie. There was just time for one more thing.

"BIIIITCH!" howled Sean.

Then the earth opened up and blackness swallowed him.

END OF PART TWO

PART THREE

In the year of one thousand seven hundred and ninety eight
A sorrowful tale the truth unto you I'll relate
Of thirty-six heroes to the world were left to be seen
By a false information were shot on Dunlavin Green.

Extract from 'Dunlavin Green' (Traditional Irish Song)

Chapter 12

A Journey
2002 – late eighteenth century

Will lay on the chair and shut his eyes, every nerve stretched to snapping point. Nothing, just a vague sense of warmth travelling up his arm. He opened his eyes slowly fearing what he might see. They were all there peering at him anxiously and he started to laugh at the absurdity of the situation.

Then the warmth changed to burning. Oh my God he was shaking. His guts churned and Will thought that he was going to fill his pants. He gritted his teeth and hung on. Then it hit him so hard that he thought his eyes would be torn from their sockets. The floor opened and he fell faster than he believed possible. Colours roared past in a crescendo of brightness. Face down now; he dropped, blinded by the intensity of the light below. He held out his arms and legs to slow himself, but a force of incredible power was sucking him deeper.

He was falling now at such speed that his face was burning and he was sick with the power and with the certainty he would be destroyed, like a meteorite re-entering the earth's atmosphere. Then he started to slow. He was sure. The colours around him began to take on form and shape. He could make out something and sounds too. The roaring in his ears stopped and he could make out voices and the buzz of traffic. He could smell car fumes and hear laughter. The picture cleared and everything came into focus.

He was suspended over a busy shopping street. Hundreds of people were milling around. It was a hot summer's day. Men were in brightly coloured T shirts, girls were in short skirts and Will could feel the heat of the sun on the back of his neck. It was odd the cars were all dated. My

God; recognition flooded over him. It looked like Carnaby Street, in its heyday, the late 1960's. The clothes, the colours, it was so real. It was amazing. He was there.

Then the picture started to fade, the heat of the sun was gone and the colours started to move past him. No not yet! He wanted to see more. Too late, he fell again.

This time it was not so violent. Images half appeared and were gone. Faces, scenes half recognised and gone, like that name on the tip of your tongue that just won't come. Suddenly it cleared again. This time it was a rural landscape, spread out below him with the sea in the distance. Again it was summer, bright blue skies around him and a noise droning overhead. The noise grew louder and rose to a roar as an aircraft zoomed past so close that Will flinched.

It did not seem in the least absurd that he was suspended above the Kent countryside watching a dogfight between a Spitfire and a Messerschmidt. It was so real. He was actually there again. It might be a drug, an illusion. It might be some narcotic induced audiovisual trick, but he didn't care. He was flying, flying through history.

Then, like the doors closing on a lift, the scene was gone. He descended again. There was no fear now, just impatience to see the next scene. It came, not in vision, but in sound. The noise grew louder, explosions that shook his very soul. Bangs and cracks were all around him. He recognised, from films, not experience, the rattle of machine guns, but it was so misty. He couldn't see anything. Or was it smoke? Suddenly the smell hit him like body blow. It was a foul stench of something evil. Was it chemical or was it rotting flesh? It clawed at his throat and made his eyes smart. Will strained to see and from the greyness in front of him appeared ghostly figures. Men, but not how he'd ever seen them, masked and wearing huge coats and helmets. They were soldiers in gas masks. He was in some great battle of the First World War!

As they came nearer he realised, to his horror, that he was not suspended above them, he was amongst them. They were coming for him! Panic consumed him and he turned to run, but he could not. He was held and could only wait. There were hundreds of these ghosts now, taking gruesome shape out of the murk. They were almost upon him, when a rattle louder than all the others consumed them all. Will held his hands over his ears and stared in horror, as the ghosts transformed again. They changed from sombre men with murder in mind to terrified and pathetic creatures, as the machine guns bullets tore into them. The ground turned into a storm of mud and body parts and the screams and gunfire grew so loud that Will howled for it to stop.

As if in answer to his pleas it became silent. The gunfire moved further off and became muffled by the fog. All around him men lay dead or dying. Not one remained upright. A shape in front of him tugged at its mask. Will watched, unable to avert his gaze. The mask came off and what was revealed was more than Will could bear. The face was a boy's. Bloody, vomit emitting from a hole in its side, where his cheek should have been. The boy held his gaze and as they made eye contact, tears running down what was left of his face, the boy raised a hand and tried to speak. No sound came out. The mouth was no longer capable of speech. The intent was obvious. He begged Will to help him. Will wanted to just hold him in the last moments of his life, but he was transfixed. He had reached out to an unknown dying boy in an unknown place in a moment of time, nearly a hundred years ago. The boy could see him, he was sure. As he tried to move to him, the image faded and was gone.

"No, no, wait!!" Will screamed out. He thrashed about trying to step forwards, but the vortex had him in its steely grip again and the boy was gone. Time rushed on. Now the images were coming quicker and less clear. Some great public event, thousands of people lining the streets – a funeral? Queen Victoria's Funeral? Will wasn't sure. It was gone too quickly. Men at a large meeting – Gladstone in Parliament? Too soon it was gone. Then there were images, so fast, one after another from exotic locations – soldiers in red uniforms in Africa? India? He could not be sure. One clear image of a train, an early steam train and then clear as day and unmistakable, the SS Great Eastern, Brunel's mighty ship and in a flash gone.

Will's spinning head could take no more, when it all slowed again. He found himself sweeping gracefully over the rooftops of London – not the London he knew, but a London of long ago. It was sensational, like a scene from Mary Poppins or Peter Pan. The Tower of London, St.Paul's Cathedral, …no, no, it was earlier than he had first thought. This was Victorian London. The London Basin bristled with the masts of tall sailing ships and the streets were teaming with life. It was filthy. Children playing in rags in the muck near the City and the smell! Will put his hand to his nose. How did people live in that? He'd never really considered it in all his studies. His Victorian England had been a world of academic research, causes and results, international relationships and economic statistics. This was life in the raw and it was pretty obvious what was raw in those streets!

He laughed and the relief of that emotion swept over him. This was the dream he had signed up for. He would return from this a richer person, with an insight into history that his nature and upbringing had prevented him from experiencing.

He was moving west. He could see Hyde Park and standing in the centre like some great ice palace – a Crystal Palace, was the most incredible glass structure. It was massive and in a moment he realised where and when he was. He laughed again. This was a new notion. When are you? The Great Exhibition lay before him.

As if with some magic VIP pass, he was swept into the building. He hovered high up in the great structure and looked down at the pageantry below. All the notables of the day were gathered as a group walked in, led by a small lady. "Oh my God," thought Will. "May 1st 1851, Queen Victoria, opening the Exhibition. The exhibits were amazing, machinery and displays of all sorts. The figures interested him most. The old man, with the whiskers with Victoria, had to be Wellington. He was very old now, at the end of his life. Will stared into his face and as he did so, the great man looked back. Will froze. Could he see him?

The face began to change and, as it did, the Exhibition Hall began to fade. The lights began to roar by again, but bizarrely the face remained. It remained and changed at the same time. It contorted, no, no, it grew younger. Wellington was growing younger! The face settled and the rest of his body took form. A cocked hat took shape on his head and a horse, the trusty Copenhagen, grew into life underneath him. Wellington's mouth opened and he roared.

Whatever sound came out was lost under the deafening crash of cannon fire. Will did not even have to think. The noise, the smoke, the chaos beneath him; it was Waterloo. This time he was not shocked or frightened. His head shot around, so as not to miss a moment of it. The British squares were there. A mass of red uniforms in a muddle of bloody strife, crumbling as a tide of French cavalry washed around them and then somehow reforming to retain their shape. Officers all around him on horses were exhorting their men to greater efforts. He could see the farm at Hougemont, where some of the fiercest fighting took place – a life and death struggle played out before his eyes.

He was enjoying it. This time it did not seem so real. It was like a computer game. For sure, it was the most realistic game he had ever seen, but not quite life, not real people. Any moment it would come up 'Game over' and, with a little disappointment, he would move on.

As these thoughts slipped into his mind, it did fade and was gone. The colours again and the vague images, nothing he could really identify. This time, though, it seemed as if he was drifting for longer. The colours vanished for a split second, hesitated and returned. It was like the system was searching for something that it could not quite find. Will remembered once, trying to tune a television, when the stations appeared and, not quite sharp enough, he had pressed the control again to move on and look for a better image.

The colours stop and bang, Will hits the ground so hard that he is stunned and winded. He lies there for a while, not sure of anything, except pain. Pain all over. He thinks he has broken his back and he cannot breathe. Slowly he realises that he is lying, face down in thick wet grass. He frantically gasps for air and finally manages to suck some cold wet breaths into his lungs. The pain begins to subside and Will tests his feet and hands, which seem to respond to his instructions. He tries to sit up. His back hurts, but, miraculously, he does not seem to be injured.

It is bitterly cold and he is already soaked through, from the patches of snow on the grass and the sleet, which are driving into his face. There is not much to see. The poor visibility only gives him a view of grass, sloping away in one direction and some windswept gorse and boulders in the other. Between the boulders runs a path. This is real, thinks Will. It must be. I can feel the cold and I can see that my clothes are wet. Wherever, or whenever I am, this is not like even the First World War experience. He stands up and takes a couple of tentative steps and sits down again. I couldn't do that on that battlefield, when I tried to run away. He casts his mind back and remembers the words from the training, 'You'll know when you're there. It will feel different, but don't worry, real as it feels, they can't see you. You'll be like a ghost. They might get a half image of you, but nothing clear.'

It had all seemed so satisfactory in those cosy lectures back at Boroughbridge. He had not taken it that seriously. What had he really thought would happen? Did he believe he would actually take part? Had he thought it would work? It is that business about being seen, which bothers him most. He is sure the soldier had seen him and for that matter, the Iron Duke too. That is quite a thought, being eye to eye with the Duke of Wellington. He is losing concentration.

Come on Will you've got to focus, he chides himself. First thing's first, where the hell is Sean? Will peers into the murk and feels like a paratrooper, who looks around the drop zone for his comrades. He cannot see another living soul. Then a terrible thought creeps into the back of his mind. It starts to grow, like a cancer and he fights hard to stop panic from paralysing his wits. Suppose Sean missed the drop zone, not by distance, but by time. Suppose he is not in the next field, suppose he is in *the next year!* The panic is bubbling up. Suppose it is him and not Sean, who has missed the right time. Then he laughs and consoles himself with the thought that he'll walk into the nearest village to catch yesterday's TV news.

That's a distraction, he tells himself. He tries to think clearly. It doesn't help that his head hurts and he feels like the morning after a pub-crawl. He stands up again and his legs feel shaky. He has to find out where he is and, most important, when he is. He has to find Sean. You're not going to do it sitting about here in the cold and wet, he thinks.

Will notices that his left hand inadvertently finds its way to the metal band on his right wrist. His escape route is still in place. He was determined back in Boroughbridge to make the very most of this opportunity. Now he has arrived at wherever and whenever he is, his resolve is weakening. Whatever he might tell himself, he knows deep down that he will twist that band at the first sign of trouble.

His thoughts return to his invisibility. He has decided that he will keep out of sight, until he is sure of himself and he will test it on some individual, not in a crowd. With the wristband checked one more time and his decision made, he feels more confident. So Will Peters, twenty-first century man, scared and cold, shoulders his bag, which feels heavier than he remembers, and heads along a path, and into, what he thinks might just be the eighteenth century.

Chapter 13

Bantry Bay, South West Ireland
Late eighteenth century

Will Peters cannot understand what the hell is going on. For the hundredth time he peers through the icy sodden grass, down into the bay and sees nothing. No sails, no ships - nothing. On a decent day it wouldn't be so bad, but the sleet, turning to snow, is beginning to settle now. The northeasterly gale, which is driving it, is cutting him in two. His hands and feet are throbbing with the cold, his head hurts and Sean is nowhere to be seen. The light is failing, as the winter night descends and Will does not know what to do. One thing is clear; he cannot stay here much longer.

What was it that had drawn him into this fool's mission? The millennium celebrations fired his imagination. Why not be the first to see the end of two centuries, as a young man? It is an historian's dream, to see it all with your own eyes, to gain that unique insight. Although he hadn't thought it possible he couldn't quite dismiss it either. Gradually he'd been sucked in. No, he tells himself, that is nonsense. It was just an easy escape hatch from the mess he was in at Oxford.

Will's mind flits back and forth. They had sold him on the idea, safely invisible and still able to see it all first hand. Indeed, his view of Waterloo, during his journey here, had been like that. If it's true why does he feel so cold and wet? And why has he started to sneeze? This is ridiculous. He is there, it seems, as large as life, a twenty-first century man, from North London, on a cliff overlooking Bantry Bay, at the close of the eighteenth century. That is, if he's not been drugged, piled in the back of a van and dumped on some windswept cliff. He has seen TV shows, where they pull stunts like this, just to see the victim's reaction. If he breaks down now, will the lights come on and Al step forward to humiliate him again? Only this time, it will be in front of millions of television viewers. Will vacillates between terror and embarrassment. He admits to himself that embarrassment and disappointment is the greater fear, if he's been duped.

Then the terror is in the ascendancy again. The doubts are gnawing at his courage. He is close to paralysis. If you were only there in spirit, why would it be dangerous to be at Waterloo? If nobody is going to see you, why have they put him in period costume? He hadn't thought about it too seriously. He hadn't wanted to. Bored, broke and forced to flee from Oxford, his desire to move on had overcome his better judgement. So he'd gone for it. What a fool. It all seemed so credible at the time. He cannot understand why he fell for it all. It was as though some other Will had made the decisions. The last few days at Boroughbridge had flown by, as if he were in a trance.

Focus on the job Will, he tells himself. You are here to see if that document was brought ashore by the French invading party, under Wolf Tone. Why did he agree to this? He knows that some of them did land, on the islands in the bay at least. There's a French boat in the museum at Bantry. So what is he playing at? Must I go out into the bay in this weather? he ponders.

Eyes stinging, he strains to see. There is no small landing party. Will cannot see a jolly boat, with a crew of hardy French sailors straining on their oars, battling the gale. He sees nothing; case for the document dismissed. Except the French were there for days. Perhaps it's tomorrow. That is fine and Will is ready to leave, but something is bothering him. He squints into the gale again.

There is no French fleet, not a single ship!

That's not right, unless, of course, it's still 2002. It niggles Will and the three-way tug of war continues, between fear, common sense and curiosity. It really is 1796. No it isn't, don't be stupid, it's a hoax. The desire for it to be true gains a temporary advantage. He knows that there is well-documented evidence that the fleet was there in Bantry Bay for several days. He has read contemporary accounts of sightings from the land; 'the fleet to consist of sixteen sail...being at a distance of at least eight leagues...' So where are they? Visibility is still poor, but between squalls he has been able to see several miles up the bay and there has been nothing. That is why Will is waiting until dusk.

Now he is shivering uncontrollably. He is soaked through, but a new fear is gripping him. Something is wrong, very wrong. It is the wrong place or the wrong date. There has to be a logical explanation. There just has to be. And on top of this, *where the hell is Sean?* If he's honest with himself, the only thing, which finally convinced him to do this, was that he wouldn't be alone. Sean was going to be at his side. Now he has disappeared.

Maybe this is just some drug induced trance or perhaps they've simply screwed his brains up and he is dead already. That is a cheerful thought. He quietly admonishes himself for giving in to the cold and wet. A rivulet of icy water runs down his back. No, this is real. If things do not seem right, it is more likely to be some elaborate form of jet lag. It would hardly be surprising - he's gone through a few time zones!

"Just go back," he catches himself saying out loud. Louder still, as if to drown out the wind, "Just twist the band and go back."

Should he go and hunt for Sean? He might be lying injured in a ditch nearby. If so, where? Or should he be brave and go down to the nearest village and establish the date and location? That's hardly going to be easy. Just stroll up to the first person he meets and enquire, in his London accent, where am I? And, is it Christmas Day? Oh, and by the way, which year? But then of course this isn't possible, because he's a ghost. He doesn't feel much like a ghost and he starts going around the whole argument again, which just makes his head hurt, on top of all his other discomforts.

Suddenly his reverie is interrupted by shouts. Did he hear something or is his imagination playing tricks on him? Is it just the moaning of the wind? Then it's unmistakable. Voices are audible above the moan of the wind and the angry waves on the shore below. He decides that he has to locate the source and peers out from his hiding place by a cluster of rocks, adjacent to the cliff top path. The wind and snow burn his eyes, but he can just make out some lights in a cluster on the path to his left. They look like lanterns and they are heading towards him. His stomach churns. Abort the mission, hide or move away? He decides to move. If these people come too close, he can just twist that wristband and be gone. He touches the reassuring metal strap yet again.

Turning around he freezes, too terrified to move. There just a couple of metres away, on a rock, sits a young redheaded boy, about twelve years old. Seemingly oblivious to the weather, he is looking directly at Will, with a puzzled expression on his face. For a moment, all Will can do is stare back at him. Then like a mime artist, Will deliberately waves one arm slowly at the boy. The boy grins and mimics Will's actions. The trickle of cold water running down Will's spine turns to ice.

The boy can see him.

Unable to think of anything more sensible to say, Will asks, "C...can you see me?"

"Why wouldn't I be able to see yers? Yer standin' right in front o' me," replies the lad.

Will's frozen brain finally seizes up. His tongue is stuck to the roof of his mouth and he can say nothing more to this strange boy. The band on his wrist and his escape plan forgotten, his mind is blank. Then suddenly all the questions flood out at once.

"Where are we? What's the year, uh, that's to say what's the date? Are there people down there, er, coming up here? I mean..."

"Yer a funny one, but yer seem pretty harmless," responds the boy. "And I wouldn't wait around here. Look at the state of yers, yer soakin' wet and the boys are after yers. Come wi' me."

The boy turns around and disappears off down a track, hidden behind him, leaving Will reeling in confusion. As his red head melts into the mist, Will's brain kicks into gear and he decides to follow, before he loses sight of him completely. Crouching low, although he's still not convinced that he needs to do so, he sets off down the path in pursuit of the young lad.

Too slow! The boy has disappeared, so Will forces his cold stiff legs to move faster, but to no avail. The boy has gone and Will has lost his bearings. At least the lanterns are lost from view and Will feels reassured by this. The daylight has pretty much gone now, which makes him feel safer from pursuit. It is even more difficult to see, so Will blunders on, with no plan in mind, except the vain hope of catching up with the lad. Then around a curve in the path appear some cottages. Instead of shelter and a refuge, more lanterns, huddled in conversation, confront him. Will hesitates. The sounds behind him seem closer again.

As he listens, wondering what to do next, he cannot rid himself of the feeling that it is him that they are hunting. What did the boy say? 'The boys are after you?' Was someone expecting him? He tries to dismiss that thought, before it paralyses him again. That icy hand of panic starts to clutch at his gut again.

Then, with a flood of relief, it dawns on him. This is a classic anxiety induced dream; running away, being pursued, by people, who can see you, even when you hide. Maybe this is an unforeseen side effect of the experiment. He'll be sure to tell them, on his return. He has to admit it is the most realistic dream he has ever had. That stuff they'd injected into him must have been a powerful hallucegenic. That's it. A bit of autosuggestion, together with the right drugs and the mind does the rest.

All these thoughts pass through Will's mind until a sharp piece of rock flies up and hits him on the side of the face. Instantly the crack of a musket whips across the wind. My God, he's been spotted and they are shooting at him! That settles it. This *is* real and he *is* scared. His mind is made up. No point in hiding any longer, Will runs, but curiously, he feels better. He is still unsure of his dates and location, but now, at least he knows what he is dealing with. No more doubts about ghosts and drugs, he had better make it to a barn he has seen on the edge of the little village. There will be shelter there, long enough to operate the wristband, before they can catch him. He can return and find out what is going on. The musket ball has come from the group on the path above him, not from the village group. Muskets were not meant to be that accurate. They must be close.

Now, with a plan, he is calmer. Muskets, he thinks, with a shiver of excitement, this must be the eighteenth century. Heh, this might be a very brief trip, yet I've done it!

As he is running, he has time to consider the absurdity of the situation. His mind is racing. All kinds of crazy thoughts burst through his efforts to concentrate on the task in hand. Is Sean legging it in a similar situation? More likely, knowing Sean, he is sitting at some bar with a pretty lass at his side, regaling her with tales of ... actually he can't think what he'd be telling her, but he knew what the result would be! Good grief! That's a point. He remembers Al's talk and his crack about 'no sex please, we're British.' Everyone had laughed. Now it hits him. If you can be shot, you can get laid. Both have fairly significant implications. He knows which situation he'd rather be in right now! What the hell's the matter with him? Why can't he concentrate? His mind feels numb, for some reason.

The cluster of buildings is closer now. There is still a group outside some sort of an inn. That's all right, as a smaller path, off the main one, leads around the back of the village and towards a squat stone barn. He should be able to reach it and hide long enough to catch his breath and make his final decision to use the wristband. Will slows to a jog to keep the noise of his steps below the level of the wind and makes his way around behind the first cottage. It is great to be sheltered from the worst of the weather, until he treads in something disgusting in the dark and nearly goes down. The entrance to the barn has a gate more than a door and he soon forces it open and is in.

Sheltering in the barn, Will feels reassured and has a moment of calm and bravery. Does he really want to end his trip so soon? What will they say about him, back at Boroughbridge, when he explains how easily he aborted his mission? He drops the shoulder bag to the ground and it spills open. Will has been carrying it around, without a moment's thought, not even thinking to eat. Inside the bag are gold coins and the reproduction Collier revolver. Where did they come from? Perhaps he can defend himself, but then should he shoot someone? He remembers that he must not change history. He never dreamt it would be so difficult.

Shouts outside the barn are very close and Will's courage dissolves in an instant and sets him fiddling with the metal band on his wrist. He shuts his eyes and waits for some sensation or lack of it, … nothing. Oh shit, nothing, no vortex no colours, not a thing. He opens his eyes. The barn is still there and the sounds of approaching voices are even louder. He twists it again and hears the comforting click. Nothing. Will is shaking so hard that he can hardly hold the metal band. Frantically he untwists and twists again, but to no avail. The tears of fear and rage well up. The door breaks open, with a splintering of wood.

"Please God, make it work," sobs Will aloud, as he falls to his knees.

It doesn't.

Despite his incredulity at all this madness, he had a blind faith in the escape route via the gadget. When it doesn't work the shock is too much for him. His heart pounds, his legs won't respond to his screaming brain. Now he needs another plan and fast, but for Will, it is way too late for plans. His mind is as numb as his cold body and, for the first time in the whole crazy series of events, the next few moments are truly dream like.

About a dozen men come at him. The first, a balding bull of a man, hits him, very hard, on the side of the head and the pain is very real, as he falls forward onto the floor. Terror consumes him and he forgets the revolver and everything else in an effort to shield himself from the blows that rain down on him. He is surrounded by faces - they are brutal, dirty, black teeth and foul breath. He is hit again and again. His head is spinning.

The last thing he remembers is the callous laughter and one voice above the rest. "I knew we'd catch the bastard. The Fox'll be very pleased, when we bring him in."

Chapter 14

Bantry
Late eighteenth century

A cold grey dawn creeps weakly through the bars of the little window, to reveal a body on the floor of the tiny storeroom. The body opens an eye. It hurts, so the eye shuts again. Slowly and painfully the reality of what has happened invades Will's mind. He doesn't want to look. He wants to pretend that it is all a bad dream. He can ignore it, with his eyes shut. He can't ignore the pain any more, but he doesn't want to discover how extensive the damage is. To cap it all, he can't ignore the stench any longer.

With a huge effort Will tries to open both eyes. The right will not respond. The left opens and gives a blurred view of a small dank storeroom, with bags, boxes and barrels piled in a muddle of filth and cobwebs. He puts his hand to the offending eye and the pain is so strong he withdraws it. As he does so, he finds a pain in his mouth. His lip seems to be pierced by a broken tooth. He can't cope with that discovery and turns his attention to the stench of stale urine. The next horror is the realisation that he is the cause of the smell. His cold damp trousers give sufficient explanation.

It is time to move. His ribs, back and hip scream in objection to any movement. The change in position causes his head to spin. Despite this, Will manages to stand and realises that he is shaking with cold and cramp. He is overcome with nausea and despair and collapses on an old wooden crate. The thought that his injuries are serious and that he has only late eighteenth century medicine to rely on, brings him close to tears.

After a few minutes of melancholy self-indulgence, Will tries to pull himself together. He had better try and eat something. Where is the bag? He turns too quickly and the sudden movement causes him to cry out with pain. Where is the bag? It is gone, along with any hopes of clean clothes, food or escape courtesy of the newly discovered coins and revolver. In despair and frustration he shouts at the walls, which earns him an angry response from somewhere just the other side of the door and a fresh shot of pain through his jaw.

The door opens and a filthy unshaven face barks at him.

"Quit yer noise, if yer knows what's good fer yers. Christ man yer stink!" the face says. A bowl of something disgusting is tossed on the floor. "Eat."

The door shuts and Will hears a bolt grind across. He looks at the bowl and his head falls into his hands. As the hours pass, Will refuses further food, but is forced to accept bowls of water. By the evening, he is retching with stomach cramps, but has nothing in his stomach to bring up. His misery knows no limits and, as night falls, Will decides to give it another night. If there is neither reprieve nor any sign of Sean, he will rush the guard in the morning. If they kill him, well he is past caring. He is so weak already, from the time travel, illness and lack of food that the plan is an absurdity. At least it gives him some crumb of comfort, as he tries to sleep.

Will is sure that he has not slept for a moment, when, around dawn, something disturbs him.

"Fer Christ sakes, wake up. We've got ter go." A familiar red head appears around the door.

"What the hell?" shouts Will and tries to stand.

"Shh. Do yer want to wake everyone up?" The young lad, whom Will met on the cliff-top, has found some means to open the door and, beckoning Will to follow him, disappears again from Will's view.

Greeted with such an unexpected chance of freedom, Will, half stumbling, part crawling, scrambles after him. He is so weak that he can barely keep up and staggers into some boxes in the corner of the yard outside. It is barely light and bitterly cold and the boy has climbed up onto the seat of an old two-wheeled cart, which is pulled by a large, but elderly brown horse. Will glances at the door to his prison. He ought to close it to cover his escape, but it's too late now.

Seizing the reins and a whip, the lad encourages the horse into action and Will is left to scrabble onto the flat back of the cart, as best he can. With an enormous effort he throws himself onto the bound bundles of sticks and frantically finds a grip to prevent being thrown off again, as the horse slips into a trot. The exertion is too much for him and he collapses face down in the sticks, as his stomach convulses with more cramps.

"That's right, keep low now. We don't want anyone ter see yers," calls out the boy, in a stage whisper. "I'll let yers know, when it's safe ter come and join me up here." With that he falls silent and guides the cart, with an expertise belying his age, through the ruts and holes, away from the village and inland.

Will has intended to climb out of the back of the cart and establish something about his rescuer and a little more of his whereabouts and whenabouts, but for Will it requires more physical and mental strength than he can summons. So he stays face down, where he has fallen and listens to the grind of the metal rims of the cartwheels on the track and tries to breathe steadily to reduce the agony in his chest. With every jolt from the rutted track spasms of pain shoot through his tortured frame.

After what seems like about half an hour, the cart comes to a halt, with a few indiscernible words from driver to horse. The young lad clambers over the back of the seat and rolls Will over onto his back.

"Let's be havin' a look at yers now." He surveys Will with the eye of an ageing doctor. "I don't like the look o' yers one little bit." He tries to pull Will a little more upright and pushes a bundle of sticks behind his back. With that accomplished, he climbs to the front again and returns with a can containing water. Removing the lid, which then serves as a drinking vessel, he fills it and holds it to Will's mouth.

The water is cool and clean and Will gulps it down. He knows that he is terribly dehydrated and indicates to the boy to give him more. After three or four cups, Will feels a little better and starts to question the boy. "Er, how did you find me? Thanks for coming to get me. Who are you? Where are we going?"

With a wave of his hand, the boy dismisses Will's words and says simply, "No time now," and indicates the height of the sun, which is trying to creep out from behind the clouds. "You rest," he orders and, leaping back onto the seat, he seizes the reins again and exhorts the horse to continue their journey.

At the inn, an elderly man, who had slept the night in his clothes, was aroused with a kick. "See ter the boy. If he dies, there'll be trouble."

With a moan he dragged himself to his feet, belched to let out the excesses of the previous night and staggered out to the yard. Stooping to fill a bowl from the pump he noticed that the door to the storeroom was open. "Oh Christ!" Dropping the bowl he scurried over to the storeroom and a quick glance confirmed his worst fears. The bird had flown.

"Oh Jesus, the Fox'll kill us! Jamie, Seamus, come quick. He's gone, he's gone," and with that cry the old man crashed back into the long room with a grubby low ceiling, which acted as a bar.

In no time everyone in the building was up and rushing around, shouting and yelling. They were all late risers, heads thick with ale. By now it was mid morning and a younger and very fat man, who appeared to be in charge, called them to order.

"Hold hard yer stupid bastards. I need ter think. If he escaped on his own, I doubt he'd ha'gon far. He'd ha got nowhere in the dark, so let's spread out and make a search." He organised his men. "You two go back up the cliff road. You two go the opposite way and I'll take the Cork road. We'll meet back here in a coupla hours." He cuffed the head of one of them, who was trying to take a swig of ale, before he went. "Sharply now, we've no time ter lose. He can't have gone far."

The fat man sounded confident, but he knew that if Will had had help, without horses, they were lost. He could hardly expect any reward from the Fox, when he discovered that they had caught the man and then lost him, whilst sleeping off a skinful of ale. There was also the small matter of the gold coins, which were discovered in the man's bag. Half of them were hidden beneath a loose floorboard behind the bar of the inn. His men had been given one apiece to keep them quiet. He'd only get away with it if they caught the man, before the Fox turned up.

As morning turned into noon, they reconvened at the inn. It was obvious that Will had made good his escape. They decided to satisfy their thirst and hunger with more ale and stale bread and extend their search in the afternoon, before the Fox arrived. As they sat down inside, the sound of horses told them that time had run out and they all looked to the fat man to build the case for the defence.

The door opened and a tall powerful man, with long shoulder length black hair, ducked into the room. He was greeted by silence, as other armed riders dismounted and followed him in. The sheer physical presence of so many armed men, in such a confined space was intimidating enough, yet it was the Fox who had the power to reduce men to cowering beasts. His pointed snout, which gave him his nickname, could sniff out the lies that men told when they were scared. His eyes burned into the tongue-tied congregation.

Before the fat man could start his excuses, the Fox had him impaled on a stare. "Where is he?" was all that he said.

The fat man stammered, "We, we've been out all the night lookin' fer 'im, but I don't think he's arrived, as of yet."

The Fox held him in his terrible gaze and then suddenly turned to the older man, who had discovered Will's absence. "Will you give me yer coat?" It was not a question, it was a demand and, without any thought, the old man stood up, slipped off his filthy long coat and handed it to the tall dark intruder.

The Fox put his hand into one of the pockets and pulled out a disgusting looking old rag. He let it drop to the floor. All the time he was staring into the eyes of the old man, who started to squirm. In went the Fox's hand again, deeper into the pocket, and out came a shiny gold coin. He simply held it up and the old man started to stammer.

"I, I found it," he said and then fell silent under fire from those pale acid eyes.

The room was deathly silent now and slowly the Fox pulled a long three-edged blade from his belt. Around fifteen inches long, it was an infantryman's bayonet, its locking ring, socket and shoulder bound with leather strips, to make a neat grip. Only too clearly it was freshly honed and even in the dull light of the inn the tip of the blade twinkled with deadly intent. He turned back to the fat man and pushed the blade against his distended belly until the cloth of his shirt started to tear.

"Alright, alright, we had 'im, but he got away," volunteered the fat one, before he was asked. "He can't be far away."

The Fox said nothing, but increased the pressure slightly on the man's belly, until a hint of blood appeared on the shirt.

"He had a bag. Quick pass it to me." The fat man gesticulated frantically to one of the others, who produced Will's bag, containing the revolver, the ammunition, a few other items and the remaining coins. The contents were soon on the table.

Still the Fox said nothing, but, with his free hand, sifted through the few coins and looked back at the fat man. The pressure on the blade increased, imperceptibly to the onlookers, but enough to produce screams from his victim.

"Behind the bar, fer the love of God man, it was fer me poor wife. Take it, take it, under the floor."

Without taking his eyes off his victim, the Fox gestured with his head to one of his gang, who, after a few moments of ferreting about produced the coins from their hiding place.

The Fox nodded and released the pressure on the blade to an audible sigh of relief, not just from the fat man, but also from his associates. It was at this moment that the Fox leaned forward again and put his full weight behind the weapon until it had disappeared up to the handle into the fat stomach and found resistance from the wooden chair behind. Then he cranked it, like the starting handle of an old machine, before removing it and letting the warm guts slip through the aperture and spill onto the dying man's lap.

"Well I'm glad we've cleared all that up," he said with a smile, as he wiped the blade clean on his victim's jacket. "Are there any more coins, now?" he enquired brightly, looking around.

The haste with which the group emptied their pockets was almost comical and, in no time, the Fox had them all gathered up and back in Will's bag.

"He'll be heading for Cork," was all he said, before turning and leading his men outside. With a clatter of hooves, they were gone.

With the sun giving a little warmth and away from the winds on the coast, Will's situation has improved and he is feeling better. He sits himself up amongst the bundles on the back of the cart and thinks to himself, I haven't a clue where the hell we are, where we're going or why, but every mile further away from those bastards who did this to me, has to be an improvement. He shudders at the thought of them. He is pretty sure that he was in Bantry Bay, but still doesn't know exactly when. He has lost a tooth and his lip is still split, but his jaw is not so sore. Besides, he thinks, the gap is at the bottom and to one side so he doesn't think it will show. He doesn't seem to have sustained any other permanent damage, but his trousers are still slightly damp. The cramps have ceased and hunger gnaws at his empty stomach. Welcome to the eighteenth century, he grins ruefully.

He cannot believe how fast he has descended into the period, filthy, hungry and not a possession to his name, except what he can barely stand up in. You've read the books now experience the discomfort. He lets out a shaky laugh, which makes the boy turn and smile.

"We'll stop for a bite t'eat, by and by," he says.

Will nods and looks around, as if expecting a van to appear, beside the road, serving burgers and chips, lorry drivers lounging about reading the sports pages of the tabloids and drinking mugs of tea. It's only now that it starts to sink in. My God it's so quiet. It hasn't occurred to him until now that he hasn't heard a car or a machine of any sort. There is no traffic noise in the distance, no drone of an aircraft overhead. As far as he can see, with his one good eye, there is nothing for miles except the road winding away between the rocks and grass and gorse and heather. With nothing he can do and still very weak, Will sits back and takes in the view.

True to his word, the boy pulls over, where the ground does not seem too boggy beside the road. Will looks around, with some anxiety, as the boy manoeuvres the cart. If the cart goes into the bog, Will realises that he's in no shape to pull it out. This area is very marshy. Dark streams criss-cross the landscape. Tufts of thick coarse grass are interspersed with patches of thick moss and pools of brown water.

He sits and watches, while the boy pulls open a cloth bag of hay. He takes out a handful and hooks the bag over the horse's neck to feed him. With the handful of hay and a tinderbox he lights a fire. Sticks from the back of the cart are soon alight and, in no time, a pot of something is balanced on some rocks over the fire.

Will worries that their pursuers will see smoke from the fire. Anxiously he tries to look back down the road, which they have travelled. His gut keeps telling him that they are being followed or is it just his stomach playing him up again? It's difficult to see from his current position and his injuries are too painful to risk standing up on the unsteady cart. What can he do if he does see someone, in any case? Run away? He shrugs, knowing that he has absolutely no control over his situation and tries, in spite of his fears, to relax. He still hasn't the strength to question the boy, so lets him continue.

At first he just watches the lad at work. Then he chides himself that he'll have to pull himself together. It's no good ignoring it any longer, he thinks, I've got to patch myself up a bit. He eases himself cautiously from the back of the cart and walks gingerly towards a little pool, adjacent to the site of their temporary camp. Very carefully he kneels down beside the water. Dipping his hands into the pool he pours the cold water over his injured face. The pain is excruciating at first. Then it numbs his skin and he begins to feel better. The damp from the boggy ground soaks into his trousers. He doesn't care. He has to clean himself up.

Noticing Will's activities, the boy approaches and points to the moss all around him. "It's a special kinda moss. It'll fix yer eye." He picks up a handful and slaps it on Will's damaged eye.

With a yell, Will pulls away and the moss falls into the pool.

"Yer do it, yerself," says the boy with a shrug and returns to his fire.

Rather more cautiously Will grabs a handful of the wet moss and tries it himself. It feels cool and relieves the pain. Maybe it's his imagination and maybe it's the effects of this natural material, but his vision does seem to be clearing in the injured eye.

After about twenty minutes the boy cautiously lifts the pot off the fire and pours the contents into two metal dishes, which he has carefully wiped on the seat of his britches. Two spoons receive the same treatment.

"Here, eat," he says and Will obliges, taking a piece of hard stale bread, which is offered.

It is some form of vegetable soup. It is mostly water and potato. No surprises there! He is so hungry that it tastes wonderful and the bread is not too bad, if you soak it for a while. When he thinks about it, this tastes better than some of the ready meals he has eaten, as a student. I guess this is 1790's equivalent to boil in the bag thinks Will and shovels it down greedily.

The boy takes the empty dish and the spoon, wipes them off with a tuft of thick marsh grass and dips them in a pool of brown peat coloured water. Water is tossed on the fire and more grass tossed over the black patch to disguise it from prying eyes. The horse has his feedbag removed and they are ready to go again. Faster than the local takeaway, thinks Will.

"Do yer want ter sit up here?" asks the boy, patting the seat beside him. "We can talk as we go."

Will feels stronger now and there are so many questions unanswered. Up he climbs and, with a jolt that nearly throws him from his new perch, they are back on the road and on their way again.

Before he can start the boy looks over and announces, "Me name's Owen."

To which Will responds, "Well I'm very pleased to meet you Owen. I'm Will and I'm very grateful to you too. I don't know what I would have done, if you hadn't come and got me. You were very brave too."

"Oh I was paid ter do it," responds Owen, as if payment overrides any fear and any further need for explanation.

Will continues, "So who paid you to rescue me?"

"I didn't know you were after bein' rescued, but I did it anyway. I can't tell yer."

Will needs a moment to follow this. "Why can't you tell me?" He gathers up his courage and asks, "Was it a man called Sean, a tall man like me?"

"I can tell yers that he was tall, like yerself, but I can't be telling yers 'is name."

This is all too confusing and frustrating for Will, so he tries a different approach. "Where did he come from, this man?"

"I don't rightly know where he comes from, but I met him in Wexford, but I don't know that he lives there," replies Owen.

"Is he my age?"

"How old are you?"

Will is starting to lose his patience and, not for the first time, looks around for the TV cameras, but there are none. "O.K. let me ask you something else."

Before he can continue, Owen asks, "What does O.K. mean?"

"It means, er, alright. Never mind that, what year is it?"

"Yer don't know what year it is?"

"Well no," admits Will. Thinking quickly he adds, "It must have been the bang on the head. I can't even remember the date."

"Well that's a trickier one, fer sure," responds Owen. "Now the year will be, er, let me see, seventeen hundert an' nointy seven. Now the day I'm not ser sure. Well, it must be around the end of February, no, no not that. It's getting on fer the end a March."

"March 1797! No wonder there were no bloody ships in the bay! I thought it was Christmas!"

"No, I'm sure about dat. 'Tis definitely not Christmas," responds Owen and they both fall silent, thinking about this exchange, as the horse plods steadily on.

After a while Will asks, "Where are we going?"

"That a way," says Owen, pointing ahead and laughing at Will's gasp of exasperation. "No, I'm just havin' a little joke. We're going ter Wexford of course, ter see the man what sent me."

Will starts to think about this. Wexford's bloody miles away! In a car, even allowing for traffic and some of the roads, it would take a few hours. On this cart, at this pace, it's going to take days. The thought of spending the next few days in this cart, his injuries punished by every rut and rock, appals him. His anger and frustration bubble up to the surface.

"Owen, did this man tell you my name, when he asked you to fetch me?"

"He described yer, just the way y'are and he said yer'd talk funny, but not ter moind and yer'd probably seem a bit stupid, which yer do, but yer were brighter than yer seemed and yer name's Will Peters, right?"

A charge like an electric shot raced through Will. "He said my name was Will Peters?"

"Fer sure."

It had to be Sean. It couldn't be anyone else. Who else knew about him? Will suddenly feels as though his world has been put back on its axis. This situation is crazy, but if Sean is there, it means that he isn't crazy. So why hasn't Sean come to get him himself? Immediately Will is plagued with doubts. Perhaps Sean is hurt or incarcerated. No that's nonsense. I bet the bastard is holed up in a pub somewhere with a couple of girls, he thinks. Then suddenly the thought pops into his mind that Canadian Bob would be with Sean and the pair will laugh at him, when he eventually shows up. The twinge of jealousy startles him. Here he is in the biggest and most bizarre mess of his life, and he is consumed with sexual jealousy. If ever I get out of this mess…, he tells himself. I wonder how many men have said that? he thinks, with a wry smile.

"How far is Wexford?" asks Will.

"From here?"

"No from Disneyworld! No, of course from here."

"The man was right. Yer do say some funny things," replies Owen. Then after some thought, "It's a few miles from here. It'll take a day a two, fer sure."

At this point Will gives up further conversation. A village is coming into view and Will is very curious to see what a real eighteenth century village looks like. He hadn't paid much attention to the last one.

With the certainty in his mind that they are heading towards Sean and with a full stomach, Will's spirits have risen to their highest point since he arrived. This is the trip of a lifetime and he wants to make the most of it.

As they come closer, the village is rather like before, a small collection of tumbledown buildings, some stone and some wood and straw. Some earthworks have been dug out of the banks on the side of the road and enlarged with turfs. Slowly it dawns on Will that they are dwellings. He has read about such things and yet nothing prepares him for the reality. How could human beings live in such squalor?

A man is scratching away in a field and does not look up. Children and pigs seem to be playing together in the muck to the side of one of the hovels. They are so covered in mud that it is difficult to distinguish child from beast. They look up as the cart appears and the children distinguish themselves by scampering indoors. Only an elderly woman, sitting on a stool on the side of the road, by the door of her house, seems to take notice of their passing. Will greets her with a wave and a cheery "Good afternoon." She responds by looking down and becoming engrossed in the vegetables, which she is preparing.

"There a sullen lot aren't they?" comments Will to Owen, as they pass by.

"Perhaps they've something to be sullen about," responds Owen. "And I wouldn't be doin' that if I was you."

"Doing what?" enquires Will.

"Doin' all that top o' the mornin' stuff."

"Why not? I was just being pleasant. They can't see too many people through here."

"Well that's fer sure, but people don't trust strangers an' we don't want to be atractin' too much notice neither."

The two fall silent again and the cart climbs a bit of a rise away from the houses. Open heath land greets their gaze on either side of the road, until they reach a group of trees at the highest point, before the road drops down again. Will realises that he's seen few trees on their journey. Perhaps it is the open exposed nature of the countryside, then his memory stirs and he remembers something he has read. By the end of the eighteenth century, short sighted and greedy landowners have chopped down most of the indigenous woodlands for timber.

He looks with renewed interest at the little copse, which comprises a few beech and ash, not yet in leaf. Swinging from a branch of one of the trees is a body. It looks like a young man, not much older than Owen, and younger than Will, but it is difficult to be certain. His hands and feet are tied and he is hanging by the neck, head tilted awkwardly to one side. The crows are dining on his eyes and other parts of his face.

Will leaps to his feet and nearly falls from the cart. "Oh my God. Who would have done that? We can't just leave him there."

In a quiet tone Owen says, "Sit down Will, it's too late to save him now." Don't forget there might be people following us, who might like ter do that ter yous."

Whilst Will and Owen were plodding steadily in the direction of Cork, the Fox pulled up his men and dismounted. Just off the road he had noticed something.

Kicking the loose grass away with his boot, he bent down to feel the ashes of an old fire. With a smile of satisfaction he noted that they were still warm.

Chapter 15

Regimental HQ Fifth Leicestershire near Midford Co.Wexford
26th March 1797

"I'll wager my purse on his majesty's hand," declared Richard Soames.

"Ah, a fool and his money… you know what they say," responded Sir Cecil Braithwaite. " That's absolute nonsense on a blind hand. You're throwing all logic to the wind, along with your wager."

"Not at all, Braithwaite. It's perfectly logical. Look how the luck has run all evening. I say it will continue. The evidence is stacked on the table."

Indeed it was. Piled high on the table were tokens, coins and a note of debt. They were all in front of the man whom they called Lucky Eddie, the King of Ireland, Edward de Guilbert. Of course, Edward was no more a king than his adversaries around the card table, Richard, local landowner, Cecil, gentleman farmer and the latest victim of Edward's relentless good fortune, a captain in Edward's regiment, John Mablethorpe.

In their different ways they all served Good King George. In Edward's case, he served his sovereign with alacrity. With wealth, power and little scrutiny, his nickname was appropriate. In reality his authority knew no bounds. Nonetheless he liked to stamp his authority on those who served under him.

Newly commissioned as captain and recently posted to serve under Colonel de Guilbert, this was Mablethorpe's first experience of a hand or two of cards in the luxurious dining room of the old house, which served as the officers' quarters. He had lost heavily all evening, mostly to his commanding officer.

Edward had three cards lying face down on the table in front of him. Mablethorpe's three cards were in his hand. His face was wrapped in thought.

"It seems only *decent*, old chap," said Edward, although any who knew him would doubt he understood the meaning of the word, "to offer you the chance to win it back. Your hand against my blind hand." He pointed to his own hidden cards. "And because you are new to this, I shall even let you break that old rule that you can't see a blind man. You bet as much as you dare and you can see me. Be courageous," he added, subtlety goading his new officer.

"That does it," continued Soames, "Come now Braithwaite, what'll you wager against my purse." By now the drink was doing all the talking. "I know, I know, I'll wager it against your fine bay gelding."

Sir Cecil declined. He hadn't indulged in Edward's fine claret as heavily as his adversary and besides, he too had lost heavily tonight and did not want to walk home to add to his troubles.

Finally, with one last glance at the three cards in his hand, the young captain placed them on the table with the words, "You know I am good for the money. I can send for it. I'll see you for the value of my note, which you have."

Edward smiled. He knew that this could cost his new captain his first year's pay. "Ace of Diamonds, Jack of Spades, Ten of Hearts. Ace high, you are brave, but I would have done the same. Good odds. So let us see."

They all leaned in closer as Edward turned over the first of his three cards.

Queen of Hearts.

"Won't beat an Ace," exclaimed Sir Cecil.

Edward just smiled and relished the look of anxiety on the face of his sub-ordinate. If this ran well, his captain would be so much in his debt that he would do anything to clear it. He certainly wouldn't be inclined to tell tales on Edward's little activities of extortion, murder and brutality. He turned the second card.

Two of clubs.

"Your luck's run dry this time," guffawed Soames. "Your gelding was safe after all, Braithwaite."

Silence descended, as the four men drew closer still and Edward placed his hand on the last card.

"Do you want to double your wager?" Edward grinned at the young nervous face opposite.

Mouth too dry to speak, Mablethorpe shook his head.

Edward turned the last card and a roar went up.

Two of Hearts.

"A pair! A pair! By Heavens Eddie, I swear you have the luck of the Devil himself!" shouted Soames.

Captain Mablethorpe rose unsteadily from the table and muttered, "With your permission sir, I think I had better turn in."

"Don't be too down, young fella. It's your first night. Your luck will run next time." Edward stood up and put a comforting arm around the younger man's shoulders. Then with a firmer squeeze added, "If you'll just sign your note again, before you go…"

There were no doubts about it. Edward de Guilbert was a lucky man. All his life he had been lucky. As a boy, the family name kept him protected from the law. Of very average academic ability, his family had paid his way through Eton. It didn't drum the badness out of the boy. There was the unfortunate business, for which nobody could be blamed, when one of Edward's classmates died, falling from the roof of the school. There were rumours of a rivalry, which escalated and some tales that Edward had been on the roof with him. Nothing was proven.

The trouble continued and they had pulled him from Eton. In an attempt to keep him out of prison, his father had bought him a commission in the army. Perhaps the army would knock it out of him or at least channel his evil nature.

Here again he had been lucky. His father had chosen the Fifth Leicestershire, the county regiment. He had influence. After a few tedious years, billeted at Melton

Mowbray, he was shipped overseas. Not for him the death sentence of the Fever Islands of the West Indies. Not for him a death or glory lottery of an adventure with the up and coming Wesley in India. A comfortable billet in Ireland, King of the colony, a law unto himself, Edward de Guilbert had found his niche. It had one huge advantage over the billet back home. He had escaped the clutches of his young wife.

In his opinion, Edward had only made one mistake. He had only had one piece of bad luck. He had been stupid enough to be born second! How could that have happened? How could God have done that to him? His elder brother had it all, the title, the estates and the vast wealth of the de Guilbert family. As the second born, he received nothing, unless, of course his elder brother died. That thought had occupied him on many occasions.

And so he had married. His father had arranged it all, while he was away at Eton. The delicate matter of a courtship and engagement did not need the interference of the young groom. Wealthy, but untitled, Sophie Steadman was perfect. She had no brothers to inherit her mother's family money, which was held in trust, by her father, until she married. From a titled family, but no money, Edward was the perfect choice to release the inheritance. The families agreed that fifteen and sixteen was not too young.

The honeymoon was brief, but fruitful. By eighteen, Edward had a son as well as a daughter. He also had a wife, who hated the children almost as much as she hated Edward. She hated his drinking, she hated his gambling, she hated his love of blood sports and most of all she hated his womanising. How lucky the posting to Ireland!

After several moves the Fifth Leicester was billeted in Jamestown. Edward, now a colonel, was the new Commanding Officer. The family money was all that had been needed, after a riding accident had taken their previous aged colonel from them suddenly.

Now he was a law unto himself. Back in Leicestershire there had been duels against weaker men, which Edward had always provoked. But he had had to be careful to pay lip service, at least, to the correct etiquette. In Ireland his lust for cruelty and violence had no restraints. With little governmental control and poor army supervision, the English troops in Ireland could do what they liked.

Under Edward de Guilbert's command, they did.

"Are we stopping already?" asks Will, as Owen encourages the horse, who Will has discovered is called 'ol' Daisy', to pull over. They stop in a little area, beside the road, which is sheltered by rocks.

Will reckons that it must be about an hour before dusk, when Owen decides to stop for the night. We don't seem to have covered much ground and they might still be pursuing us, thinks Will. I suppose that they'd have caught us by now, if they were going to. Yes, for sure, we must be all right, by now. I'll certainly be pleased to get off this damn cart and stretch my legs again. He rubs his chin and flinches again. He has a good growth of stubble and this is mixed with the matted blood, which was too painful to remove, when they stopped earlier. I could do with a shave, he thinks, but I don't fancy taking an eighteenth century blade to this lot just yet, even if I can find one.

"I need some daylight ter catch yer supper," explains Owen and jumps down from the cart. He motions Will to do the same, while he unhitches the horse.

The countryside has changed. It is less boggy and exposed here. There are bushes, stunted trees and grassy hillsides. Will has noticed plenty of rabbits around. Great, but how to catch one?

Owen lifts up the seat of the cart to reveal the compartment, where he keeps his possessions. One by one they all come out onto the ground. When the compartment is empty, Owen fiddles around and lifts the bottom board out to reveal a secret compartment. From this he pulls out a fishing-net. He turns to Will and puts his finger to his lips.

"They'd hang me, if they found this," he says.

Will starts to laugh and then realises that Owen is serious. So instead, glancing at the tiny rivulet a few yards away, he says, "Where are we going to catch fish?"

Owen responds with a big grin. "They were right about yers. Yer do say some odd things. Rabbits of course! I need yer help."

All Will is required or trusted to do is to double around behind an area of open grassland. As he walks from the top of this space to the bottom, the rabbits are disturbed and gradually move towards the area, where the two plan to set up camp. They cannot scamper to the left, because of the stream. There is dense undergrowth to their right and ahead.

After about fifty metres, Will makes his best attempt at a gentle run and waves his arms around, feeling very foolish and the rabbits scatter. At this point Owen appears to the left and the rabbits panic and change direction, racing into the bushes ahead of them, where Owen's net is concealed. Most escape, but two are hopelessly tangled up and present Owen with no problem to seize and wring their necks.

It all seems so easy, except that Will feels that, had he done it, the result would have been very different. This lad has an instinct for survival and Will likes the simplicity of his approach to all life's little challenges. How would he cope with the world, which Will has left, of compulsory education and social services? What does it matter? Will is only too pleased to let this young lad look after him and enjoy fresh rabbit meat over a fire.

The night has turned cold, but mercifully dry, and Will edges as close to the fire as he dares, without burning the blankets. Exhausted as he is, the turmoil of the last forty-eight hours prevents him sleeping. He drifts in and out of consciousness, as all the events, since his arrival in Ireland unfold before his eyes. From Owen there is not a sound.

Through the flickering glow of the fire Will thinks he notices something move on the edge of their little camping place. It's probably an animal or maybe I'm dreaming, Will tells himself. The orange embers of the fire form shapes in his head and he drifts off again. From the circle of darkness beyond the reach of the dying fire, dark forms take shape.

The Fox and his men have found Will.

They take their places surrounding the fire and sit like a pack of trained hunting dogs. Harmless and obedient, whilst under the control of their master, one word and they will strike mercilessly. The Fox is in no hurry to wake Will. Whilst his men watch, he stoops over Will's slumbering form and examines him.

After a while, Will stirs. Maybe he is aware of the presence of the intruders. With a shock he looks into the cold eyes of the Fox. He tries to rise, but a hand from the Fox on his shoulder forces him back down.

"Who, who are you?" stammers Will. He is suddenly aware of the other threatening shapes surrounding him. Then he tries to take in this stranger. He is a large man, lean and strong, with a scar on his left cheek. Clad in knee-length black leather boots and trousers, wide leather belt, white shirt, front and cuffs decorated with lace, and a long black leather coat. The look is vaguely reminiscent of something. Will takes in the shoulder length hair and reckons that this guy could front a '70's heavy metal band perfectly. He looks every inch the rock star, until you catch those eyes.

"I've been looking for you," replies the Fox, ignoring Will's question. "You can't believe how long we've all been waiting for you, Will Peters."

The words send a shiver down Will's spine, far colder than the night air. "You know who I am?"

"Oh, I know who you are and why you are here," replies the Fox and smiles at Will's shocked expression.

A silence falls between the two men. Will's mind is spinning and he does not know what to think or say. The Fox, without taking his eyes off Will, pulls the bayonet from his belt. With a wicked smile and only a glance at his target he impales a scrap of rabbit meat, from the fire, and eats the black morsel.

"Hmm, burnt. I should have got here sooner," he grins.

Hypnotised, like some frightened rabbit himself, Will tries to make his brain work. "Do you know Sean?" he finally manages to ask.

"Sean?" the Fox considers for a moment. "That'll be Sean O'Grady?"

Will nods, even more amazed.

"Oh I know Sean very well. We go back a long time," he smiles. "But it's you I'm interested in. Rumours have spread throughout the South West, even into the North." He leans forward and whispers; "I think they've even heard about you in Dublin Castle."

Will didn't think he could become any more scared and confused. He is wrong and his face reveals it, so the Fox explains.

"You have become something of a folk legend, Will Peters. For some years the rumours have spread like a fire in the heather, flaring up here and there and then disappearing, only to come up again, somewhere else."

The Fox pauses to see the effect his words are having on Will and continues. "The legend says, that a man will appear one winter's day in the South West. He will come from afar. He will be an Englishman. Yes, an Englishman. An Englishman will free Ireland from the English!"

The words shake Will to his core. My God, I am changing history, he thinks. This wasn't meant to happen and it's all my fault.

The Fox hasn't finished. "You are the Messiah!" He waves his hand, still holding the bayonet, in the air in a theatrical manner. "You will free us from the cursed yoke of the English! Like Moses, you will lead us to the Promised Land. Will you part the Irish Sea, Will? Then I look at you and ask myself," he leans forward again, so his face is inches from Will's and whispers coarsely, "Have you got the balls?"

After a time, which seems to Will long enough for the earth to circle the sun three times, the Fox leans back and says, "We will see. We will see."

He tucks the bayonet back in his belt and enquires casually, "Is there anything you need for the journey?" He shakes his head, as if suddenly remembering. "I have something of yours." He turns to one of his followers. "Pat, the bag."

From the shadows a bag is tossed to the Fox, who catches it neatly. Will recognises the bag immediately. The Fox stretches out a hand and passes it to Will, who opens it with some hesitation.

"It's all there," says the Fox, as if reading Will's mind. "Well almost all of it. I removed a few coins to cover my expenses. That's not unreasonable is it?"

"No, no, not at all," stammers Will. He can hardly believe, that this terrifying figure and his gang, who have found them so easily in the night, wish him and Owen no harm. That's a point, where the hell is Owen? He is beginning to realise that Owen has a real skill for self-preservation. Who can blame him? He'd still be locked up, if it weren't for the kid.

Will suddenly asks, "How did you get hold of this?"

To this the Fox gives him a long hard look and simply replies, touching the bayonet handle, "Oh, I have ways of persuading people who step out of line."

For a few moments the Fox looks at Will, as if he is trying to make up his mind what to do. Will finds this very unnerving and tries to tell himself that he has nothing to fear here. If this man had wanted to harm him, he could have easily done it by now and why then would he have returned Will's bag? Why indeed? Is he playing some cruel game? Is Will now to be obligated to return the favour? If so, what kind of a favour will an eighteenth century gang leader call in?

In desperation to learn more, he overcomes his fear and ventures, under the guise of politeness, "To whom do I owe my gratitude for returning the bag?"

The dark figure smiles. "My name is my business. They call me the Fox."

The Fox clearly does not take kindly to being questioned, but Will pushes his luck a little further. "Well thanks anyway. You and your group, er, who do you represent?" Tongue-tied under this ferocious gaze, Will curses himself for his clumsy question.

At first the Fox does not reply. Eventually he responds. "I suppose you'd call us Defenders. You could hardly call us Whiteboys." He laughs and holds out his arms, so that Will can admire his black coat. "It wouldn't seem quite appropriate would it?" He doesn't wait for a response. He is not interested in Will's opinion. "You do know what I'm talking about, don't you Will? Of course you do."

There is a pregnant pause. The Fox takes a couple of steps towards him and Will suddenly realises that, this time, the man is expecting a response. Like a schoolboy caught daydreaming, he blurts out. "Of course, uh, of course. The Whiteboys used to be called that, because they wore white shirts over their heads. The Defenders came later, defending the interests of the poor rural Catholics."

As the words tumble out of his mouth, Will curses his naivety again. How must that have sounded? This isn't a history class. This is real. This is now. Does it arouse suspicions in the Fox?

"Defending the interests eh? Ha, ha." It is a humourless guffaw. "I like that. Did you hear that boys? We've certainly defended a few interests in our time eh?" Obediently there is a ripple of murderous laughter from the pack of dogs.

The Fox considers. "I'll be honest. I don't know what to do with you Will Peters." He stares at Will, who decides to keep quiet this time. "So I think the best thing to do is…

nothing. I'm going to leave you to continue on your journey. Avoid Cork. There are too many prying eyes and ears there and a garrison of English troops. You'll attract too much attention. Then continue to Wexford, but remember, I won't be far away."

With a sign to his men the Fox turns and in an instant they have disappeared into the darkness and are gone, leaving Will squatting by the fire in a state of relief and complete confusion. Was that a threat? Or was it a promise of help, if he needed it? As his head starts to clear and his heart beats a little more steadily, it hits him. How the hell did he know I was going to Wexford?

Chapter 16

Between Cork and Wexford
27th March 1797

The next few days passed without incident for Will. They took the Fox's advice and gave Cork a wide berth. It was not easy and young Owen cussed and muttered at the condition of some of the tracks. Once or twice Will had to help him manhandle the cart. He didn't mind. His strength was gradually returning and, as his vision improved, he had stopped worrying that he would lose the sight in his eye.

He continued to marvel at Owen's extraordinary talent for catching, stealing and bargaining for anything edible. Will too, became skilled at catching rabbits and there were trout to be had from the larger streams and small rivers. A pheasant was Owen's masterpiece. Will was impressed, not only with his skill in catching it, but also the speed with which its colourful neck was wrung and the dead bird stashed away in the compartment under the seat. Later that night, when they were sure that they were alone, Owen retrieved his catch from its hiding place and held it up, with it's head hanging pathetically to one side on a limp neck.

"Pheasants. They're good, but if yer gets caught…" Owen rolled his eyes and, picking up the head, let it flop again. The message was clear enough.

Will was becoming very fond of the boy. He was such an odd mixture of youth and maturity. He took a childish delight in the simplest matters. He had soon learnt that Will had a knowledge of all manner of things, seemingly beyond the boy's experience and he pestered Will to tell him stories about England. This led to fairy tales about machines, which people could climb into and travel from place to place on rails or, most exciting, through the air.

In contrast, Will knew that the boy had taken him on and become his carer. That was the word. The realisation was a little shocking. Will could do nothing without him. Without Owen he couldn't eat, couldn't find his way and wouldn't know how to track Sean down. Owen was full of good advice about making himself fit again, like the moss in the bog, which had improved his eye remarkably. His gratitude encouraged him to help Owen, as much as he could and to be ever more inventive with the tales.

Between the stories and the forays for food, Will had plenty of time to consider his situation. His thoughts always returned to the same key question. Whatever had happened to Sean? If Owen was to be believed, Sean was in Wexford and in the present time. Will's present that was. He must be in control of his situation to have sent Owen. What Will couldn't figure out was why he hadn't come to meet him in person. Come to think of it, how was it that half of Southern Ireland seemed to know his whereabouts and his business too? Why the hell had they beaten him up? Perhaps they were just robbing him. That couldn't be right, they were expecting him. And what about the prophecy that the Fox had mentioned?

Maybe Sean had put these stories about to be sure of finding him. Then another thought struck Will. To do such a thing Sean must not only be well established, he must have been there for some time. How long? Hadn't the Fox said that he'd known him for ages? If the positions had been reversed, Will would have kept a low profile and gone to look for Sean in person. He wouldn't have alerted everyone. He certainly would not have concocted some story about arriving to start a revolution, not in the Ireland of 1796 or '97 or whatever it was.

Oh my God, perhaps Sean had done it to have him caught or killed. No that was paranoid nonsense. Why would Sean do that? He shook his head to toss such foolish ideas free from his mind.

Owen noticed the movement. "Are you O.K.?"

"You mustn't say that," replied Will. "It'll make you sound odd, like me."

"O.K." responded Owen, with a wink.

Will was about to reprimand him again, when he caught the cheeky grin on the lad's face and laughed.

When Will managed to put thoughts of Sean and his predicament to the back of his mind, it was a carefree existence. He might have been less carefree had he known that his easy passage was down to the Fox. He and his gang were never far away, a small group ahead of them and another, just out of sight behind. They ensured that the man and the boy were clear of Cork and then the Fox had other more pressing matters to attend to.

Three days beyond Cork, with a collection of rabbits hidden under the cart, they came across an isolated cottage, white washed walls, in need of a new coat. As night approached the temperature fell sharply. Will was beginning to wonder where Owen would choose to stop. Clear skies, it would be a cold night to be out in the open. Owen had other plans.

With a gentle tug on the reigns, he pulled up by the cottage and bid Will remain seated. He disappeared into the old building, which seemed deserted, no smoke rising from the little chimney, poking out of the turf roof. Minutes later he emerged alone.

"Come on now Will. Grab some sticks from the back of the cart. A couple of bundles now," cried Owen.

Will did as he was told and had to duck, as he followed Owen, who had retrieved the rabbits and potatoes. Convinced that Owen had found an abandoned dwelling, the scene, which greeted him, was a shock. A dim light from two candles, fixed to the stonewall, threw long shadows, across the sparsely furnished single room. A family of at least three generations was huddled close together against the cold night air, which crept under the poorly fitted wooden door. A smell of damp filled Will's nostrils and he shuddered.

"Will, come on now, set the fire," instructed Owen, pointing at the empty hearth. "I'll just settle 'ol' Daisy' around the back, out of sight."

Will felt like a child on a visit to a distant relative, clumsy and unsure; wanting to please, worried at causing offence. He followed his instructions and, as he set the fire, frightened eyes watching him. Owen returned with more sticks and made reassuring sounds to the family.

Will, now familiar with the use of Owen's tinderbox, soon had a blaze roaring. It brightened the room and he moved back and looked around. A woman, whom Will took to be the mother, together with the eldest girl were already butchering the rabbits, with expert hands. An elderly lady was preparing the vegetables. It was soon simmering in a pot over Will's fire. A young girl of about fourteen was cuddling a baby. Will could not be sure if she was the mother or simply caring for a younger sibling. A grubby little boy of about seven had taken a liking to Will.

"We've ter thank yers for our supper and a warm," said the boy, with wide eyes.

"Er, that's nothing," replied Will, with embarrassment. "Er, do you often have meat?"

"Oh we can have meat whenever we choose," responded the lad. "But we don't often choose.

Will was bemused.

"Follow me." The boy seized Will's hand and led out of the back of the cottage and into the yard, where four chickens were cooped up.

"If we have meat, we can't have eggs," he explained to Will, as if he had just revealed one of the fundamental truths of the universe.

"No I can see that." Will felt stupid and spoilt. An egg to this child was one of life's treats. No wonder he had thanked him for the rabbits and the fire. While he was building the fire, he had been wondering what these people do. They survive he now realised. They do, that is, if they're lucky.

As the food was cooked the aroma of wood smoke and rabbit stew filled their senses. A teenage lad had given up his stool for Will to sit on. The bag containing the gun was stashed under it. The younger children, barelegged, played marbles. Polished pebbles served for the bright glass objects with which Will was familiar and a pitch had been marked out in the dirt on the floor. An old man, masticating with shrunken gums, looked on with disinterest. Encouraged by Owen, Will helped put some old blankets up at the windows to keep out the cold. The lad muttered that it would be better not to show too much light and one of the girls agreed.

A silence fell on the cottage, nobody knowing what to say, Will full of questions and not knowing how to ask them. Eventually the food was slopped out into wooden bowls and one china plate for Will. They nodded their appreciation to Will and Owen and, to Will's surprise ate slowly and deliberately, savouring every mouthful. Will felt like a pig, as he shovelled it down. He forced himself to slow down and match their pace.

When every last scrap had been consumed, they embarrassed Will further with the profusion of their thanks. Will was trying to think of an appropriate response, when the man, who seemed like the head of the family, held up his hand for silence.

"What was that?" he whispered.

Will thought that he had heard something outside. It was like the sound of hushed voices.

"Oh sweet Mary, no," cried one of the older women.

"Quick Will, out the back." Owen was on his feet and tugging at Will's arm.

They rushed for the door and then Will remembered his bag. As he turned, the bag, thrown by one of the family, was already in the air. Will held out his arms to catch it, but it went to Owen. To Will's amazement it was the baby which landed in his arms. They were pushed out through the back door and into the black cold of the night. They just had time to pull the back door shut behind them, when they heard the crash of the front bursting open. Within seconds of sitting replete in front of a wood fire, Will found himself shivering beneath a starry sky with a baby smiling placidly up at him. Who says that eighteenth century life was slow, he thought to himself.

"What's going on?" demanded Will of Owen.

"Shh, shh," responded the lad and beckoned Will to peer through a crack in the door.

By crouching low and close together, they could see through a long horizontal split between the panels in the lower section of the old warped wooden door. Will squinted through the gap, glancing down first to ensure that the baby would not give them away. It was asleep.

Six men had broken into the cottage. They were not in uniform, so clearly not soldiers. Each was armed with a heavy wooden club, except one, who carried an old fowling piece. It looked like a shotgun with an enlarged opening to the end of the barrel, like the end of a trumpet. There was a lot of shouting, which was so fast and guttural, that Will struggled to follow it. The aggression seemed to be directed towards the women, who were holding their hands apart, as though denying something. He thought that he heard the word 'baby' and froze, as he looked down at the innocent infant. Why would a babe in arms be the object of all this fuss?

Will's head span. A panic took him over and all logic evaporated from his mind. Over the last few days, with the thought of meeting Sean soon, he had started to come to terms with his bizarre circumstances. Now he was on the point of losing all self-control. The strangest idea had popped into his head. Had he completely altered history and these were Herod's men searching for the baby Jesus? Was he holding the Christ child in his arms? The world began to spin around him until Owen caught his arm and brought him back to his senses.

Owen seemed totally unfazed by it all and, with the widest of grins, whispered in his ear, "I think this time yer've really bin left holding the baby!"

Will seized Owen's sleeve in a fierce grip. "What's the baby called?"

Owen looked puzzled. "Theresa, I think. Why would yer be wantin' ter know that, at a moment like this?"

Will forced a smile. "Thank God for that. Why are they looking for her?"

Owen shrugged at Will's odd behaviour and responded. "Tithes and taxes."

"What do you mean, tithes and taxes?"

"Yer have ter pay a tithe for a baby," said Owen casually, as though he were talking about the duty on a pack of cigarettes.

"For a baby?!" Will was trying to remember his Irish Laws for the period, but was confused for the moment. "Does it go to the church?"

"Yes ter the *English* Church." Owen emphasised the difference between Catholic and Protestant with great certainty. Then with less confidence added, "Or sometimes ter the squire or his agent or maybe…" He paused for thought. "Ah, 'tis difficult. I'm not too sure now." He shrugged again. "They're all at it."

Will suddenly remembered the baby and looked down at the little bundle in his arms. To his relief the infant was still asleep.

Following his gaze, Owen, like an experienced father of many, added, "Just fed, yer see."

Things had quietened down a little inside, when a loud shriek went up, followed by a lot of shouting and the sound of the few bits of furniture being smashed. It startled the two outside and the baby stirred. The two nearly banged their heads together in their rush to peer through the door again. It was difficult to make out what was happening. A melee seemed to have broken out inside. As the throng parted for a split second, Will could see the men holding the other members of the family back, while one of the larger of the intruders was ripping the clothes off the girl, who had been nursing the baby.

"For Chrissake," exclaimed Will. "Give me the bag. I want the gun."

Owen held the bag away from Will. "If yer go in there. Yer'll have ter kill them all, Will. There mustn't be anyone ter tell tales. Are yer prepared ter do that?"

Will hesitated. Could he really do that? Could he march in there and shoot half a dozen unknown men in cold blood? His mind wandered back to Game Show Al and his rules. It had all seemed like a joke then. Was this some kind of a test? He looked over at Owen. "I can't just stand here and let them be raped." He hesitated. "You do know what I mean don't you?"

"Oh, I know about rapin'" reassured the boy, "but that's not what they're up ter. They're after checkin' if there's anyone feedin' a baby. Yer can tell yer know, by checkin' the breasts." He nodded sagely.

Will stared at Owen incredulously and then at the baby and then back through the crack in the door. His brain just did not want to work. It was difficult to see exactly what was happening inside. Then another yell went up and two of the men rushed up the little open wooden staircase. A lot of crashing and banging could be heard from above.

"There lookin' fer the baby. They'll be out here next," said Owen. "Come on." He motioned Will to follow him over the little stonewall, which skirted the yard.

Owen's sense of self-preservation had not deserted him and within minutes, two of the gang were out in the yard, waving a lantern about.

"It'll not be out in this cold," barked one of the thugs.

"Na, it'll be with some bloody aunt, somewheres," snapped another.

"Heh, but these'll do fer payment!" The first had opened the little wooden hutch, which served as a roost for the chickens. "Heh hold up that light."

Will heard a lot of flapping of wings and a couple of squawks, which told him exactly what was occurring, beyond the line of vision from his hiding place. The lantern disappeared inside and there was more yelling and shouting, followed by silence. A few minutes later the young boy, who had shown Will the hens appeared.

"Yer can come back inside, they've gone. They've taken the hens."

Will knew. He could only imagine the misery of this little family. They would be eating neither meat nor eggs, after tonight. Inside, what little they had by way of furniture, seemed smashed. The women were sobbing. The men were cussing with the agony and anger, which comes from helplessness. Will understood that. He felt a mixture of frustration, inadequacy and guilt. They thanked him profusely for taking the babe and that made him feel worse.

Will did not sleep well that night. He could not make himself comfortable in the corner of the room, but that was not his real problem. His mind kept revolving around the same conundrum. Next time he would do something, anything to help. Then he kept telling himself that it would be interfering and he was not supposed to do that. Or was that just an excuse for being a coward and taking the easy way out. God he wished Sean was there. He would know what was best.

They left early the following morning. Will was awake and eager to press on to Wexford. Overcome with guilt, Will offered the family a coin from his precious collection. They refused, although they were clearly tempted. To spend such wealth would attract attention, they told him. Will realised that a family like theirs could only acquire such riches by theft. Renegade groups had robbed many of the big houses in the area in recent months. They would be assumed guilty without trial.

Will and Owen rode in silence for the first few miles. It was more difficult now to avoid humanity. The land was more wooded. The villages bigger and more frequently encountered. Farming was more developed and there were big houses that could be glimpsed through the trees. As they approached the largest village so far on their route, Owen advised Will to conceal himself again at the back of the cart beneath their load. It was not so easy now. Much of it had gone up in smoke, keeping them warm over the last few days. Nonetheless, with Owen's help, Will managed to conceal himself, lying flat on the floor of the cart, wrapped in the blanket, with piles of sticks built over him. He was quite comfortable and had a good view, rearwards from the back of the cart.

It was a view that Will would remember for the rest of his life and would rapidly erase the memories of the incidents of the previous night.

As they entered the village it was obvious that things were not as they should be. From his hiding place, Will could smell smoke, before he could see it. Given his immediate surroundings, it made him extremely nervous. He wanted to shout to Owen to pull up, but the sight of red-coated troops, beside the road, prevented him revealing himself and, he realised, probably prevented Owen from stopping, without attracting attention.

Then he saw it, first one and then two cottages on fire. There seemed to be no attempt being made to extinguish the conflagrations. Will heard someone shouting at Owen and the cart swung to one side and came to a halt. It gave Will a clear view over the centre of the village. It was not really a square, more a slightly wider part of the road, as it made its way through the centre of the houses and past an old inn. The street was packed and everyone was jeering and shouting at the troops, who had formed lines, on either side of the street to keep the crowds away from the middle of the thoroughfare.

In the centre of the road a couple of wooden contraptions had been set up. The first was made of three pieces of heavy timber, fixed together at the top. With the legs spread at the base it formed a pyramid shape. Will knew it to be the dreaded triangle. Its use was obvious from a glance at a large trooper, who stood beside it, cat o' nine tails whip in hand. To his left and just behind him two other men were standing by a metal brazier contraption, which looked a bit like a modern barbecue. Something was smoking in a pot over the heat. Adjacent to them was a frame on a base with wooden wheels. Will remembered sitting in the library upstairs at University College, looking at contemporary drawings of these machines. It stood like a set of miniature rugby posts, only the cross bar, at about seven or eight feet above the ground was made of rope. The troops would slip a noose around the neck of a terrified victim and then, throwing the rope over the cross bar, choke him until he talked. Half hanging, it was called.

A man was dragged from out of the crowd by two redcoats. He tried to escape, but was clubbed on the back of the head with the stock of a musket. As he fell to his knees, he was dragged to the wooden triangle, where his arms were tied above his head to its upper ends. Will went cold, as he realised what he was about to witness. He had heard how the troops would beat men, until they confessed where rebels were hiding or where pikes and stolen muskets had been stashed.

These troops made no attempt to interrogate him. There seemed no reason for theses brutal actions, except to flaunt their power and inflict cruelty and humiliation on the defenceless villagers. The victim was flogged until the trooper was too exhausted to lift his weapon. Will could not watch. By the time they cut the bloody body down from the triangle, the man was already dead. For the second time in less than twelve hours Will watched helpless as the most appalling scenes were played out in front of him. Worse was to come.

Next a boy was dragged from the crowd. A woman broke free from the throng and pulled at one of the redcoat's sleeves. She received the same vicious treatment as the man, from the soldier's musket stock. The boy too was clubbed hard with a musket to quieten him down and dragged to the little stove. While two soldiers held his arms apart and put their boots to the middle of his back, a third lifted a container of something smoking. He held it high for everyone to see. The boy was now frantic in his efforts to free himself. It was to no avail. With a shout of triumph the soldier poured the cocktail of hot tar and gunpowder onto the boy's head. His screams made Will weep in rage and despair. Troops everywhere, his bag with the gun hidden under Owen's seat, he knew that there was nothing he could do. He hated himself for his uselessness.

Will shut his eyes. Until now he had only thought about his own plight, *his* violent treatment at the hands of his captors, *his* escape back to Boroughbridge and *his* search for Sean. This was not *his* time, not *his* problem. It was history and whilst his intellect told him that it had happened, his instincts told him that somehow it wasn't real. It was like a fable, perhaps based on an event in the past, but not true, like your own personal experience. The present could be explained by the past, but nonetheless it was an intellectual exercise, an academic pursuit.

Now Will was more sickened than at any time in his sheltered life. He had felt upset and indignant at things, which he had seen on the news. This was so different. It was immediate and it was wrong. He also had the benefit of hindsight. He knew where this was leading. Had he not lectured on how it was the one time in history, when a genuine opportunity had arisen to bring the different sides together and make something better? Could he just sit and watch?

Eventually the streets were cleared and Owen permitted to continue on his way. After about thirty minutes, Owen stopped the cart to let Will out. Will ran to a ditch and vomited. Owen looked at Will and said nothing. When Will climbed back onto the cart, Owen passed him water in the tin cup. Will drank and then said, "I want to get to Wexford, as quick as you can."

Owen nodded and encouraged the horse. The two rode on in silence.

It took another night under the stars for them to reach Wexford and it was late and dark on the following evening, as they slipped between the houses and into the town. Owen had wanted to stop earlier. Will wouldn't hear of it and they had pressed on. Will had had time to collect his thoughts, after the traumas of the previous day. The sort of scene he had witnessed in the village centre was well recorded. This kind of event had been commonplace in 1798. The army had driven the population to desperation and it had culminated in the uprising of that year, which was so brutally suppressed. If Owen was to be believed, it was 1797 and no attempted French landing had been made. This should not be happening. Something was not right. Will, now frantic to catch up with Sean, tried to suppress his fears.

The cartwheels clattered over the cobblestones and the sounds echoed off the moonlit walls. Owen pulled up in a back street, just short of the old town wall. They were outside a bar. Light and raucous laughter spilled out on the silent street. Will looked at Owen quizzically.

"What yer waitin' fer? Down yer get!" ordered Owen.

"Is this it?" asked Will. "Aren't you coming in with me?"

Will was sweating. Was Sean really there? How would he react to see him again? Could he go into a busy late eighteenth Irish bar alone? Since he had arrived, he had been unable to function without the help of a young, but admittedly remarkable boy.

He pushed the door open. The place was packed. Will swallowed hard. He realised that the only coins he possessed would be valuable enough to attract all manner of undesired attention. Oh Christ, you'd better be here, Sean, he muttered under his breath.

He entered.

If Will had been painted bright orange he could not have felt more conspicuous. Thank God nobody took the slightest notice of him, so he pushed his way through the throng, looking over the heads for the familiar form of Sean. A medley of pungent smells, stale beer, staler sweat, filthy clothes and bad breath filled his nostrils. Smoke hung in a thick blanket between the sea of heads and the low ceiling. Will strained to pick out that familiar tone amongst the cacophony of voices. He observed that the bar ran the full length of the left hand side of the room. Behind it, an army of barmaids struggled to satisfy the noisy demands of jostling crowds yelling for attention. To his right more young women, pots of ale in either hand, ran the gauntlet of lecherous hands to serve the privileged, seated at wooden tables. Will's heart sank as he searched in vain through this riotous historic scene for the only link with his own lost world.

Beyond was a step up to a second bar, partly obscured by a staircase that ran to an upper floor. Will pushed on towards the back. He climbed the single step to give himself a view of a huge table where at least a dozen men sat engaged in a rowdy card game. Will scanned them. As his eyes rested on the back of a familiar head, it turned and a smile transformed into a huge grin. In moments the two men embraced.

"Holy Mary, Will. You took yer bloody time!" cried Sean.

They both laughed. Sean made his excuses to the group around the table and threw down a few coins and his cards. He ushered Will upstairs to a private room, yelling to one of the girls to bring them drinks. With the door safely shut behind them the men embraced again and then stepped back and grinned at each other.

Will spoke first. "So, if I took my time to get here, how long have you been here, yer smart ass?"

The smile fell from Sean's face. "Uh, well see that's a bit of a long tale."

"Go on Sean, try me," said Will.

There was a long silence, before Sean responded. "About two years."

Chapter 17

Regimental HQ Fifth Leicestershire near Midford Co. Wexford
31st March 1797

"What the bloody hell do you want at this hour?" bellowed Edward de Guilbert, from the fireside.

"It's a message from Dublin, Sir. It seems that there was an attack on the mail service, but that the mail has now been retrieved," quivered Lewis, the young orderly, from outside Eddie's room.

The door burst open and Lewis jumped back.

The veins stood out on the colonel's face. "This had better be good. I am not in the mood for any more messages tonight. Make it quick."

It was nearly midnight and only a couple of hours earlier he had received Lady Squires' servant, with a message, rather than Lady Squires herself. The note was brief; her husband had returned unexpectedly from Parliament in Dublin. There would be another evening.

He snatched the note from the outstretched tray and slammed the door in the young man's face.

Returning to the fireplace he seized a knife and broke open the seal. The de Guilbert coat of arms was the first thing to catch his attention. Then he saw his mother's familiar hand. He threw the letter casually on the table beside the fireplace and thrust a taper into the fire to relight his cigar. Puffing vigorously, he scanned the letter quickly. The cigar fell from his mouth and smouldered at his feet.

"Dear God, in his infinite wisdom…"

He read the letter again, slowly and carefully, while the cigar burnt a hole in the rug. There was no mistake. Elated he rushed to the door, and stuck his head out onto the landing.

"Lewis, LEWIS!"

The young man stumbled on the stairs in his haste to respond.

"Yes Sir?"

"Sir? I think 'my lord' would be more fitting," smiled de Guilbert.

"Sir?"

"Never mind, never mind. I want all the officers and the N.C.O.'s in the drawing room," snapped de Guilbert.

"And the N.C.O.s? Now? Uh Sir."

"Now? No next bloody week, you dunderhead! Of course now! And I want champagne, the decent stuff."

The servant hesitated, caught the look on his master's face and decided against further questions.

Fifteen minutes later, in various states of undress, Captain Mablethorpe, Lieutenant Davies, Sergeant Jeffreys and Corporals Johnson and O'Connell were muttering anxiously to each other around the large table. Only the second time that the corporals had seen the inside of the magnificent room, it did not portend well. Lucky Eddie, a fresh cigar between his lips and the letter in his hand stood before them grinning broadly. Lewis appeared with the champagne and glasses rattling precariously on a large silver tray. He clattered them onto the table in front of his colonel and, obeying a flap of de Guilbert's hand, disappeared promptly. To the amazement of the small congregation, the colonel poured the champagne himself. A silence descended, as the last glass was filled.

"Gentlemen," he beamed, "I have a very sad announcement to make." His facial expression belied the message. "I have received, this evening, a letter from my dearest mama." He flapped it in their faces, daring them to disbelieve him.

Nobody was brave enough to react.

"She tells me," he continued, "that my older and much respected brother, Robert, was struck down by a fever. Despite the prompt and expert administrations of an excellent physician, sadly he passed away the following day." He paused again to wipe a tear from his eye. "He will be sorely missed by us all." The grin had returned.

His assembled subordinates, not sure how to respond murmured their commiserations.

"On a brighter note," continued de Guilbert. The room fell silent. "You may like to join me in drinking a toast."

He handed out the glasses.

"You might like to join me in drinking the health of the ninth Earl of Eastshire... your beloved commanding officer!"

Obediently they all raised their glasses and chanted, "The ninth Earl!" At least the champagne was good, if a little warm.

His more experienced inferiors knew when to keep quiet. Young Mablethorpe, as second in command, felt the need to make conversation with his commanding officer.

"I, I hope that his lordship, that is your brother, didn't suffer," the young officer ventured.

De Guilbert stared at him in amazement.

"That is, um, will you be attending his funeral?" he blundered on, whilst his colleagues gazed into their glasses or at the walls, anywhere rather than catch the eye of their commanding officer.

The new Earl rose to his feet. "How the bloody hell would I know if he suffered. My mother hasn't described his last dying twitches." He leant across the table and stared at the frightened junior officer. "As for his funeral, I hope they've buried him by now or there'll be a hell of a stink." He considered his own gaffe for a moment. "Quite literally, I should think..." He picked up his mother's note from the table and waved it in Mablethorpe's face, "This letter has taken nearly a month to get here. It's a bloody disgrace!"

In silence, Mablethorpe joined the others in examining the pattern of the drawing room carpet. De Guilbert puffed on his cigar and the uncomfortable silence continued.

Eventually de Guilbert continued. "And that brings us to you Mablethorpe."

All eyes stayed glued to the carpet at this stage, except for the captain, who was now obliged to meet the withering gaze of his commanding officer.

"Sir?" enquired Mablethorpe anxiously.

"Sir?" boomed the colonel. "I'll give you 'Sir?' What in hell's name are you planning to do about these outrages on our postal service? You are supposed to advise me. You and this bunch of useless excuses for manhood sit about playing soldiers, whilst the countryside is descending into chaos."

He was into his stride now and, crashing his glass onto the table, tore into his second in command, disregarding any protocol, in front of junior officers and N.C.O.'s. It would weaken Mablethorpe's authority in front of his men, which suited Eddie perfectly. There was only one authority in his regiment.

"The word from Dublin castle was that attacks on the post would signal the outbreak of a revolution. *Yes, a revolution*. Well it's not going to happen, not while I'm in command.

And another thing, I have new instructions from the castle. They've sent that damnable fool Abercrombie back to London, thank God. Did you hear what the general said about His Majesty's forces in Ireland?"

They had all heard. Not a soul in Ireland had missed his damning summary of the state of the army of occupation, but none of them were going to volunteer it, so de Guilbert was forced to continue.

"He said," and the colonel tried to recall the exact words, "it is in a state of licentiousness rendering it a hazard to all except the enemy, or something of that sort. It's a damned abominable outrage.

Fortunately the Prime Minister, Mr. Pitt, has had the sense to recall him and we have our own General Lake to put things right. And he, in his wisdom, has issued orders for the army to go out into the country and seek free quarters."

This finally provoked a response from Lieutenant Davies, an old hand in his thirties and too poor to buy promotion. Normally taciturn in his resentment of senior officers he felt compelled to ask, "Colonel, we can move at will in the countryside seizing houses and food as we wish?"

"That is what I have always understood to be meant by free quarters lieutenant," scowled the colonel. "And that leads me back to you Mablethorpe. What are you going to do about it?"

The young captain, hopeful that the colonel had forgotten him, was forced to respond. "Uh, I shall mobilise the men in the morning, Sir and," his brain floundered about for something appropriate to say, "I will advise you of our target, when you inspect the parade."

De Guilbert stared at him. "I want to know first thing, which village is the most fervent hotbed of these filthy disloyal rebels and we will flush them out. You have General Lake's orders to follow and, by God, you will carry them out. I intend to supervise this personally. Now get to bed. You have King George's work to do tomorrow."

Having dismissed them all, Lucky Eddie poured himself another glass of champagne, relit his cigar and put his feet up on the table. Tomorrow was going to be an interesting day. As the Earl of Midshire, Colonel of his regiment and armed with Lake's orders, he wasn't just King of Ireland, he was God and he was going to enjoy it.

While Eddie was savouring his nightcap, the N.C.O.'s headed back to the west end of the old stable block, which had been converted into their quarters. They all knew what the colonel's personal attention entailed and they discussed what the morning would bring.

"There'll be Irish blood spilt tomorrow," remarked Sergeant Jeffreys to the two corporals. He was a huge cockney and a veteran of many campaigns. Everyone knew that it was he, not the officers, who ran the regiment. He knew every scam and every dodge. He had to. No prize money and fewer carnal pleasures were to be had, with a posting to Ireland. In overseas campaigns it was common to let the army run amok for a couple of days, after breaking a siege. Neither women nor possessions were safe and Jeffreys had enjoyed his share of that. His rackets were only a small supplement to his meagre army pay, but that was about to change. 'Free quarters' was a licence to rob and rape, particularly under Colonel de Guilbert's regime.

"And a bit o' fun fer the boys," winked Johnson.

"Knowin' the colonel, 'e'll be wantin' 'is share too," laughed Jeffreys.

O'Connell did not share their enthusiasm. He was an Irishman, like so many in the English army and had only enlisted to escape gaol, for stealing on the streets of Liverpool. Bizarely, he was originally a Wexford boy and now not far from home. He hated the English and most of all he hated his commanding officer.

"I can't sleep after all that fancy French stuff," announced O'Connell. "I'm going fer a walk an' a smoke."

"Do what yer like, Paul, but don't be late in the morning or his bleedin' lordship'll have yer balls fer breakfast," replied his Sergeant, before turning in.

O'Connell was alone. He could probably be absent for about an hour, without arousing suspicion. Not long enough to reach the village and return, but sufficient time to reach the old keeper's cottage on the edge of the woods. He could put word out of the regiment's new orders. The news would be in Wexford, before dawn.

For a time, Will could only repeat Sean's words. "Two bloody years." He studied Sean's face. "What the hell happened, Sean? Did they get the dosage wrong?"

Sean's thoughts raced back to those last moments in the chair at Boroughbridge, the panic and the sheer damn rage. That Canadian bitch and Jones, they'd really screwed him over. He had been over and over it in his mind so many times, in those two long years, trying to find a way back, wanting to even the score with them. They'd been far too smart for that. There was no way back. He should have seen it coming; that's what hurt. Once that damn stuff was racing through his veins, there was nothing he could do. He had been seized in a down draught of light and energy, far too powerful to fight, which had sucked him backwards into the past.

His first thought had been to try and think of something in the immediate past, an incident from the last few days. Maybe he could limit the damage and just reappear a week earlier. It didn't seem to work and as the downward flight continued, something popped into his consciousness. He'd been reading about it, just the night before. He tried to stop it, but all of a sudden it was in his mind, the meeting of the members of the fledgling United Irish movement on Cave Hill. Of all the things he could have thought about. Thank Christ it hadn't been the Roman Invasion of Britain!

Bang, and there he was, the opposite end of Ireland from what had been intended and over two hundred years adrift from *his own* time. He knew immediately, where and when it was. Belfast, May 1795. The image had been so clear, just before he landed. At first he was too angry to think straight. The more so, with the realisation of how he had been set up. No thought of Will or anyone else, he had twisted the bracelet to try and return. A click and then… nothing. The bastards. He'd really been had. God he'd get his revenge, but how the hell was he going to escape the past?

It had taken a long time for that anger to subside and it had driven him. At first he went out of his way to flout Al's so called rules. He went looking for trouble in Belfast and found it easily. He had no compunction about shooting his way out of a bar, when some local thugs had tried to relieve him of his money. He didn't worry either about bedding a young girl, who had latched on to him, after the incident. What did it matter? It wasn't real was it?

Thank God he'd stolen the coins and guns.

Gradually that thought had led his mind back to Will. Jesus, was he in the same godamn mess? If Will was, it was in no small part down to him. Sean tried to kid himself that they had both been set up; that they were both victims. It did not stand up to close scrutiny. He had helped them recruit and con Will. He felt guilty and responsible and so he had gone in search of him. He looked at Will now, filthy, stinking, face slightly swollen and scarred.

"What the hell happened to you? Yer look like yer've bin sleepin' with Molly O'Reilly's prize pig. I hope it was a good lookin' one."

"What happened to me? What happened to me? I'll tell you what the hell happened. I got kidnapped and had the crap beaten out of me, by a bunch of lunatics. If it hadn't been for Owen, I'd still be locked up in some stinking shed in Bantry. And where the fuck were you when all this was going on?" Will's voice was becoming higher as all the miseries of the last couple of weeks came flooding back.

Sean held up his hands defensively. "Alright, alright. We'll soon have you cleaned up and I did come lookin' for yer, ol' son, honest I did. To be precise, twice. Here sit yerself down, I figured you could do with some food first and a drink. Ah and right on cue, here's Maggie with somethin' to eat and drink. I expect yer could do with it. Let's sit down and I'll tell you all about it."

Sean smiled to himself at Will's reaction to Maggie's appearance. In spite of his misfortunes and discomfort, Will's eyes went not to the two beers and the plate of bread and broth, but to what were revealed by the low cut, tight fitting brown dress on the attractive young brunette. She leant forward to ensure that Will could fully appreciate her bosom, as she put down the tray. Then with a smile to Will and a wink to Sean, she was gone.

"Yer don't get too many of them to the pound and I can vouch fer that personally." Sean cupped his hands in the appropriate gesture.

Will tried to ignore Sean's comments and returned to the attack. "Twice? What do you mean? What happened to you and how did you end up here? Why did you send Owen, instead of coming yourself? Oh, and what happened in the end? Did the French invade? What's the date? Oh, and where did the gun and money come from? Christ Sean, what the fuck am I talking about? Have you found a way to get back? Does your bracelet work? This piece of crap is useless!"

Sean held up his hands. "Whoa, hold on there! I'll tell yer what. You eat and I'll talk and I'll try to fill yer in as best I can."

They sat down, either side of an old trestle table and, after a glance to check that the door was shut, Sean started his version of the events of the previous couple of years.

"I knew that I was supposed to land next to you to clock this French invasion. I don't know whether they got the dosage wrong or whether it was down to me, not being as clued up as you on dates and stuff. Either way, I landed in the wrong place, at the wrong time. Cave Hill, May 1795. I was reading about the United Irishmen meeting there, yer see."

Will choked on his bread. "Cave Hill? Good God, that's Belfast and about eighteen months too early. Couldn't those bloody imbeciles at Boroughbridge get anything right? Wait a minute. You didn't see…"

Sean interrupted him, "Yeah, yeah. The full bit. Tone, Nielson, Russell, McCracken, the lot of them."

"Did you speak to them?" asked Will excitedly, forgetting his anger for a moment.

Sean was amused at how easily his friend was distracted. If Will only knew the half of what had happened, but that could wait. "Well hardly. I couldn't just stroll up to them and say, 'what a coincidence, I was just reading about you and did yer know yer'll all be dead in no time,' now could I? Besides, I wasn't really in the mood, at the time."

"No I suppose not." Will recalled his own confusion, when he landed that cold day in Bantry Bay. "My God, that reminds me, weren't we supposed to be ghosts or something? Nobody could see us?"

Sean nodded. "I never really bought all that. Otherwise why would you have Al's little 'no shaggin' or killin' pep talk and all the dressin' up bullshit? Mind you, I never really bought into the whole time travel bit either. Christ, I sure got that wrong didn't I?"

Before Will could respond Sean continued. "The bracelets? Well they were a bloody con too, weren't they? Those lying bastards certainly stuffed us there. Here I'm still wearin' mine." Sean too, now flushed with anger, reddened and pulled up the sleeve of his shirt to reveal the shiny metal band, which matched Will's. "God knows why. I suppose I'm still clinging to the hope that I'll wake up one morning and it'll be glowin or somethin', 'cause some silly sod has remembered to switch it on at the other end." He pulled a face. "I've bin thinkin' about that too. Trouble is, with all this time stuff, it might take decades of our time for someone to walk across the room at Boroughbridge and flick a switch. You an' me'll pop back, before they've even noticed we've gone, an' be ready ter collect yer Queen's Telegram!"

Sean had tried to lighten his own mood, as well as Will's, but instead Will's face fell further. Clearly he had hoped that Sean would have the answers to all his problems.

Sean put a reassuring hand on Will's arm. "I guess I've had a bit more time to get used to the idea. I could get the thing taken off by a blacksmith, but somehow I can't bring myself to do it. It'd be like being marooned on a desert island, after yer ship had sunk, and burning the life raft to keep warm. It's the only way off this island and, despite everything, I *do* still believe that it could work. We just need to work out what we've been doing wrong. Now you're here," he added brightly, "I'm sure we'll crack it."

Sean did not believe this for a second, but it had the desired effect on Will. God, it seemed strange to see him sitting there! There were more than a few occasions when even Sean had woken up in the middle of the night and doubted that he ever would see Will again.

"Did you manage to hear any of it?" Will asked suddenly.

"Hear what?" responded Sean.

"The business at Cave Hill. It was when they made their pledge to free Ireland of the English. After that Tone went off to America to contact the French via their ambassador in Philadelphia." In spite of everything Will grinned for the first time, "Christ, I can't believe you saw that."

Sean looked at him quizzically. "Have you lost a tooth?"

Will's hand flew to his mouth. "Does it show?"

"Only when you smile, but don't worry, there's not much to smile about in eighteenth century Ireland!"

Immediately Will's visage revealed the underlying despair.

"Oh Christ, It ain't that bad Will. The world isn't such a different place. If yer've got money in yer pocket and a smile on yer face... oh sorry, yer tooth really doesn't show much... the girls can be very appreciative." Sean tapped the side of his nose. "No more cold lonely nights for you Will Peters. Young Maggie's with me, but there's plenty more, where she came from. I reckon you might be a very popular addition to the team, with the girls here, but I think we might need to get yer cleaned up a bit first." He put his finger to his nose. "They're not so fussy here, but there are limits!"

Will did not seem to appreciate Sean's comments, so Sean went to the door and yelled for more ale. Only after it had been delivered and the door closed behind Maggie again, did he try a different approach with Will.

"The date? It's the, er, let me see, fifteenth of March 1797. So how long have yer bin here? About a couple of weeks?"

Will nodded.

"So you missed yer date too? But only by a couple of months, I guess." Sean thought for a moment. "So yer weren't there in December, when the French were meant to land?"

This time Will shook his head. "No, I missed it. Did anyone get ashore?"

Sean took a drink and considered his answer. "I don't think it happened. The French fleet in Bantry Bay an' all that, I mean. They didn't come."

Will put down his ale. "What do you mean? 'They didn't come.' Of course they bloody came. It was just a question of whether they put some men ashore with that document. We *know* that they arrived in Bantry Bay. By the time the storm blew them away, half the world knew they'd been there!"

Sean shifted his position in his chair. "Will, I don't rightly know how to explain this. Things don't seem to be quite the way they're meant ter be." He smiled at Will. "I'm really glad ye're here now, 'cause maybe you can help me a bit, you being a bit more clued up on the history an' all that. There are some things, which don't seem like I read about them and I'm not sure if it's me, and I just don't remember 'em right, or if it's all different. You know, like we're in a parallel universe and things are kinda the same, but a mite different."

Will had finished eating by now. He pushed the bowl to one side. "What do you mean? What sort of things are different?"

Sean scratched his ear. "It's difficult to say exactly. Let's start with this French landing. I've heard nothing about it and from what you told me, back in Boroughbridge, half the country was shouting about it. On top of that, the place is in uproar. The army is running around killing anything that moves and burning anything that doesn't. This seems to have been going on some time and that doesn't exactly fit in with what you told me about 1796 and '97."

Will was listening intently and so Sean continued, "It's like a powder keg out there and, if I was a gambling man, I'd say it was all about to kick off now. I can't see it lasting another year, not till 1798. All it will take is for the Government to up the ante and push the people a little more. Then I reckon they'll have a war on their hands."

"I know what you mean, Sean," acknowledged Will. "I've witnessed some terrible scenes, floggings, hangings, pitch capping, the works." He shuddered. "It was awful. I just watched it and couldn't do a thing to help those poor people." His eyes started to moisten. "How could people do things like that?" He pulled himself together. "I'm sure that sort of thing went on all the time, but I didn't think it got out of hand like that until '97 and '98. There again, perhaps the history books played it down. A lot of the stuff was written by the English. You know what they say, history is always written by the winning side. You haven't been dragged into it, have you?"

To be honest with you, I put me money into this place..." Sean indicated the room around them, "and I've had to put together a little group of boys to, er, protect me interests."

Will's eyes widened, "You own the bar?"

"Sure," Sean laughed. "I had to do something to make a living and I've always fancied a bar. If you could work out a way that we could ship it exactly like it is, back to the present, that is our present, I reckon we'd make a fortune."

Will wasn't so easily distracted this time. "What kind of group of boys? What's going on Sean? What are you up to?"

Sean was tired with consoling Will. "Heh, it's alright for you. You've just arrived and you haven't had to survive here on your own. I bet you reckon that you're going to find some miraculous way of getting back. Forget it. I've thought about fuck all else for nearly two bloody years and I haven't come up with a thing. It may never happen. In the meantime you're gonna have to make yer way. It took me a while to get my head around that."

Will tried to interrupt, but Sean talked him down.

"You want to know what's going on? I'll tell yer what's goin' on. Forget your bloody books and your fancy little study groups, sittin' around drinkin' tea at Oxford. This place is in fuckin' turmoil. The only reason that the bloody army don't ride into town is that they know that they'd have a fight on their hands. It's like the Wild West ol' son. Besides I pay the buggers to stay away."

"You're bribing the army?!"

"Course I am! Those bastards would have burnt this place down by now, if I didn't slip 'em a share of the profits. I think of it like income tax. Don't look at me like that! Oh fuck off Will! Can you imagine what it's been like here on me own. I couldn't be sure you'd turn up. For all I knew you'd be dropped into Wales or somewhere, fifty years ahead of me."

Will nodded. "O.K. O.K. I'm sorry." He sighed. "Why the hell did we agree to it, Sean? How did we let them talk us into it?"

Sean had had more than enough time to consider this over the last two years. He had resolved to come clean with Will, if and when he eventually appeared. Now the moment was here it didn't seem like the right time. He would explain to Will how he had been drawn in by the Boston connection and how his father had been instrumental in it, at least in part. He would explain all this to Will and make him understand, just not now. There was too much going on and he could not afford to fall out with Will just at the moment.

He had hoped that Will would turn up, but he could never be sure. He had been forced to set things in motion without him and hope for the best. At what point had he resolved to do as Jones, the Bostonians and his father had bid him? He could not be sure. Neither was he sure why he'd decided to do it. Deep down that anger against those, who had tricked him, was still smouldering. So why do what they wanted? Perhaps it was inculcated in him. Perhaps there was a little germ of a thought that, only by doing this would they allow him to return. It didn't seem very logical, but the idea was there. Perhaps it just sickened him to see what was going on, knowing where it was leading. At least the idealists of the time, Wolf Tone and the rest had a dream that it would all come right. They didn't know the death, misery and humiliation, which was in front of them. They did not know what the next two hundred years would bring, history repeating itself at Easter in 1916. How idealistic would they be, if they knew what there best efforts would bring? Whatever the reasons, Sean had not been idle over those two years.

He looked at Will and resolved to tell him later.

"I'm damned if I know, Will. I don't really think I believed in it and just went along for the ride and the money. What about you?"

Will gazed into space. "I'm not really sure either. It's odd; it all seems like a dream now. Valerie was very persuasive, you know. Now I'm not so sure about her. She seemed really keen on me." He laughed, "and I was dead sure that she was after you."

"The ways of women! Who knows what they're thinking? I've had plenty of women in me time and never understood a single one of 'em." He smiled again at Will, "I'm sure she liked yer, mate. She picked you for the night out didn't she?"

"Yeah, I suppose so," admitted Will, unconvinced.

Sean could see that the beer and tiredness were taking a hold of Will. "Why don't yer get some sleep 'ol son and we can pick this up again tomorrow. I'll take you out for a look around and you can get a feel for what's goin' on."

"Hold on a minute. I still want to know why you didn't come and meet me. If it had been me, I'd have been turning the country upside down for you. Why did you send Owen? And where did you find him anyway?"

"Ah Owen, I didn't so much find him, as he found me. He sorta' attached himself to me, that first night in Belfast. Just as well really or I'd probably got into even more trouble." Sean hesitated while he decided how to explain it all. "When I realised that I was in the wrong place at the wrong time, I decided I'd better go and look for you. I couldn't do anything about the date, but I could do something about the location." Sean laughed, as he recalled it, "I guess you kinda' think that it's all like it was in our time. I had this idea that I'd just pop down to Bantry and have a look fer yers. In a decent car you could drive it in a day." He paused for a drink. "It took me bloody weeks. It was like Hercules' tasks or Hannibal crossing the Alps or something. Everywhere you went there were delays and distractions." Sean decided not to mention the week he'd spent in a cottage, near Kildare, with a young woman, whose husband had disappeared whilst on a trip to Dublin.

"Eventually I bought a horse. Well I stole it actually. And that was another diversion. Never mind, by the time I arrived in Bantry, it was the back end of the summer and, of course, there was no sign of you. I asked about a bit, but it was difficult to explain, so I just described yers' and said that you were coming by sea."

"That explains it," interrupted Will. "How they all knew about me, but why did this gang catch me and beat me up?"

"Ah so that's how you lost yer tooth," replied Sean. "But don't blame me for that! I just said that I was lookin' fer a dull lookin' English fella, about your size and that you were all right, 'cause you were one of us. Besides that was over a year ago. I went back again, this Christmas just gone by." He hesitated, "That's how I know that the French never turned up," he added hastily.

"You must have bloody done something Sean. When I turned up, it seemed like half the country was looking for me. Yeah, and come to think of it, The Fox knew all about me. Told me I was a legend or something. He seemed to know all about me and said that Ireland was expecting me to liberate them from the English, or something like that."

Sean gaped at Will. "The Fox? You met The Fox? And he knew all about you?"

Will was wide-awake again by now. "Yeah, it was weird really. He and his gang came chasing after me. I thought they were going to kill us, but all he did was return the bag, which I'd had stolen at Bantry. And then he came out with all this stuff about knowing who I was and why I was here. He also reckoned he knew you too."

"What?!" Sean shot upright in his seat. "I've never met him. Sure, I've heard about him. Every bugger's heard of him. He rides around the place like Robin bloody Hood, killin' off the landowners and stealin' everything. Supposedly he gives it all to the Catholic poor, except I doubt much of it reaches them. And he's committed some real atrocities. He crucified, yeah, actually nailed some guy to the door of his house, while his family watched. The fella was the head of one of those Catholic families, who'd crossed the line and turned Protestant, just to cosy up to the Ascendancy lot to get land and stuff. Yer don't want ter go messin' with *him*."

Will reddened, "Well it wasn't exactly by choice! He followed us, came out with all this prophecy stuff, returned my bag and then just left. I've got to be honest; he frightened the bloody life out of me. And he definitely reckoned he knew you. 'We go way back' or something like that, he said."

"I don't know what to say to yers' and that's the truth. I've never met the guy and don't especially want to. He's never been in here, or not to my knowledge. Let's face it he's not the sort of fella that you'd forget in a hurry. What did he look like?"

Will cast his mind back to the night by the campfire. "He was tall, dressed in black, shoulder length dark hair. He looked like the lead singer for some heavy metal band. Oh, and he had a scar on his cheek, about here." Will indicated a place just below his right eye. "Or maybe it was the other side, I can't really remember. Like the sort of scar people get, if they've had a glass smashed in their face."

Sean went very pale. "Well, it's a bit of a mystery to me. All I can say to you Will is that I haven't been sending out gangs of murderers on lost luggage duty. When you didn't turn up, I was pretty depressed, I don't mind tellin' yer, but then I figured that, if I could land at the wrong time, so could you. I just hoped the place would be right and so I sent young Owen to wander about and sure enough here you are and it really is grand to see yers'." He smiled at Will, who looked exhausted.

"Why don't yer get some sleep, Will? Yer look all in. We have, as they say, all the time in the world to catch up. I've got a room for yer. You can clean up in the morning. Just dump all those clothes by the door. I'll fix you up with a hot bath in the morning and some new clothes. I can also sort you out with a razor too. Heh you know the best bit?" Sean leaned forward conspiratorially, "I've even got something pretty close to soft bog roll. They never mention that in books and films, but, believe me it's important."

Sean showed Will up a narrow staircase to a room under the eaves of the old building. "Just leave yer stuff out here and get yer head down. I'll arrange a bit of a look around tomorrow and you can tell me all that Fox stuff again. Maybe we can find out a bit more about him, too. Oh, and by the way, when yer needin' a piss, use the pot. The neighbours complain, if yer use the window. See yer tomorrow."

With a pat on Will's back Sean left him and went down to check the bar. He had a lot of thinking to do and he had a very bad feeling about The Fox.

Chapter 18

As Sean descended the stairs into the main bar, Maggie and two of the other girls were throwing out the last few stragglers.

"Go on wi' yer now. Have yer no home ter go ter?"

"And yer can keep yer hands ter yersel', Seamus O'Malley. Yer've a wife at home fer all that kinda' thing."

They looked up as Sean appeared.

"Are yer all right? You look kinda pale," asked Maggie.

Sean brushed his hand over his face, "Get me some coffee."

Maggie frowned.

Noticing her reaction, Sean apologised. "Sorry, I didn't mean ter shout at yers. I'm a bit worried, that's all."

"That's fine. Is everything all right wi' yer friend? He is the one yer've bin lookin' fer, isn't he?" asked Maggie with genuine concern.

"Oh, fine, fine. He's had a spot o' trouble on the way here, but he'll be fine, when he's had some sleep."

"Yer could do wi' a bit a shut eye yersel' Sean, by the look o' yers." She brushed her hair behind her ear and took his hand in hers. "Would yer like me ter come up ter yer room?"

Sean switched on the smile, as he put his arms around her waist. "Now normally there's nothing I'd rather, 'cause yer know yer the prettiest girl this side of Galway, but tonight I've got a couple o' things that I need to think about. Besides, Maggie McGee, if you come up to my room it'll not be sleeping I'll be doing!"

The young woman grinned up at Sean. He looked into her pretty green eyes. "Well perhaps yer might want ter stop in my room and I'll be up in an hour or so."

The barmaid nodded. "Will yer be sure to wake me?"

Sean kissed her on the lips. "You can rely on it. Now young serving wench, get me my coffee or I'll have ter throw you out on the street!"

"Oh no Sir! Don't be doin' that," she laughed.

Much as Sean was tempted by Maggie's charms, he needed thinking time. Things were moving apace and he felt as though he was losing control. Damn it, he could have done with Will arriving at Christmas, as was intended. Never mind, he was here now and Will had clearly been affected by the atrocities he had seen. That could be useful, thought Sean, I can exploit that.

He sat in the backroom of the bar, where they had been playing cards earlier. The large wooden table, now cleared and scrubbed, was ideal to spread out the map he had released from its hiding place, behind a wooden wall panel. He turned up the oil lamps, which hung from the beams over the table.

Maggie returned with a metal pot of coffee and a cup. She placed them on the table to the side of the map. She showed no interest in the document, clearly used to seeing such things. As she left, she caught Sean's eye, slipped her dress provocatively off one shoulder and blew him a kiss, while ascending the stairs.

Sean blew her a kiss in return and then turned his attention to the map. It was a work of art and he had laboured on it for hours over recent months. Based on a simple work from a Dublin printer, Sean had used his network of contacts and informers to add the details of all the army barracks and camps. To this he had added the locations and dates of all the attacks on nearby villages and towns. In red ink, he had written details of the locations of a number of fictitious attacks and the number of troops involved. A false key to this was clearly written on the side of the map, just into the Irish Sea. If the map fell into the wrong hands anyone seeing this would not easily realise that the red figures indicated the location of hidden pikes and muskets and not army activities.

Where would they strike next? Sean and his supporters were just about ready for them, but he wanted an incident to unite the disparate groups into one co-ordinated rising. If the army carried on its relentless, but piecemeal suppression, the key people, including himself of course, would be winkled out. One by one the weapons stashes would be unearthed and confiscated. The battle would be lost before it was even fought, just like it had been in the '98 revolution that he had studied back at Boroughbridge.

Rumours were coming out of Dublin that the army was about to escalate its activities. That might incite the uprising, which he sought. Better would be an incident, which would provoke the army to commit itself rashly. He wanted to fight an action, big enough to weaken the local militia and buy him some time to mobilise his forces. It also needed to be significant enough to show the people that the army could be beaten. On the other hand he didn't want a major defeat, a massacre of the local peasantry.

Tap, tap, tap. Sean was startled by a noise at the back door of the bar. He looked around. Everything was in darkness, except for one lamp, which burnt low over the table. The other lamp had burnt out. Oh Christ, he must have fallen asleep. What a way to be found, draped across his map! Talk about being caught red handed!

Sean hastily folded the incriminating document and stashed it away in its hiding place, removing his pistol from behind the panel at the same time. He turned down the lamp until it was only the faintest glow. Then he approached the door cautiously. It opened onto a very narrow alleyway in which two people could not pass without touching shoulders. With no form of lighting to show you the way after dark, it had been infamous for muggings and beatings, before Sean had taken over the bar. Cocking the pistol, he slid open a little panel in the heavy wooden door.

"Announce yerself," he rasped.

"Sean, Sean, it's me Ryan. Let me in, I've got news fer yers," came a little voice from outside.

Sean, pistol raised, slid back the bolts and stepped back into the gloom. "Come in."

A young man's form took shape in the doorway. His eyes used to the dark of the alley, focused on the pistol in Sean's hand.

"Fer the love of Jesus, put that away Sean, yer scaring the life outa me."

"Bolt the door, Ryan and come in."

The youth did as he was told and, with the door secure, Sean turned up the lamp to reveal a figure, not much more than a boy. He was sweating profusely, despite the cold night air and he was breathing heavily. Clearly he was frightened.

Sean glanced at the cold coffee pot on the table. "Do yer want a beer, son?"

Despite his fear and exertions, Ryan's eyes lit up. "Oh, that would be grand Sean, if it's no trouble."

It was, because Sean had to find another lamp, light it and go through to the backroom behind the bar for the ale. Not to worry, it would give the lad a chance to catch his breath. It must be something important to have him risk coming here at this time of night. If the army caught him, he'd be lucky to escape without a beating. Returning with the ale and some water for himself, Sean let the young man drink.

"Alright now, what's this all about? What time is it anyways?"

"I, I'm not sure. It must be late, maybe about four or five o' the morning." The young man bowed his head, "I'm sorry ter disturb yers, but I had ter come. Me Da told me ter."

"That's fine now. What have yers got fer me?"

Ryan was calmer now and, with a deep breath started to explain.

"It was O'Connell, yer know, Corporal O'Connell, at the barracks, he came to see me Da, late last night, about midnight, I guess. He told me Da that the army has new orders." He scratched the top of his head, "Now let me get this right. They've ter take free quarters in the country. Yes, that's it, free quarters, he said." He looked up at Sean for approval.

Sean leant forward and seized the young man's arms. "Are you sure that was the message Ryan?"

"Yeah that was it, fer sure. And he said that they all bin a drinkin' chimney or something fancy like that."

"Champagne?" offered Sean.

"That was it, Champagne. They'd all bin drinkin' that stuff, 'cause the Colonel, yer know with de funny name."

"De Guilbert?"

"That's yer man, de Guilber' His brother had died, or somethin' so they were all celebratin'. I don't understand it mesel'. I can't stand me brothers, but I wouldn't want ter see them die."

Sean's mind was whirring while young Ryan drank the ale. Free quarters he knew about, from his reading. It had come sooner than it should have done according to Sean's history and that was surely, as a result of his rebellious activities. It was what he wanted, but they had to move fast or all their work would be undone, as the army ravished the country.

De Guilbert's brother? What the hell was that all about? Then the pieces dropped into place. If the bastard's brother were dead, he'd be the new duke or earl or whatever he was. He was a prize target before, but now… Oh my God, a top drawer English Lord within his sights. If they took him out, it would cause a national outcry.

Sean smiled at Ryan, "Did he say what they were planning to do? Or where they were planning to go? Think carefully now."

Ryan shook his head. "No nothin'. That was it, just free quarters an' De what's 'is name's brother was dead."

"Give me a minute, Ryan." Sean thought hard. He did not want to display his map to this honest, but rather dull young man. Midford was perfect. It was about half way, between Wexford and the barracks and surprisingly it had not been raided yet.

"Ryan, listen carefully. Can yer get a message back to O'Connell?"

Ryan nodded, "Me sister cleans up there. She goes up there every mornin'."

"You'll never get back in time."

"Ah, that's where yer wrong. I've gotta horse," the young man puffed his chest out proudly. "It's me uncle's an' it's goin' ter win the big race in June. I' left it outside o' the town so as not ter get caught."

"Well in that case Ryan, get this message to O'Connell. Tell him to take them to Midford. Midford, now, remember."

Ryan nodded.

Sean thought for a moment. "Tell them there's a big stash of pikes and muskets, hidden in the village."

Ryan's eyes opened wide. "I can't do that."

"It's a trick Ryan. It's not really true." In fact it was true, but Sean did not want to confuse the young man with that burden.

Ryan's eyes lit up again. "Oh, a trick. That's alright then."

"And one more thing. He must bring De Guilbert. Is that clear? Somehow he must get De Guilbert to come too. He's an evil bastard, he'll probably enjoy seeing a few houses burnt down. Now have yer got all that?"

Sean had Ryan repeat it all twice to him and then, with a cautious look out into the alley, sent him on his way. With a pot of ale in him and a horse ride ahead, Sean had his doubts whether he'd make it in time. Come on Ryan, go for it old son. I need you to come good for me, he thought, as he bolted the door. Suddenly he remembered Will upstairs. It was ironical; he didn't have the luxury of time to play Will in gently.

Tomorrow could well be a baptism of fire, Sean thought, as he finally headed up to a couple of brief hours in the warmth of a plump feather bed and Maggie's arms. He doubted whether he'd be able to wake her now or, indeed, whether he'd bother.

Chapter 19

Regimental HQ Fifth Leicestershire, near Midford Co. Wexford
April 1st 1797

De Guilbert awoke late, head thick with Champagne and cigar smoke. The entire garrison had been turned out three hours earlier, after the threats of the night before, the officers left with restless troops and nowhere to go. The N.C.O.'s snarled at the troops, who moaned and complained at the early rousting from their slumbers, only to be drilled and abandoned to stand about aimlessly.

For Mablethorpe it was a Godsend. It gave him time to think. What on earth should he recommend to the colonel? His stomach knotted as he thrashed about for an answer to his predicament. New to the regiment and without an established informant network of his own, he was forced to rely on others. But whom could he trust? Lieutenant Davies, his junior officer, but many years his senior, resented him and was as unhelpful as he dared, short of insubordination. He was wise enough to recognise that Sergeant Jeffreys held the men in his grasp. He knew that he needed to befriend the giant sergeant, but that was easier said than done. In the meantime salvation came from an unexpected quarter, Corporal O'Connell.

"If you've a moment, Sir?" enquired O'Connell of his Captain.

He had been desperate for hours to catch a word with Mablethorpe, out of earshot of the sergeant. Jeffreys would never allow discourse between him and the captain. At any time De Guilbert could appear and the chance would be gone. At just after 9 a.m. Mablethorpe had shown the courage to stand the men down and this finally presented the much-needed opportunity.

"What is it O'Connell? Won't it wait?" came the captain's blunt response.

"I, er, I probably shouldn't tell you about this Sir," O'Connell chose his words carefully, "but with so many weapons stashed away, Sir, I felt that it could present a threat to the regiment."

That did it. He had Mablethorpe hooked.

"What weapons, O'Connell? Speak up man, it's your duty."

"Well Sir, I should have said something last night, but I thought that it would be better to come to you Sir, being as you're in charge, so to speak. It's something I heard the night before last and well it's a bit difficult, Sir."

"This is no time to beat about the bush, Corporal. Speak up or you'll answer to me."

"Well Sir, it's just that I heard it in the village inn at Midford and er well, we're not meant to go there, Sir.

"I see." Mablethorpe pretended to consider, but was far too eager to hear O'Connell's news to worry about any minor transgressions.

"Spit it out, man. If the information is sound enough, I might decide to overlook your misdemeanour on this occasion, but you'll have to put a stop to it. It's bad for discipline with the men."

O'Connell knew full well that Sergeant Jeffreys sold passes to the men to visit the local inn and also controlled the visits to a nearby farm, which doubled as the local whorehouse. Now was not the time to mention that.

"Thank you Sir, I appreciate your tact and understanding, 'specially as this is such a *major* rebel stronghold." He nodded and smiled at his captain.

"Get on with it man. I haven't got all day. The colonel will be down any minute."

"Of course, of course. Well it's like this. I was just sitting in the corner having a quiet drink, when a group o' the boys comes in and starts drinking heavy like. Well, they takes ner notice o' me Sir, on account of the fact that I'm, well, an Irish lad meself. Well after a few beers they starts shoutin' an' braggin' about how they're goin' ter teach the army a lesson, 'cause they got all these weapons hidden in all the houses in the village. Not only that, but they've been trainin' the local boys ter fight at night. Someone even mentioned them havin' a small canon, but I don't believe that fer a minute. I reckon 'twas just the drink talkin'."

"A canon, a canon, by God. What makes you think *any* of this is true?" The young captain could hardly contain his excitement, yet he needed to be sure.

"Well I might have put this down ter high spirits, but well I don't know if I ought ter tell yer this Sir." O'Connell paused and prayed that nobody had noticed this conversation.

"Go on, go on man. You've gone too far to stop now."

"Well Sir, I should have bin back 'ere, but I followed them. Yer know, after they left the inn. I was takin a 'elluva risk. If they'd 'av caught me, they'd 'av killed me. Anyway there they were, bold as brass, drillin' the boys in a field by moonlight an' all o' them wi' a musket."

"Good God! How many of the devils were there?"

"Twas difficult to say fer sure Sir, bein as it was dark. I'd say maybe twenty or thirty of them."

Mablethorpe's face was a picture of concentration. He didn't need Davies or Jeffreys. He would repeat this direct to his colonel.

"O'Connell are you absolutely sure of this? You weren't drunk were you?"

"Oh no, heaven forbid Sir. I'm not a big drinker Sir. I just likes the one with a smoke Sir. It helps me sleep."

"Very well, but if this turns out to be a tale, I'll see to it that you're flogged. And this was in Midford?"

"Yes Sir. And you'll not say where this came from Sir?"

"Provided your information is sound, they'll be no mention of your name."

"Thank you Sir. I hope yer don't mind me tellin' yer Sir."

"Get about your business corporal and O'Connell…"

"Yes Sir?"

"If you hear any more like this, you make sure that you come to me and nobody else. Is that clear?"

"Yes Sir."

Still unobserved by Jeffreys, O'Connell grinned to himself, as he left his captain to run to the colonel.

Will awoke with a start as the two young barmaids burst into his room. It was still dark, which meant that it was early and he had hoped to be able to lie in. His thoughts were soon distracted.

"Wake up now Mr. Peters. I'm goin ter shave yers and then we;re both goin' ter bath you," trilled one as the other giggled and pulled the covers off him.

At the sight of his dirty naked body in the light of her lamp, they both shrieked with laughter.

"Don't worry now, we'll soon have you lathered up," squealed the other and they both convulsed with giggles.

It was not what Will had expected, but now rested he could see that the situation had endless possibilities. The shave came first, a tricky operation with an open razor and by lamplight. He sat as still as he could, shivering in a blanket. The girl with the razor, who introduced herself as Anna, was remarkably skilled. Nonetheless there were mishaps, but Will determined to be brave, when she did cut him, until he discovered that any nick had to be kissed better, by the other girl, whose name was Margaret. Then he made a fuss at every opportunity.

"Oh, don't take on so. I've lather all over me lips," protested Margaret. "Fer God's sakes Anna, be more careful," she exhorted her partner in crime.

The bath was something of a different ordeal. The girls dragged him downstairs and out to a yard, at the back of an enormous long old kitchen, where huge metal containers of water had been warmed on the range. They stood him in a horse trough in the yard and with a shriek ripped his blanket away. They then set about him with soap, water and coarse brushes. His skin howled in protest and so did Will. Between them they made so much noise that it attracted an audience.

As the first light of dawn crept over the inn, Will resigned himself to the public humiliation and took up mock-heroic poses to wolf whistles of appreciation from the young women watching. The curtain came down, when he was doused in ice cold water. With a wink to each other, the two girls turned, dropped their brushes and seized two wooden buckets, which they'd filled earlier from the pump.

"This should calm yers down a bit", they shrieked and threw the contents over him. Will howled and the audience cheered. The girls were right. It was remarkably effective.

Will seized the blanket, which he now noticed smelt of horse and made his escape to the sanctuary of the kitchen and its wood fired range. He dried himself as best he could and was given hot tea to stop his teeth chattering, by an elderly woman who, Will could see, had few of her own teeth left to chatter. Her wide grin at his predicament revealed a couple of stumps. She hardly took her eyes off Will, as she started to prepare something on the range.

Anna and Margaret soon returned, this time with fresh clothes for Will. He was given dark brown breeches, which fastened below the knee, a clean fine white shirt, which laced at the neck, a cream waistcoat and a three quarter length pale brown jacket, which sported double rows of buttons and fastenings and an intricate green motif embroidered into the lapels. He was not so keen on the knee length stockings, but his dismay was soon overcome by the appearance of smart new brown leather boots, which came to just below the knee. They were made from very soft leather and were obviously expensive.

Before Will could admire himself, Sean breezed into the kitchen. He looked tired, but grinned broadly at the sight of Will.

"Well, who's a pretty boy then? You *have* scrubbed up well! Does everything fit? I just got everything about one size too small for mesel' The stuff's bin hanging around weeks waiting for yers."

"The boots are a bit tight, but they're soft and I guess they'll stretch," replied Will. "I'm starving. What's she cooking?"

By now the kitchen had filled with the smell of bacon and eggs and the two men sat down to eat.

"How are you on a horse, Will?" asked Sean, as they ate. "I'm not great mesel', but I've had ter get the hang of it. It's just we're going out, as soon as yer've finished. I want ter take yers to a village near here. I'm planning to meet up there with some friends o' mine."

"I've ridden a bit, but it'd have to be something pretty docile," replied Will.

"Not a problem. I've just the beast for yer." Sean wiped the egg off his chin. "Come on now. We're gonna be late.

He took Will back to the table, where he had fallen asleep over the map, picked up Will's bag and tossed it to him. Will caught it and noticed that it was lighter.

Reading his face, Sean said, "I've put the money away safe, but keep the gun handy. Yer never know when yer might need it around here. Keep it outa sight mind, especially in town."

Before Will could give it any more thought, Sean led him out of the back of the inn, through the door, which Ryan had used earlier that morning and down the alley. As they walked briskly through the streets, one or two heads turned in their direction, but everyone was careful not to hold their gaze too long. At the edge of the town they encountered a patrol of four English soldiers. Their classic red coats looked dull and dirty, as they came closer. Will found himself slipping his hand into the bag to reassure himself with the feel of the carved surface of the butt of the revolver. There was no need. The soldiers said nothing and simply nodded to Sean, as they passed. Apart from a slight dip of the head Sean showed no reaction.

They arrived outside an inn on the outskirts of Wexford. Without a word or a glance at his companion Sean led Will into the stables at the back. Before Will's eyes could adjust to the gloom inside, Sean had introduced him to three men, who emerged from between the horses. Formalities were kept to a minimum and first names only were used.

"Will this is Pat, Rikki and Michael. Boys, this is the fella I told yers about, Will. I see the horses are ready. We've no time to lose. Let's be goin'."

Pat, a larger man than the others squared up to Will, "Are you straight?" he enquired.

Will was taken aback at the directness of the question and then it flooded back to him. He had read these words many times, but never thought that he would be asked the question in earnest.

"I am."

"How straight?"

"As straight as a rush – in truth, in trust, in unity and liberty."

Rikki beamed at the words of this Englishman thrust in their midst.

"What have you got in your hand?"

By now, Will was in his stride and knew these to be the secret words of greeting of the United Irishmen. "A green bough."

"Where did it first grow?"

"In America."

"Where did it bud?"

"In France."

"Where are you going to plant it?"

"In the crown of Great Britain."

They all shook hands and then one of them showed Will to a large, but seemingly placid beast and helped him into the saddle. They rode towards the northeast, as fast as Will's limited skills would permit. Sean prayed silently that young Ryan had done his job.

"Show him in, show him in," urged Lucky Eddie of Lewis impatiently. Eggs and kidneys washed down by a glass of claret had improved his mood and now, polished boots on the table, he was ready to start the day's proceedings.

Mablethorpe entered eagerly. "My lord, I…"

The ninth Earl raised his hand, cigar smoking between his fingers, to silence the captain. "You can save that for the Regimental Ball. Sir or Colonel will do when we are discussing military matters." He leaned forward. "Now what have you got for me? Whose little world are we to turn upside down this morning?"

He expected to watch his new subordinate squirm, knowing that it was Jeffreys who was the source of all information for the regiment. He hated the Sergeant and his games, but was wise enough to recognise his uses and not to challenge the order of things in the lower ranks. Had Mablethorpe been forced to go cap in hand to the man or would he now bluster, before admitting that he had no plan?

"Sir, I have received information about a major arms stash, very close to our barracks. We should march there immediately and seize the weapons," announced Mablethorpe proudly.

De Guilbert puffed on his cigar and scrutinised the officer standing in front of him. "And who might be the source of this vital information?"

"I er, I am not in a position to reveal that Sir."

"Oh you are not in a position to reveal your source, aren't you? Might it be…" the colonel puffed on his cigar, "Sergeant Jeffreys?" He waited for Mablethorpe to blush, but he did not.

"No, sir. I can tell you that it is not from Sergeant Jeffreys.

De Guilbert took his feet off the table and leaned forward again. "Not Jeffreys? Hm, you *are* full of surprises, Captain. And where is this den of rebels and thieves?"

"Midford, sir, just a few miles southwest of here."

"Yes, yes, I know where Midford is, man. What makes you think that Midford is a centre for hidden weapons? Are they really stupid enough to hide them so close to our base?"

"I have reason to believe that they are not only hoarding arms, but training men in their use, sir. I gather that we have never carried out a detailed search of Midford, Sir."

De Guilbert considered this. Was it just possible that the regiment had never turned over Midford, because Sergeant Jeffreys had never unearthed any information to cause them to do so? Was that fact in any way connected with the endless supplies of drink and tobacco, which came Jeffreys way? If they marched on Midford he could not lose. A wasted trip would humiliate the captain and still show the locals, who was running the country. A successful venture and it would put a stop to one of Jeffreys' little dodges and remove the threat on their doorstep. Besides, he had seen one or two very pretty wenches, whilst passing through the place. It might just be diverting!

De Guilbert beamed at Mablethorpe. "Excellent work, young man. I can see that you'll be a fine addition to the regiment. Are we ready to march? I think I might just come along to ensure that the job's done properly."

As the colonel sat astride his white stallion, he was amused to hear Jeffreys' protestations at their plans. It reinforced his suspicions and he insisted, when they had divided the troops into two operational forces, that Jeffreys should accompany them to Midford. Another force under the command of Lieutenant Davies was to travel north and descend on a village of Jeffreys' choosing. Daniel O'Connell was relieved to find that he was assigned to

Davies. Jeffreys sulked and exacted his revenge by replacing Mablethorpe's usual reliable mount with a skittish young gelding, which they had stolen during one of their forays.

After hours of waiting the men were eager to make a start. News of the new orders had spread rapidly through the regiment. In an ill humour the huge sergeant barked orders at the men, who simply became more aroused in anticipation of visiting mayhem on the local populace. They set of at a quick march and within two hours entered the village. Warning shouts went up from the fields surrounding the road from the barracks. They were to no avail. Jeffreys knew that with Eddie's eyes on him, he had better show no signs of weakness.

Without warning the inhabitants, Jeffreys ordered the first four houses to be burnt. Pitch soaked faggots were lit and thrown onto the thatched roofs. With screams women and children rushed into the road to be driven before the troops into the centre of the village.

"That's the job, boys. That should loosen their tongues! Bring out the whips! Boil up the pitch. Remember you're doing the King's work,"
bellowed Eddie brandishing his sword. The world looked a perfect place from atop his stallion. Meanwhile Mablethorpe held back, totally preoccupied with controlling his mount, which bucked wildly at the scent of smoke.

In minutes the British army showed what a fine military machine could achieve, when roared into action by an enthusiastic sergeant. The troops had fanned out, fifteen-inch bayonets fitted to muskets, to ensure that nobody slipped away in the panic. The triangle was set up in the middle of the street and Sergeant Jeffreys was flexing his whip arm, as the first victim, a young man of about fourteen, was dragged screaming and crying to the fore and tied to the blood stained beams.

As Jeffreys' arm rose to make the first blow and De Guilbert licked his lips in anticipation of the pain and anguish, a gaggle of young women ran out and threw themselves at the huge sergeant. Caught by surprise, the big man lost his balance and nearly fell.

"Leave him alone yer murdering filth," screamed the oldest, a young woman of about twenty. "He's done nothin' ter yers."

Jeffreys regained his balance, kicked and shouldered the two younger girls into the welcoming arms of the troops standing by and grabbing the eldest by the hair. She tried to kick him, but by now he had the measure of her. Whip still in one hand he swung her around by her hair, as she let out squeals of pain, accompanied by cheers from the men. Finally he brought her under control by pinning her arm painfully behind her back and pulling her close to him.

"Such a pretty girl, but such a temper. Methinks you need something to calm yer down," breathed the sergeant into her ear. He admired her jet-black hair and ivory complexion. Vivid green eyes burned out above classic high cheekbones.

"I got one like you, sarge," yelled an unshaven private as he struggled to control one of the other girls. They were clearly sisters. The others laughed and tossed the youngest of the three, a girl of about thirteen, between them. She tried in vain to scratch at their lecherous faces, which leered and jeered at her.

Jeffreys looked up at his men and then back at his captive. "What you need, my dear, is a large helping of roast beef."

The men roared their approval, as the girl swore and spat and struggled to free herself.

"I think she needs a few helpings of roast beef!" chirped up a cockney voice hopefully.

"Show her yer beef, sarge!" roared the men.

The girl squirmed in panic and in desperation turned to the assembled crowd and screamed, "Help me! What's the matter with yer, yer cowards? Fer the love of God, someone?"

Ignoring the youth strapped to the triangle, Jeffreys tossed his whip to a private and took both hands to rip the girls dress from the neck down. A loud cheer went up at the glimpse of her breasts. At that moment a voice boomed out.

"Sergeant, let the woman alone. I'll deal with this," shouted Lucky Eddie.

He dismounted and handed the reins of his horse over to a young trooper to an audible sigh of disappointment from the troops. He marched briskly up to the scene of the imminent rape.

"Come here, my dear." He held out his hand and caught her as the sergeant released his hold.

As he marched her a couple of paces away from his men she panted, "Oh thank yer, sir. I knew there would be a gentleman amongst yers."

He pulled her close to him, so she could feel his pelvis against her belly and whispered in her ear. "You have a simple choice. You can come with me into one of these cottages and give yourself freely or…" he smiled at the look of shock in her pretty brown eyes, "you can enjoy the attentions of my sergeant, in front of the men. He probably won't be so gentle…" She started to struggle again. "Nor will the rest of his men, I daresay. If you're good I might even let your sisters go. They do seem a little young to be enjoying such fun, but no matter, I'm sure the men won't mind. What will it be?"

At a little stone bridge over Brannigan's brook, two miles from Midford, Sean, Will and their three companions were joined by two more horsemen. The Magnificent Seven, thought Sean sombrely and tried to remember how many of the seven survived. Where the hell were the others? His question was answered immediately by the thud of hooves on earth and another six arrived.

"Sorry we're late, Sean" panted the first rider.

"Are there any more?" demanded Sean.

The riders shook their heads. Great, thought Sean, thirteen. He forced a smile at Will. "Keep that pistol handy."

Sean hesitated and then made his decision. "Give me the sword Rory," he said to one of the new intake to their little band.

A sword was tossed to him and he fastened it around his waist.

"What are you waiting for?" Sean asked and put his heels to the flanks of his mount.

They rode until their route passed through a small copse of tall trees and turned to the left. They were less than a mile from Midford now. As they emerged from the trees and the road straightened several of the group let out a yell.

"Look Sean, smoke! The bastards are burning the place!"

"Christ, I hope we're not too late," exclaimed Sean. Turning to Will, he asked, "Can you manage a gallop?"

Will pulled a face. "Go for it. I'll give it a try."

Sean led the way and two of the others kept either side of Will to encourage him. It wasn't pretty, yet somehow they covered the ground quickly and without further thought or preparation, crashed into the village and past the burning cottages. For a moment the smoke obscured their vision and suddenly they burst upon a scene, which reminded Will of the one he had witnessed from the back of Owen's cart.

Sean and his men clattered to a sudden halt. There was an extraordinary silence. Nobody moved. The entire village, troops and villagers alike, stood and stared at this unexpected intrusion.

Will surveyed the scene, a mixture of emotions churning inside him. He saw the brazier heating up the pitch and knew what this portended. He surveyed the now familiar triangle, with its dark dried bloodstains. He saw the whip, now back in Jeffreys' hand. He noticed the young girl, dress ripped, at the feet of the English officer. Slowly he dismounted. His boots hurt, but it was not important.

Without taking his eyes off the officer he held up his hand to Sean, "Give me the sword, I'm fucked if I'm going to sit through this again."

A strange smile played on Sean's lips, as he unsheathed the blade and handed it to Will. "Now mind you don't hurt anybody with this thing. And while you're playing Zorro, it might be an idea to give me your pistol, so I'll be sure to have a shot to put yer out of your misery at the end of it all."

Will and Sean exchanged weapons and glances and Will strode purposefully towards the young woman and the English officer.

"My this *will* be interestin'," muttered Sean as he too dismounted and drew his own revolver. Quickly he closed the gap between him and the English troops to give himself a chance of hitting someone, should it come to that. He knew that it would.

"Hey you, leave her alone! She's done nothing to deserve that treatment!" yelled Will. It was rather stilted, but it certainly attracted Eddie's attention.

Unaccustomed to interruptions from a downtrodden populace, the English officer did not notice the London accent. "My, my. What have we got here? Is it a local boy, who can't wait any longer to meet his Catholic God?" asked de Guilbert looking at the approaching figure, sword in hand.

"Shall I take care of him for you sir?" enquired the burly sergeant.

"No, no, sergeant. Leave this one to me," responded de Guilbert. "It'll be a pleasure. Will anyone wager a drink on this upstart?"

There were no takers.

Turning to the young woman, he pulled her hair away from her tearful face. "You have a hero. Don't be foolish enough to think he will be your salvation. I want you to admire my skill as I fillet him like a joint of pork." He looked into her eyes. "Ah there now, don't be sad. I won't kill him. I'll just cut off his manhood and let him watch us, to see what he's missing."

He laughed and the girl still had the spirit to spit in his face, as de Guilbert's men laughed and cheered.

Will pulled up and stood off from the English officer. De Guilbert took his time and rose slowly and deliberately. He drew his sword inch by inch, as if relishing the imminent kill. As the point emerged from his scabbard, he was on Will in a flash. It startled Will and he automatically drew back, tumbling backwards over the extended boot of one of the Redcoats. His guard was down and in that instant, de Guilbert's blade shot forward.

Somehow Will managed to raise his own blade to defend himself. He used his adversary's momentum to direct him to one side and into his own men. There was a tangle of arms and legs, while de Guilbert cursed his soldiers and regained his composure. It was long enough for Will to find his feet and step away from the enemy troops. He drew de Guilbert towards him and into the open space. Sean stepped to one side slightly to keep a clear line on his targets.

Will assumed the fencing pose, side on to his opponent, weight equally balanced on either foot, blade raised and extended, left arm held behind him. It prompted a little whistle of amusement from his enemy, before he rushed him again. This time Will was prepared and parried the incoming blade. Forcing it wide he ran his blade along de Guilbert's upper sword arm and drew blood from his arm and the side of his head. It was not lethal or even particularly skilful. It was painful.

The English officer let out a roar. "You filthy Irish pig. You'll pay for that."

This was not meant to happen in front of his men. He was the King of Ireland and this bog-swilling bastard had better know it. He turned and, with a bellow, flew at Will with mesmerising speed. Far too slowly Will realised that his defences were breached and he was forced to throw himself to one side. For the second time in as many minutes he found himself sprawled in the mud. This was not fencing, as Will knew it, and he'd better learn this new game quickly or he might not have another lesson. The man was quick and strong, but he was clumsy and not as skilled as Will.

Scrabbling to his feet Will put a few yards between himself and the other man. Away from the supporting troops and on more even ground, he found space and time to see his man coming. De Guilbert collected himself, unable to believe how Will had escaped his attack.

This time Will took the initiative and attacked. The officer began to realise that he was not up against some stupid Irish rebel. Too late now, he wished that he'd left this one to his sergeant. He was up against a trained swordsman.

For moments the men fought gaining and giving ground. Will's anger had dissipated and so had his fear. For de Guilbert the doubts grew. His debauched lifestyle was catching up with him. Will, fully recovered from his illnesses and his beating, grew in stature. Calmer now, he looked for a way to disable the other man.

In the end it was de Guilbert, who decided it. He drew back. "Well now young sir," he panted, catching his breath, his sword arm limp at his side. "I clearly underestimated you." He held out his left hand to Will and approached him. "I'm sure we can talk about all this. There's clearly been some misunderstanding."

It was too laboured, too theatrical and Will noticed the tip of his sword surreptitiously rising. De Guilbert was standing about four yards distant, chest heaving, when he rushed Will. It was the same old dog, with the same old trick and this time he was slower than before. Will parried the blade and instinctively aimed for the throat. Defences beaten, there would be no chance of a riposte. His execution was perfect. The force of his own last desperate assault threw de Guilbert viciously onto the point of Will's blade. It penetrated deep into his throat. Harsh shiny steel sliced windpipe, nerves and arteries. It ground into spinal column and severed consciousness.

Death was instantaneous. De Guilbert sank to his knees and fell forwards, while Will, in shock and panic, frantically tried to withdraw his weapon and distance himself from the cavity in the man's throat, which was jetting blood up Will's sword arm.

All his anger and adrenalin had dissipated in an instant. Will muttered, "I never mean to… I just wanted…"

Lucky Eddie's luck had finally run out. The King of Ireland's reign was over and, with the eighth earl barely cold the de Guilbert family would be looking for the tenth. Shock waves would reverberate through every aristocratic estate in England and the Irish Ascendancy would quake. A response would be sure, quick and merciless.

As their blades clashed a spark flew into the dry brush and the flame had caught and burned and roared and started a conflagration, which would set all of Ireland aflame.

Just a few yards apart Sean watched blue English blood soak into rich dark Irish soil and he smiled. This had turned out better than even his wildest dreams.

"Game on," he whispered, "April the first, how appropriate, and just in time."

Chapter 20

Midford Co. Wexford
April 1st 1797

Sean was the first to react, as the shock of what they had just witnessed stunned everyone. He rushed past Will, pistol in each hand yelling, "Wake up ol' son or they'll be on you."

In seconds he was in front of Jeffreys. He raised the pistol in his left hand to the sergeant's face and pulled the trigger. The huge head exploded in a shower of brains, blood and skull bone. The report of the gun woke everyone from his paralysis and all hell broke loose.

Mablethorpe's horse reared up. He wrestled to control it and to keep his seat.

Will looked up from De Guilbert's body to the girl. She eyed him warily and tried to pull her torn dress together.

"You've nothing to fear from me. Cover yourself up and go."

She looked at her feet and mumbled, "Thank you, sir." Then suddenly looking up, "What about my sisters and brother?"

"What?"

"They have my sisters and the boy tied up is my brother."

With no plan in mind Will inadvertently blurted out, "Don't worry I'll save them." He turned towards the bedlam unfolding in front of him and did not notice the intensity of the gaze in those big green eyes.

Sean's gang kicked their mounts into life, aiming muskets and pistols.

As the troops lifted their weapons, Sean stepped back and fired the pistol in his right hand at the first to bring his weapon to bear. Seeing him discharge both pieces the men now roared and turned on him. Mr Collier's engineering did not let him down. With a little dance step back and a grimace Sean took the life from the next to raise his musket and the next. Time hung for a split second while the troops hesitated, trying to take it in.

Then it happened.

With screams of anguish the villagers were amongst them. With knives, stones, tools, chairs, anything that they could lay their hands upon, they tore into the outnumbered troops.

It was a massacre.

The screams and yells were too much for Mablethorpe's mount. It bolted and the captain could do nothing except cling on to the reins.

Sean and Will stepped away and watched in horror, as the men, women and children of Midford dismembered the troops of the Fifth Leicester.

Will was appalled at what he had instigated.

"Well that was fuckin' great," said Sean eventually. "Game show Al would be proud of you. You haven't gotten anyone pregnant, while me back was turned have you?"

Will was silent. He leaned wearily on his sword.

"You'd better hang on to that," said Sean, nodding at the weapon. "You seem to know what you're doin' with it. I'd only stick it in me foot or somethin'."

"I was runner up in the Public Schools' Epee Championship, you know." Will struggled for something to explain his actions.

"Glad you weren't runner up today," grinned Sean.

Will looked at Sean and said nothing for a moment. Then he added, "I just couldn't let it happen again. I just couldn't let them do that to innocent people."

They both fell silent again.

"You know who you've killed, don't you?"

Will shook his head.

"That was Edward de Guilbert, Earl or somethin' of Eastshire. Top drawer English aristocrat."

"Oh, bloody hell. I…I didn't mean to kill him. I just wanted to stop him molesting the girl. It all happened so quickly. I just…"

Will's words trailed off. He was fighting the urge to retch. They both watched, mesmerised, as the villagers stripped the troops of everything they possessed. Rings were cut from fingers, clothes stripped from backs, corpses disfigured. They were like jackals picking over the remains of a lion's kill.

Sean, noticing Will's distress snapped, "You didn't think it through did you? Oh, and by the way you could've gotten me killed and me mates an' all."

"I'm sorry Sean. This is a mess and it's all my fault."

"Too fuckin' right it is. You didn't give me a choice, but to wade in and kill a bunch of them, myself."

Will's face contorted with shock, grief and guilt and Sean realised that he better go no further. He had played the guilt card enough and needed to act quickly to prevent him breaking down.

"Will, I wouldn't lose too much sleep over it. What's done is done. We've more pressing matters to think about."

"What do you mean?"

"What do you think the army will do now, Will? Just say 'never mind, we'll put that one down to experience.' They'll go fuckin' ballistic. We've just massacred their finest *and* some bloody English earl. They'll be back by the morning with everything they can throw at us and burn this place to the ground."

"Christ, Sean. What are we going to do?"

"Well, I think the best thing I can do is to organise the boys and maybe try and get the rest of them up here."

"What can I do?"

"Gather up all the weapons you can. You know about all these things. There's bound to be loads more hidden away. Teach this lot to use them."

"But, but I can't just line them up for shooting practice."

Sean turned to Will and seized his arm aggressively. "See this bloody mess." He pointed to the bodies strewn around the street. "This'll be nothing compared to what it'll look like tomorrow. They'll be nothing left standing and they'll gang rape every livin' soul, men, women and children. Do you want to watch that little show? Oh, and by the way, don't you think that they'll single you out for somethin' special? What do you think they'll do to an Englishman who's turned traitor and murdered a member of the House of Lords?"

Will didn't answer.

"Well, that's settled it," continued Sean. "I'll hang around long enough to help you get started and I'll leave a couple o' the boys with you." He looked at Will, who still seemed mesmerised. "Come on Will you're gonna have to get your arse into gear!"

Before Will could reply an elderly man approached him. "Er, beggin' your pardon, Sir, have you finished wi' 'im?" he asked, indicating the body of de Guilbert, which had remained unmolested on the ground, where he had fallen.

Will looked at the man, bemused and shrugged.

Sean stepped in. "Just a minute. Will, take his sword. It's better than mine. Besides, it must be worth a bit."

Will nodded and stared at the bloody corpse.

"Christ Will, don't throw your guts up now, not in front o' them all. Here I'll get it." Sean picked up de Guilbert's blade, where he had dropped it and pulled the sheath and sash from under the dead man. He made the exchange for his own blade with Will. "Besides," he said quietly to himself with a little smile, "we want the world to know that you're the great hero who slayed the evil oppressor."

Sean indicated that the old man could take what he wanted from the body, dressed in all its finery. With a nod of acknowledgement the wizened old form turned and stood over de Gilbert, studying him, as if undecided what to take.

Then he pulled down his britches and urinated. The warm stream steamed and splashed over the colonel's tailored uniform. When he had finished, he gave Will a little nod of appreciation, pulled up his britches and ambled away up the street.

This seemed to announce open house for the rest of the villagers, who rifled through his pockets, but left him dressed, apart from his boots and tied him to the triangle, from which the young boy had recently been released.

"This won't do," said Sean, "we need to get crackin'." He grabbed the nearest person, a young man. "Who's your top man? Who's in charge here?"

The man hesitated. "I think you're meanin' Luke Kilpatrick, Sir." He said indicating a man in his thirties, about ten yards away.

"That'll do, thanks," said Sean patting the man on the back, " Oh, and do me a favour. Bring that over here, I think it belongs to him."

Sean nodded at Will and indicated de Guilbert's white stallion, which was being led back into the village. It too must have bolted, when the private minding it had been killed.

The man left to retrieve the horse, while Sean dragged Will over to meet Kilpatrick. He and Sean had already met, which made it easy to have him issue instructions to round up both weapons and volunteers for Will's platoon to defend the village from the forthcoming English attack. Sean explained that Will knew everything worth knowing about weapons, an explanation which was readily accepted, after Will's demonstration of swordsmanship.

Sean's plan worked well in focusing Will's mind on something other than the recent horrors. Will soon had a small army of volunteers, eager to help their new hero. Muskets and ammunition had been stripped from the dead soldiers and more guns and pikes were produced, as if by magic. The adulation was very flattering and Will found it easy to conjure up enthusiasm in himself and those around him for the newfound task. From nowhere Owen reappeared and fought his way through the throng surrounding Will.

"What have you been doin'?" the young lad enquired, eyes agog.

Before Will could answer a chorus of voices interrupted with versions of recent events. To Will's amazement the tale he was hearing already bore scant relation to the truth. This was already a folk legend and he was the epicentre of it.

"Sounds like I've missed all the fun. It's good to see you again, Will."

"It's good to see you too, Owen," replied Will and he meant it. "It's not the same, when you're not around."

"Make the most of me, Will. I can't hang around forever."

On the southern side of the village was an open field, which swept down to an embankment at the bottom. Anybody wandering into the copse behind it could easily be shot, once they started practising with the muskets. Oh well, thought Will, it was not ideal but the noise will frighten them off. The slight down slope would serve his purposes well in one respect; it would train them to aim low. The inaccuracy of these unrifled weapons, together with the recoil from them in inexperienced hands made it very easy to fire well over the heads of the intended targets.

Sean had stayed behind in the village centre, leaving Will and Owen to the job of forming and training the defence force.

"I'll catch up with you in a while, before I go. I've some things to sort out. I'll bring a couple of the boys to help you out."

Willing hands set up targets at the bottom of the field. It was a gruesome sight. Salvaged bits of the soldiers' uniforms were stuffed with straw and anything that could be found. While these were mounted on poles, Will had all the weapons brought to him for inspection. One by one he checked that the firing mechanisms worked and that the barrels were clean and unblocked. As he put some of the muskets to one side for further maintenance, Owen watched attentively. Will noticed that he had another audience. The young woman, he had rescued, together with her sisters and brother had gathered about thirty yards away, higher up the field and they were all watching Will attentively. He looked up from his work and smiled.

The woman immediately looked down to avoid eye contact. Will might have felt disappointed, except that he was sure there was a hint of a blush, before her face disappeared under her beautiful hair. My God, how does she look like that? thought Will, as he looked around at the other villagers in the field, dirty clothes and faces, many ugly and disfigured. For Will it was as though there was nobody else in the field except him and her. The boy and the middle sister grinned and the youngest girl waved enthusiastically until her eldest sibling tugged at her arm to stop her.

Will needed to select his platoon and impose some kind of order on what was fast becoming a carnival outing. It would wait a little longer.

"Don't let anyone touch these," he instructed Owen and walked towards the little family party. His action prompted a frenzy of giggles and elbowing between the girls.

"How are you? Not hurt I trust?"

Like a comedy act the two younger girls turned towards the eldest, while the boy piped up, "I'm fine now thanks."

The young girls collapsed into giggles again. "Not you Kevin. He's asking Mary."

"How was I to know?" muttered Kevin and kicked the ground.

Mary, as Will now knew her to be called, could not avoid his gaze any longer. Her face was red with embarrassment, but that was not what took Will's breath away. Her eyes met his gaze and Will's throat tightened.

"I, I…" stammered Will and the girls convulsed with giggles yet again.

It was Mary who came to his rescue. Her dress had been hastily repaired. "I'm fine thank you, Sir. My family and I will always be in your debt."

"Oooh!" exclaimed the youngest girl at her sister's well-spoken words and flapped her hand around, as if fanning her face.

In the aftermath of the duel Will had not noticed. Now he was entranced by her soft accent. It was not broad like the others but gentle, although he suspected that she had modified it for his benefit.

A sharp look from Mary silenced her sister.

She continued, "I trust you were not injured in your encounter?"

Will cleared his throat, as Mary scowled her sisters into silence. "No. I'm fine actually. I was pleased to be of assistance. It was very fortunate that we arrived when we did."

Will's initial confidence was collapsing and he felt that he was embarrassing her. "I should be attending to the weapons training."

He turned to go.

"Um, er, can I assist you in any way? Perhaps I could help you choose the best people to shoot the guns?" Another scowl silenced the irrepressible sisters.

"Er, that would be very helpful," replied Will. "Shouldn't we be introduced?"

"Oh, of course. My name is Mary O'Neill."

She held out her hand in such a way that Will was not sure whether he was meant to kiss it or shake it. He took it, gave a little bow and their eyes met again and locked far too long to go unnoticed by the precocious younger girls.

Reluctantly Will broke the moment and responded. "I am Will Peters. I have travelled a long way to be here."

"And I suppose I'd better introduce my brother and sisters or they'll only introduce themselves." She smiled and turned to them. "This is Annie. She is sixteen."

"I'm nearly seventeen," protested Annie and did a little bob.

"This is Kevin. He's fifteen and this is Liza, who is…"

"Older than yer think!" interrupted the youngest. She pushed past her sister and seized Will's hand, shaking it vigorously.

"Are your mother and father around?" enquired Will.

"Our mother passed away a year gone by. Our father, well he was taken by the English troops and they well…" Her eyes filled up. "We don't rightly know what happened to him." Mary looked away.

"I'm very sorry to hear that," hastened Will. "Well, you seem to be doing a fine job looking after them all."

She beamed with pleasure. "Do yer think so?"

"Without a doubt. Now do you want to come and help?"

Will led Mary to one side and directed the others towards Owen.

"How many do yer want?" asked Mary indicating the melee in front of them.

"Well, I've about forty muskets but around ten of them are damaged or don't look like they're new enough to use. Let's see if we can choose thirty, maybe thirty-two. Will it be all men or will any of the women join in?"

Mary shot Will a look of amazement, "You'd consider a woman?"

Will wondered if he had made a huge gaff, then emboldened, continued, "Naturally, there's no reason, why a woman can't shoot as well as a man, if she's trained properly."

"I think it's mainly men, who will help, but can I learn to shoot?"

Their eyes met again.

"Of course you can," he said.

She beamed again and Will decided that he could spend the rest of his life trying to make her smile at him like that.

Mary stood beside Will and looked down the slope at the crowd, who were milling around, talking excitedly.

"Who do you suggest?" enquired Will.

She pointed to a group of four young men talking together and jostling each other good-naturedly. "The O'Driscoll boys are a good family. Pick them to start. And Old Pat; he's a bit of an old rogue, but he'll stand by you. And young Rory there; he's my cousin and as brave as they come."

Will pointed to a stocky man in his early thirties. "What about him? He looks strong."

She shook her head. "That's Seamus Donnelly. He talks tough and the others, the weaker ones, will follow him, but he's a bully and a coward. When the English come he'll run and he might take the others with him. You don't want the likes of him."

"I don't know what I'd have done without you, Mary." It was the first time he had addressed her by her name. They both smiled.

"It is the very least I can do," she hesitated, "Will."

They smiled again. No words were spoken. An understanding passed silently between the man and the woman, born two hundred years apart. Their lives had become linked in a way that neither could have dreamed possible. What both did understand was that, quietly, their lives had changed forever.

Reluctantly Will called the crowd together. With Mary at his side he pointed to the chosen few and Mary called out their names. Unnoticed by either of them, Owen looked on, an old and tired smile on his face.

They picked thirty-eight volunteers and issued them each with a weapon. Will explained that only thirty of the weapons were in working order, but at least they would have some extra people trained up. To replace the dead, he thought grimly, but he kept that bit to himself. He did not dwell on that and threw himself into the training. First he showed them how the musket worked and lectured them on the basics of safety. Never point the weapon at anyone, whether or not it was loaded. Always ram the charge and the ball down the barrel before priming the pan, for obvious reasons. He also explained how important it was to ensure that the ramrod was removed from the barrel. They laughed, but he knew that, in the heat of a battle many a soldier had fired a ramrod harmlessly at the enemy, instead of a musket ball. Then he explained that the recoil on the weapons was sufficient to break a collarbone, if it wasn't held tight into the shoulder. Finally he loaded a musket and fired it down the field to let them become used to the noise.

Without powder or shot, he then had them miming the loading sequence, as Sean strode down the slope, accompanied by Pat, Rikki and Michael, whom Will had first met that morning at the inn outside Wexford. Will smiled to greet them. Was it only a few hours since that encounter? So much had happened in those few hours.

Will indicated the pantomime, which was playing out in the field. Dropped muskets, jammed ramrods and people tumbling into each other. "Lads, lend a hand to that lot a minute, while I talk to Will."

Sean put his arm around Will and they walked a few metres away to be out of earshot. "How's it goin'?"

Will pulled a face. "It'll take some time, but they'll get there. They're a pretty good bunch." He couldn't stop himself grinning. "I had a bit of help picking the best ones." He nodded towards Mary, who was shouting at her cousin for nearly putting her eye out with his ramrod.

"I think you've a bit of a fan club there, Will," said Sean.

Will could feel himself blushing. "I think she likes me."

"You think she likes you?!" Sean burst out laughing. "Oh Will Peters, I've met some cases in my time, but you take the rosette at the County Show. Have you any idea what you've done for her? Let's just put to one side the fact that you saved her from the classic fate worse than death and likely her sisters too. She's probably spent her entire life barely straying more than a mile from here and never seen a half decent fella. The most excitin' thing ter happen in this place was probably when Mother O'Reilly's sow had a litter. Half the blokes around here are either old, married or interbred so long they're barmy. I bet she'll have been considerin' marrying some dirty old pervert, just to put a meal on the table for her and her family. And then suddenly this good lookin' bloody hero comes along and is prepared to die for her."

Sean paused for breath. "And what did you do, after you'd saved her? Most fellas around here would've seized their reward and raped her themselves. What do you do? You act like Prince Charming. Christ, ol' son, if you don't watch out, you'll never get rid o' that one. She'll follow you to your grave. Mind you, if you don't sort that lot out, that mightn't be too long."

Will, amazed at Sean's tirade, couldn't help smiling at the image of himself as the hero. "I've told you. I only did what I had to. I wasn't going to stand by and let that happen."

"I know, I know, but you'd better train this lot up well or we'll all be dead in the morning. I'm going ter leave Rikki and Pat with you. They know what they're doing, if you get any trouble and they can help with training some lads up. Why don't you get them teachin' another group to use the pikes, while you work with the muskets. I'm goin' back to Wexford with Michael. I'll be back by dawn with some more men and some more weapons."

Will had a moment of panic at the thought of his friend's departure and it showed on his face.

"Don't worry Will, I won't leave you to face the music alone. I will be back. Now whip those boys inter shape."

With a reassuring slap on the back, Sean was on his way. He shouted to Michael and waved to the other two. Will watched the two walk back up the rest of the slope. Without turning, Sean and Michael walked up the lane and were gone. Will fought off a wave of loneliness and, putting a determined smile on his face, returned to his duties.

It was another hour, before Will felt confident enough to let them fire the muskets. He divided them into three groups of just over a dozen, the first under his supervision and the other two under the watchful eyes of Pat and Rikki, who seemed more than capable of the task. He ensured that Mary was in his group and she turned out to be the most capable of them all. Nonetheless by the end of the afternoon, they were all reasonably competent and he decided to risk forming them into a platoon of three ranks of ten, using all the working muskets. The front rank fired first then stepped back between the other two ranks to reload and give the second rank free line of fire. The second rank, now at the front, repeated the actions of the first rank, finally giving the third rank the chance to fire.

They repeated the exercise three times until it ran smoothly and Rikki and Michael came over to Will afterwards to congratulate him. Mary's eyes shone with pride at her own achievements and at the cheers, which they gave Will at the end. Momentarily elated, Will soon started to worry if they would be able to do this, when an enemy was coming down on them. Tomorrow would bring him his answer.

In the meantime, the muskets had to be cleaned and Will insisted that they were all kept together in one place. He didn't want them to go missing, when they would be needed in the morning. Mary volunteered her cottage as a temporary arsenal and they all took their weapons and the powder and musket balls to her dwelling. Gradually they dispersed and Rikki and Pat agreed to organise a group of sentries and come back to Will to confirm the arrangements.

Will suddenly found himself alone with Mary outside a tiny little cottage, quite similar to the one where he and Owen had hidden. Even the rest of the family had left them for the moment.

"You must stay here tonight Will," she said. "We haven't much room, but I'm sure that we can squeeze you in."

Will could feel his ears going red. "I don't want to impose upon you."

"Not at all," she interrupted. "And besides," she flashed a half smile at him, her eyes wide, "I'd feel so much safer, if you were close by."

She moved close and stroked his arm and Will hoped that she could not see the effect that she was having on him. He wanted to kiss her, but Owen popped up at that moment. He really did have an uncanny ability to appear and disappear.

"You'll be pleased to hear that I've found a place to stay."

Was that sarcasm in Owen's voice? Will was not sure. He felt slightly guilty, for after his genuine words of affection to Owen, he had completely forgotten all about him, distracted as he was with Mary.

"That's great Owen. I think that I'm stopping here tonight. Are they looking after you?"

"Oh to be sure they are," chirped Owen and added with a cheeky little grin, "Mind not as well as you'll be looked after, I'll wager."

Will could not look at Mary. He preoccupied himself with impressing on Owen the importance of being ready early in the morning.

As Owen departed, Mary's family returned and their chance to be alone was gone. Within moments Rikki and Pat arrived and Will was forced to dismiss any romantic thoughts from his mind. Mary and her sisters went inside to prepare the evening meal and Will set off with the two men to inspect the village's defences and discuss tactics for the morning.

The village of Midford lies on a slight rise above the damp surrounding countryside. It is built along one main street, which runs almost due east west. Will and Sean had come from the southeast and the Wexford road turns onto the eastern end of the main street. The Fifth Leicester was garrisoned a few miles to the north. The road along which they had arrived joined this same route in from the east.

"They'll come along this road in the morning," advised Pat.

"For sure, it'll be this way. It's the obvious route in from the barracks. They'll just come in like we did, this morning,'" concurred Rikki.

Will said nothing. They had walked out of the village to the east to re-examine their route into the village. He looked across the fields to the north.

Eventually Will said, "I want to ride out to the north and come in the way they will. We must be quick, it'll be dark soon."

Nonplussed and with a few rumblings of impatience, Rikki and Pat concurred and they returned to the village Smithy, where the horses were stabled. Will decided that he was not up to riding De Guilbert's white charger and took the horse he had arrived on. They urged the horses back east up the road to where it intersected south to Wexford or north towards their enemy. Will reined in his mount and turned to look back up the road.

It was narrow, with a ditch on the south side and an earth bank to the north. To Will's eye you would struggle to drive anything more than a four-wheel drive vehicle down it. He tried to think like an eighteenth century soldier. It would only be possible to march five or at most six abreast down it. With numerical superiority only a fool would bring his troops in this way. True they had come in that way this morning, but then they were not expecting any opposition. He turned and rode north.

About half a mile further the road broadened out and, apart from a very narrow ditch, it was easy to enter a clear open field, which sloped down and then gently up towards the north side of the village. Astride his mount, even in the fading light, Will could see that fifty abreast could march on the village from here. A force of several hundred could be deployed effectively. Oh God, thought Will, if they bring that many we'll all die. He shivered as the cold night closed in.

"Come on," he called to the others, as he spurred his horse into life. "We can just about make it back this way if we go now."

Will wondered if he'd made a mistake in testing his riding skills across the open ground in poor light. Fortunately his horse was steady and the route yielded one more piece of vital information. With wet ground to the left and rocks and thick undergrowth to the right, he hadn't realised from the road that an approach this way narrowed for the only access to the village from this side. The soldiers would be forced to pass a stone barn, where riflemen could be deployed. If only he had some! Muskets would have to do. Then the enemy would turn slightly to their left and come into a gap about ten metres wide between the wall that ran from the barn and a cottage; Mary's cottage. Once through this gap they could spread out and the village would be theirs.

This was the place to make a stand.

From the road it looked more open. In fact it was a trap and they would be exposed to fire from three sides. Would they spot this and come up the road as Pat and Rikki reckoned? If they did Will would have minutes to reorganise his troops. With experienced soldiers it would be possible, but with these raw recruits he would have no chance. He had better decide. He couldn't wait till the English were advancing.

"I'd like to look again in the morning," he said half to himself and partly to his two companions.

"They'll come up the road," was all Pat said and Rikki nodded.

The group fell silent as they dismounted and handed over their horses for the night. The village was practically deserted as many had decided that it was safer to sleep in the fields and ditches.

Will walked silently and alone up the dark unlit street to the little cottage, which could well be the centre of the fighting in the morning. He hoped that Sean would bring an army with him. Mostly he hoped that Sean would return.

His mind absorbed in the tactics of the morning, Will was not prepared for what greeted him, when he entered Mary's cottage. Somehow he thought from her well kempt appearance that Mary's cottage would be better than the hovel he and Owen had visited. It was not.

He had difficulty in not letting his face reveal his feelings.

It was virtually dark in the dwelling, tiny windows letting none of the remnants of twilight through. Two candles mercifully revealed little of the interior. It was the smell that hit Will, an animal smell, like a barn.

As his eyes became accustomed to the gloom they searched for furniture. Apart from a table, six stools, and an old wooden armchair, there was none. A more pleasant aroma came from a pot held over a hearth by a metal contraption.

Stairs, not much more than a ladder, lead up into the gloom. Will did not need halogen lighting to know that there would be little more than straw up there.

What Will expected to happen that evening in the little cottage, he was not quite sure. What had transpired was a series of embarrassments, interspersed with moments of complete panic, when he considered what was likely to happen in the morning. It was made worse because they all seemed to have a blind faith in him. They expected him to conjure up some extraordinary victory over an enemy, which would undoubtedly outnumber them and be much better equipped and trained.

The girls continued to giggle and nudge each other as he chased a solitary piece of meat around a muddy pond of vegetables in a wooden bowl. Not daring to make eye contact with Mary in front of them, his gaze rested on these innocent children. Thoughts of the morning crept into his tired mind and, cold though it was in the cottage, he started to sweat. Fighting the nausea building in his stomach, he struggled to force the meal down, while the others squabbled over the few scraps remaining, after Mary had stretched their paltry meal to provide for him.

Amongst all this mess was one miracle, Mary. She spoke openly and frankly about everything, including the inadequate sleeping arrangements. They all slept in one room upstairs; the girls at one end the boy at the other. Where did he want to sleep? Ignoring the snorts from the girls, he opted for the chair downstairs. She seemed to understand his embarrassment. Instead of disparaging him for it, she seemed flattered, almost honoured that he should feel that way. Quick stolen glances were always rewarded with a smile, before she too averted her gaze. He felt like a kid on his first date, invited to tea with the parents, only, bizarrely, it was he and Mary who were playing the role of parents, embarrassed in front of the children.

Finally he managed to converse with her alone outside the cottage. Understanding his need to talk to her, she insisted that the others clear up.

"Tomorrow…" Will started.

"I know, I know. We don't have much hope do we?" she interrupted.

"Well it all depends on how many they send. It might not be too bad," Will lied badly.

"You don't have to pretend, Will, not to me. For the younger ones we must be brave. It won't help if they're terrified."

Will nodded. "I feel like it's my fault. If I hadn't killed De Guilbert, you know the colonel…"

She put her hand to his mouth, "…my brother would be dead and I, well you know… So don't you go blaming yourself." She sighed. "I'm sure there are some that will, but then some always do. It's always someone else's fault, someone else's responsibility. They were quite happy to sit back and let those English bastards do that to us. They're all bastards, those English." She put her hand to her own mouth. "I didn't mean you…"

Will looked at her shocked expression and laughed aloud. She joined him and then they kissed.

After that there seemed nothing else to say. They sat together on a stone bench and looked out into the damp darkness to where the army would probably come in about eight hours and kill them both.

The noise of squabbling inside the cottage eventually forced them inside.

Then, for Will, the night was endless and, without a watch or any means of telling the time, he hung in limbo, too tired to rise, too scared and cold to sleep. He was petrified that he would drift off just before dawn and awake to an English bayonet in his stomach. Around and around his head the same thoughts spun. Would they come? How many? Would his new recruits fight or, under fire, run away? Could he face an enemy or would his nerve crack? Would Sean return and with how many? And in the morning he must make a decision. Where to fight? On the road or by the cottage? It was his decision and he dare not get it wrong.

As the cold night crawled by he prayed for daylight to release him from this purgatory, but dreaded what the dawn would bring.

Chapter 21

Near Midford Co. Wexford
April 2nd 1797

Captain Mablethorpe had barely gained control of his mount when he reached the intersection, which Will was to study later that day. Shaking hands pulled up on the reins. Silence, but for the panting of his horse and the thumping of his heart, he strained to see the village.

The colonel was dead; he'd seen that, but what of the rest of his men? Yes, *his* men. They were his men now. He should find out. To what purpose, if he too was killed? His bright uniform would soon be spotted. It was easy to convince himself that returning safe to the barracks, to plan his revenge, was the responsible course.

Arriving well before Lieutenant Davies, he was received in silence. Nobody dared question him. He hurried to his quarters. An hour later he heard shouts and cheers. The men had returned in high spirits.

Davies' voice accompanied a knock on his door.

"Captain Mablethorpe? Sir?"

"Come in *Lieutenant*." Mablethorpe's words, barely steady, emphasised his subordinate's rank.

"Where is everyone? What happened? For God's sake, why have you come back alone… er, Sir?" Davies pulled up just short of insubordination.

"I think that you had better sit down, Davies. Something terrible has happened. It's a miracle I escaped."

Davies took the seat he was offered and eyed his captain suspiciously. Mablethorpe was his senior, but younger and inexperienced. He hated these young men from wealthy families. They were a liability and he always prayed they'd be killed, before they caused the death of too many good men.

"What happened, *Sir*?" Davies spat out the words.

The events of the day tumbled from Mablethorpe's nervous lips.

For a moment Davies struggled to comprehend, his mind reverberating. "I can't believe it," he exclaimed. "How many of them were there? And who was this man, this skilful swordsman? For Chrissake, *Sir,* they were a bunch of unarmed peasants. What were *you* doing when all this took place?"

There it was again that note of sarcasm.

"It was that bloody horse they put me on. It bolted." He could feel a schoolboy whine creeping into his voice. "I don't know, damn it, man. They were a local rebel gang, a few dozen of them," lied Mablethorpe, reluctant to admit how few had destroyed them. Soon the whisper of cowardice would work its insidious passage amongst the men. He had to prove himself quickly. Worse was to come.

"Didn't you owe the colonel money?" sneered Davies. He had gone too far now, but it was too late.

Mablethorpe turned puce. "How dare you? Damn you Davies, I'll have you reduced to the ranks! No family, no breeding, you're not fit to be an officer. Just remember I'm in charge now."

"That's another way you have profited from the colonel's death," Davies mumbled beneath his breath.

"What's that? What's that you say?" Mablethorpe was shaking. "You will do well to remember who is the senior officer here."

He realised that he had better act quickly or he was lost. "You *will* do as I say. Now go! Muster the men on the parade ground. I will address them and give my orders."

As Davies departed, Mablethorpe collapsed. "What am I to do? I am ruined," he sobbed. An act of revenge was needed. He'd burn that damn village to the ground. That morning he had found the thought abhorrent. Now it was different. His honour, his career, and damn it, his whole life was at stake.

His speech to the men convinced nobody, least of all himself. Only one course of action remained, to mount an attack and quickly.

"As your acting commanding officer…" Mablethorpe summoned every last ounce of dignity and raised his voice to be heard over the rumble of dissension, "…I shall personally lead you tomorrow at dawn to show these barbarians that they will rue the day that they inflicted this atrocity on our proud regiment."

It sounded ponderous. Nonetheless some of the troops managed a feeble cheer at the prospect of committing God alone knew what atrocities on the villagers. Others, including Lieutenant Davies, seemed far less enthusiastic. Corporal O'Connell looked pale.

That night Mablethorpe dined alone. Although a regiment in name, their numbers were short. Davies knew that they needed reinforcements, but without an invitation to join his superior he dared not approach him again.

All night O'Connell thrashed around in search of a way to redirect Mablethorpe's plans.

None of them slept easily.

Will woke to a sharp jab in the ribs from the barrel of a rifle. He jumped out of the old chair and winced with pain at the stiffness in his neck and back.

"That's what we like to see, a man who can sleep soundly on the eve of a battle. I'm proud of you!" boomed Sean, as he pulled his bleary eyed friend to his feet.

"Christ Sean, you scared the bloody life out of me," moaned Will. "I'm glad to see you, though. How many have you brought?"

Sean pulled a face. "It's always better to have quality than quantity and I've brought five of the finest."

"Five! Five! Christ Sean, is that all?"

"What's all this noise? I'll not have blaspheming under my roof." Mary appeared at the top of the stairs and shot a fierce look at Will. Then with a forgiving smile she added, "Who wants a hot drink?"

Despite his state of agitation Will wondered what she'd make and if he could hold it down. "Thank you Mary. That would be very nice."

As she went out to the back to draw some water, Will turned to Sean again. "What time is it? Is it nearly dawn?"

"I reckon that we've about an hour, maybe two, till they get here." Sean took a good look at Will, now he was standing. "You look like shit. Go an' clean yourself up and we'll discuss our plans in a minute."

About ten minutes later Will, Sean and Mary, together with Sean's three companions from the previous day, gathered around the cottage table. Mary had dispatched the children to wake up the members of Will's platoon, as it now seemed to be called.

"You've seen the lie of the land, Will. What are your thoughts?" Sean opened the discussion.

They all turned to Will, who steeled himself to make a decision.

"I've been thinking about what you both said overnight," he nodded to Pat and Rikki. "You could be right, but on balance I still think they'll cut away from the road. They must have more than fifty, probably nearer one hundred?" he looked around the table for a reaction to his assessment and received a number of shrugs.

"Not more surely?" Will tried to keep the fear out of his voice.

"We reckon about eighty to a hundred, don't we lads?" said Sean and received the same shrugs.

"Alright. With those numbers they'll come across the field from the road and hit the village right here."

Mary started as Will indicated her own home around them. "Here?"

Pat and Rikki started to interrupt, until Sean held up his hands. "What makes you so sure, Will?"

"Why would you bring a hundred troops into a narrow road, where they can't form up and where they can be attacked from between the buildings?"

"But they'll have to squeeze between the buildings here," interjected Pat.

"I know that," argued Will. "They'll burn this place first to be sure nobody's at their backs and…"

Mary's eyes widened in terror.

Rikki tried to interrupt. "That doesn't make sense, Will…"

Sean clapped his hands. "That's enough. We've no more time to debate this. It's Will's fight." He turned to Will. "It's your call."

"We stand here by the cottage. What are you going to do Sean?"

Sean grinned. "Get a look at this baby." He stood up and reached behind him for a rifle. It was a work of art, ornately decorated on the stock and barrel. "This is the best of them, but we've a couple more. I wanted to get my hands on a Baker rifle, but nobody seems to have them over here. If they're coming across the field, me and Pat and Michael can take 'em out from the roof of the barn."

Will looked at Sean, he could feel his pulse racing, his anger rising. This was not a game. It was all very well for Sean to sit up on the roof at rifle range and let the rest of them fight at close quarters and then… No, these doubts were ridiculous, Will chided himself.

"Of course you couldn't get a bloody Baker, they won't bring in Bakers for three years yet," he blurted out. Will tried to control his emotions and added hastily, "Are you really going to sit on a straw roof and fire a flintlock rifle?"

"What do you mean?"

"C'mon Sean, a few sparks and you'll burn the bloody place down yourself."

"Oh it'll be fine. Them roofs are all old and damp and half of 'em are turfs and not straw. Don't look so worried.

We'll not be far away and we can do loads of damage before they even get close. They won't be expectin' that."

Will couldn't think of a counter argument, so instead he asked, "Where did you get them anyway?"

Sean looked rather shifty. "Er, well we paid a wee visit on one o' the local squires and, er, how shall I put it? – Persuaded him to loan them to us."

Will eyed Sean suspiciously. Had he been riding around with some rebel band, which slashed the legs of livestock and raided the houses of the landed gentry? Even two hundred years later the debate still raged. Did the Protestant landowners deserve it or were the brutal reprisals justified? This was not the time to fall out with Sean. Will needed to act.

"Alright, Sean, you Pat and Michael get yourselves sorted out on the roofs with good firing positions. Rikki, you and me will walk the field again. Are you with me now?"

To Will's relief Rikki nodded.

"Good," continued Will and looked up to see a friendly face. "Hello Owen, It's good to see you. Will you help us? We want to walk the route that we expect the army to take and we can place some rocks at various distances to show us how far away they are, as they come at us."

Owen responded with enthusiastic nods. As the two men and the boy left the cottage Mary offered to help round up all their troops and they agreed to meet back by the cottage in thirty minutes. Will kept glancing at the band on his wrist, forgetting that it was not a watch. The thought slipped into his head again. If it all went wrong in the next couple of hours, would the wristband suddenly work and whisk him away from here and back to the safety of Boroughbridge? He doubted it, but then, could he bring himself to run out on these people and, especially, Mary and her family?

He must focus he reprimanded himself and, while he paced the distance from the back of the cottage into the field, he had Owen and Rikki collect and place little piles of rocks at key intervals.

"We'll start here at about thirty yards," he called out, stopping for the others to come to him. "From around here they'll probably charge at us." He wasn't sure about that, but tried to sound confident. "From here we'll mark at every ten yards, up to one hundred. Beyond one hundred, we'll be wasting our time with muskets. Whatever happens we must not fire before they reach here or we'll just waste ammunition."

For the riflemen's benefit he paced to one hundred and fifty and two hundred yards. It would be an approximation for Sean and his men on the roofs, but it might help. He had Owen gather up light coloured stones and showed him how to put them in piles as markers. Looking back towards Sean he realised that it was still too dark for them to appreciate his efforts. He prayed that Sean had learned how to use that damn rifle.

Will returned to the two hundred marker. Beyond this even the rifles would be of little use. If only he had some modern weapons. It was a ridiculous thought. An army would never march in formation against modern weapons. Millions paid with their lives before the Generals of the First World War learned that lesson. Why hadn't they studied the American Civil War more closely? As these thoughts played through his mind Will felt older and wiser and his confidence grew. There was no point in going further. He turned and counted the time back to their line of defence, marching at the pace the drummer boys would drive the troops forward.

As he approached the cottage the first glimmer of dawn crept over the Eastern horizon and Will shuddered, his newfound confidence quick to evaporate in the cold, damp air. He fought hard against the temptation to run the last few yards. Then, as the light improved, it struck him, where the hell were all his troops? Oh God, what if they were still hiding in ditches and fields dotted around the countryside?

He rushed past the cottage and out onto the street, forgetting Rikki and Owen, behind him. His relief to see them gathering on the road was short-lived. It was a shambles. They all started to shout at once.

"I've left me musket at the cottage, shall I go an' get it?"

"You were meant to leave it at Mary's cottage! Yes, yes go quickly!"

"I was havin a bit o' a practice an I seem to 'ave got the ramrod stuck…"

"Rikki, Rikki, help him with this."

"I don't want me son to fight with you…"

"Mary, Mary, can you talk to her?"

The light was growing steadily and with it the panic in Will's gut.

A shout went up from the rooftop behind him. "I can see them! They're here! They're here!"

Christ not yet! Will's mind raced. Which direction? They were already on the road. Should he stop here or move his troops behind the cottage? He'd better look. He turned back and started to run around the cottage to see for himself. No, no time. He stopped and Rikki, who was close behind, ran into his back.

"For Christ sake, what are you doin'?"

Before Will could reply another shout went up. It was Sean. "They've left the road. They're in the field."

He'd guessed right. No time to be smug, he pushed Rikki to one side and ran back to the villagers. Even the warning shouts hadn't stirred them.

"What are you playing at? They're coming, they're coming," screamed Will.

As soon as the words left his mouth, he knew he'd made a fatal mistake. The effect of his outburst was immediate and disastrous. They all leapt up, colliding with each other, as they tried to seize their weapons, and fell over in a muddle of curses and clattering muskets. One went off, frightening everyone and narrowly missing young Patrick

Murphy, who seemed to go into a state of shock. Paralysed with fear, nobody could make him pick up his own musket and join the others.

Driven by desperation Will managed to herd them into the field behind the yard wall. Persuading them to form three ranks was beyond him. Come the moment for action, all of them had forgotten their training. Panic was in his throat. He was screaming again.

"For God's sake form up, they'll be on us in minutes."

He scowled at old Davie O'Connell, whose musket had gone off, "Can't you get that damn thing loaded again?"

His voice cracking, Will despaired. If he'd lost control of himself, how on earth would he control the others?

Shouts rang out as the enemy formed up.

In the grip of terror, Will knew he was about to fall apart. Damn it, he should have been tougher and instilled some discipline.

"Will," Mary's voice was calm in his ear.

He turned to her. "What's the matter with them?" he wailed. "Don't they realise we'll all be dead in minutes, if they don't get their act together."

"Will, I don't know about acting." She squeezed his arm. "But I do know *them*. They're not like you and Sean. They're frightened. There's no good in shouting at them. They need to be reassured. Let me try."

Before Will could protest, Mary was on an upturned bucket clapping her hands. To his amazement she had their attention instantly, all except Davie O'Connell, whose hands were shaking so much that he was spilling powder over his torn britches.

"Davie don't you go worrying about that. No harm was done and we probably gave the English a fright." He gave a nervous laugh. She turned to a tall fair-headed boy with no shoes.

"Dermot you're loaded aren't you?" The fourteen-year-old lad nodded. Youngest of eight and always supervised, he was having the time of his life, out on his own and playing with guns.

"Help Davie load his musket. He'll be fine when he's loaded. The rest of you need to form up in your three lines… I mean ranks," she added with an embarrassed glance at Will.

Mablethorpe bellowed and, like a great ocean liner, the body of men was set in motion.

Amazed, Will felt resentful at how quickly she had calmed them and taken control. He glanced towards the field. To his horror he saw that the soldiers were already formed into ranks and advancing. They couldn't be more than a quarter of a mile away. How many? - Around a hundred? Will's stomach churned. Oh God, don't let him be sick.

"Mary, hurry, hurry. They're coming." Will tried to sound calm.

Though gathered and armed, they were not lined up. Mary caught the look of despair on Will's face. She smiled reassuringly. "Will, draw that sword so everyone can see it and stand at the front there." She pointed.

The enemy ship gathered speed.

Like a child, told to play linesman, as consolation for not making the team, Will walked forward, drew his sword and had the presence of mind to check his Collier. He, at least would be ready. He looked up at Mary for approval. She was gesticulating madly. Why didn't she get them ready?

"Not there Will. You'll be in the…" she struggled for the right words, "line of fire?"

Will blushed, his misery complete. Standing between the villagers and the approaching army, he would surely be the first casualty of the battle, killed by his own troops! He moved to one side, closer to the cottage wall.

The villagers were yet to form ranks.

O'Connell dressed his lines straighter and further increased the pace.

"Right, who's in the front line?" asked Mary.

Nobody raised a hand in reply. Will could not believe what he was seeing. Had nobody remembered a thing from yesterday?

At three hundred yards the drummer boys set to work. They gave it their all. The beat was fast.

It sent a chill through Will's soul.

Rikki had gathered a group of about forty men and boys with pikes, wicked looking steels blades with hooks on long poles. Christ, he'd forgotten about them too!

"Well never mind," Mary said in a steady voice. "I want you ten," she pointed, "to come to the front and you, yes you too, Davie and you Laura to step in there…"

The first rays of sunlight reflected off fifteen-inch English bayonets.

Slowly the group settled into some semblance of order. One middle-aged man at the back was clearly thinking about dropping his weapon and running.

"And where do you think you're going Daniel O'Shaunessey? You'd better turn around like the rest or I might tell your wife what you've been up to."

A titter ran around the group and a shamefaced Daniel O'Shaunessey took his place again.

The enemy passed the two hundred yard marker rocks and a hundred mouths roared in time with the drumbeat. The officer on the large horse urged them on.

"And as for you young Liam," she was addressing a young boy close to tears, "just think how proud your mother'll be when I tell her how brave you are."

The boy smiled weakly and stood more upright.

Shots rang out from the rooftop and Will stared frantically at the line of advancing troops. None fell.

He turned and looked at his own troops. Not one of them had a musket raised. "For Chrissake get on with it, Mary"

"There'll be no cause for blaspheming, Will Peters," she chided him.

"Sorry," Will muttered. Taking a deep breath he added, "They'll have to come through me to get to you."

Mary's face lit up with pride and instantly Will knew that he would never use the wristband.

With renewed vigour she turned to her platoon. "Front rank I will want you to fire first. Only the front rank now, I don't want anyone to get hurt."

Hurt? Even Will had to smile. Better to die like this than die of boredom in an Oxford college.

The enemy passed the one hundred and fifty yard marker.

Three more shots rang out, crack, crack…crack.

The ball from Sean's rifle flicked the ear of Mablethorpe's horse, causing it to rear up. No matter, the round piece of metal, coated in scraps of powder and leather, continued its path into the captain's stomach, with such force it took him out of the saddle. Soon the pro tem commander of the Fifth Leicester would pray to every living God to let him die.

The other two shots found their targets. Luckier than their captain both drummer boys died instantly and the beat with them. Thank God for that, thought Will.

The enemy slowed, as it passed the one hundred yard marker.

Still Mary wasn't ready. "Now mind that you pull your muskets into your shoulders properly, just like Will showed you."

His name on the lips of an eighteenth century woman, how strange it sounded.

Less than one hundred yards, light improving, and he could see their faces clearly. They were just a sprint away and only one officer and two boys down. Will knew how this was going to end. Strangely his stomach had settled. Death? He didn't care anymore. Would the history books remember him?

Crack, crack, crack. Three shots rang out again in close succession. They reloaded fast, thought Will, encouraged.

Lieutenant Davies fell next. For a few brief moments the acting commanding officer of his regiment, his sash and sword had made him Sean's next target. He died, as he feared he might, the victim of a senior officer's folly.

At this range Sean's riflemen could pick out the N.C.O.'s. Daniel O'Connell was just another tragic victim of the Irish conflict. Had Pat known that he was killing his second cousin, he might have picked a different target. Instead, he shot an English corporal and grunted with satisfaction.

The third shot took out a large man in the forefront of the approaching group. His death would never be recorded.

The Fifth Leicester was now a ship running without a helmsman.

Will dared to hope. Oh God those muskets still needed to do some damage. What the hell was Mary playing at!

At last she had her front rank ready, but the soldiers must be barely eighty yards away. Leaderless they might charge and create panic. Not a shot would be fired!

Very quietly and steadily Mary spoke. *She* had remembered it all. "Only fire on my command and all of you, *aim low*."

Ten muskets lowered their aim.

Will was caught in a dream. He turned back to the approaching troops. Now was the time. Stand or never look in the mirror again.

"FIRE"

CRASH!

Only ten muskets, it deafened Will.

As the smoke cleared he saw a ramrod impaled in the soft ground, vibrating ridiculously, fifty yards away. Somebody forgot to remove it. Nonetheless it was a miracle, they'd fire in unison!

Organised fire, the shock was massive to the inexperienced soldiers. Only two fell, but the pace slowed perceptibly.

Mary was busy again. "Now all you first ones step back, you can have another turn in a minute."

Forty yards, the second volley, aimed perfectly low, devastated. Knees exploded, faces erupted in showers of blood and bone. Arms were ripped off at the shoulder.

The advance faltered. Three more fell to the rifles on the roofs.

At twenty yards a yell went up from the troops and they charged. CRASH! It was met by the third volley.

Those hit at the front were lifted from their feet and thrown back amongst their comrades. Less than seventy men broke to cover the last ten yards towards Will and his allies.

Now I'm ready to die, thought Will.

"RIKKI, PIKES!" he roared and flew at the first man to bear down on Mary. Fired with the madness of battle, he thrust his sword at the soldier's chest. Parried by a bayonet, he head-butted the man away and was upon the next. The blade found his enemy's stomach and stuck. He was but two short yards from Mary. Her hands were over her face as the English wave broke over them all and she slipped from view.

Rikki's pikes ploughed into the mass of English troops. The huge weapons stemmed the tide only to be embroiled in the melee.

Crack, crack, Sean was killing the men around Will. Still he was trapped. Frantic to reach Mary, he wrenched his sword free and hacked a path forward. A giant of a man was felled with the Collier and he was there. No time to lift her from the ground, he stood between her and the furious horde. With Mary at his back, the Collier roared and he chopped and thrust until he could lift his sword no more.

Then it was over.

His lungs screaming for air, Will stood before a small mountain of bodies. His clothes and face were drenched in blood. His frame shook from the emotion and exhaustion of the life and death struggle.

Between them, they had killed at least fifty. The rest were running for the road and escape.

"You fuckin' mad bastard!" grinned Rikki staggering towards Will. "I had me doubts about you Will Peters. Not any more!"

Will was not listening. Dropping his weapons he held Mary in his arms. "You're safe. You're safe now," he panted. Then taking her head in his hands, he bent close. "You were amazing," he whispered. "I couldn't do it. We'd all be dead but for you." He kissed her on the lips.

From behind Will a group of dark riders appeared and a familiar voice froze the sweat on his back.

"Well what a romantic little scene this is, fer sure. I think I'm goin' to fuckin' cry." The Fox took it all in with one calculating glance. "I'll be back to talk to you in a minute. First, boys, we've work to do."

With that, he drew his sword, put his spurs to the flanks of his mount and he and his gang flew after the retreating English. Some had made the road and salvation in the woods beyond. Others were slower. Within view of the villagers, they rode down the stragglers, slowed by injuries and, with swishing cavalry swords, butchered them all.

Some of the villagers cheered. Some were exhausted and indifferent. Others were too preoccupied with their own injuries to notice.

Mary watched aghast. "Oh, Dear Lord, Will, we're no better than them."

Will had no time to think, before The Fox returned, all smiles, his gruesome work complete.

"What the fuck are you lookin'at?" he said to Will, wiping the gore from his blade. "You're no bloody different from me. Look around you. I'm quite impressed. You're a killin' machine. Now to business, where's your mate?"

Will and Mary looked around. Sean was nowhere to be seen. Owen too, had done one of his disappearing acts.

"I don't know. He was up on the roof, with his rifle."

The Fox laughed. "That's about right for him, not too close to the action. He doesn't mind if *you* get your guts ripped out!" He slid his weapon into its scabbard. "Ah well, I don't suppose he wants to bump into me. Pity, I was quite lookin' forward to it. Never mind. He can't avoid me forever. It'll wait. I'll just have to make do wi' you."

The Fox slid from his horse and Mary slipped away to help the other women tend to the wounded.

"Let's get a drink," The Fox put his hand on Will's shoulder and ushered him along the road to the old cottage, which stood for an inn. "A couple of pints for breakfast'll set you up for the day. By the look o' you, you could do with a drink."

Covered in mud, blood and powder stains, Will needed a bath and a change of clothes. Indifferent, The Fox steered him to a small table in the corner of the little bar. Quite relaxed in the post battle chaos, The Fox was charm itself, organising beers and food. Exhausted and too weak to argue, Will collapsed into a chair. His tongue was stuck to the roof of his mouth and he threw two beers down in quick succession into his empty rebellious stomach. Eggs and bread did not sit too well on the mixture. Will, now slightly drunk, didn't care if he was sick on The Fox, as long as he left him to sleep.

Embarking on his third beer and pushing another in front of Will, The Fox smiled, "Well I'm sorry we missed most o' the fun. The boys and myself just couldn't quite make it in time. Never mind, you've done good."

"We didn't do so badly in the end did we?" replied Will unable to keep a brief note of pride from his voice.

"So what are you plans now?"

"Plans? What plans? I don't have any," spluttered Will, "except maybe staying alive." Why couldn't this nightmare of a man just leave him to sleep across the table?

The Fox had other ideas. "This country has been waiting for you. You slay the evil English baron and then win a great victory. Ireland expects! You can't just leave it there. Do you think you can ride off into the sunset with the girl on your arm? This hasn't finished. This has only just kicked off."

Will's concentration had started to drift. The Fox was virtually shouting. Will shook his head to clear it.

"Look, I just stepped in when I saw what they were doing to them. I didn't want to start a war."

"Well that's what you've done. Can't you see that?" The Fox seized Will by the shoulders and shook him. "Whatever you do, it won't stop now. If you leave it, they'll send in more and more troops, and not just here. It'll be the whole county. They'll likely burn Wexford as a warning. Do you want that on you conscience?"

His conscience? No way! Or should he try and change history? Right now he was too damn tired to think. He knew what had happened in his old world. The Wexford rebels declared a republic and within weeks, defeated, the ringleaders were rounded up and hanged.

Will tried to collect his thoughts. "That's how Sean spoke to me, after de Guilbert's death." He described it like an unfortunate car accident, as though he were devoid of all responsibility.

"Well me lad sure got that one right. Yer see Will," continued the Fox, forcing his face uncomfortably close to Will's. The ragged detail of the scar on The Fox's cheek was clear to see. Whoever had done it had nearly taken his eye.

"I can't help feelin' that you still think o' this as some kind of a game or maybe the sort o' thing that happens to other people, but not to the likes of you. Well, it's not a fuckin' game, not to us."

Then to Will's relief The Fox slid back in his chair and took a swig of his beer. The relief was short-lived as the silence became unbearable. Wide-awake now and mind racing, what should he say to rid himself of this man?

The Fox was in control and knew it. He eyed Will with a mixture of amusement and disdain. Eventually he said, "The trouble is Will, if you're not very lucky, you're gonna get yersel' killed. Now why get yersel' killed for a game, when yer might as well die fer a cause?"

Will said nothing and tried to avoid The Fox's penetrating gaze.

"I think that you need a cause, Will Peters. I think that's what you've been missing, all your life. Maybe that's why you came. Or maybe you've got another reason now. Perhaps it's that pretty wee thing, I caught you cuddlin', that'll make you fight. I don't know. One thing I do know, Will, you've made yourself a bit of a hit around here and these people need a hero. Lovable as I am," he stroked his scar, "I don't think they'll follow me the way they might follow you."

The Fox paused and drank and Will wished he were anywhere or any time other than here and now.

"And there's another thing, I think you understand a lot o' what's goin' on around here." He waved his hand in the air, "and that might be useful to us."

To Will's surprise and relief, The Fox suddenly rose from the table. He seemed about to leave and then turned and was back inches from Will's face. "You'd better make your mind up, Will Peters," he smiled, "but don't take too long. The tide may have receded for the moment, but you know the trouble with tides…"

He patted Will on the cheek. It was not a reassuring feeling.

With the relief that followed The Fox's departure exhaustion swept over Will again. Would they notice if he slept here? Did he care?

The door opened and Mary rushed in.

"Where's Will?" she gasped.

Fingers pointed to the filthy body slouched over the end of the table.

"Will, Will, wake up! Wake up!" She shook him rudely. "They've taken Owen."

Chapter 22

Midford Co. Wexford
April 2nd 1797

Sean was prepared for the attack. I hope to God you're ready soon Will, he thought, watching the chaos in front of the cottage. The English troops were already on the move. No point in worrying, just focus on your own job, he told himself. You've only got a couple of minutes before that red tide sweeps over them. You and the two boys have practised this. Take out as many as you can. It's all you can do.

Only three against so many, their task seemed impossible; the hunting rifles might be beautiful, but they were slow to load. At least they had two a piece. Preloaded, it evened the odds a bit. He hadn't explained this to Will. No need for more difficult explanations about the source of these prize weapons. Will didn't need all that just now. He had enough on his plate.

Dear God, what the hell was Will doing? Then Sean realised. It was sheer genius to give the girl the job of calling the shots. To stand in front, sword drawn, where his men could see him, was real eighteenth century stuff. Good thinking but oh, so exposed. Don't get yourself killed Will. I can spare Rikki, but not you. Besides, Rikki can look after himself.

"Boys, do as we said, long shot into the thick of 'em, then its take out the officers, drummers and N.C.O.'s. If you've anything left after that, kill the bastards around Will!"

Heads nodded, rifle butts were squeezed into taut shoulders. Each man had a partner to load and to watch his back. Nothing for the riflemen to do except concentrate and kill.

Sean directed his attention down the sights of the weapon. With Pat to his left and Michael to his right, they all knew what they had to do. Sean mind filled with the smell and feel of the weapon. Despite all his preparations with the sights, the rifle shot to the left. Aim to miss the target to the right. It took conviction to do that. The other weapon was true. Concentrate Sean boy. You mustn't waste a shot.

"Alright boys, let's do it! Fire as soon as you like!"

Their first three shots took out two redcoats from the back of the advancing enemy. From the cottage they wouldn't see. Sean wasn't looking anyway. He'd studied and practised hard. In the back of his mind it was ingrained. Don't look at the last shot, look for the next.

CRACK! CRACK! Pat and Michael were doing the job.

For Sean the rest was a blur, until the melee engulfed Will and Rikki and he dared fire no longer. He threw the spent rifle to Danny, his backup and reached for the Collier, as he turned to descend. Then he saw them, in the street behind the cottage. Cavalry! Immediately they were gone from view, as he slid down the back of the barn roof. Frantically he scrabbled his feet to grip and climb back for another look.

Stuffing the Collier back in his belt, he clawed his way back and dragged his head over the ridge. There was about forty of them. Not cavalry, thank God, rebels. Relief washed over him to freeze immediately, when he recognised the outline of The Fox. What in hell's name was he doing? His hand was raised holding his men back. By now Pat and Michael were beside Sean.

"For Christ's sakes, why doesn't he lead 'em in?" murmured Michael.

"What's he playing at?" added Pat.

"I'll tell yer the game he's playin'," growled Sean. "He's playin' the waitin' game. He's playin' the 'let's see who comes out on top game." Sean was shaking with fury. "He's playin' the let's let 'em fuckin' kill each other first game. Come on lads, let's help 'em."

Sean made to move, when Pat held his arm. "Look! Look! It's over. They're running. They've bloody done it!"

For the second time Sean had to regain his balance and look again. "Holy Mother, you're right." He looked hard. "Oh dear God, would you look at that. Yer man's still standing! Oh, at 'er boy Will. How sweet are the fruits of victory!"

Sean smiled at Will's embrace of Mary and then glanced towards The Fox, who was finally on the move. Satisfied that Will had survived and that the soldiers were vanquished, Sean's mind raced on to other pressing matters.

"On reflection, I think I'll let our friends bask in the warm sunshine of their victory. I'm not much for tending to the wounded, anyway," said Sean. "Pat, keep an eye on that bastard and 'is boys," he indicated The Fox. "Although he seems to be satisfying his need to hurt defenceless creatures." Sean gazed for a moment as the horsemen rode down the retreating stragglers. "There's no fuckin' need for that! Mind, I'd rather he was doin' it to them," he added with a shrug.

The three men slid down the roof to the top of the wall behind it and jumped to the ground.

"Danny, Michael, you two come with me. The rest of you, go with Pat," continued Sean, putting his arms around the two men. "We're off to meet a fisherman in Wexford harbour. Let's hope he's got a good catch for us," he added with a wink. "Tell Will I'll be back well before sundown."

In the event the sun was setting over the hills in the West when Sean rode back and slid down from his saddle outside Mary's cottage. He sent the others on to the inn, with his mount, and with a slight rap on the door ducked under the lintel.

"Where's me lad?" he enquired of Mary, who was preparing food in the area at the open hearth. Her hair was tied back with a piece of old cloth, her clothes soiled.

"He's sleeping," she replied, without looking up. "I made him. He wanted to rush after Owen, but I wouldn't let him, not in that state. They'd have killed him."

She turned to look at Sean. Her face was etched with grey lines and her eyes were red from crying. "He was so angry, with the soldiers, with Owen, with himself. I've never seen him like that."

She spoke as though she had known Will for years, not a matter of hours. She returned to cutting vegetables. "Will you go and talk to him? He's upstairs where I sleep."

Sean raised an eyebrow, unnoticed by Mary. Then, pulling himself together, rested his rifle against the wall. "Sure I can," he murmured and climbed upstairs to the gloom of the upper floor.

Will stirred at the sound of Sean's boots on the stair. He sat up suddenly and squinted in Sean's direction. "Oh my God! What time is it? I've got to get up!"

Sean pushed him back onto the straw. "You're not goin' anywhere till I know what's been goin' on? What's all this about Owen? And have you taken up cross-dressing? What in the name of God are you wearing?"

Will looked down at himself, dressed in what looked like an old worn dress. He reddened. "It's a ladies night er, thing. She didn't have anything else. My clothes were filthy in mud and blood," he blurted. "Oh, and I threw up on my new trousers," he added more quietly.

"Oh Will, Will, I have to say that you're a bit of a disappointment to me. The last time I saw you, you were the proud conquering hero, your enemies vanquished and a fair maiden in your arms. I leave you for five minutes and here you are dressing up in women's' clothing and sleeping *on your own* in her bed. I think we need to have a wee talk about the birds and the bees." He leant forward and whispered, "You're not o' the other persuasion are you? That's fine. I don't have a problem with that."

Will grabbed Sean's coat and opened his mouth to remonstrate with him, when he caught the twinkle in his friend's eye. He let the coat slip and put his hand to his head and laughed. "Oh my God, what have you got me into? What would they say back at Oxford, if they could see me now?"

"I thought it was at Cambridge that they preferred that sort of thing." Sean looked puzzled. Then added with a smile, "Thank God you survived and without hardly a scratch by the look of you."

"I don't know how we did it, but we did," replied Will. "Mind you my head's really sore from head butting some guy. I think I did it wrong." He shrugged, "We don't do a lot of that behind the Conservative Club in Harrow."

"That's not what I've heard," Sean laughed and the two men embraced.

There was a noise on the stairs and they separated hastily, embarrassed. "Blimey…" Sean was about to make some joke when they both saw Mary's face.

"Are you rested Will?" she said.

"Have you been crying?" replied Will

"I think I'll leave the two of you for a bit," interrupted Sean. "I'll get meself a drink an' come back in a while."

Sean, with a nod to Mary, squeezed past her and was gone.

"There's quite a celebration going on at the inn," she called after him and then, turning to Will, added, "I really don't know what there is to celebrate. So much killing and some of our friends so badly hurt."

She started to cry again and Will held her in his arms and drew her down onto the straw. They lay together, her head on his chest, until Will was convinced that the sobs had subsided.

"We had no choice," said Will softly. "The only alternative was to run away and how could you do that with your family dependent on you? They'd have only taken it out on the rest of the village anyway. You didn't ask for them to come to the village and do what they did. Why *did* they pick on your brother anyway?"

Mary shifted herself onto her elbows, her face a few inches from Will. "I don't really know. The soldiers often pick on the blacksmiths and their apprentices. They're the ones who know where all the pike heads are, as it's them who make them. Maybe they thought he worked for the smithy."

They fell silent and gazed at each other.

"Will, what do we do now?"

"I don't think I've got a choice. I'll have to look for Owen. He risked his life for me over and over again. I can't just leave him. I'll go first thing tomorrow. Perhaps Sean's group will have heard some news."

Mary sat up and wiped her face with her grubby apron. "I've seen Owen's cart. We can take that. It'll be much less suspicious."

"We? I don't think so. I shall go with Sean and Rikki, if they'll come. If not, I'll go alone."

"You're not going anywhere without me, Will Peters." Her voice was raised. "Where would you have been this morning, without my help?"

Will sat up pushing her to one side on the bed. "I'm not completely useless. You know what would have happened to you if I hadn't arrived yesterday, when I did!"

"I know that, but you didn't have to kill Lord, Sir, whatever he was! If you hadn't done that they might have gone away."

"Don't be bloody stupid!"

"Don't you dare swear at me, Will Peters!"

"Swear at you! Have you any idea what will happen when General Lake sends his troops…?"

Will stopped short, realising that he was about to explain the events of the next two years to her. Besides she was crying openly now, no attempt to disguise it or wipe away the tears.

A movement distracted them and they both looked around to see Sean's head appear at the top of the stairs.

"Well that's romantic. Are you two having yer first row?" He registered the look on their faces. "I'll come back in a bit," he said and was gone.

"I, I'm sorry…" Will started.

She put her hand gently over his mouth. "It's not your fault, it's just everything and…" the tears were running down her cheeks.

"It's alright…" he whispered.

"No, it's not. Let me finish. Will, I couldn't bear to lose you, not now. I'd rather die myself. I have never met anyone like you. Nobody has ever done anything like that for me and well, you know, not expected something in return. You've done it twice now. Perhaps I'm selfish. It's wonderful that you've risked your life for me and I suppose it's that I don't want you to do it for anyone else."

Will held her tight and they kissed. It was like nothing Will had ever experienced. She kissed him with complete abandon. She was giving her life to him. And he to her.

"Whatever we do, we will do it together," he murmured.

She pulled away to look at him and it was there again, that look she'd given him, when he stood before her, sword in hand, as the troops advanced. He grinned back at her and they sat grinning at each other like two perfect fools.

"Well I'm glad you two have managed to patch things up. I knew you would and I'm sorry to interrupt…"

Will glared at him.

Sean shrugged. "It's just that they've run out of food at the inn and I've hardly eaten all day and I can smell…"

"Oh my life, the supper," gasped Mary and rushed past Sean. A moment later a call came up the stairs. "It's alright and of course you can stay to supper, Sean." She reappeared again with Will's clothes. "They're not quite dry. It's the best I can do," and she threw them to him.

Sean went down to the kitchen as Will dressed and was instructed to set the table for three. Of the children, there was no sign.

As Will, Sean and Mary pulled up chairs, Sean said, "Oh, I've managed to bring a couple of jugs of ale. I reckon they'll be running out of that soon as well." He stood up to retrieve it from by the door, where he'd left it.

"I think Will has had enough ale for one day thank you Sean," interjected Mary, without looking up from the table.

"Your reasons for this unseemly disturbance had better be sound. I've left a table and a damn fine one at that," boomed Earl Camden, Viceroy of Ireland, bursting into the once splendid stateroom in Dublin Castle. Tall and in his late thirties, he looked every bit the British aristocrat, formerly attired in his cloak and chains of office. Moderate and fair he had held office for only two years, but already his handsome face was worn with the relentless struggle against the selfishness and prejudices of the old guard, who held the real power in Dublin.

"You know that I would not have disturbed you, my lord, if it were not of the utmost importance," responded chief Secretary Thomas Pelham, his pale complexion and moist lips due perhaps to nerves or illness.

"Hmph, it seems I'm not the only one whose evening has been spoiled," added Camden, taking in the other five, gathered on the faded silk carpet.

All except the twenty eight year old Castlereagh were older than him. Only this young Cambridge graduate was not opposed to concessions to the Catholics or relief for the poor. How to bring about change? Camden was only too aware that his predecessor, Lord Fitzwilliam, had sacked two of the men before him, John Beresford, Chief Commissioner and the Undersecretary, Edward Cooke, only to lose the support of Pitt and his own job, whilst the two cronies were reinstated. All hope of a fairer Ireland and real equality for the Catholics had sailed from Dublin harbour with the dismissed Fitzwilliam.

No less formidable opponents were John Foster, nearly sixty and Speaker of the Irish Parliament and the Lord Chancellor, Lord Clare, who, even this evening, was carrying a pistol and was known to brandish it at any who stood in his path. Like Camden, they were not amused to be dragged into the castle at this late hour. Only Castlereagh, relaxing on a chaise longue, seemed unperturbed by the interruption to his evening. Camden knew well how often this brilliant young rising star had used his presence and oratory to bring the hot heads of the Parliament back from the brink.

Camden beckoned them to be seated and nodded to Pelham.

The Secretary, report in hand, took a breath to present his news, when another figure slipped in. William Elliot, nicknamed the Castle Spectre, made even Pelham appear healthy.

"Ehem,"

Pelham was unsure if the cough was due to his condition or the need to draw his attention.

"What is it?" he hissed impatiently.

"I have further news from Wexford." He passed Pelham a document on a silver salver and disappeared as befitted his epithet.

"Damn it man, get on with it." It was Clare and not Camden, who interrupted. "John is not the only one whose dinner has been interrupted. May we proceed?"

Camden took a seat and nodded again to Pelham, who took up a position, centre stage, in front of the fire that had been hastily encouraged back to life.

"I crave your indulgence a moment," blustered Pelham, as he pulled on spectacles and tried to digest the latest information. His pale complexion turned ashen. "Uh, um, where to start?"

Beresford and Clare muttered impatiently.

"There has been something of an, um, uh, uprising near Wexford."

"Damn it," roared Foster. Turning to Camden, "I warned you this would happen."

Camden raised his hand to silence him. "Let the Secretary continue."

"The soldiers were going about their business in the usual manner, we understand, when a band of renegades appeared and attacked them. Heavily outnumbered, the troops fought back bravely, but were, uh, defeated."

It was Clare, who interrupted next. "It's hopeless using these local militia for this kind of work. They're not trained or equipped for it. We must use the regular army."

"You're aware, John," responded Camden, "that I have constantly petitioned London for reinforcements, to no avail. They fob me off with tales of unrest at home and I'm to understand that the south of England is in constant distress with the fear of invasion."

"My Lords," continued Pelham, "these were regular troops, the Fifth Leicester."

"What?"

"Impossible!"

The room was in uproar. Only Castlereagh was calm. "Isn't that De Guilbert's regiment? Is Edward hurt?"

All eyes focused on Pelham. The Secretary shifted uncomfortably from one foot to the other, his eyes fixed on the report in his hands.

"It appears, from the information we have received…" the air lay heavy with fear and anticipation. "…that he was killed by the rebels."

Clare strode over to Pelham and snatched the documents from his hands. "Give me that!" he growled and scanned the report. His face turned puce.

"This is it. This is the final straw, the limit. They're bloody barbarians, worse than barbarians, animals! It says that they captured poor Eddie and hung him naked from a post!"

Foster, Cooke and Beresford were all on their feet, roaring and shouting. Clare was reading the second document, brought in by Elliot. He held up his hands for silence.

"There's more and it's grim. A Captain Mablethorpe survived the first incident and heroically lead the regiment back to the village, only to be wiped out by a small army, which was lying in wait. Mablethorpe was killed."

The Lord Chancellor folded the reports and placed them on a coffee table. Once again he held up his hands for silence.

"Gentlemen, this is no disorganised peasant riot. This is the organised uprising, we had feared."

They all turned to Camden.

"You have no choice now, John," growled Foster to the Viceroy. "They need a clear message. You must send Lake to Wexford, rout out the rebels and burn that traitorous town to the ground!"

Sean had grave misgivings about the expedition to rescue Owen, about taking Mary and about risking Will, who seemed obsessed with saving the lad. He had further misgivings about leaving the rifles and swords behind and sitting on manure, which concealed the Colliers and two daggers, in the back of Owen's cart. All in all Sean had grave misgivings about almost everything that morning as he and Rikki, dressed in old smocks and breeches, bounced along behind Will and Mary.

At least it gave him time to think. Will's conviction and passion were more than he could have expected, from his psychological profile, which he had read, back at Boroughbridge. This expedition would only help, provided, of course, that Will wasn't killed. That was Sean's greatest concern.

This phase was crucial. He had hardly dared hope that it would start so well. From now onwards the timing was even more critical. This excursion was an unforeseen waste of time and worse, a hell of a risk. The duel had been a godsend. The battle was a calculated risk. Today was neither. The wretched boy was not important. He was not worth any swordplay or fancy heroics. He didn't need Will for that. Reluctantly he had agreed to join Will, only to show support. Will's job was yet to come and his commitment and trust were vital.

The military stuff Sean had grasped. The strategic stuff was obvious. Making it happen naturally wasn't so easy. That didn't seem such a hurdle now the race was on. It was what came next that confounded Sean. How on earth was he going to sort out all these disparate groups and pull them together into some cohesive force? That had been the biggest challenge in the 1798 Rebellion that he had studied back at Boroughbridge. A challenge they had failed to meet. The problem was that there had not been enough time even for his quick mind to grasp all that information. Maybe it was the time travel or perhaps the two years, which had elapsed. Maybe part of him had not wanted to absorb it all. He wasn't sure. Now he was struggling with the names and groups. It was such a muddle and he needed help.

That's why he needed Will. What was it that Will had said back at Boroughbridge? Something about it not being simple, not just Irish versus English or Protestant versus Catholic. His intellect agreed and yet somehow his upbringing or his instincts told him that it *was* just that damn simple. And in his mind was another dichotomy. He wanted so badly to change all this, to change it *his* way. Oh what a glorious achievement that would be, only sullied by the thought that he was doing someone else's bidding. There it was again, just below the surface, bubbling away, that anger at how he'd been tricked and coerced. What would Will think if he knew that he, more than Sean, was a victim of coercion? What would he think of me? considered Sean.

Sean swivelled around to look at Will, eyes set on the road ahead, upright, strong and determined. My God, had he changed in the last few days! And the girl! What was that all about? Will and she were latched onto each other like a pair of limpets. He really needed to talk to Will on his own, but Sean just could not separate them. Will seemed determined to involve her in everything.

The wagon jogged on towards Enniscorthy. It was to here that the stragglers from the battle had fled, according to recent reports.

Sean sat back again and glanced at Rikki. He was dozing in the morning sunshine. What a star! He was so cool. Sean knew that he could rely on him implicitly. Sean's thoughts returned to Will. He was a different story. He had turned out to be a bit of a surprise package. Could Will be controlled, especially now he'd found his feet? If he couldn't, would Sean do what his father and the Boston men expected of him? No orders had been given. Sean just knew. It was all right shooting these eighteenth century toy soldiers, but Will? He'd have to be so careful, if he were to avoid that. How much should he reveal to Will? It must be enough to enable him to help and yet not so much that he rebelled against the cause.

The sound of voices disturbed Sean's thoughts and he climbed to his knees and turned to see what was happening ahead. They were about to join the road to Enniscorthy, which ran parallel to the western bank of the River Slaney. It was only a minor dirt road. The main road that linked their destination with Wexford lay on the eastern bank of the river. That led to the bridge and the southeast gate into the town. Sean and his party had decided they were less likely to attract attention if they went around to the northwest and entered by the Duffrey Gate. They had expected their route to be quiet. Surprisingly the road was packed with travellers, on horses, in carts, but mostly on foot. All were heading in one direction, north, away from Wexford.

As they overtook a man with a chair and a bundle, over his shoulder, Sean hailed him. "'Tis a fine mornin'. What takes you to Enniscorthy?"

It was unusually warm for April and the man was sweating under his burden.

"It might be a fine mornin' from up there," the man replied. "For the rest of us 'tis a terrible day indeed."

"And why so?" Sean managed to keep his voice steady.

"Where have you been? Have you not heard? There was a parade last night in Wexford, after dark. Hundreds out on the streets, parading caps on pikes, torches and all and burning the houses of loyal folk. The militia was called out and all hell broke loose. Screaming and killing and allsorts. Next thing we know they all up and left." He nodded as if that explained it all.

The cart was leaving the man behind and Sean wanted to hear more. He leapt down and fell in step with the man.

"Who's left? Left for where?" Sean asked urgently.

The man eyed him suspiciously. "Who wants to know? Aren't you the one who owns the bar near the Old Town Wall?"

"Fer sure I am. You know me."

"I don't know nothin'," insisted the man, hoisting his load up a little higher and dropping his head to ignore Sean.

Sean gave up on him and ran after the cart. Rikki had woken and was sitting up.

"What's goin' on Sean?" he asked looking around at the traffic heading north.

"I don't exactly know, except yer man there says there was some kind of a riot in Wexford last night an' everyone's leaving. The North Cork militia was called out, but I don't know who's running away."

"If they were rebels, they wouldn't be heading north on the road, they'd have legged it over the fields." Will had turned to whisper to them. "I bet the militia and the local yeomanry have bunked it up the main road to Enniscorthy. It's going to be lively there. We'll have to scout around quietly to see if we can trace Owen. Word will have got out about what we did and I expect most of the county is rising up, as we speak. We're going to have to do something, but we'd better focus on Owen first."

"Are you alright Sean?" asked Rikki. "You look kind of upset. Don't worry the pub'll be fine. They won't have burned that down, now will they?"

"I'm fine, just fine. It's well, uh, I just didn't think that the news would get about quite so fast," said Sean. Oh God, I hope that it's got to Dublin. If they haven't heard yet it'll be too late, by the time they do, thought Sean. I hope my messages have been delivered.

For the rest of their journey they kept conversation to a minimum. There were so many on the road that anything could be overheard and Will's accent would certainly attract attention. By the time they reached the outskirts of their destination, the throng was so thick that it seemed the best subterfuge was simply to be herded in with the rest of the flock and take the direct route in from the southeast. Will was forced to pull up on the reins and halt the cart about a hundred yards from the bridge, as hoards of refugees from the south jostled for places to enter the town.

Rumours started to reverberate around the impatient crowd. A Captain Snowe had attempted to shut the gates, for fear of rebel infiltration. It was in vain. They had been overwhelmed. So great were the numbers pouring in, the troops of the Enniscorthy Infantry had abandoned their posts. Shots and yells could be heard from within the town and stories were spreading that the troops were about to withdraw, but not before they had exterminated the known rebels.

Panic was spreading amongst the crowd. Some at the back were pressing forward to make their way to the gate. Others at the front were having second thoughts and trying to go back. Caught in the middle and with Owen's old horse sidestepping nervously, Sean jumped up between Will and Mary and seized the reins and whip. Encouraging the horse forward and laying about with the whip, he forced the cart forward and through the gate. The few troops remaining showed no appetite for stopping them.

Far from finding refuge within the ancient walls, the scene before them was pandemonium. Troops, people, cattle and horses were running everywhere. Shots rang out from the upstairs windows, killing at random in the turmoil below. As casualties fell down, people and horses stumbled over them and, in turn, fell causing more chaos.

Sean fought his way forward, trying desperately to control the skittish horse. At last the street opened up onto a small market square. Sean pulled up quickly as a line of militia stood across his path. This area, at least, seemed to be under military control.

A crash of musket fire tore the air. As the smoke cleared, they could see the results of the troops handiwork. A pile of bodies lay, where the victims had fallen. More prisoners, men, women and children stood, blindfolded, hands tied behind their backs, waiting their turn. It was just one last wanton act before the Enniscorthy militia, too, fled north.

Sean's eyes swept the square. Apart from the firing squad, which was busy reloading, there must have been about two hundred troops, militia and yeomanry. A row of carts had been overturned to form a makeshift backstop for the firing squad. There was little else of significance except for a small crudely constructed scaffold. Below it were two barrels, one on top of the other. Standing on the uppermost barrel, rope around his neck was a young boy. Owen!

"Thank God, we're just in time," panted Will. "Now we need a plan."

Sean watched a soldier march quickly over to the barrels. He put his shoulder to them and pushed. The barrels wobbled for a moment and fell. Owen dropped suddenly, about four feet. The rope went tight and Owen's neck jerked sharply to the left. His feet kicked a little dance and were still.

Mesmerised as he was with the scene before him, Sean noticed a sudden movement to his right. Will was out of his seat and about to leap down. Sean swung his body to the left and kicked out to his right, taking Will's legs from under him, as he leapt from the cart.

"No, Will. Stop!" cried Mary.

Throwing the reins at Mary, Sean jumped on top of Will and held him to the ground.

"Help me Rikki," Sean yelled.

In a moment Rikki was down and, as Will broke free from Sean's grasp, Rikki hit him hard. Will sank to his knees, winded and Sean and Rikki bundled him into the back of the cart.

Sean, jumping on top of him, yelled, "Rikki, get us out of here. Now!"

Rikki ran round to the front and seized the reins. "Yah! Geetup!" he coaxed the frightened horse into action and down another side street, away from the main body of troops.

In the back Will was regaining his breath and wrestling with Sean, as the cart rocked through the streets, amidst the noise and commotion. Sean was torn between holding Will down and repelling boarders, who saw the rapidly moving cart as an escape route from the madness around them.

"Mary, help me with him! I don't want to have to hit him again," bellowed Sean.

Mary stood up as the horse found a clear path and shot forwards, tossing her backwards on top of Sean and Will. There was a tangle of arms and legs until finally Mary held Will close. Both were crying.

"It's not your fault, Will. You tried. You couldn't have done anything. Shh. Shh." She held his head against her, as Rikki miraculously found his way through a narrow lane and out of the town, avoiding the main gates. He found a little track and forced the horse on as fast as it would go.

As soon as Rikki dared, he pulled up behind a ruined cottage about a mile from the town. The horse's sides were heaving with the exertion and the cart's wheels were groaning ominously.

Sean jumped down and leaned on the side of the cart.

"Jesus, Will, you nearly had us all killed back there." Then noting the tears still in Will's eyes, added, "Look, I'm sorry about that. We didn't want to hurt you, but it was hopeless. They'd have mown you down, before you'd gone five yards. Besides, it was too late for the boy."

Will sat up and shouted. "I should have tried. You shouldn't have stopped me. What gives *you* the right, anyway?" He paused for breath and, jumping down beside Sean, added more softly, "It's just, I dunno, I should have done something."

"Don't be a fool. You'd have died a hero and what good is that? And you weren't thinking of the rest of us were you? What about young Mary, there?"

She and Rikki were both beside them now.

Will's temper rose again. "Don't you bloody tell me about thinking of others! If you'd come back a bit sooner yesterday, we could have gone last night."

Will looked at Mary, Sean and Rikki, who were both standing around, silently studying the ground.

Will kicked the wheel of the cart. "The bastards, the fucking bastards! What had *he* done? He was only a child. It was just a game to him. He was just trying to help, just caught up in it all."

Unexpectantly Sean found his eyes filling up. He stepped forwards and put his arms around Will.

"Now you understand," whispered Sean.

Chapter 23

South of Enniscorthy Co. Wexford
April 3rd 1797

Emotions ran high before the day's end and tempers flared up again. In their haste to leave they had brought insufficient food and drink. The cart's axle was damaged and could not be fixed without tools, which they'd forgotten to bring. Each blamed the other. Owen's old horse was exhausted and they struggled on for about ten miles, before she refused to go any further.

It was no use. They had to abandon the cart and Rikki suggested that they turn the horse loose. It seemed to Will the last act of betrayal and they argued. Sean was desperate to return to Wexford immediately to see what was happening, whilst Mary felt compelled to return to her village, afraid, in all this uproar, for her family. To cap it all, Sean insisted that Will come with him, which he refused point blank. His duty, he explained, was to see Mary back safely. The arguing continued.

Finally it was Mary, who settled it. She wanted Will to come with her, but could see that Sean had need of his help. She would be fine, if Rikki went with her for protection. In some ways it was an arrangement that suited nobody and yet they all agreed to it. They were emotionally drained and too tired to argue further.

They parted company reluctantly and, at last, Sean had Will alone. Sean did not want to risk another row. He would have preferred to wait until they were back in Wexford, with some food and drink inside them and yet time was pressing and the events of the day had shocked him more than he liked to admit. He needed a second opinion. He broached the subject cautiously.

"Thanks for coming with me, Will. The Lord knows what kind of a mess I'm going to face, when we get back to Wexford."

"Hm."

Sean tried a different tack.

"What do yer think will happen now that word seems to have got out about our little battle?"

Will shrugged and they strode on.

It was the middle of the afternoon, the road was curiously deserted now and they had some miles to cover, if they were to arrive before nightfall. The day was running away from him and Sean pushed the pace as fast as he dared. What he would have given for a car, a motorbike, even a bicycle!

"My kingdom for a horse, eh Will?"

"Well Rikki shouldn't have been in such a hurry to get rid of Owen's then should he?"

Sean sighed. "Will, I need to talk to you. This has got out of hand. I need you to help me sort it out."

Sean stopped marching and held Will by the sleeve.

"Will you help me? I really need it."

Will hesitated. "Yeh. Course I will. It's a bloody mess isn't it?" He managed a smile. "In every sense of the word."

Sean smiled too. "You sure said a mouthful there, kid".

"Look, whether we like it or not, this thing has taken off. We can sit around all day blaming ourselves. I guess that's what I've been doing over Owen." Will glanced at the sky and the position of the sun. "We'd better get going. We can talk as we walk."

They continued on their way.

"Funny how you start doing that, isn't it?" said Will.

"Doing what?"

"Glancing at the sun, to guess at the time."

"Sure."

Sean did not press Will, now that his mood seemed to have lifted. Several hours walking were in front of them and he decided to let Will take his time.

"Where the hell is everyone?" continued Will.

"Search me. Anyway at least we can talk, without worrying who's listening."

"Alright then. It is a mess, but probably not as big a mess, as the original rebellion, which came about a year later, if that's any consolation." Will sighed. "Look I'm sorry that I've been a bit, well you know, strung out about all this. You've had longer to get your head around it all. For me it's been a bit of a shock. I guess I'm not used to all this blood and guts stuff either. Fencing, with all the gear on, is just not the same. I need to think about it."

They marched on, with the sun descending behind them. Sean waited patiently for Will's thoughts.

"Sean, I guess it's quite simple really. Since we're here and everything is different anyway, we might just as well do what we can to make a difference for the good. It's too late now to start worrying about changing history. It's already changed. I don't even think that we should worry about making it close to the history we know. We should try and minimise the human damage done and try and improve things. Does that make sense?"

"Sounds good to me," nodded Sean. This sounded very encouraging. Sean breathed deeply, trying to be patient, whilst Will plodded through his ideas.

"Right then. This has gone too far already to put the lid back on it. Even if you and I could hop in a carriage and shoot up to Dublin Castle, it wouldn't help. We could say to old Camden, 'Excuse me, old chap, there's been a bit of a mix up and we're all frightfully sorry and won't do it again.' Do you think it would all end there?"

"I think the only decision would be whether to shoot us or hang us," responded Sean and immediately wished he hadn't. To his relief his gaffe didn't seem to stop Will's flow.

"So what's the alternative? We have to make this revolution succeed, as quickly and bloodlessly as possible. Don't you agree?"

It was all Sean could do not to punch the air.

"Seems sensible. How do we go about it?" he asked calmly.

"The theory is simple. Well not that simple, really. You know the principles of any guerrilla war, quick surprise attacks, never get caught in a major formal engagement. That's what went wrong at Vinegar Hill. My God, I didn't even think about it! It's only just up the road from where we were at Enniscorthy, this morning."

"Go on," encouraged Sean, smiling.

"We know that the rebels will have numbers, maybe ten thousand could be put into the field at one time. For the Government, much less. If they put two thousand together, they'll be stripping the capital bare. That's not the point. The rebels will be poorly armed, poorly trained and poorly led. Get them fired up and in a street fight and the army will have a fight on its hands. That happened on several occasions. Put them in a formal engagement and, under fire, they'll probably run.

The army is not very disciplined, not like it was under Wellington in India or ten years from…" Will smiled, "…now. They are better, than the rebels, though, and they are well armed. The key is artillery. They know that running up a hill against thousands of pikes is suicide. It's the same for cavalry, so they don't bother. They sit back and pound you to death with their guns. Simple. There's nothing the rebels can do against it and nobody's going to stand much of that either. They'll run. And when that happens the pikes are useless. The cavalry will run them down."

"So what can we do about it?" asked Sean.

"It's not so easy. They've got the big guns and unless you can take them off them, those are the rules. It upsets the balance of eighteenth century warfare. If both sides are evenly matched, it's different. It's like a dance. Closed formation is a target for the artillery, so you break formation. Then you're exposed to cavalry, so you close up for volley fire and to form a wall of bayonets. You're cavalry is useless now. They'll be slaughtered, so you need your artillery and so on."

"Hm. So we need to capture some artillery. Mind we haven't got any cavalry either, Will, except for The Fox and his boys, of course, and he only likes to turn up, when everyone else is going home."

"He said something similar about you, Sean."

"Did he, by Christ? And when was that?"

"After the battle. He took me for a couple of drinks. Fair enough, he did apologise for not arriving sooner and said something about you always keeping out of harm's way."

"Did he now? Did he also tell you that he an' his boys waited outside the inn until you lot had done all the real fighting?"

Will stopped in his tracks.

"What?"

"I thought not. He forgot to mention that didn't he? Me and the other boys could see him from the top of the barn. I had a hell of a fright, 'cause I thought for a minute they were army cavalry."

"Are you sure?"

Sean nodded.

"The lying bastard. He's never done anything except help and yet he scares the hell out of me. Mind, I never took him for a coward."

"Oh, I don't think he's a coward. He just doesn't give a damn for anybody else and he likes seeing folk get hurt. I think it turns him on."

"I thought you didn't know him. He was on about you enough and he said he wanted to meet you."

"Everyone knows The Fox in these parts and I'm sure that he does know about me. I've something of a following myself these days."

They walked on in silence for a while. Will hadn't told Sean anything that he didn't already know. He needed more.

"Alright, so we need to get this guerrilla war going. What do you suggest?"

"It won't be easy. The other big problem that they had was they were so disorganised and the Dublin leadership did nothing. It was hardly surprising, most of them and been sold out to the government and captured. The traitors' activities spread like a cancer through 1797. This year!

I can see things have changed somehow already from what I know but if the leadership in Dublin is still intact and we can winkle out the traitors… I wonder. Better still we could use them to feed duff information back to Dublin Castle."

"Will, do you know who all these guys are?"

"The traitors you mean? Well I wouldn't exactly know them, if I bumped into them in the street. I do know their names, or the famous ones at any rate and I do know where they were."

Sean stopped and turned to Will. "Who were they?"

"Well it's a matter of historical record. Let me see, there was Francis Magan. He was on the United Irish Executive, right at the top. Leonard McNally was one of the best-remembered spies. M's, there was another. Oh yes, Nicholas Mageen; he was on the Down Directory."

"What about here in the South?"

"Good grief, Sean, I'm trying to remember. Thomas Reynolds. He was on the Leinster Directory."

Sean wiped his brow. "Never mind 'was', he is and I know him. Jesus, what have I told him?"

Will studied Sean's face. "You've met him?"

"Oh I've met him on a trip, er, on the way to Dublin. Who else is there?"

"There are loads more. I need to stop and think about it. You might have trouble convincing people that these guys are spies. A lot of folk won't want to believe it, just on my say so."

"You're right. Course you are. C'mon let's get back to Wexford and you can write it all down. Keep thinkin'. Like them game shows, I'll give you a pint for every one you can remember." He laughed. "Only I want the names, before you start on the beer!"

In better spirits the two men increased their pace, until they reached a part of the route, where a rocky bluff overlooked the road. Known locally as Three Rocks, it was here that Will noticed something unusual first. Somebody had dumped something in the bushes, beside the road. On closer inspection the ditches and undergrowth were full of rubbish. Sean was eager to press on. Will paused to take a closer look.

"Oh my God. Sean, Sean, look. They're bodies."

Sean's stomach turned at the sight. Hastily thrown into the undergrowth were the bodies and possessions of about thirty militiamen. It was hardly possible to recognise them, their uniforms were so torn. Sean did not want to spend longer looking at the hideously mutilated corpses.

"C'mon. This is no place to hang around. Whatever happened, I don't want to be caught out here, a witness to this lot."

Too late! A crunching of boots on the road alerted the two that they were no longer alone.

"Stand hard or you'll be joinin' them!"

Sean and Will spun around, hands reaching inside their coats for their revolvers.

"Don't you even think about using those things. I've men all around you. We'll cut you down like the rest of them."

They were confronted by a group of men, armed with a mixture of muskets and blunderbusses. Their coats and breeches were covered in mud and they each wore a small brown bowler hat. Clipped in the bands of their hats were what appeared to be remnants of ladies petticoats, lacy, frilly and dyed green.

Sean started to laugh, when more figures, similarly attired emerged from the bushes and trees, although they were easily outnumbered and outgunned.

"Well I hope your sister's not gonna catch cold, Thomas. The boys haven't stolen her bloomers as well, have they?"

"Sean, Sean man, I didn't recognise yer. Where have yer been? We've been scouring the county for you," exclaimed the man, Sean had addressed as Thomas. "And who's this fine fella, you've brought with you?"

Sean stowed his pistol out of sight and Will followed suit.

"Ah, this is a fella you have to meet. He is that rare and wondrous creature, an honest Englishman."

There was a hiss from the group, which was now spilling onto the road.

"No, no, boys," Sean held up his hands. "I'm serious. This is yer man that led our boys to victory, at Midford. This is Will Peters, the man who sent Lord Edward de Guilbert on a one way journey to the place downstairs!"

A roar went up.

Thomas rushed forwards. "In that case I'd like to be the first to shake your hand."

In a moment Will was surrounded by men, green lace bobbing enthusiastically, slapping him on the back and shaking his hand.

"Well boys, what's been goin' on here?" Sean nodded in the direction of the ditch and its gruesome contents.

"Well," responded Thomas, putting his thumbs in his waistband and standing erect, "we've had a little bit of a victory here of our own." A cheer went up from the assembled band. "When the boys took over the town, last night."

"So it's true," interrupted Sean. "What happened? Was anyone hurt?"

"Ah, 'twas a wondrous sight! As a man the whole town rose up and was out on the streets. They all gathered in the Bull Ring, in front of the Court House. They were all a cryin' for you, Sean. And some was calling to go home and was shouted down. That Mr. Smithson, the magistrate got up and a couple of the boys seized him and they was all yellin' to string him up like he'd done to the Jameson boys, last month."

Will looked at Sean aghast. So the uprising really had taken place.

"And I think they'd have hung him, if the military hadn't arrived," continued Thomas. "Colonel Foote and his troops came charging down Main Street from the barracks and he tells 'em to fire their muskets in the air. Well that put the fear of God into us and I don't mind telling you. But nobody moves. We're all just stood there looking at 'em. And then it's their turn to be scared. So the colonel tells us all to disperse, or some such, but still nobody moves."

Thomas stopped his tale for a moment to take a drink from a very ornate silver hip flask, which he had recently acquired.

"Alright, the next thing it all starts to go wild. You see 'cause there's still folk flooding inter the Bull Ring, down from the Cornmarket, but also from down Main Street behind the troops. The colonel, seeing this, next orders the troops to return to the barracks and not to shoot anyone, 'cause he doesn't want anyone to get hurt! Oh that's a goodun!

Now it all starts sort of orderly like, with the troops kind of marching and everyone following and keeping away from them bayonets. Well that's fine till about the Flesh Market, when some o' the colonel's boys sees how many folk are pourin' into the Main Street from the side streets and some o' them starts to panic. Then the next thing you know, it's like race day. The troops running for the barracks, a couple of guns goes off and everyone is shouting and running after them.

That's when people started to get hurt. Some was shot, others was trampled under the crowd and some of the soldiers, what got left behind – well they just got pulled apart."

Thomas was about to drink from the flask again, when Sean took it from him and demanded, "What the hell were you all playing at? I thought I told you not to do anything until I came back."

Will gave Sean a curious look.

"Look Sean, don't you go blaming me for what happened. I didn't start it. It just happened, when the news came back about your battle and defeating the army." He pointed at Sean and Will. "If it's down to anyone, it's you and your man there. If you two will go around slaughtering English soldiers," he grinned. "Well the rest of us just thought it was time to show them what we can do."

"And what the hell's all this about?" Sean pointed to the bodies in the ditches. "For that matter, where did this come from?" Sean held up the almost empty silver hip flask.

Thomas grinned again. "Well that belonged to the colonel, but I don't think he'll be needing it, where he's gone. Mind he might be needing a drink down there."

At this comment there was much laughing and cheering from the others.

"Oh Christ, is this the garrison?" demanded Sean.

"What's left of it, aye. The rest of 'em legged as fast as they could for Enniscorthy."

"You mean you let some of them get away to tell tales." It suited Sean perfectly. It would send the Wexford message back writ large. He didn't let his face reveal his delight. "I think you'd best tell me what happened," growled Sean hanging on to the flask.

"Well it was like this. The colonel and his boys was locked up in the barracks and didn't want to come out. So eventually Colonel Foote steps up and we all agrees that we'll let them go if they leaves the cannon and their guns behind. They wouldn't agree to that so me and Mr Richards suggests that we'll clear the streets and let 'em pass unhindered at midday. And that's what we done."

Thomas paused and gave a conspiratorial wink. "What they don't know is that me and all the boys set off about nine this morning and was waiting for them here at Three Rocks. They was so busy looking behind them to see if we was following them that they didn't see us waiting for them, till it was too late."

Another cheer went up. Will's face was in his hands.

"You mean," said Sean, "that you promised them safe conduct and then killed them."

"Oh come on Sean, you've been telling us for ages, especially, when you came back, that this is a war. These boys would only have come back to kill us."

At this point Will interrupted. "What's going on back in Wexford now?"

Thomas shrugged, "What do you mean?"

"Well who's in charge? What's happening with the loyalists in the town?"

"Well I don't know, I suppose…"

Will didn't give him time to finish. "Come on Sean, we'd better get there quick or you might have a bloodbath on your hands.

Sean nodded. He tossed the flask back to its new owner. "Thomas, pick a dozen to stay here and watch the road. Any troops, give 'em a few warning shots and then get word back to me." He looked up, "The rest of you come with me. And for Christ sake, bury those bodies. In a few days they'll be more dangerous dead than alive."

Sean glanced at Will as they set off. This had not been expected. He knew that there were more questions coming and he'd better be ready with some answers. In the short term he had a reprieve. There were too many ears listening and too much haste needed to cover the last couple of miles to Wexford.

Sean had hoped to slip back into Wexford unnoticed. It was an absurd notion. It seemed that the colonel was not the only one who had liquor with him and the seventy or so, who had ambushed the militia had drunk their fair share. It was a boisterous group that he and Will led back into the town.

"Heh boys, look who we've found!"

"Tis Sean, come back to lead us to more victories!"

The responses were no less animated.

"Sean, Sean, you've missed all the fun."

"Sean, get back to that pub of yours. We've much to celebrate."

"Sean, you're back. We're declaring a republic and you've to be President."

At every cry from the hordes, Sean could feel Will's eyes on the back of his neck.

How could he have come to know these people so well and still been naïve enough to think that he could keep a lid on all this and control them. It was like a carnival in the town. Everyone had put up banners, declaring their support. Every window had a green emblem in it. Probably to save it from being smashed, thought Sean. Some had already been kicked in and some houses were on fire.

The whole town was out of control and hundreds were out on the streets, many of them drunk.

Will spoke first. "Since you clearly have a lot of influence around here, you'd better do something. You know that they piked ninety-seven loyalists on the bridge, first time around. Don't let it happen again, Sean. Remember what we agreed."

Sean nodded. "I'll round up some of the boys I can trust and we'll try and get people off the street. Will you help me?"

"Of course," agreed Will.

Sean's own pub was packed, when they arrived and Sean was carried shoulder high and placed on the bar. It gave him the platform to address the crowd. Eventually he calmed them down and mustered about twenty men, who were, at least, slightly less drunk than the majority and they went out to make a show of force.

There followed several dangerous, exhausting hours of breaking up fights, putting out fires and organising groups to protect the known loyalists. The only solution had been to round them up and move them to a couple of houses, which could be protected. It was not easy, as many of them were too frightened to leave the protection of their own homes or too scared of what might happen to their property, if left unguarded.

Sean shot one man, who was drunk and refused to drop his pike. Barely more than a kid, he had disembowelled a man in his own living room and was about to do the same to his widow.

Sean was at the point of abandoning their efforts, when, mercifully, the rain came. Cold driving squalls from the southeast achieved in moments what they had failed to do all evening. The fires were dowsed and the streets were cleared. Aided by the few sober men that he could trust, Sean imposed a curfew, at threat of shooting, until daybreak.

It had been a nightmare.

At around midnight, they returned to Sean's pub. It was quieter now. Not quiet enough for Sean. He threw them all out at gunpoint and collapsed into a chair. Turning to Maggie, behind the bar, he said, "I don't care what it is, but get me somethin' ter eat."

Hair fallen down around her shoulders and wet with perspiration, even her smile had worn a bit thin. "Do yer know what time it is, Sean? I'm not cooking at this time of night."

Sean turned to her and drew the Collier. "Do you want me to use this on you?"

"Sean O'Grady, put that thing away or you'll feel the back o'my hand, so you will. Now they tell me in this here new republic, that the women will be the same as the men.

So maybe you'd like to go and fetch me something to eat." She winked at him mischievously.

With a groan Sean forced himself to his feet, put the Collier on the table and strode over to the bar. "Will you come around here a minute, Maggie?"

She put down the cloth she was using to wipe up and walked around to Sean's side of the bar.

He put his arms around her waist and squeezed her until her breasts were almost popping out of her blouse. "Now, young Maggie, from where I'm standing this woman will never be the same as the men." She giggled and he kissed her. "And I thank the good Lord for that, but you've a point and I do agree that we ought to give the women more of a say in things. But could we start all that tomorrow? I've hardly eaten a thing all day and I'm just about dead on me feet. Pleeease?" He kissed her again. "You do want me to keep me strength up, don't you?" He squeezed her buttocks.

"Oh, alright, but it'll have to be cold. I'm not starting the fire up, not at this hour."

"You're a little darling. If they make me President, I'll make you Mrs President."

"Yeah, yeah, you're all talk, Sean O'Grady. If you want a drink, you'll have to do it yourself. You can remember how to do that can't you?" she added and was gone out to the back.

The others had dispersed, leaving Will and Sean alone in the bar.

"Pint?" enquired Sean.

"God, yeah, I could murder one," gasped Will.

Sean pulled the pints, dreading the questions that would follow, now they were alone. To his relief and amazement, Will said nothing. He too had collapsed in a chair and drank his beer, presumably too tired to probe Sean further on the events of the day and Sean's involvement in them.

The new day would bring difficult questions and even more difficult decisions.

Chapter 24

Wexford
April 4th 1797

Will descended the stairs from the room he had occupied on his first night in Wexford and found Sean at his usual table. A group of men, strangers to Will, huddled around Sean, studying his precious map. It was clear from the debris of cups and plates strewn across the table that they had been there for some considerable time.

"What time is it? You should have woken me," cried Will.

Sean looked up. He forced a smile. "Well, you had a helluva day yesterday and I didn't like to wake you. Never mind, you're here now. Go and see Maggie in the kitchen and she'll fix you up with something to eat. Then come and join me. I think we need to have a talk."

Will walked through to the kitchen. It seemed to him a lifetime, since the day he'd been washed down in the yard and fitted with his new clothes. There was no sign of the elderly lady or the two girls. How familiar and normal it all now looked; no longer like a tableau in a museum, with waxwork characters. The smell of bacon frying and coffee on the range called him. This was life. It was real.

Maggie was real enough too. It wasn't difficult to appreciate what Sean saw in her. Apart from her more obvious charms, she was full of energy, living every moment to the full.

"Well, so you've decided to join the living have you? Now I was about to eat this lot myself," she said turning the bacon. "Ah now, don't worry. There's plenty more and eggs and all. So you make yourself useful and pour some coffee and cut some bread and you can join me and we'll have a little chat. Won't that be nice?"

Driven by hunger Will quickly found cups and knives and set two places at the old wooden table, its surface worn and uneven from years of scrubbing.

"There you are." Maggie slapped two platefuls on the table and there wasn't much chatting, while they both ate.

"More coffee?" Maggie enquired and topped Will's cup up in response to his nod and then finished her bacon.

She seemed impervious to the chaos that had shaken the town. The world might be coming to an end, but a man still needed bacon and eggs. Rested, fed and for the moment safe, he paused a moment to take it all in. He was living in the late eighteenth century, just like Maggie and all the others and yet he knew so much more than they. How to use that knowledge? That was the question.

Will looked at her over his cup. She was very pretty, all curves and curls; not at all like Mary. Mary had something more. Her unique natural beauty disturbed and excited him. No woman had ever looked at him the way she did. There was something else. Different from each other and from any in his former life, they had one thing in common. They were strong and that strength was supportive, not challenging. If the militia came through the door right now, he'd rather have Maggie standing beside him with a pan of hot fat in her hand, than just about any man he'd ever met.

"You're thoughtful this morning. I heard that you fought like a demon, against them English soldiers." She gazed intently at Will as she said this and Will couldn't help but smile at this mild flirtation.

"Well, we all fought hard and none more than Mary. She's my, uh…" Will was unsure how to describe her. "I saved her from the troops and she, well, saved me, I suppose," he finished lamely and could feel himself blushing.

"Ah, so you've a sweetheart! There's more to you than meets the eye, Will. The girls here will be very disappointed." She leaned forward, wide eyed. "You must tell me everything that happened. I like a good story."

She made Will relate the whole tale of the rescue and when he'd finished, she said, "Well, you're a proper hero and no mistake. Now, why can't I get Sean to rescue me? To take me from this place and make a proper lady of me? Whenever he goes away he never takes me with him. I'd love to go to Dublin and see all those fine folk in their carriages."

"Does he go away often?" enquired Will casually.

"Oh, all the time. I can never keep track of him," she smiled.

Will stiffened, trying to keep his voice steady. "Just for a day or so or does he go away longer?"

"Oh just for a day or maybe a night and then I always want to know what he's been up to."

Now alert, Will enquired, "But never longer?"

"Well he sometimes goes to Dublin and then he's away a few days, but he always tells me." She hesitated for a moment. "Mind there was the time that he was gone for weeks and I was getting to wondering if I'd ever see him again."

Will, alarm bells ringing in his head, nodded to encourage her to continue.

"Then one fine day up he strides up like he's just been to market, not a care in the world and not a word. Wouldn't say where he'd been, no matter what I did." She fluttered her eyelashes and wiggled her breasts. "I gave him quite a row in the end."

He strove to keep his tone casual. "Oh, he's a case and no mistake. When was that Maggie? Recently?"

"Oh no, 'twas last year, towards the end of the summer. Yes that was it, about harvest time he left and was back, oh I don't know, but it was weeks later. Why so interested?"

"Uh, no reason. It was just that I was trying to get in touch with him and couldn't track him down for a while, that's all."

Maggie smiled at Will. "How long have you known him? Where did you meet?"

"Well that's a bit difficult to say, really. We met at University…"

"University now! My, my…Oh, now you're teasing me, Will Peters. I can see I'll have to watch you. Where did you really meet?"

Maggie's reaction to Will's unguarded response set him back for a moment. Then, wasn't a half-truth better than a lie? And he certainly couldn't tell her the full story.

"Well alright, we met in a public house really."

"Now that's more like it! Why would you be tellin' me tales of universities?"

"It was near a university, I suppose, in England and he sort of invited me to come and visit him."

"It all sounds a bit strange to me, Will, but I'm glad you came and, well, did what you did."

Will could see that he could gain nothing more from this conversation and only risk slipping into deeper water, so he made his excuses and summoned the courage to face what Sean might tell him. The sooner he tackled him, the better. He walked through to the bar, where Sean was now alone. Noting his expression, Sean began first.

"Will, it's time I levelled with you. I haven't told you the whole story." He held up his hands to prevent Will from interjecting. "I know, I know. I said that I'd told you what had happened. There's a bit more to it and it's only fair that I tell you now."

He steered Will into a seat, before he could say a word and sat opposite him across the table.

"Don't look at me like that, Will. You'd just arrived and you were in a hell of a state. I didn't want to dump all this on you on top of everything you'd been through, now did I? Anyway in no time at all, that business with de

Guilbert kicked off and there just wasn't time. So listen up now and I'll set the record straight."

Sean, having silenced Will, composed himself.

"Will, you've got to understand. You know me. You know what I'm like. I'm not like you. I didn't know what I was getting into, when I came back. I didn't take it all that seriously and then it kind of took me over. I couldn't help myself. This is my country. You know what I'm saying?"

Will shrugged.

Sean continued. "I know we weren't meant to interfere. That was fine sitting in a lecture room in Boroughbridge. That was all bullshit like the rest of it. Think about it. If they didn't want us to kill anyone, it was pretty bloody silly to train us up and give us guns. Besides, that was fine, when we knew we could twist the bracelets and go home. I don't know about you, but to say it was a show stopper, when the thing didn't work, is the understatement of the century."

Sean pulled up his shirtsleeve to reveal the bracelet. Suddenly he shot out his right hand and seized Will's arm. With his left he pulled up Will's sleeve. He fixed Will with his gaze.

"We're in the same bloody boat now, Will, you and me. What the hell does it matter what we were told? I just couldn't bear to stand around and watch what was happening, all the bullying and killing, the sheer bloody injustice of it all. At first I did a few things to even the score, a bit of robbery. I thought I could play Robin Hood, or something.

It started like that and then it got a bit crazy. People started getting hurt, but I didn't start all that."

Will nodded and Sean released his arm.

"Will, I need your help. I know I've said this before. Now, more than ever, we can make a difference. There's just one problem." He laughed. "I don't know what the hell to do."

Will remained silent.

"Talk to me, Will," urged Sean.

Will gazed longingly at the metal object on his wrist. Then he rose and walked around the room, collecting his thoughts, while Sean's anxious eyes followed him. He turned to Sean.

"I need some answers first. And they'd better be straight ones. If you mess me about that's it. I'll take my money and Mary and I'm out of here. I don't know what I'll do, but I'm not hanging around, while you kill us all rewriting history. Do you understand?"

It was Sean's turn to nod.

"Tell me what you've been doing, Sean. Exactly how far has the Robin Hood stuff gone? Have you been working on your own little revolution here?"

"You could say that," murmured Sean, shifting in his chair.

"A bit more than robbing the rich and giving to the poor, eh?"

"Yeah."

"These trips to Dublin; you've been meeting with the United Irishmen?"

"A couple of times." Sean smiled. "You've been talking to Maggie and put it all together, haven't you?"

Will ignored the question. "Where did you go last year? And I don't mean in our time, I mean here, in Ireland."

Sean caught Will's eye. "Last year?"

"Don't piss about, Sean. Maggie said you disappeared for weeks and you wouldn't tell her where you'd been. Where did you go?"

Sean held Will's stare. He grinned. "How well do you know me? What do you think I was doing?"

Will did not respond.

"Oh come on, Will. What do I always do? Why do you think I didn't tell Maggie? She was gorgeous, lips to die for and she had money. It was another woman, you bloody idiot. I met her in Dublin. She lived in one of those fancy new houses they've just built on Merrion Square. You know how it is. I got, well, distracted for a time.

Look, I'm not proud of myself. I think the world of Maggie. I wish I could change, be a bit more like you. This gorgeous thing and I got talking and she invited me to stay in this beautiful place her family owned. Separate rooms, of course, well to begin with…"

Will watched Sean intently.

"…Anyway, after a while I got bored and even I had a twinge of guilt, thought I'd better get back to the job in hand and my loving Maggie."

Sean's face did not contort during his explanation. His hands and body were relaxed. Could Will be sure that this was the truth?

Sean had observed people like this himself. "I know what you're thinking. If I can tell a tale to Maggie, why not to you? What would be the point? I told Maggie that I got caught by the militia for a while and couldn't get word to her. Sure that was a lie. I've had enough practice with the ladies. I could hardly come back and say, 'Sorry I'm late, love, I've been bonking the brains out of some rich piece in Dublin, while her Dad's been plying me with his best Claret,' now could I? Well not if I didn't want me manhood served up as dish of the day, by the lovely Mags. You've seen what she's like."

"No, I guess not," admitted Will. He smiled. "You'll never change, Sean, will you? I have to admit that I was a bit jealous of you and the women, back at Boroughbridge. Now I think it might be better being me."

"Ah, words of wisdom. I envy you, Will Peters, when I see the way that your Mary looks at you. I'd give it all up for a woman, who'd look at me like that. Mostly they just want to know if I've been up to something. Mind you," he grinned, "that's usually because I have!

Now can we get back to business? I really do need your advice, and not just about the ladies."

"No hang on a minute. You never answered my question. You said things got out of hand and people got hurt. What exactly happened?"

"Oh that. Well, it started off by hitting a few army and militia patrols, just to get some weapons. Then it got a bit more organised. You know, sort of heading off the militia when they were going in to a village or maybe taking the stuff back off them, after they'd taken it and returning it. The bastards will just take anything, food, furniture, livestock. Half the time they just wreck it and chuck it away.

We never hit civilian targets. It was always the military. I'll not hold with all this sectarian stuff. God knows there's enough of that trouble without going looking for it.

So are you happy with that? Can we get on? Only time's pressing, now you've had your beauty sleep."

"There's one other thing."

"Go on."

"You said before that you didn't make contact with the United Irishmen in Belfast. Is that true?"

Sean shrugged. "I didn't lie about that. I was just a bit economical with the truth. I said that I didn't make contact with them, *when I arrived.* I went back and met them the following day."

"You did what!"

"Look Will, I didn't know how to explain it to you at the time. That day I landed; I couldn't believe what had happened or where I was. Besides I was so angry. I wasn't ready to go back in time. I reckon they drugged me. To be honest, I think they drugged you too."

"What do you mean? What are you on about?"

"We were doped. I'm damn sure of it. It was all a bit confusing, but it's the only explanation I can think of. You said to me, 'Why did we do it?' Why else would two bright guys like us do something as bloody silly and get into a mess like this?"

"Oh my God! That explains it all. It was all a dream, those last few days at Boroughbridge." Will rolled his eyes and looked up to the ceiling. His gaze returned to Sean. "Was it like that for you, the last few days, I mean, just before we were sent here?"

Sean nodded. "That's why I just ran away from the United Irish guys on Cave Hill. I literally just appeared and there they were. I was groggy and I didn't know what was going on or what the hell to do." He winced. "I'm not exactly proud of this. Dr. Sean O'Grady, the great intellectual, had a brilliant response to this on the day. I went and got drunk.

The following day, when I came round and took it all in, how much money they'd given me and the pistol and ammunition. That's when I started to think. I realised that all that nonsense they'd told us about being invisible and the rest was just that, nonsense. Then I decided to go back to Cave Hill and they were still there, or at least they were back again."

"So what happened? How did you introduce yourself?" interrupted Will.

"It was a joke, so easy. I just strolled up, told them I was a supporter, who wanted to help fund them and showed them some of the cash. I told them that I'd read their stuff and heard them speak. Then I quoted a few bits and pieces. You'll laugh. I had a bit of a panic at that point, because I thought I might have come out with something that they hadn't written yet! But it was all right and they took me at face value.

I don't know about you, but they all struck me as being a bit too trusting, maybe a bit naïve. They could do with a trip to our time. A short stint working for Bush or Blair would wise them up, ready for what they've got coming with Pitt and the rest."

Will smiled and Sean sensed that his mood was lightening.

"To cut a long story short," continued Sean, "I promised to help them and support their cause. And that's pretty much what I've been doing ever since, after running round the country looking for you, of course."

Sean leaned forward and stared hard at Will.

"I know I haven't been very straight with you and that you don't really trust me right now. I can understand that, but look at it from my point of view. I've had two years of dealing with all the lies and double-dealing. They set me up at Boroughbridge and I don't reckon I can trust any of them back there, given what they did to me. How do I know that you weren't in on it? How do I know that you aren't working with that lot?"

Will shot up from his seat.

"All right, all right, cool it," continued Sean. "All I know is that we were meant to come here together and you turned up two years later. How do I know you're not going to disappear again and pop home for a hot shower and a shave? Meantime I'll just hang around here in all the filth waiting for you to grace me with another visit."

Before Will could reply, Sean seized his arm again and pulled up his sleeve. Placing his arm next to Will's, bracelets adjacent, he demanded, "Are you really telling me that you don't know how to work these things?"

Will shook his head. "Sean, I feel terrible now. You found yourself in this mess and came looking for me. Do you know what I did when those bastards in Bantry caught me? I grabbed the bracelet and twisted it. I didn't stop to think about you, where you'd gone or if you needed my help. I was so bloody scared I'd have done anything to get back to Boroughbridge. Do you think I'd still be here, if this thing worked?"

Sean eyed him, "Really?"

Will's mind filled with an image of Mary. "Well maybe not." He sighed. "I don't know what to do now."

"So we really are in the same boat, eh?" Sean shook his head. "And, just for the record, I don't blame you. Besides," he added brightly, "you've more than made up for it. You're a local hero now.

Why don't I see if the lovely Maggie can fix us some coffee? Come to think of it, I've come by a small amount of decent Darjeeling." He tapped his nose. "No questions asked and taxes paid. Do you fancy some of that?"

"Tea! No taxes paid? You could start a revolution over something like that. Go for it!"

"That's agreed then." He rose and disappeared into the kitchen to seek Maggie and the tea.

Will eased back in his chair, more relaxed, his conversation with Sean now concluded. How could he have coped had he not found Sean? What would he have done, if they'd sent him alone?

The sounds of a lively debate reached Will from the kitchen, the volume increased, as the door opened and Sean reappeared.

"Great, that's that. The tea's on its way and so is Maggie. I've been told," he winked, "that we're not drinking that on our own. Oh, and by the by, it's time I started treating her like an equal. You've not been filling her head with wicked stuff like votes for women and wearing trousers, now have you? There aren't many benefits in living in the eighteenth century, but the women doing as they're told is most definitely one of them.

She's not coming back with the surname Thatcher, is she?"

Will laughed. "It would serve you right if she did. She'd love to go to Dublin with you, you know. She told me. You treat her like shit and she's great. She'd do anything for you."

Sean ran his fingers through his hair. "Can I help it, if the ladies find me irresistible?"

Will frowned at him.

"All right, all right, I'll be a bit nicer to her and when things settle down a bit, I'll take her on a bargain break, somewhere. Are you happy now?

"O.K."

"Now, before she comes in and we get the travel brochures out, can we *please* go back to the stuff about tactics?"

"Sure," agreed Will. "Now let's see, the theory is simple, although I don't know how you're going to do it. Firstly, you've got to sort this place out. You've got to get people involved and show them that the place can be run by democratic means. It ought to work. That part of it actually worked quite well the first time around. And you must instil some law and order. If this descends into yet another sectarian killing spree, what's the point? We might just as well sit in here and get legless!"

Will paused to ensure that Sean was following. "Next, you need time to get people armed and trained. Not just here, but all over Ireland. We both know there'll be repercussions from recent events. There's only one thing that'll stop them sending a huge army down here and that's the fear that, whilst their forces are here, they'll be exposed elsewhere, especially Dublin. They can't afford to leave the capital undefended."

"So what do I do?" asked Sean.

"You need to keep them guessing. If you can organise little uprisings all over the country, they'll never know where the biggest danger is. But, and here's the big but, don't let your men engage the army on a grand scale; no set piece battles. A major formal engagement will be a disaster. We're just not ready. You'll get us all killed, if you do that.

Think about it. It's classic guerrilla tactics. Hit them hard and run away, only to pop up again elsewhere. Think what the Cong did to the Americans in Vietnam. All that fire power, all that military might and in the end, the Yanks fled with their tails between their legs."

Will, fired with enthusiasm, continued. "There's one other really important lesson to learn, since we have the benefit of hindsight. In the original '98 uprising, the rebels found themselves boxed in and couldn't break out of the county to join forces and inspire the other groups. If you look at the geography it's obvious."

He leant over Sean's map and pointed. "To the south and east is the sea. Don't even think about taking on the navy. To the west, you need to take New Ross and that opens up the whole south west of Ireland. To the north is Arklow, the gate to Dublin and the rest of the country. The rebels lost these key battles in the '98. Mind you, it was damn close at New Ross. From that point there was nowhere to go, except escape to the hills.

If you have the rebellion focused on Wexford County alone, history will repeat itself. You won't be able to link up with the others and they'll trap us all, in this little corner of Ireland. A decent general like John Moore will destroy us in no time."

Sean's brow furrowed at this.

"Don't look so worried." It was Will's turn to encourage Sean. "We *do* have the advantage of hindsight. If we can set fires burning all over the country, until we're ready, we can pull this off. I know it's frustrating and we'll not give them a killer knockout blow like this. We just need to be patient, not long, just for a couple of months. While this is going on we can train more troops.

There's another thing we can do. We can lead them a dance at the Castle. I can tell you who a lot of the traitors and informers are. Don't let's weed them out, much better to use them to our advantage. We can feed them all sorts of duff information and have them pass it back to their masters in Dublin. We can start by telling them about the huge rebellion about to blow up in Donegal. I don't think anyone up there gives a monkey's about a rebellion. The French discovered that when they landed in August '98. That'd send them up to the opposite end of the country to us."

Will grinned at the idea. "Do you think you can do that? Do you know enough people to feed it out?"

Sean seemed less enthusiastic. "I don't know. I suppose I could. I'll need some help though, to pick these informers out. Are you sure you can remember them. You didn't seem so confident on the road back from Enniscorthy."

"Well, I was a bit stressed out at the time. I've had some sleep and a bit more time to think. You need to take me to Dublin, though. Your Maggie will have to miss out on that trip." Will's enthusiasm ebbed suddenly.

"What's the matter?" enquired Sean.

"There is one thing I need to do first."

"What's that?"

"I'm sorry Sean. I have to go back to Mary. I have to make sure she's safe. I know. I know. I ought to look at the bigger picture. Just not right now. Not when it comes to her."

"Oh dear, oh dear. You have caught the love bug, haven't you?"

Will didn't respond.

Sean thought for a minute. "That's fine. I need a few days to sort this bloody town out. You're right about that and it'll take me a while to get messages out to my contacts. You know what it's like here. What wouldn't I do for a few mobile phones?

You go on back to your lady and, while you're there, train up a few more troops. I'll send more weapons to you, as they come in, and some reinforcements. That way you're moving things on and, at the same time, setting up a unit, which will protect young Mary and her family."

Will smiled, relieved.

Maggie came bustling into the room with a tray of cups and a teapot. Both men looked up.

"Will's going to be leaving us shortly to go back and take care of his girl, Mary," explained Sean.

"Well, I've had some surprises in my life, but I have to say that's not one of them. These are dangerous times and a man's place is by the side of his woman, at all times. Isn't that right, Sean?"

"For sure it is and that's why I'm here with you, my love. And I've been thinking that, when all the troubles die down, perhaps we might take a little trip together."

Maggie crashed the tray down on the table and, hands on hips, stared at Sean. "Now, *that's* a surprise." Beaming, she turned to catch Will's eye. "I think we need to invite you more often. You seem to be a good influence on him. Mind you," a frown appeared, as she turned back to Sean, "you're full of good intentions. And, as they say, the road to hell…" She sat down and poured the tea.

The three chatted and enjoyed the Darjeeling, until Will felt it was time to leave.

"Will you be alright going back on your own? Do you need a guide?" asked Sean.

Will shook his head. "No need. Just a decent horse and I'll be fine. I've got the sword and the pistol. Nobody's going to mess with me."

He said it with such confidence that both Maggie and Sean were impressed. He was probably right.

Sean departed in search of a mount, leaving Will to collect his belongings, which didn't amount to much. Left alone again with Maggie, she called to him, when he returned downstairs.

"Will, Will, I have something for you." She rummaged in her apron pocket and fished out a little silver ring. "Here, take this and give it to your Mary as a keepsake."

Will examined the ring in her outstretched hand. With a little heart shape on one side, it looked tacky; the sort of thing that a lovelorn schoolboy would buy his girlfriend on a seaside pier.

"Will she like it?" Will enquired ungratefully.

"Oh, you men, you know nothing about women. Of course she'll like it. Now give it to her, but don't tell her it's from me. She won't want it then. Tell her you bought it or some such."

"Of course, thank you," replied Will hastily, ashamed of his thoughtlessness. It was clearly precious to her. "But, er, I shouldn't take such a nice thing from you."

"Ooh, you are such a darling. Just you tell her you love her." She kissed him on the cheek. "And you might mention to Sean," she laughed wiggling her wedding ring finger in his face, "that I'd rather like a ring myself."

The pub door opened and Sean gave a shout.

Will's journey back to the village passed without incident. Sensing his inexperience the huge placid gelding plodded steadily on in the spring sunshine, which followed the previous night's rain. Having cleared the air with Sean and heading back to the woman he loved, his mood was light. And yet something was nagging at the back of his mind. What was it? Something about Sean and the rifles and what he'd said. It was there and it was gone. Never mind. It was just too good being out in the country, with the sun on your face.

When he sighted the village, Will pushed his mount into something approaching a canter. Mary's cottage came into view, smoke billowing from the chimney, a good sign.

She was watching for him.

His heart leapt as she ran from the cottage door towards him. Had he not caught his foot in the stirrup, it would have been the perfect reunion. As it was, he fell, taking her to the ground with him. They laughed till the laughter turned to kisses, while the horse nonchalantly munched the roadside grass.

"Thank God you're safe, Will," she eventually managed to gasp.

"I was worried about you, too, Mary. I should have stayed in Wexford longer, but I had to be sure you were all right."

She smiled.

"Besides, I couldn't wait any longer to see you."

She beamed.

He helped her to her feet. "Oh, and I have something for you." He reached into his pocket and produced the little ring. "I, um, don't know if you like it. There wasn't much…"

"Oh Will, it's beautiful." She snatched it from him and then hesitated. Engaging him with her green eyes, she slipped it slowly and deliberately onto the third finger of her left hand.

He didn't stop her.

For Will, the days that followed were the happiest of his life. In the mornings he trained an ever-growing army of eager volunteers. Weapons flooded in, as did young men from the surrounding villages. His confidence grew with every session and this rubbed off on his followers. His stature and control over his men increased with every day that passed.

At around noon he would call a break and return to Mary's cottage. Alone, with Mary's siblings in the fields or the hedge school, they retired upstairs and made love. They both knew it was mad, even wrong. Who cared? Who was there to stop them? They would probably be dead inside a month, so why not live for today? Both were consumed with the same wild abandon and nothing else mattered except being together.

Sean was in full flow, before an assembly of representatives from all over Ireland. Key men had come down from Dublin. So many were crowded around the table at the back of the bar that many were forced to stand. All were straining to see Sean, who was holding court in the middle, his secret map the centrepiece of his presentation.

"Now is the time to be bold," boomed Sean, thumping the table. "We have shown you what can be achieved, here in Wexford. And now we are enjoying the fruits of our toils. You are gathered here in the Republic of Wexford, where all men are equal and answer only to themselves." He paused for effect. "Today Wexford, tomorrow all of Ireland!"

A roar of approval shook the building.

Maggie and the other girls moved easily between them, replenishing tankards and collecting money. Sean had made it clear to them that political freedom was one thing, free beer quite another.

"We will lead you to the freedom your fathers could only dream about. We have the strength and we have the resources to defeat the enemy at the gates of the New Republic. Until that time I do not want any of you to risk your lives. Your time will come. Sharpen your pikes, clean your muskets, but do not show them, not yet.

General Lake and his filthy army of scoundrels and rogues will descend on us and we will fight him near the Three Rocks and drive him back to Dublin itself."

Thanks in part to the beer; Sean's rhetoric fell on fertile ground. They cheered and clapped each other on the back. The plan to let these reckless revolutionaries in Wexford do the job for them was an easy one to follow. How simple it would be to take this message home to their nervous and divided committees.

"Once Wexford county is free and the army defeated, that will be the time to call you to arms," concluded Sean.

"And we will answer!" roared the room.

After questions and pledges the meeting finally broke up and they drifted away. One man held back, requested by Sean to wait until the others had gone. As the last one marched fearlessly out of the front door, Sean went over to the bar and pulled out a bottle.

"I know that you've a long journey in front of you, but I wanted a word, just the two of us, man to man. Do you fancy a drop of the decent stuff to set you on your way? It's on me." He waved a bottle and two glasses.

The man agreed readily.

Sean ushered him back to the table, where he had left the map. Sitting next to the man he explained, "I just thought that, given your senior standing, you deserved a little background. I figured that you're wise enough to handle it." Sean uncorked the bottle and poured two large measures.

They both raised their glasses.

"Erin go Brach!"

"It's um, not quite as rosy a picture as I might have painted to the others." Sean put his arm around his companion. "You can keep this to yourself, can't you?"

The man assured him that he could.

"Well, you see, we're not really ready for them, not yet. Give us a month and we'll be there, I'm sure, but not yet. I didn't want to dampen their enthusiasm. I need to keep morale up. You can understand that, I'm sure."

The man agreed enthusiastically.

"To be honest, we were lucky to take the town. If Lake came down here with half his army tomorrow, they'd go through us like a hot knife through butter. We need, say, to the end of May. So just tell your lot to be patient. We'll get there; don't worry, just not yet. I don't want to go too soon and be responsible for a massacre."

The man drank and said nothing.

"That's great. You can't imagine how much better I feel for getting that off my chest. Now I'd better not hold you up any more."

Sean drained his glass and stood up. His companion took the hint and made ready to leave.

At the door they shook hands.

"I can trust you to be discreet with that, can't I?" asked Sean before releasing the man's hand.

"To be sure you can, my friend," said Leonard McNally and walked out into the damp spring sunshine.

Chapter 25

Midford Co. Wexford
April 10th 1797

"Stop it, stop it now," squealed Mary, running from the cottage door and into the front yard.

The laughter lines around her eyes told Will that stopping was the last thing that she desired. He chased after her, seizing her slim waist and pulling her to him. "Oh Mary you are…"

A cough from a tall stranger at the gate pulled him up. Mary, suddenly anxious, clung tightly to Will's arm, as she surveyed the intruder.

The stranger shifted his feet uneasily in the dirt. "Begging your pardon, Sir, I've a message for you. That is, I have, if you're Mr Will Peters."

Will nodded to the man cautiously, pushing himself between Mary and the newcomer. He noticed that the stranger had a companion, holding two horses, a few yards distant. Both men were armed.

"Go back to the cottage and fetch my pistol," he whispered in Mary's ear, as he steered her back towards the sanctuary of the cottage. "Keep it hidden under your apron. Now go."

"Who's looking for Will Peters and who's the message from?" enquired Will steadily.

"My name is Ryan MacIvoy and that there's my friend, Jamie O'Toole. We've a message from Sean O'Grady…"

Will stiffened, trying to loosen his tongue from his dry mouth.

"… But I've to make sure that you're Will Peters," continued Ryan MacIvoy, clearly not fooled by Will's evasive response, "and to let you know that I really come from Sean." He paused.

Will, relieved, felt that Ryan's unease came from uncertainty and lack of confidence, and was not a prelude to unleashing some act of violence.

"Go on," encouraged Will, puzzled.

"Oh, uh, yes. I've to ask you, let me see, if you'd met a lady from somewhere called, er, Canada, what would she be called?"

Will smiled. "Would it be Bob?"

Ryan grinned in response. "That's the right answer."

Mary appeared at the door and Will moved to her side. "It's alright, don't worry. These two are fine, but just wait here a moment."

Young Ryan scratched his head. "There was something else. Oh, that's it. I've to tell you about a man called Al. What was it? He was game or something. That doesn't sound right." His face creased in worry. He looked expectantly at Will. "Does that make any sense to you?"

Laughing, Will slapped his shoulder. "Sense enough, Ryan MacIvoy. Do you and your friend want to come in for a rest and to tell me your message?"

The young man eagerly beckoned his companion. Having tethered the horses at the gate, the pair entered the gloom of the cottage and sat down. Unrequested, Mary stoked some life back into the fire and went to draw water, leaving the pistol handy by the window.

"Relax lads, your message can wait a minute, till Mary returns. I want her to hear it too. What's the news from Wexford and how is Sean?"

"Oh Sean is fine and he says to send his best regards to you and your Mary. As for Wexford, well that's another story," sighed Ryan. He turned to his friend. "What shall we say about it, Jamie?"

Jamie, even taller than Ryan and lanky, seemed more confident than the messenger that he'd clearly been sent to look after. "In some ways it's better than it was. There's no troops nor no militia and the magistrate's in jail. In some ways it's worse." He paused to choose his words carefully.

"People are afraid, not just of the army coming in, but of each other. In the old days you knew who to be afraid of and who was who. Now you're not so sure. And everyone has put a green bough or a ribbon in their window to show that they support the republic, even when you know that only last month they were with the government.

Lots have left the town and gone into the country. They've taken to sleeping in the ditches and under hedges for fear of having their houses burnt, while they're sleeping. But then they get too cold or it rains and they have to go home again.

What's more, Father Barker said to me only yesterday that he'd never been so busy with confirmations. All sorts of folks, he said, have come to him. They gave him all sorts of reasons that they weren't Protestants at all, like the priest who did it was in the wrong parish or some such."

He glanced at Ryan who showed his concern with a frown.

"Oh and the magistrate," continued Jamie, as if he had just remembered that he'd left him in jail, "is going to be hanged, some say. Now I say that's all he deserves, but not his wife and children and kinfolk. You can't blame a child if his father's a bad man, now can you?"

Will listened with increasing anxiety, impatient for Mary to join them. She had returned and was arranging the kettle over the fire.

"Now let's find out what Sean's been up to," she said, when she finally took her seat.

All eyes turned to the messenger, as he fiddled with a loose button on his jacket, unused to this kind of attention.

"It's like this, see," he started uncertainly. "Sean has asked me to tell you that this message is very serious and you've to act upon it right away."

Mary and Will glanced at each other in anticipation.

Ryan took a deep breath and burst into the speech that he'd rehearsed all the way from Wexford. "A large English army is approaching Wexford and is only two days away according to…"

"What?" interrupted Will, aghast. "Are you sure? Where did you get this message, I mean where did Sean get it? Is that two days from now?" Will's mind filled with images of prints he'd seen; the battles of 1798, the defeat of the rebels, the aftermath of persecution. It was all too easy to transpose those images onto these people he had grown to love. It was his worst nightmare, a set piece battle. His brain whirled. How could Sean have let this happen?

Bewildered by Will's reaction and the barrage of questions, Ryan looked to Jamie for support.

"Just tell them Ryan," encouraged Jamie.

"It was only late last night that I heard all this," continued Ryan. "I suppose the English army will be here tomorrow," he shrugged casually and then noticing the look of horror on Will's face, added hastily, "or maybe the day after tomorrow."

Will leapt from his seat. "Tomorrow! Tomorrow! Christ, that's no time. Why didn't you say when you arrived?"

"Will, my love, sit down. It's not his fault." Mary's voice was calm and steady. "Let them give you the rest of the message."

Will managed a smile and let Mary pull him back into his seat. "Alright, alright, I'm sorry fellas. What else do you have to tell us?"

Ryan and Jamie exchanged looks.

"That's about all," said Ryan, "except to tell you that you are to gather up all your troops and bring them to defend Wexford right away." He placed both hands on the table and exhaled slowly, relieved to have unburdened himself of his message.

"And that's it? Nothing else? Oh that's bloody marvellous!" exclaimed Will.

Mary put her hand on his arm. "What else is there to know? And if we are to do this, Will, we must remain calm.

They must not panic." She engaged Will with a knowing look, not reproachful, just a warning.

It was not lost on Will. He turned slowly to the two young Irishmen and smiled. "Thank you for bringing this news. Be assured that we will act on it immediately."

Both men smiled, their task accomplished.

"Kindly convey my compliments to Sean," added Will, "and say that we will come tomorrow, as early as we can." He glanced at Mary, who nodded in agreement.

An embarrassed silence followed, until Jamie nudged Ryan, who spluttered, "Uh, um, I don't think that we were expecting to take back a reply. You see, because Sean said he was about to leave and wouldn't say where he was going or when he would be back."

It was Mary's turn to look nonplussed. "He can't have gone. Gone where? Who's in charge in Wexford?" she asked.

"Well that's sort of what I've been saying," replied Jamie. "It was bad before, but now it's going to get worse. That's why we need Will there."

Will sat silently looking at the three, as they all turned to him. This really was his worst nightmare and, to cap it all, Sean had run away. All his doubts about this man, whose adventure he was sharing, bubbled to the surface. He looked at the worried faces, depending on him. It was up to him now. If this is my fate, he reflected, I'd better make a better job of it than the last battle.

"Lads, is Rikki still there?"

"To be sure he is," they both said.

"Tell him we'll be there for midday and that I want to see him, as soon as we get there."

It was late in the afternoon, before Will and Mary, followed by a caravan of villagers, reached the outskirts of Wexford. Will had thought long and hard over the last few weeks about battles and skirmishing. He had not dreamt how difficult it would be to organise such a disparate group and move them a few miles to the outskirts of Wexford. Despite all his efforts he was obliged to admit defeat and his fighting troop, now swollen to nearly two hundred, was accompanied by animals, relatives and a bewildering array of personal possessions.

Under Mary's watchful eye Will remained outwardly calm and they followed him blindly, carefree, like an excursion to the seaside. Confident in their dashing young talisman, they sang and even danced as they accompanied him on their daytrip to drive the old enemy into the Irish Sea, once and for all.

Will tied his horse to the back of a cart he had commandeered. Once on the move and sitting beside Mary, he tried to focus on a battle plan. When they arrived he would leave them to camp out of sight, find Rikki and reconnoitre. He badly needed Rikki's calm assurance and clear head. Beyond this he could not plan. Dark thoughts kept creeping in and it was all he could do to keep these from his face. And he had remembered what had worried him about Sean and those beautiful hunting rifles.

Unable to acquire the famous army issue Baker rifles, which would not appear for a couple of years, hadn't Sean admitted to stealing them from one of the landed gentry? Will was convinced he had said that. It was the only place to procure such expensive and rare items. If this were true it made a lie of his claim to have hit only military targets and to have avoided sectarian violence. If Sean were lying about this, what else was he lying about? Had he found it too difficult to organise affairs in Wexford and run out on everyone? Was it all part of his plan to leave them to slaughter the old order and clear the way for the new? Was he just in it for what he could get? Was in the pay of the English? No, that was mad, impossible.

Will smiled and encouraged those around him. Inside he fought to keep the demons at bay. The next twenty-four hours would change their lives, or maybe end them.

The outskirts of Wexford were approaching.

"Will, Will," Mary was tugging at his sleeve. "Don't take them into the town. They'll disappear into the streets and bars and you'll never get them to the battlefield."

'Battlefield.' Did she have any idea what that word meant, thought Will. Did he? The business at the village had been nothing but a skirmish. This would be something totally different, something he'd only ever seen in films. Was he strong enough to handle it?

"Oh, no you're right. Shall we stop here and I can take my horse and ride on ahead to meet Rikki? Are you alright to wait here?" He wondered how Rikki would assess the situation.

She agreed to his plan and to organise it so that he lost no time in meeting Rikki. They were already hours later than promised. Will drew the cart to a halt and, handing her the reins, slipped down and untethered the horse that Sean had given him. It seemed that he was barely out of Mary's sight when he was practically ridden down by Rikki and two companions galloping in the opposite direction. They all pulled up hard in a melee of curses, mud and reins.

"Where the hell have you been? They're only about ten miles away and the town's in absolute bloody chaos. I haven't got a fucking clue where Sean is. You'd better get a move on. How many men have you got? Oh my God, you're not alone are you?" Rikki's eyes were blazing, his skin was an odd shade and he looked like he hadn't slept since Will last saw him.

"Whoa, steady on. Who is ten miles away? The English? Which direction? No hang on, let's dismount and sort this out. And no, I'm not alone. The rest of them are just up the road." Will tried to calm himself, his horse and his newly met allies.

They dismounted and found a tree for tethering their horses. The ground was too damp to sit and so they gathered in a huddle by the roadside.

Will took the initiative. "It's good to see you, Rikki." He seized the man, he had grown to know and trust and they embraced.

"Yes, it's good to see you too, Will. I'm sorry about that, just now. It's that we were expecting you earlier and things are moving fast. If I'm honest I was beginning to think that you might not show up."

It was extraordinary, thought Will. Here was a man from a different time and place, whom he had known for no time at all. For him, Will Peters, to ignore his call for help, to refuse to stand by him, even to the death, was impossible to contemplate. Will was still terrified at what the morning might bring, but to run way would bring nothing more than a slower death of shame and misery.

"Who are these brave lads?" Will indicated Rikki's companions, who smiled at this description and were quickly introduced.

"So tell me about the enemy first and then I want to hear what's happening in Wexford," continued Will.

"We've had men tracking their progress, practically all the way from Dublin," explained Rikki. "They retook Enniscorthy this morning and will be here by tonight or the morning, at the latest."

"How many?"

"Well there have been all sorts of wild tales, so I sent Pat. You remember him? He has just come back and reckons they must have at least a couple of thousand and some field pieces and of course some cavalry. I'm not sure how many horsemen they have. It's most of the Dublin garrison as well as the garrison that pulled out of Enniscorthy."

As if Mary were at his shoulder, Will smiled, while his heart sank to his boots. "Not so bad then, eh? If they'd been properly organised, they could probably have put at least five, maybe ten thousand into the field. Who's in charge? Sir John Moore?"

Will's forced smile was infectious and Rikki laughed, "I suppose it's not so bad." Then his face fell. "We've heard that General Lake himself is leading the army."

"Lake? That's brilliant. He might be an evil bastard, but he couldn't find a whore in a brothel. Moore's a different case altogether. He's a fair man and a gentleman. He's also a superb commander of men. So how many men have you got and where are they?"

"I reckon that we have around a couple of thousand. The only thing is, they're not all properly armed and..." Rikki glanced at his two companions, as if seeking support, "... when it comes to it, I'm not sure how many of them will stand up and be counted.

"That's to be expected, Rikki. We need to put our trained troops amongst them, to give them confidence. I've brought about two hundred with me. It's not many, but they do know how to handle their muskets and have had plenty of practice using powder and ball. It's the English way of training and it works. We'll give them a taste of their own medicine eh? Now where are your troops?"

Rikki explained that practically half the town had headed a couple of miles north to a rise of land that barred the road into Wexford. They decided on a plan to skirt the town with Will's group, so that they could all join up that evening and be ready for an expected attack in the morning. The four men remounted and rode to join Will's villagers. Quickly they agreed that Rikki's two companions would stay with Mary to show her the route, whilst Will and Rikki went ahead to reconnoitre the land and discuss tactics.

Rikki pushed the pace around to the north of the town. Taking all his concentration to keep his seat, Will had no time to talk, until they cleared a small rise, emerging from a copse and the intended battlefield came into view. Pausing to survey the scene Will could see that it was a classic defensive position. In the distance the road from Enniscorthy topped a rise and then descended into a wide valley to cross a stream by a few farm buildings and cottages. The stream itself was a trickle and would not form a defensive barrier, but Will could appreciate that from that crossing the road rose steeply up to the crest of another hill, before it dropped again into Wexford. He could see a great gathering on the ridge of the hill on the Wexford side.

"Rikki, it's a fine place to make a stand, but wouldn't it be better to do this at Three Rocks, where they killed the local regiment? It's a much narrower position and won't give the English the chance to deploy their cavalry."

Rikki grimaced. "You're right of course, Will. It's just we can't get them there. A crowd of them set up camp, where you see and then more joined them and now it's like the biggest party you've ever seen. We can't shift them. I've tried. I could take a group of well trained men to the Three Rocks and hold them up, but I couldn't hold them forever."

"Let me think for a moment," said Will, pulling out the telescope, which Sean had given him. He could see groups gathered around fires, drinking and dancing. "I see what you mean about the party. How many men do you have that you can rely on? I'm talking about men that know how to use their weapons and have seen some action; men that won't run away."

"A few hundred that can fight, I suppose, but would I trust them all, to stand with me to the death? Maybe only about fifty."

"That's what I guessed. I love the idea of making them pay dearly at Three Rocks. If we had more reliable men it'd be the obvious thing to do. It's just we can't afford to lose our fifty best men, knowing that they'll eventually pass. Besides if you did get back from there I'm afraid you might arrive back here to find this lot had gone home and left you to fight the whole army on your own. We're going to need good men to hold this lot from running, when the artillery start up."

"So what's the plan, Will?"

"I might change it a bit, when I get up there, so don't shout at me if I do," he smiled at Rikki, who couldn't help but laugh, despite their predicament. "For the moment, it seems to me that the best we can do is to try and hold as big a group as possible. That way we'll look like a formidable force. I'm not convinced that the English rabble is any too disciplined themselves. Look what happened before, when they didn't expect to face a united front.

If I put my lot in the centre, three ranks of about forty either side of me. We'll split whatever we've got up there on the hill either side of my position. Can you split your few hundred and put them on either flank? If we've got reliable troops either side, it will protect our flanks and may even keep the partygoers in line. Have you got reliable deputies, as you can't be on both flanks at the same time."

"Yes, that's not a problem," agreed Rikki.

"We've got the little cannon we captured. It won't do much and it won't have the range that they'll have. Never mind we can lob a few shots into their cavalry. Maybe we'll get a lucky shot amongst their guns. Have we got any mounted troops?"

"The same fifty or so that I can really trust."

"Hm, we can't use them twice. They'd be so useful to make their mounted troops think a bit and it makes them very manoeuvrable. We'll have to use them like that. What about the Fox? I'm bloody sure just having him and his men milling around might help. They frighten me and they certainly decimated the remains of the troops at Mary's village. Have you seen him?"

"Not a sign. Maybe he'll turn up, but you can't depend on him, Will."

"It's not much of a plan, but it's the best I can do. I don't want to make it too complicated. My troops can shoot volleys quickly and they won't run. I can't make them do complicated manoeuvres. You know, turn direction or form proper squares. It ain't Waterloo!"

"Waterloo?"

"Huh, oh yes. If we're still alive this time tomorrow, I'll try and explain," laughed Will. He knew that he wouldn't. Besides tomorrow evening didn't seem very likely to happen.

They set off for the hilltop and the scene didn't improve as it came closer. Will was close to despair, as he witnessed drunken men chasing equally drunken women around huge campfires, which would show their position for miles around. What did it matter? It might make them appear stronger than they were. There was only one thing that mattered. Who was in charge of this rabble? He needed to find them and gain some kind of control. For an age he and Rikki hunted about and were sent from one to another, in search of anyone who held sway. Eventually they identified men who might be relied on to organise this crowd. Will was not convinced.

Mary finally led Will's followers into the throng. She too was appalled at the scenes she witnessed. "We must not let them mix with them," she announced dramatically.

"How do we stop them?" asked Will. "If they get drunk tonight, they'll never fight in the morning. If the English come it'll be at dawn. Oh my God, where the hell are they? I must talk to Rikki and find out where his scouts are."

"Go, Will, go. This is my job. You've an army to organise."

At around five in the morning Will managed a few minutes sleep or so it seemed to him.

He was woken by Rikki. "We have company. Come and see."

Will crawled out from beside Mary under the cart and shook the cold and stiffness from his limbs. He walked with Rikki to the brow of the hill. In a moment Mary was beside him rubbing her eyes and clinging to his arm for warmth and support. It was barely light and they were there, on the hillside opposite. A few at first and gradually, revealed by the growing dawn, there were many.

The three stood on their hill and watched, mesmerised as the enemy deployed. The English made no attempt to disguise their numbers or their intentions. They poured over the hill and down the little road, spreading out over the hillside like an incoming tide. A troop of gunners finally came down the road and the threesome watched, as they unlimbered their heavy weapons. Will fancied he could hear the clink of the chains as they unhitched the horses from the gun carriages. He knew what those guns would do to them. At least they had brought up the rear and no more troops had followed them down that road.

He looked up from the gun crews to the road. Then more troops appeared. They were followed by cavalry, who spread out behind the gunners and to the left, away from the noise, which he knew would come. More troops arrived. Will tried to assess their numbers, at least two thousand, probably nearer three and still they came. "Oh Sean, what have you done?" he muttered audibly.

His two companions cast him nervous glances.

Pulling himself together, Will blustered cheerfully, "No point in gawping, you two. We need to get ready and don't let's fool ourselves, it won't be quick. Rikki, your men are deployed on either flank, whistle up your platoon leaders. I want them to take charge, leaving you free to help me to get the rabble organised. Mary, if you can have our men formed up and ready, that leaves me to work with Rikki.

Now listen, both of you…" They hung on Will's every word. "…Whatever you do, you must keep all your people behind the brow of the hill. Post a couple of lookouts and tell them to keep telling everyone what is happening. That'll keep the curious at bay. Behind the hills, those big guns are just wasting ammunition. It'll just go over our heads. Rikki and I will have to make sure that they pull in tighter to the hill from the back. The shot has to land somewhere.

On the front of the hill, they will slaughter us. Lake will be quite happy to save his men and let the gunners do the job for him."

"And we've got nothing to counter the guns," added Rikki.

"Well not quite. We've a handful of rifles. Can you get them in close enough to shoot a couple of the gunners? It might just cause them to move back or at least to slow up their rate of fire. Watch out for their cavalry, though," said Will.

"I reckon I could get in from our right, away from the cavalry, with a few men," offered Rikki.

"Sorry Rikki, not you, I can't afford to lose you. You'll have to give that job to someone else. There'll be plenty of opportunities for dying later in the day."

"Understood. I know who to pick."

"Great, let's get to it."

Will and Rikki had tracked down again the men who claimed to hold some kind of sway over the gathering. It was to these men that the two turned their attention. Once word was out that the English had arrived it proved easy to gather the troops, in spite of sore heads, lost weapons and clothing. It was much more difficult to keep them out of sight of the big guns, until the first report echoed across the valley towards them.

It was a pure flook, a tester for the gun team. The fourteen-pound ball roared across the divide, between the opposing teams, landing about forty feet below the crest of the hill and skidded another twenty feet along the ground, removing a small shrub, a lot of damp grass and the legs of an elderly man, who had come to watch the fun. The stampede for safety behind the hill threatened to turn into a rout at the first shot. Nobody thought to attend to the crippled man, moaning pitifully, where he had been felled. Will shouted for the medical team, who scooped him up onto a makeshift stretcher. The youngest member of the team, a teenage boy, hesitated before picking up the remains of the legs and tossing them onto the stretcher alongside their former owner.

Will cursed as they took him to a tent that he had thought to erect the previous night. All that they would achieve would be to let the man die with some dignity and away from the fearful eyes of his comrades. After that minor success the English guns banged away for half an hour or so until they either realised that they were wasting their time or had satisfied themselves that the range was set.

Silence fell on the field, broken briefly by the crack, crack of rifle fire. Will guessed correctly. The riflemen caused the gunners to take cover, but not to move their guns. The English cavalry threatened. The riflemen retreated and silence fell again. It was fully light now and there had been one casualty. A phoney war, thought Will. Why don't they get on with it?

He surveyed his own lines. To his amazement, they looked reasonably organised. Just too few. He surveyed the enemy. Dear God, his little army was outnumbered at least two to one. In reality, if he counted only the trained men, it was nearer ten to one. The thought made him shudder. Why didn't they attack? It would be over before lunch. Then he realised. They don't know. They have no idea how many we are, he pondered. No doubt the reports have been exaggerated. They probably think I've got thirty thousand men behind this hill. In that case let's not disillusion them.

He called to Rikki, who was on horseback fifty yards away and explained his thoughts. "Rikki, do you think that we can get everybody to spread out across the whole length of the hilltop and show themselves, say about three deep? From over there it will look like we have about ten times the number we really have."

"I should think so, only what good will it do?" asked Rikki.

"I don't really know, except it might make them hesitate to commit all their force. It could make them want to talk or, maybe even hold off the attack, if they think they're outnumbered."

Rikki shrugged. "I suppose anything is worth a try. If they throw that lot at us in one go, we both know what the outcome will be," he added grimly and set off to organise it.

Mary joined Will at the brow of the hill. After explaining his plan, they stood arm in arm to watch the reaction, taking turns with the telescope. At first there seemed to be no response, although Will could see a group of officers training their lenses on the his hilltop, pointing and exchanging opinions. Suddenly a man mounted a horse and rode away from the group. Astonished, Will watched as two large groups of troops, maybe a whole battalion, shouldered arms, turned and retreated back up the hill and to one side of the cavalry.

"Oh look, Will, look. You've done it, they've started to run away." She thrust the telescope back into his hand to check for himself.

Then a small detachment moved forward and descended to the foot of the slope and entered the little group of farm buildings by the stream. They disappeared into the cottages to emerge a few moments later dragging what looked like a young man out into the field. Will started to sweat. It had never occurred to him that the buildings were still inhabited.

After a brief tussle the man broke free and started to run. He had covered but a few yards, when a shot rang out. He fell, only to struggle back to his feet. He had been shot in the leg. They shot him again. He thrashed around until a soldier marched up to the injured man and shot him in the head. Worse was to come.

A silence fell over the Irish line, even when smoke started to pour from one of the cottages. Two men and a woman rushed out. They shot the men and seized the woman, their intentions plain. Will took the telescope from his eye, unable to watch it any longer. He looked as thousands of Irish eyes watched helplessly.

Then with a roar the line broke. It was like an avalanche. A few started down the hill and suddenly there were hundreds. They were unstoppable, as they screamed vengeance on the English murderers.

"NOOO!" howled Will. "STOP! STOP!"

It was hopeless. This avalanche would not stop until it had reached the bottom of the valley. Will could only hope to stop his own men from rushing to their deaths. By running in front of them and firing his pistol in the air he turned them. He looked about. Somehow Rikki's men had been held too. For the rest it was a different story. He turned his attention back, as events unfolded on the valley floor.

The soldiers, who had committed the atrocities, had gone. Killed or retreated, it was impossible to say. The hordes of Irish were milling around, with nobody to wreak revenge upon. They were still unaware of the imminent danger. From Will's vantage point it was clear. The troops, he had so recently thought were retreating, had left the way free for the cavalry. Gathering speed, the horsemen formed their own avalanche, which would not stop until it had smothered the first light fall of Irish rebels.

Will watched the bulk of his army look up, watched the realisation dawn and anger turn, with wicked speed, to fear, retreat and despair. It was done with ruthless efficiency and cunning. Not typical of the cavalry at all, thought Will. The horsemen split into two formations. The first rode their victims down. The second rode wide and moved ahead of their victims on foot, cutting off their line of retreat. Driven in front of the English infantry lines, Will's troops were shot down by beautifully disciplined volleys. Barely a few score made it back to the safety of their own lines.

They did not stop, when they reached the brow of the hill. Like moisture evaporating on a hot road, they were gone, taking the hangers on and the voyeurs with them. In around twenty minutes Will's rabble army had gone like a shower on the wind. Only his own men, flanked by Rikki's two platoons remained. Mary, ignored by him throughout the entire episode, was shaking in shock and grief. Her tears would not come. He held her close, pushing her head against his chest.

"It's alright. It's alright," he murmured, his eyes riveted to the English lines. They were moving, all of them. Wave after red wave was approaching. They were twenty minutes away, probably less.

"Mary, Mary, I need to pull our lines together. The gaps are too great between us. They'll cut us apart."

She let him release her.

"Rikki, Rikki, bring them to the centre!" he shouted, waving his arms above his head. "Form them up on my flanks."

Rikki, waved his arm in acknowledgement, mounted his horse and was gone to issue the orders.

"How long have we got?" asked Mary.

The valley floor was running red with advancing English troops.

"Maybe fifteen minutes."

Even with Rikki's men forming either side of them, they were pathetically few now. Perhaps I should let them run, thought Will. Do it now, before the cavalry can cut them down. That way at least they have a chance.

Mary was watching his face. "Will, I want you to promise me one thing."

He stared at her uncomprehending.

"Promise me, Will and I won't be scared."

Still he did not understand.

"Your pistol, the one with the five shots. You must save the last shot."

Realisation broke through his defences.

"It won't come to that, my love. It'll be alright."

"No it won't, Will. You know it won't. Don't die and leave me to them." She took his hands and formed them around the crucifix at her throat. "Promise me."

"I promise," he whispered, fighting back the tears. Taking a sharp breath he held her at arms length. "Now we must be brave, for the others."

Mary smiled and walked deliberately forward so that her fellow villagers could see her. Will was about to follow her, when something caught his attention. The sun had risen high in the morning sky and he had noticed a flash of light on a hill to the East, about a mile away. It was nothing. Will had more pressing matters to attend to. There it was again. Will pulled out his telescope and trained it on the hill. Curiosity turned to shock. More troops were pouring over the hill to the east, in the direction from the coast. That was it. He should make his troops run, before they were cut off. They might make it to New Ross, in the West and beyond.

Will snapped his telescope shut, decided. Then he hesitated and opened it again to take another look. Something bothered him. Something was not right. He squinted through the lens. They were coming over the hill at an incredible rate. Bastards probably don't want this lot to steal all the glory, he thought. He must be decisive and move quickly.

He spun around to tell Mary, but she was too far away, encouraging her fellow villagers. She was a wonder. She never stopped. More than they, she understood what was about to happen and yet she showed no signs of fear. What was the point in sharing this new misery with her? Oh God, what would they do to her village if they ran.

Will turned back to watch this new enemy deploy. He put his telescope to his eye again to follow them more closely. They were good. Damn, they were good. He could clearly see the gunners unhitching their weapons, just like he had watched earlier. These were different weapons and these guys were quicker than their comrades. A giant of a man was laying about him like a madman with a huge bullwhip, roaring his men on. What the hell was the hurry?

More blue uniforms poured over the hill. Blue? Which regiment was that? What did it matter? Did he care which regiment killed him? Blue? Damn it, who were they? It was stupid, yet it bothered him.

Blue? Blue! Oh my good God! They couldn't be! He twisted the instrument frantically to focus. Damn it, his eye was too wet. Wiping his eye and then the lens on his sleeve, he tried again. Mounted troops in blue with plumes in their hats were hastening past the gunners.

"Oh Sean, you crafty bastard. It's April 1797. How could I have forgotten? How to land an army on the East coast? When the Royal Navy is on strike!!"

"Mary! MARY!" he shrieked in excitement.

He ran after her and seized her hand, dragging her around and ramming the telescope in her eye in his haste.

"Will, stop it. You're hurting me. Don't let us down now. You mustn't let the others see you're…"

"No, no look," he interrupted her. He steered her in front of him. Stuffing the telescope in his coat pocket, he held her head between his hands and twisted it viciously to face the far hill, where the activity was now clearly visible with the naked eye. "Look!"

"Oh my life, not more of them. What are we to do, Will?" she gasped.

Will spun her around to face him, holding her head he kissed her. "You don't understand. They're, they're French!"

Fighting him off, she spun back to see for herself. "Holy bloody Mother of God, they're not, are they?" she shouted and her hand flew over her mouth to cover her blasphemy.

Chapter 26

North of Wexford
April 11th 1797

For a moment it was as if only Will and Mary had noticed the arrival of the French. Then, with a roar and a thud, the first shot flew out from one of the French guns. It was wildly short of its target, but unmistakably directed at the English and not the Irish lines. As a man the battlefield turned and peered east.

At first there was no discernible reaction. The English military machine, set in motion whilst Will was distracted, continued to trundle forwards, as if on rails. The cavalry, horses recovered from their earlier exertions, accompanied the infantry to their flanks. The Irish stared, comprehending neither the identity nor the significance of the interlopers.

Rikki raced up, his horse's eyes wild with fear and tension. "What's happening? Who are they?"

"They, Rikki my friend, are the reason that you may yet see your grandchildren. They're French," replied Will, trying to control his grin.

"Bloody hell! They're bloody not, are they? How did they get here?" shouted Rikki, swivelling around in his saddle for a better view.

Will looked again at the advancing English army. Was there a hesitancy about them? It was hard to tell. The drummer boys drove them forwards. The cavalry troops were certainly now looking closely at the new enemy, as if weighing up how long it would take them to close the distance between the two forces. There was no time to lose. The Irish lines might break in their excitement on realising that salvation was at hand. The French were too far away and the English approaching fast.

"Come on, Rikki. They've still got time to slaughter us and get home for tea. Keep your lines tight and…" Will's last words were drowned in the noise of three more shots from the French cannon. Two ploughed into the English lines and one flew a few yards from his own.

Nobody was in any doubt now of the presence of a new player on the board.

"That's it," Will shouted. "Let's give 'em a taste of Irish hospitality. Don't let's give the French all the glory. On my orders, I want disciplined volley fire. Are you with me, Rikki?"

"A pleasure," grinned Rikki and threw Will a flamboyant salute, before riding back to his men.

It was a gamble. The range was still too great. It might provoke a cavalry charge or it might be just enough to make them turn and retreat. At least, thought Will, my men will be under control and throwing up a defensive barrage. He could not bear to see them scythed down like their compatriots had been earlier. Will ran a few yards to where his horse was still tethered to the cart. He needed to be visible to his men. The risk of being hit against men, marching with muskets, was minimal: too late to worry about such things now.

"Will, where are you going?" Mary called after him.

He turned. "Sorry, I need to be on a horse, to direct the fire. You can wait behind the lines, if you want. It will be safer."

"Will Peters, if you think for one minute that I'm going to stand here, while you're all fighting. Have you forgotten that it was me who…"

Will held up his hands, no time for a domestic row. "No, no, of course not. Go quickly and be ready for my signal."

She smiled and ran back to her position, like a child released from detention.

Sword drawn, Will rode to a position level with the front line of his men. He glanced east. More guns were in position. Puffs of smoke were swiftly followed by the noise of the shots. Looking ahead he was appalled at the proximity of the English line. French cavalry were pouring over the hills, between the gun positions. He looked again at the English. If Lake halted his infantry now, he could bring them back to a defensive position on the hill opposite. His cavalry did indeed have plenty of time to sweep into the Irish ranks and be safely behind their own guns and bayonets, before a Frenchman could touch them. Large bodies of French infantry could be seen. Like pawns at the wrong end of the chessboard, they would not play a part in this endgame.

The enemy were still too far away, considered Will. He fought the urge to make his men fire, just to prove he could do it. At a quarter of a mile it was a waste of time. He'd wait until two hundred yards. Even then it would have little effect, except to serve as a warning, but it would give his raw recruits time to reload. Something he had failed to make them do by the cottage.

Oh God, I hope they can do this: I hope I can, thought Will.

He looked at his men and prepared to give the order. At two hundred yards he'd bring them up to the firing position. Now he was waiting, bizarrely, the enemy seemed to be taking an age to cover the ground. He peered at their lines. It was impossible, a miracle. They had stopped. Lake had brought his infantry to a halt. There would be no need to fight after all.

He turned back to his line, a cheer on his lips, when he noticed the movement from the corner of his eye. The infantry were giving way to the cavalry and with a body blow he recognised them. With their scarlet and gold tunics, black pants, silver helmets with red plumes; they were the King's Own Cavalry; the sons of the gentry, direct from the polo ground of Windsor to the battlefield of Wexford. They were the best and two hundred of them were bearing down on him fast. Six hundred yards and their riders were urging them to the gallop; less than a minute to reorganise his infantry and have three ranks fire. Reloading no longer mattered.

It was a terrible risk. They had practised it and now if they did it wrong or did not stand their ground it would all be over in a squalid massacre of cavalry hooves and swords.

A rumble of hooves reached Will's ears.

"ALL RANKS…" They started to raise their muskets. "… FIX BAYONETS."

Nobody moved. Frozen at the sight of the advancing cavalry and awaiting the firing order, their brains could not cope with the unexpected.

Will kept his tone steady and firm.

"ALL RANKS FIX BAYONETS. SMARTLY NOW, WE DON'T WANT TO KEEP THEM WAITING."

Will's resolute tone broke their paralysis. One or two lowered their muskets to the floor and pulled out the fifteen inch steel blades from their belts. Slowly comprehension penetrated their frightened brains. A few started to respond. Gradually others followed until it became a wave and it became easier to respond than not. In a sudden flurry of movement and curses and cut fingers it was done.

Four hundred yards, the sound of hoof on turf was filling Will's senses.

"I will order you to fire by ranks, starting with the front. On firing your weapon, the first two ranks will kneel and present your bayonets to the enemy."

A murmur of fear and dissent swept the ranks. Kneeling in front of two hundred pretend horses was fine to practise in your village. This was very different.

"We've practised this. You can do it. If you turn you'll die. If you hold firm you'll live. Will you hold firm?"

"Aye, Will," a few muttered.

"I said, WILL YOU HOLD FIRM FOR IRELAND?"

"AYE, WILL," they yelled with a little more enthusiasm.

Two hundred yards and twenty seconds to impact; no more time; it had to work.

"Front rank, PRESENT.

Two hundred clicks told Will that the weapons were cocked.

Wait, wait, it was still too far to be effective, Will told himself. Dear God, this was going to be tight to get three rounds away. They must be approaching one hundred yards.

"FIRE!"

Two hundred muskets released their deadly load. Will flinched at the noise. To his relief his mount remained steady. He had never considered the effect of the noise on his horse.

The thunder of hooves was overwhelming. The front rank stood motionless peering into the impenetrable wall of their own smoke.

"FRONT RANK, KNEEL AND PRESENT BAYONETS!"

The front rank, as a man, knelt.

"SECOND RANK, PRESENT…FIRE"

CRASH!

No time to look, too much smoke to see, screams of men and horses.

"THIRD RANK, FIRE"

More screams. Where were they? And then they burst through the fog.

Why wouldn't the old fool release them? This bunch of Irish bog waders would be fine sport. They'd already slaughtered thousands, without a casualty. Why be so damned careful?

Now it was obvious. God knows from where, but the French were here. That left time for only one option. The cavalry had time to do the job and get out.

Major JJ Johnson, JJ to his friends, held his men in check. Shielded by the infantry, they kept pace around two hundred paces behind and to their left.

A young ensign galloped up to the major.

"Compliments of General Lake, Major Johnson. The General has asked me to draw your attention to the arrival of a French force, Sir."

"Thank you Ensign. I'm not as young as I once was, but my eyesight hasn't failed me completely. Where in hell's name did they come from? Why didn't the navy blow them out of the water?"

"There seems to be something of a problem with the navy, Sir."

"Problem, problem, what sort of a problem?"

"Uh, we're not entirely sure, Sir."

"Never mind all that. What are the General's orders?"

"He asks if you would be so good as to wait until he has turned the infantry and then would be beholding to you if you would destroy the remaining rebel forces. Begging your pardon, Sir, but he has asked me to issue you orders to make one sweep only and return directly to our lines, on account of the…"

"…The French. Yes I'm not a complete fool. Kindly inform the General that it will be my pleasure and that we will return directly."

The ensign saluted his superior, reined his mount around, removed his hat and waved it over his head to indicate that the orders had been delivered and accepted.

Major Johnson did not have to issue orders to his men. The ensign's message had been overheard and it spread through the eager troops in moments. The front riders increased their pace and edged forward, until the major was forced to pull them back, for fear of running down their own troops. In their eagerness to destroy the last few rebels or perhaps to complete their task ahead of the arrival of the French, the rear ranks pressed too close upon the heels of the forward lines.

In the heat of the moment the regulation twelve-pace gap between the ranks was forgotten. What did it matter anyway? It was designed to give the rear ranks a chance to avoid or jump those fallen in front. Nobody was going to fall against this lot. Those at the back feared they might miss the fun.

The troops cleared from their line of approach and J J spurred his huge mount forward, no further attempt to hold his boys back. Hooves thundered, the wind rushed past them and there was no greater joy on earth than the charge. The fixing of bayonets went unnoticed; the organisation of ranks was immaterial. This lot would run at any moment and then the sport would start.

Smoke rose from the line ahead and, before the crash hit his ears, the major became aware of rushing into a sudden squall. Men and horses collapsed around him and yet he rode on, unaware of the number that fell behind him, crashing into their fallen comrades.

The line in front had disappeared behind a wall of smoke. Through that wall the second volley cut into the front ranks like a cheese wire. Two hundred musket balls, at fifty yards, all found targets. Hooves were severed, legs and joints smashed. Horses fell as if the rolling turf was ripped from under them. Remarkably few riders were hit. Will's exhortations to fire low had been heard and learnt well. The deaths were caused as men fell under the weight of horse and rider from behind.

Still JJ rode on, though now aware of his thinning ranks.

At fifteen yards the volley threw even charging horses back, such was its force. Had Will been able to see the damage he was inflicting, he would have been appalled and exhilarated. Becher's Brook on National Day came nowhere close to the carnage to man and horse that his actions had caused. It was a horsemeat factory and still more men drove their steeds into the fallen animals ahead. Fetlocks snapped and riders shattered necks and spines as they hit the earth.

As the sound of the third volley died, JJ heard his men weeping and their horses squealing in their death throes. Sword above his head he flew through a wall of smoke, which gave onto a wall of steel.

As if by instinct his huge mount swerved right and its momentum carried him along an impenetrable line of bayonets. Others were less fortunate. Some were driven onto the waiting blades, like a ship thrown onto the rocks by a powerful tide. Less fortunate still were those who fell into them, writhing in agony without touching the soft moist turf.

Will held his breath and then it landed. Not the expected tidal wave, cutting a swathe through his ranks, but the wave that threatens much, then subsides pathetically, all force spent, hardly touching the weakest of sand castles.

Barely twenty emerged from the smoke, but a couple, driven forward by those behind fell onto the line of bayonets. Young Danny O'Rourke screamed as a huge bay stallion fell on top of him. Yet he held his bayonet up until he died, crushed. The remaining horses, some riderless, reared up and then swung to Will's left and down the line, as if trying to find a break in the steel hedge.

His line had held, resolute in their faith in him. He may have shouted with pride and relief. He was not sure.

Then the line broke and the Irish fought – each other. With elbows and knees and musket butts they fought to reach the few remaining mounted cavalry. Horses blown, deflected by the bayonets, the English horsemen were overwhelmed. Bayonets jabbed horses' flanks, cut reins and saddle straps. Those deadly cavalry blades found not unprotected backs and necks but forests of bayonets. Will's men pulled them from their saddles, these intruders, with their fancy uniforms, expensive saddles and beautiful horses and butchered them.

The smoke cleared to reveal to Will a scene like the most appalling motorway pile-up he could imagine. The musket volleys had taken their toll. He could see lines of corpses, man and horse in three stages. He could also see how, in their arrogance and eagerness, they had ridden in tight formation, the riders at the rear piling into their fallen comrades in front.

His men saw the carnage too and rushed to kill and plunder amongst the fallen.

Unnoticed by Will, his horse had taken him a few yards to the right and forward of his lines. It mattered little until a mounted figure somehow broke free from the avenging horde. He seemed the only survivor of the two hundred strong cavalry troop. A huge man on a huge black charger, from his epaulettes he was clearly an officer. Face contorted in fury and despair, JJ kicked the flanks of his exhausted horse to charge for Will. His intention was obvious. It was the final act of a desperate man.

Will kicked his own horse. It showed no reaction and bent to crop the lush damp grass. How absurd thought Will, slightly detached with the stress of the previous few minutes. One man, alone, is about to kill me, just yards from six hundred allies, none of whom are loaded.

No time to sheath it, Will dropped his sword and pulled out the Collier. Cocking it, he rested it across his saddle and swore that he would buy Mr Collier any drink in the house if he lived long enough. At ten yards Will raised the pistol, aiming for the huge chest, waited and fired. He had no time even to duck as the huge horse raced by and he was soaked in a hot, wet spray.

Will's horse did not look up.

Suddenly he remembered Mary. Swinging around, his eyes searched frantically amongst the chaos, his recent danger immediately forgotten. His survival would mean nothing had she fallen beneath those few riders to break on his line.

Mary too had held her breath as one huge cavalry officer, breaking from the melee in front of her, had ridden for Will. The incident was over in an instant and she rushed to Will's side, as he slid from his mount to hold her in his arms.

"This is getting bloody monotonous," moaned a familiar voice and they both looked up to see the Fox, astride his horse, surrounded by mounted men.

"I might agree with that," prickled Will. "A little late again?"

"Ah, brave words from a man who just lost two thirds of his army, without firing a shot. Never mind Will, you've done a grand job with this lot; such pretty uniforms and some decent horseflesh too. Our friend General Lake will be a busy boy at his writing desk tonight.

I wish I could see it, in all those posh English houses. Picture the scene; there is a knock at the drawing room door and some ponsey butler, all wig and white gloves, enters with a message on a silver platter. Your precious boy's had his lungs ripped out by some Irish peasant, trained up by a renegade Englishman." He put the back of his hand to his brow, in a theatrical show of distress. "Oh the tears, oh the trauma." He roared with laughter. "It's turned out nice after all."

The Fox ignored Will for a moment, looking past him to the surviving loose horses, milling about nervously; Irish hands trying to capture them. He turned to a companion. "That one, the black one with the white blaze, looks unharmed. It's a fine looking mount. I think I'll have that one. Would you mind, Charlie?"

As Charlie rode off to collect the beast, The Fox turned his attention to Will again. "Ah Will, if you've learned nothing else from today," he nodded towards the fast approaching French cavalry, "you must appreciate, in warfare, as in most of life, timing is everything."

Will glared at The Fox in an effort to show that he wasn't afraid. He could think of nothing to say. The Fox seized the opportunity to continue.

The Fox grabbed the reins of Will's horse, which stopped feeding and stood shoulder to shoulder with The Fox's mount. "I thought he was on drugs," laughed The Fox.

He beckoned Will closer and for reasons he could not explain Will released Mary and complied.

Leaning over close to Will, The Fox rasped, "And another thing, the Frogs; let them serve their purpose and then they will suffer. They will not spread their empire on Irish soil." His smile, so close to Will's face, was more of a snarl. "As for The Wolf, you're a sentimental fool, Will Peters, he will not prevail over The Fox. Be a good boy and work with me on this. You know it makes sense."

The words scared Will to his core. It was ridiculous. Only moments earlier he had expected to die and was prepared to do so. Now he felt couched and intimidated by this coward and bully, a man who was not prepared to face his enemy, as Will had. There was something in his words that frightened Will, awoke doubts in him that this time travel had initiated. Had he changed history? Would he end the world? Would he slide through some crack in time to wander lost forever?

The Fox was watching his reaction. "It gets to yer, doesn't it? Stick with me son and you'll be fine." He looked up. "Now what have we here? Look, your mate's back. Typical of him, he thinks he's a bloody hero!"

Will turned to look. The French cavalry swept past, with barely a glance at Will and his men, bent on engaging the English. Unnoticed by Will, the French artillery were banging away at the English lines and now they had found their range. Following close behind was a horseman in a blue uniform, but distinct from the cavalry. It was Sean.

As he rode level with Will, the Irish started to cheer and Sean removed his hat and bowed to the troops. The Fox, still smiling, withdrew a few yards to take in the scene. Released from his spell, Will's pent up fears and emotions took over. Still shaking with fear and shock, the relief at the deliverance by the French gave way rapidly to anger and resentment. He had been such a fool! Sean had lied to him. His friend, the man he trusted, in whom he had confided, had fooled and used him. So many had died and so many more had come so close. He had been but a heartbeat from shooting the woman he loved, so this popinjay could strut arrogantly in front of them and play the conquering hero.

Sean caught sight of Will and swung his horse towards him. As he rode up Will extended a hand towards him, which Sean leant forward from his saddle to seize with alacrity. With a firm grip on Sean's hand and his friend leaning forward, it was easy to pull him from the saddle. As Sean hit the ground, the air exploded from his lungs and he felt Will's Collier, thrust into his throat.

"You lying, two-faced bastard," erupted Will. "Have you any idea what you've done to us? Do you know how many died today and I felt responsible? Responsibility, I suppose, is not a word you understand." Will was shaking uncontrollably with a real chance that the Collier would go off, intended or not. "I nearly, nearly shot her. Do you have any idea?"

Mary gently placed her hand on Will's arm. "Will, Will, hasn't there been enough killing today? Give me the gun."

Will exhaled steadily and lowered the cock on the pistol. "You're right," he conceded and handed her the weapon. He stood up and wiped the weariness and perspiration from his brow. It was not meant to be like this.

Sean sighed with relief and leant forward to stand up, only to be forced back down by the Collier, this time in Mary's hand.

"There are things going on here that I don't understand," whispered Mary, "but if you do that to Will and me again, just remember one thing, Sean O'Grady, you're Will's friend but not mine." She cocked the weapon. "And I will not hesitate. Do you understand me?"

Sean dared not breath.

"I asked a question. Do you understand me?"

Sean nodded as slowly and gently as he possibly could.

"Good. I think we understand each other, don't you?"

Sean said nothing.

"I asked you a question."

Sean nodded with more vigour than was prudent and Mary removed the pistol from his larynx.

"Dear Lord, Mary, what are you doing?" cried Will, aghast.

She turned to him and Will saw the fire burning in her eyes. "Will, I am not sure why you are here or what you have come to do. I don't understand all that. I do understand one thing. I love you and I will not let you waste your life. God forgive me, I will kill any man, who comes between us."

Sean now forgotten on the grass, Will held her in his arms again, lost in this wonderful woman, except to lower the cock on the pistol in her hand.

The moment was not to last long. The French cavalry had returned, their chase of the English abandoned beneath the English guns and the prospect of English infantry volley fire. Even with a retreating enemy, without infantry support, which was still distant, nobody but a fool would have pursued it further. Capitaine Jean-Luc Bapaume was not a fool and he had seen it all.

"Mon dieu, what is happening? I was impressed with the discipline of the your volley fire. I had feared that you Irish would not stand and fight. Now I see this. You fight amongst yourselves and worst," he turned to Will, "you assault a man in the uniform of the Army of France. Explain yourself immediately."

It was too much for Will. If the pistol had been in his hand and not Mary's he might have shot the French captain out of sheer frustration. Fortunately Sean came to his rescue. He stood up, brushed some mud from his uniform and saluted Bapaume.

"It's my fault, Capitaine," interrupted Sean. "It was a misunderstanding. He thought we were about to attack his men and not the English. He is in fact an old friend of mine and a key leader in the struggle against the English imperialism. He has long been an admirer of the Revolution.

May I introduce, my friend," Sean seized Will's arm in a gesture of friendship, "Will Peters."

Will had the good sense to bow low and blustered his apologies.

"Since you speak so highly of him I shall let it go," continued Bapaume. "I shall view it in the light of the passions, which are aroused by battle, but we will not tolerate indiscipline, now that we are in charge. Attacking a French officer is punishable by death, do I make myself clear, Monsieur Peters."

"Of course, Capitaine," Will replied hastily.

Bapaume was clearly not convinced by Sean's explanation. Nonetheless he was intelligent enough to realise that it was probably not a good start, if his first act of aggression on Irish soil was to execute one of their leaders. He made some attempt at reconciliation.

"I am Capitaine Bapaume of the Fourth Cavalry. Are you the man, who led this small but magnificent army, Monsieur Peters?"

Will had finally collected his thoughts. "You are very kind, Capitaine Bapaume. We are so grateful for your arrival. My men would not have lasted long against the full might of General Lake's force. Will you convey my thanks to General Hoche?"

"General Hoche? Who is General Hoche?"

Will floundered. "Uh your General, General Hoche."

"I am sorry you are mistaken. Our army is led by the hero of Toulon. He threw out the invading Royalist forces of King George. Our leader is General Bonaparte."

Will's mind whirled. It wasn't possible. Napoleon would go to Egypt, his fleet to be destroyed by Nelson at the Nile. If Napoleon were to conquer Ireland he would make it a vassal state like Naples and Spain and so many others. "Are you sure?" he mumbled between dry lips.

"Do you think I don't know the identity of my own General? Are you saying I am a fool? Be careful Mr Peters. You may have led your men bravely today, but we French will not tolerate such outbursts.

Now, I have things to do. My compliments to your brave soldiers, my comrades will be with you soon. I must go." With a touch of his hat he pulled his mount's head to one side, kicked its flanks and was gone.

"You were pushing your luck there, old son," said Sean. "Don't worry, there's no need to thank me for saving you from the guillotine."

Will glared at him.

The Fox drifted back towards them and looking at Sean announced, "You're looking well and I do like the fancy outfit, but is blue really your colour, I ask myself. Never mind, you got the Frogs here. The famous Royal Navy is on strike, with a bit of help from the Irish, eh? Not a ship at sea, what a blessing!"

Sean glared at The Fox, reddened noticeably and, for once, had nothing to say.

The Fox continued, "Can't see what they're all cheering about. You made a right balls of it. Bring the English army to a decisive battle and destroy them, now that would've been worth sacrificing a few Irish souls for. As it is, well, the real job's still to be done."

Will stared hard at Sean to discern his reaction. Sean looked at his feet.

The Fox turned his attention to the departing French cavalry officer. "Cocky little sod, wasn't he? I think he might need taking down a peg or two, don't you, Will?"

Will shrugged. Despite the traumas of the last hour, he could not help but notice Sean's reaction to The Fox, a man who claimed to know Sean and whom Sean denied ever meeting. His friend immediately appeared withdrawn and fearful, even subservient.

The Fox dismounted and, with a twinkle in his eye, asked Will, "Aren't you going to introduce me to your mate?"

Will could feel the tension between the two men as he made the introduction. He felt foolish calling this man 'The Fox.' Mary watched the interchange closely. Something had startled her.

Still holding Sean's hand, The Fox pulled him close and whispered in his ear, "The girl's beginning to irritate me. Perhaps we should arrange a little accident, what do you think?"

Any further deliberations were interrupted by Rikki's arrival. "Come on fellas, ...oh good to see you Sean, I thought we'd lost you. Now we'd better get our men organised, before the entire French army marches past."

He was right. The French infantry were arriving in force and Will's men were still picking over the remains of the English cavalry. He and Mary rushed to bring them under control.

It was much later that day before Mary and Will had time alone together. They sat on the grass. Mary had found them some bread and roast meat.

"Will, you look tired. Eat some of this and you'll feel better."

They ate silently, too hungry and exhausted to talk.

"It's not just the battle is it?" enquired Mary eventually. "It's something more. It's Sean and what he did. Or is it that French officer? Who does he think he is, threatening you?"

Will gazed at her and finished his bread.

"That's not it either is it? Something about their general, boney something, upset you, didn't it? Will, tell me. I want to help. I only ask one thing and that is that you're honest with me."

Will's stomach churned. Maybe it was the meat on an empty belly, maybe the quandary of the truth, his truth. How could he tell this woman everything? And yet perhaps he should.

Mary could see the dilemma on his face. "Is it The Fox? You're right not to trust him. He's dangerous. He's your enemy, not Sean, I'm sure. Still there's one thing that you all have in common."

"What's that?"

"It's difficult to explain. You talk to each other in an odd way, say things I don't understand."

Will could not look her in the eye.

"And another thing…"

"Go on."

"You all three of you wear the same funny metal bracelets."

"WHAT?"

END OF PART THREE

PART FOUR

It is mortifying, but that is too poor a word; I could tear my flesh with rage and vexation but that advances nothing, and so I hold my tongue in general and devour my melancholy as I can. To come so near, and then to fail, if we are to fail!

Extract from the Journals of Wolf Tone (Bantry Bay December 23rd 1796

Chapter 27

Wexford
May 6th 1797

"What's the matter with you this morning?" enquired Maggie of Sean, slumped over the kitchen table gazing into the bottom of his tankard.

"What the hell do you think is wrong with me?" he snapped back.

"Well you won't find the answer to your problems in there, Sean O'Grady! I'd have thought you'd have known that by now. You've served enough of that stuff in your time or, more to the point, you've had me serve it. Oh and that reminds me. It's about time you started pulling your weight around here. There's a lot more to do now the French have taken over this place. It's not like the old days."

"Don't remind me," groaned Sean.

"So that's your trouble is it? You've nobody to blame but yourself. You brought them here and now they're running the show. Whose fault is it but yours?" She stood with her hands on her hips staring down at Sean.

He stood up and tried to put his arms around her slim waist. She pulled away.

"Oh now, don't think you're going to get around me like that," she said, pushing his hands away. "You've been a picture of misery, ever since you came back. I haven't seen hide nor hair of Will or Mary... ah, they're a lovely couple, ...since the French threw them out of the top room and they went to stay at Mrs O'Connell's. Have you two fallen out? Is that what's eating you?"

Sean considered for a moment. How much should he confide in her? It was not his style to take her into his confidence. She understood him far too well as it was, without sharing his innermost thoughts and yet he needed to talk to someone and at least he knew that he could trust her.

"It's Will," said Sean.

"Aha, I thought so," clucked Maggie.

"I know you'll say it's my own fault. I lied to him and now he's angry with me and, what's more, he doesn't trust me."

"Oh now, what a surprise. You've told one of your usual tales and it's come back to bite you. You're right, Sean, it *is* your own fault. So what are you going to do about it?"

"I don't know for sure. I do know that I need to get him back trusting me again."

"Right again, Sean. There's nobody else you can trust amongst this French lot and, as for The Fox, well, I think I trust him less than the French. How come he's so friendly with them now?"

"The Fox! What a bloody silly name that is, that he's given himself." Sean's face creased with anxiety. "Have you heard they've made him a captain in the cavalry? I've no idea how he pulled that trick."

Sean slumped back in his chair. How the hell was he going to tell Will the truth? How could he conceal it any longer? Will had probably guessed by now or, if he hadn't, he soon would. He'd better tell him something.

"What are you going to do, Sean? You can't carry on like this. The French have been here nearly a month and all you've done is mope around the place. You brought them here. Why won't they talk to you?"

"I don't know, Maggie. I was expecting a different man to be in charge, a General Hoche. This Napoleon, I know that Wolf Tone met him, but I haven't and he won't talk to me, even in my own bloody pub! I don't know what I'm going to do and that's for sure."

"Well you can start by seeing, Will and setting that right."

"And how am I going to do that?"

"Well, why not start with an apology and finish by telling him the truth?"

"Come on, Will you can't lie in bed all day, can you? What good will it do to lie there?"

Will sat up and, leaning on one elbow, studied Mary, as she tried to clean a dirty mark from the tunic of his new French Army uniform. On top of all that had happened with Sean and the French and their inexplicable delay in advancing from Wexford, he was worried about her. She looked pale, she wasn't eating properly and the other day she had been violently sick. He knew that he should be doing something. He just didn't know what and so he had started to slip into his old lethargy.

"Will, I don't understand about the French and what they're doing. I do know that I don't like them. They were supposed to come here to free us from the English and it just seems as if we have changed one set of masters for another.

I know something else as well. I don't like what Sean did, any more than you do. He lied and played games with our lives and I have to say that it'll be a long time before I can trust him again. Just the same he is your friend and you don't have too many of those here. Apart from Rikki I don't think you can rely on anyone. If Sean won't come to see you, you'll have to go and see him. What do you think?"

"You're right, you're right." Will swung his legs out of bed and walked over and kissed her. "You usually are."

"That's settled then. Put on your uniform and we'll go around there and see if there's any breakfast. It's the least he can do."

The streets were unusually quiet, which Will concluded was due to the restrictions that the French had imposed. Identity passes had been issued and French troops controlled the roads in and out of the town. He understood that they also had roadblocks on the 'borders', which lay about ten miles away. Will had played no part in these matters in spite of his rank of lieutenant in the army. He had been commissioned by Napoleon himself, a tale to tell if he lived to tell it.

In truth it had been an anti-climax. The great man was pre-occupied with other matters and was in no mood to talk to Will let alone engage in debate on either strategic or political matters. Will had been ushered quickly in and out of the great presence. He had the impression that refusing the honour of a commission was not an option. And then nothing. He had been dismissed to local lodgings with instructions not to leave Wexford and to be available at a moment's notice.

Nearly a month had passed and the French showed no sign of moving. It was inexplicable. They had had the huge advantage of surprise and Will could not imagine why Napoleon had not seized the initiative. Rumours abounded. The most plausible was that reinforcements were expected. None had arrived. In no time the French fleet was gone, high tailing it back to France before the Royal Navy could sort itself out. No other French ships appeared and now it was rumoured that the English fleet was back at sea. The official line was that the sailors were still in dispute with the Admiralty. Some of the fishermen reckoned to have seen ships of the line off the coast. Will thought this more likely.

Will voiced his thoughts to Mary as they walked towards Sean's inn. "Why don't they make a move? The longer they leave it, the more likely the English army will be reinforced. If they bring troops into Dublin harbour there will be nothing that we can do to prevent it."

It was more a vent for his frustration than a question expecting an answer.

Mary nodded. She had heard it all before. They turned the corner and saw the inn. "Will look. There's Sean. He's heading this way."

Sean glanced up and smiled at them both. Will had seen Sean use that smile before.

"I was just coming to meet you folks. How are you both? I like the uniform, Will," chirped Sean.

"Of course you were coming to see us, Sean," responded Will.

Mary tugged at Will's sleeve. He turned to her and she scowled at him.

"We're both fine, thank you Sean. We were on our way to see you. So there's a coincidence. How's Maggie?"

Retaining the smile, Sean replied to Mary. "She's very well. She has managed to hide some of that good tea from the French. How would you like to join us for a late breakfast?"

"That sounds grand. We'd love to wouldn't we Will?" replied Mary with enthusiasm.

Will grunted his agreement.

Maggie was effusive in her welcome and when the food was served the two women sat on one side of the table, leaving the men to sit side by side. An uncomfortable silence fell over the group and each was relieved that eating overcame the need to make conversation.

When Maggie had cleared the plates and poured more tea Sean cleared his throat. "I think it's up to me to say something here and I'd like to start by making you all an apology." Maggie encouraged him with a smile. "I haven't been honest with any of you and I've done some terrible things. I should have confided in you all, but I was too arrogant. I thought I was smarter and made decisions for you, which were yours to make. I had no right to do that and I am truly sorry. I did it for the right reasons, but that is no excuse. I took away your right to choose and risked your lives.

I am not looking for you to forgive me; I am simply asking you to understand and I want to be straight with you now. I just hope that you can accept that and believe me that I won't do it again. I hope that I have learnt from my mistakes.

We are in a very difficult situation that none of us foresaw." Sean paused to catch Will's eye. "We do not know who we can rely on and it's more important than ever that we stick together."

Will seemed unmoved by Sean's words and glared into his mug of tea.

"Look I never intended it to go so far," continued Sean. "I thought that the French would turn up much sooner. If you knew how frantic I was to get them ashore…"

"And what would have happened to Mary and I, not to mention Rikki and all the others, if they'd arrived just an hour later?" butted in Will. "What about all those folk who were slaughtered before you deigned to put in an appearance?"

Before Sean could respond Mary interrupted. "It was terrible and I never want to see things like that again, but it's done now. Sean can't change that, Will. I was there too and could have died. Let Sean explain."

Sean nodded his appreciation to Mary. "We must talk about that some more. Right now I must tell you some other things if we are to wipe the slate clean. It's about The Fox.

I lied to you about him too. I told you that I'd never met him. I met him in Boston."

Maggie was the first to react. "Boston! Where's that?"

"It's in America," replied Will.

"America! Isn't that, well it's over the ocean isn't it? When did you go to America?" gaped Maggie.

"It was before I met you, my dear," answered Sean.

"Or was it after?" added Will. "And I bet you sailed on a very fast ship. How long did it take to get there, Sean?"

Sean scowled a warning at Will. "Let me explain, before you say anything. I was sent over as part of the recruitment process and I met these very strange men. They came from Ireland originally. Will, they never explained what they wanted me to do, honestly. They just asked lots of questions about me. I needed the money and I never thought I'd end up here, even when my father got involved."

"Your father? What has he got to do with it all? Who is your father?" demanded Will.

"My father? Ah well how shall I explain?" Sean caught Will's eye and then let his gaze move pointedly to the two girls. "He was, er is, very involved in the movement to free Ireland from the English, if you understand what I mean."

"Oh I understand exactly what you mean," snapped Will. "And what were his instructions to his loving son? Were they to make sure that everybody found a nice way of power sharing so that nobody got hurt? Or were they different? What was the plan after the English were kicked out, Sean? Maybe a little tidying up to do?"

Will's voice had risen to a level that risked attracting the attention of the French boarding upstairs and Maggie and Mary looked both bemused and frightened.

"I don't understand all this," interrupted Mary. "I thought you were sent to free Ireland, Will. What is Sean meant to be doing and what about The Fox? Who is he, Sean?"

"Good questions, Sean. Any good answers?" added Will.

"I am meant to get the English out. After that I am not too sure. I didn't have a clue that they were going to send anyone else, but I kind of guessed who The Fox was. Honestly Will I didn't know that he was coming here and that really is God's honest truth."

"Let's just suppose for a moment that I believe you, Sean. What about all that stuff at Durham? Ooh I hope we get in! I'm sure you'll make it, Will!" sneered Will, mocking Sean's accent. "It was all a charade wasn't it?"

Sean was examining a speck of dirt in his cuticles. He looked up to face Will. "Yes, it was. I recruited you."

Will leapt out of his seat. "You bastard, you fucking two faced bastard. I don't give a shit what you were supposed to do. I'm out of here!"

Without a glance at Mary, he stormed out of the kitchen, through the bar and into the street.

Mary was on her feet and after him.

Maggie glared at Sean. "What in heaven's name have you done, Sean?" she cried and raced after Mary.

Sean put his head in his hands and groaned.

"Will, Will, Will!" shouted the girls, as they chased after him.

They were all attracting far too much attention from the French troops on the street, but Will did not care.

At the end of the street Mary and Maggie caught up with him and seized his sleeve.

"Please Will, please, don't run off, not like this," they pleaded.

"Will, I don't understand what is happening here. You're scaring me. I'm scared that I'm going to lose you too," cried Mary.

"Will, please don't be so angry with him. I know he lies. He does it to me, probably more than I know. He can't help it. He's like a child sometimes. It's like he's never grown up and learnt the difference between right and wrong. Please don't leave us. We need you. Sean doesn't realise it. He needs you too. He needs you to do the right thing. Haven't you ever done something that you've regretted?" added Maggie.

Will thought of Suki's twisted body on his bed in Oxford. "Oh, I don't know. I don't know anything anymore. I don't understand it myself." He looked at the two anxious faces. "Oh, I'm sorry. It's not your fault. None of this is your fault."

"I don't know what you mean by that. It's just that we need you, Will. You are our…" Mary laughed. "You're our hero."

"So you are," added Maggie and both girls kissed him.

Will smiled. "Oh for goodness sake, can't a man be angry if he wants? Has any man ever said no to either of you two?"

Maggie and Mary looked at each other and grinned. "Not that I can recall," they both chirped.

Will let out a long sigh. "Come on then," he took one on each arm, "let's go and sort this out. How did I ever get into this mess?"

Back at the kitchen door they found Sean sitting, head still in his hands.

"Do you want us to leave you two alone?" asked Mary.

Will nodded.

Sean looked up, relieved. "You're back."

"I'm back," concurred Will. He sat opposite Sean. "Right let's have it. No bullshit. What are you doing here? Who is this Fox and what is he supposed to do?"

Sean looked up, the strain apparent on his face. "You want answers Will? Join the club. All I can do is tell you what I know and perhaps we can work it out from there.

You can guess my background, Catholic family, generations involved in the Republican movement. I walked away from all that, or so I thought. The trouble is, you never can. My father leant on me. You know the scene, all that stuff about heritage and duty. The guys in Boston didn't spell it out. They didn't need to.

So why did I go along with it? Simple. I thought it was all bollocks. I needed the cash. So I went along with it. I never dreamt, for all the saints, that we'd be sitting here now like this.

Honestly I'm sorry I conned you. I really am. I just never thought it would happen like this. I reckoned that the worst I was doing was wasting your time while you made some cash.

I did it again, didn't I? I took away your freedom to choose.

So I'm a complete jerk, but since we're here, what are we going to do about the French?"

Will eyed Sean carefully. "Oh Sean, you haven't changed. I don't give a damn about the French right now. What about The Fox? Do you think I should just shoot him?"

Sean blanched. "Christ no! I don't think that that's a solution to anything. Besides he might know about getting back to our time. I sure don't and that is not a lie either. Do you think I'd be here if I did? I'd probably have gone back and left you here," he added ruefully. "And, if we do get back, I don't think that you want to be explaining why you killed him to some committee at Boroughbridge."

Sean thought for a moment and sighed. "Look, if it comes to that, I'll do it. It's the least I can do. You leave The Fox to me. He's my problem. I'll sort him out. I'm sure there's a way without resorting to murder.

Can we get back to the main issue," continued Sean, " what we're going to do about the French and the English? I've been plotting like mad, since I've been here. The only thing is I was just thinking about kicking the English out. I hadn't given the rest of it much thought."

Will studied Sean's furrowed brow. "Given your background, Sean, I find that difficult to believe. You must have thought about it. You can't imagine that we'll wave our hankies at the departing English ships on the quayside and then all live happily ever after. Who's going to run this country and what will they do about the divisions left behind? What sort of Ireland do you want to build, Sean? In the words of the song, what colours will you wear?" He held Sean's eyes in a firm stare.

Sean hesitated. "I don't know, Will. Surely the United Irishmen, Wolf Tone and the rest will sort all that out. I just thought I might make a fast buck and go back to the pub. That is, if I can't get back to our time."

"I don't believe for a moment that you thought that. You've met these guys and studied them. They're wonderful people with high ideals, heads ringing with the words of Tom Paine. There's just one problem. They couldn't run a piss up in a brewery. They'll get slaughtered by the tough guys, men like The Fox. And what sort of Ireland do you think he wants?"

Will offered Sean a chance to respond. He simply shrugged.

"Alright I'll spell it out for you. He'll seize power, provided he can kick the French out. He's probably got a plan for that already. Or the guys at Boston worked one out for him. Then it'll start. All the landowners, the Protestant ones that is, will be massacred. Didn't you tell me that The Fox nailed someone to his barn door or something? Then it'll be anyone one with any English blood in his or her family. It'll be like Nazi Germany, with the knock on the door in the middle of the night and the death camps. What did we call it in our time, ethnic cleansing?"

Will was out of his seat and leaning on the table, his face inches from Sean, the veins bulging around his eyes. "Is that the Ireland you want to build? Is that an Ireland to die for?"

Sean shifted backwards in his seat and put some distance between him and Will's angry face. "Look Will, it's not like that. I really didn't give this a lot of thought and you know why. I just thought it was all a load of crap, the guys in Boston, the twats at Boroughbridge and even my Dad, whom I genuinely thought had lost the plot. All I had to do was go along with their stupid little fantasy and take the money. It was all so simple."

Sean's put his head in his hands again.

For moments neither man spoke.

It was Will who broke the silence first. "Sean perhaps we should put together a plan, work something out. It's just that I need to, er, know what you're going to do. Are you going to fight for what's right or are you going to sit back and watch them turn this country into a police state or maybe a French puppet state?"

Sean made no move.

"Sean I've got to know."

Sean looked up. "Will… Let me tell you something. I've always run away from this stuff. I guess I can't do that any more can I?" He smiled at Will. It was an odd sort of a smile, not a Sean smile at all. "I didn't come all this way to recreate all the stuff that terrified me as a kid and nearly took over my life."

Will noticed that Sean's smile had turned into something else. His jaw was set and the muscles in his neck twitched. He was trying to hold back the tears. Was it an act?

Sean looked up. "Will, I've never done much that I'm proud of and hardly think that I'm going to undergo a personality change. Things like that rarely happen, but…" he sighed, "…since we are, as they say, where we are, for once in my life let me try and make a difference and do the right thing. Perhaps together we can do something for the good. Perhaps that's the real reason we are here. Maybe there are other forces at work that we don't understand. Whatever it is, can we try together?"

Sean could see the doubts still lingering in Will's eyes. "I wouldn't blame you if you said no. I probably deserve that. It's just that now is probably a good starting point. I have no plans, no schemes and no plots. There are no hares that I've set running. From here on in what happens depends on what we do together."

Will still hesitated so Sean added with a laugh, "I haven't got the American army landing in Galway next Tuesday." He looked at Will. "Actually they're landing in Derry!

Come on Will, I'm only kidding," he added.

Will looked at his fellow time traveller. "What is the matter with me? The girls can wind me round their little fingers and now you! Go on Sean, but if you double cross me again, so help me, I'll end your time travelling once and for all."

They did not stand and embrace. Sean caught Will's eye and said, "Will if it's…"

He never finished his sentence. The door opened and the men looked up to greet the girls. It was Bapaume.

"Gentlemen, do you not rise when a senior officer enters the room?"

To their joint irritation they both rose involuntarily from their seats.

"Excellent! I had feared that with this inactivity you would forget that you were soldiers. You may sit."

Seething at their spontaneity, Sean and Will immediately sat down and seethed again.

"I have news for you. I am well aware of your frustration at the lack of action. All that is about to change. I have your orders. You are going to war!"

They were a mixed bunch sitting upstairs above a warehouse in a secret location in Dublin. In truth it was a poorly kept secret but that didn't matter now that the English and the Ascendancy were on the run. The city was teetering on the verge of panic and the harbour in Dublin was a hive of activity. Many of the great and the wealthy were loading everything they could crate up onto any vessel they could hire. They were prepared to sail anywhere to escape the French and the explosion of popular hatred that would surely come at anytime.

"Gentleman, we must make a start," called a large, ugly man at the centre of the room.

It was difficult to discern who was in charge. With no agenda or minutes being taken and no structure to the discussion, there was little danger of this bunch of rebels starting a revolution. The ugly man, Napper Tandy banged the arm of his chair to call order. Aged fifty-eight, he claimed authority, having arrived with the French. In practice he undermined the efforts of others, was indecisive and was determined to let only the others expose themselves to the risks of battle.

In marked contrast, to his left, sat Lord Edward Fitzgerald. Only thirty-five, handsome, hair cropped in the French style, he and his beautiful French wife were the celebrities of their day. A utopian revolutionary by disposition, not birth, he was looked upon, in spite of his limited experience, as the military leader.

To his left was an equally good looking man of the same age. Previously the MP for Philipstown, Arthur O'Connor had only joined the United Irishmen in the last two years. His craving for power had overridden his judgement and he too was considered something of a military strategist, based on wafer thin experience. Unknown to his lordship, O'Connor was sleeping with Fitzgerald's sister.

A shorter man, resplendent in a green uniform sat in the next seat. William Drennan had written the so-called 'test' for the United Irish. From Ulster Presbyterian stock his views were almost as narrow as the opening to his purse.

It was impossible to miss the man to his left. An eccentric giant, Hamilton Rowan, somehow reappeared from America, towered over them. His reputation for fighting and duelling matched his physique. News of his return had arrived on the desk at Dublin Castle, before he could unpack his vast luggage.

Leonard McNally, the spy, was back in Dublin and noted everything in a small book on his lap, whilst at one end of the gathering was Wolf Tone. Wearing his French Army Uniform, which he had smuggled into the meeting in a bag, he was trying to impose his authority on the gathering, a situation that Tandy would not permit.

The debate was, as ever, about the timing and method of orchestrating the uprising.

"Move now and strike, before they have a chance to reinforce," insisted Fitzgerald.

"We should not be so hasty. Let us wait until the French are at the gates of the city," argued the cowardly Tandy.

"Gentlemen, we should follow the instructions of our revolutionary allies, the French. We should..." Tone's words were shouted down by first O'Connor and then Drennan.

McNally sat quietly scribbling.

It is unlikely that any more would have been resolved than at the previous day's meeting. Then the door burst open and five heavily armed men rushed in.

"My Lord, gentlemen, pray forgive this unseemly intrusion. There is something to which I must attend urgently," announced their leader grandly.

The Fox drew his Collier and shot Leonard McNally between the eyes.

Chapter 28

Dublin
May 6th 1797

"Well that's got your attention!" beamed The Fox, as the smoke cleared from his shot and a stunned silence descended. "I'm good at this. I should have been a teacher. Oh and I wouldn't do that your Lordship," he added as Fitzgerald, the first to recover, reached inside his cloak. "We've enough firepower between us to wipe out half of Dublin, besides…" he pointed the Collier to the wall above Fitzgerald's head, "…this little beauty has a neat trick, it fires more than one shot."

The gun roared again and pieces of plaster fell out of the wall. Edward Fitzgerald put his hands of the arms of the chair, where they could be seen.

"That's much better," smiled The Fox.

Bravely Wolf Tone spoke up. "What is the meaning of this, murdering one of our colleagues in cold blood? How dare you? When we were introduced I was lead to believe that your role was to liaise between our organisation and the French expeditionary force. What in God's name are you playing at man?"

"Ah, Lieutenant Tone, a man with a voice, excellent." The Fox put the Collier back in his waistband and pulled up a spare seat. His four accomplices stood, weapons drawn.

"It is not in my nature to explain my actions and yet, on this occasion, I will do so. After all, you are all intelligent men and very shortly, it is my express wish, you will be forming the new government of our proud country. Our revolutionary colleagues from the French Republic have empowered me to communicate this to you.

Bur first, the late Mr McNally! Please accept my apologies for such drastic measures. I feared he might have been armed.

Mr McNally, a colleague, I don't think so. Have any of you known how long he has been reporting your meetings, your every plan, and your every action back to the men in Dublin Castle? He was a traitor and died too easily for his betrayal."

"No, surely not..." There was a ripple of response around the room.

"Prove it!" O'Connor demanded.

"Prove it? With pleasure." The Fox beamed. Turning to Drennan, he demanded, "Pass me the spy's notes."

Drennan demurred at touching the body, which had been blown from his chair and was lying on the floor, the head an unrecognisable mess of gore.

"Oh for God's sake, you fellows are going to have to toughen up. We're fighting a war, not organising a church social." He bent down and picked up the papers, scattered around the corpse. Wiping the brains from the top sheet with the dead man's arm, he held it up. "Look. Every detail of your discussions has been noted down."

"That doesn't prove a thing," boomed Rowan. "He may just be keeping a record for himself."

The Fox held the giant of a man in his withering gaze. "You're a bloody fool if you think that. What kind of a secret organisation let's its members take notes from the meeting?"

Rowan fell silent.

"Besides," continued The Fox, "I have proof." He reached into an inside pocket and produced a document, which he unfolded slowly and deliberately. "Here," he held it up, "is your proof. This letter is addressed to Lord Camden at Dublin Castle. It contains details of this location." He stared at them all. "How do you think I found you? And look at the handwriting. It matches our dead friend's notes exactly!"

"Give me those," demanded Fitzgerald.

The Fox passed him the papers, which he studied carefully.

After a few moments Fitzgerald looked up. "He's right."

The Fox made a bow like a magician who had just completed his trick. Turning to his men he said, "Put your guns away, boys. We don't need them in this company."

Immediately The Fox's men lowered their guns and tucked them away. The man in black removed his hat and pulled up a chair.

"Look," he said in a softer tone, "I'm really sorry about that," he indicated McNally's corpse. "It was stupid of me to use such violence. I was just trying to make the point that you must tighten up your security." He put his hand over his mouth. "Oh dear, I think I feel sick. Can you cover him over boys? Use one of the curtains."

His men quickly obeyed.

"With security in mind, we had better move on," he continued, suddenly recovered from his brief bout of nausea, now the body was covered. "I have a further document to show you." He withdrew another sheet from inside his coat. "This is signed by General Bonaparte himself and refers to me in person. It gives me authority from the French commander to enforce his instructions to the Irish Revolutionary Movement. He appoints me as his official representative in Ireland and commands me to issue you with these orders."

Too much for the assembled officers of the United Irishmen to swallow, they broke into loud dissension. "Let us see that," they all roared. The Fox smiled and passed the document to the nearest outstretched hand.

After a few moments of jostling and peering, Drennan looked up from the document at The Fox, "Who's this?" he demanded indicating the name on the page. "Seamus who?"

"Ah well that's me," grinned The Fox. "Capitaine Seamus O'Malley," I think it says. You see he wasn't too comfortable about putting The Fox or Capitaine Renard, if you see what I mean. So he put my name down. As you probably worked out already, The Fox is not my real name."

"I see," was all Drennan replied.

"What are these orders?" demanded Tone.

"Quite simple really; do nothing until I tell you."

The Fox and his men left soon after and thoughtfully took McNally's corpse with them. Downstairs The Fox stopped his men, as they were about to leave with it.

"Hold hard, there's something I need to do with him."

The face was sufficiently destroyed to make it easy to slice through his tongue like a piece of meat and remove it.

"Let them see what we do to informers," smiled The Fox. "There'll not be many keening over this one now," he added and slipped the tongue in his pocket.

"This is bloody ridiculous," moaned Will.

"I think you may have mentioned that about a hundred times already. Change the record, Will."

The two men had slowed the pace after an hour's hard riding, chasing the French army, which had left the previous day under the direction of General Couteaux, towards New Ross. "Alright, alright, I know I've been going on a bit," conceded Will, "but just think about it. This isn't chance. It's deliberate. They want us out of the way, while they press north to Dublin. Or maybe they want us killed in some stupid battle that won't make the blindest bit of difference to anything. We don't have a big enough force to do this and Couteaux is a head case."

"Catch on to yourself, Will. Aren't you the one that told me all about the battle of New Ross and how it was critical to break out of the county to the west?"

"Well yeah, but that was when there wasn't a bloody great French army on Irish soil. It was a bit different from all this."

"Who's trying to kill us Will? You're paranoid. Why would Napoleon want to kill us?"

"Because they see us as a threat. We could lead an uprising against them."

"Hm, I don't think so, Will. Unfortunately you might be over-rating our power. Just the same it does seem odd that they'd send us off on our own, leaving all of our forces behind. I do agree that I don't like the idea of them all going north without us. We aren't going to do much down here."

"And we both know who that leaves."

"Yeah, I've been thinking about him too. Maybe he's behind this."

"Maybe he's trying to kill us."

"Maybe, but if he was, I think he'd just shoot you or something. Maybe he's trying to keep us out of the main action. We might be useful to him."

"Oh sure. How the hell does he have so much influence anyway?"

"I've been thinking about that too. There's something I was going to tell you."

Will pulled up on the reins so hard that Sean, who had been riding alongside, shot ahead and had to pull up sharply and turn his mount around. Sean noticed the cold expression on Will's face knew instantly.

"No, no, Will. It's not like that, not like that at all. It's not something I know, just more something I'm guessing. Something I want to share with you and get your thoughts."

"Go on, Sean."

"Well, it was when I was in Paris. You know I was in Paris, don't you?"

"I guessed."

Sean continued. "I was there with Tone and Tandy turned up. We waited forever for meetings with the Directory. Then finally we were granted a meeting with Napoleon. I knew who he was of course, Wolf Tone wasn't so sure." He laughed. "It sounds silly doesn't it? Well I missed the meeting."

"What? You didn't go? What the hell were you doing?"

"Yes, well no, it wasn't like that. I didn't hear about it until too late, I was with…what are you laughing at?"

"Oh Sean," chuckled Will. "Was she blonde, in a French maid's outfit? You're priceless, absolutely bloody priceless."

"It wasn't funny. I'd hung around for weeks. Stop laughing."

"I can't wait for your next mission, mate. 'Sean O'Grady what went wrong, you were meant to stop them dropping the atomic bomb on Hiroshima?' 'Well there was this cute Japanese chick and she had a twin sister!' Sean, you're hopeless. You ought to be locked up."

Sean started to laugh too. "Oh you're right, Will. I am a waste of time. Look, I've almost forgotten what I was going to tell and it's important.

I was apologising to Tone afterwards, because I was supposed to supply the cash and support his arguments, but he said it was fine. A substantial sum had been provided *in gold sovereigns*, like the ones we had. Tone didn't know where it had come from. He was so elated that it was going ahead. I was so relieved that it was going ahead to my schedule. You know, not late 1796, but Spring 1797. So where did the cash come from?"

"You think…"

"Yeah, it had to be The Fox. Who else? And if he provided all that, there would have been strings attached, a captaincy and more important, influence and a role in the uprising."

"You really don't know?"

"No, but I bet I'm right. It explains it all."

"You had no idea that he was in France?"

"No, Will, I didn't know and, yes, if I'd been a bit more responsible, I might have found out. Come on, we'd better get moving again."

"Alright let's get going, but there's something else," replied Will. "If The Fox has all this influence and he's behind our being seconded to Couteaux, what's he up to? Is he trying to get us killed or just get us out of the way?"

"Hm, I've been thinking about that too," said Sean. "For sure he's getting us away from the main action. Killed? I don't know about that. You've seen him in action. If he wanted us dead he'd just kill us. He's had the chance, especially you. I think he might be keeping us out of the line of fire. The question is, why?"

"I don't know about that. Wait a minute, if we're being kept safe, what will happen to the others, Mary and all of them?"

"Oh, I'm sure they'll be fine," replied Sean confidently. He did not let Will catch the expression on his face.

The two men rode on.

Late in the afternoon they encountered the first signs of the French Army, a motley assortment of wagons, animals and camp followers. Soon they were within sight of New Ross and were directed by a cavalry officer to a house on a hillside, overlooking the town. French soldiers guarded the door.

"You are expected, messieurs, please follow me."

They were led inside into a whitewashed room, which served as a kitchen and dining room and up a flight of open wooden stairs to a small landing. The guard knocked on the door and opened it to let them in.

The sight that greeted them was a surprise to Sean, if not to Will, who had read about Couteaux's eccentricities. The General, in full uniform, was sitting up in bed, next to, they assumed, his wife, dressed in a white night dress and bed cap.

"Ah, the Irish. Welcome, welcome," enthused the General, while his wife nodded and beamed.

It seemed to be the full extent of the General's English and an aide de camp, assisted by Sean translated the General's orders. It seemed that the two companions had a specific mission to fulfil, a mission which Sean grasped quickly, whilst Will was ushered out, uncertain as to their role.

"What the hell was all that about?" enquired Will, when they had left the house.

"Very straightforward really. All we have to do is to trot down to the gates of the town in the morning and get them to surrender."

"Shit, I thought that's what he was saying," exclaimed Will. "No chance, not a prayer, they'll never surrender and probably shoot us for our cheek. What are we going to do?"

"You're the military strategist. I was rather hoping that you'd have the answer to that one."

"Alright, I've got an idea. Let's see if the French Army has anything to drink."

"Sound suggestion and I forgot to mention, we've been invited to dinner tonight by the General and his wife. It sounded a bit like an invitation to the last supper. I hope they get out of bed!"

Shortly before dawn the following morning, Sean and Will were woken from their tent. Thick heads, they accepted with alacrity something remotely like coffee. With no excuses to cling to, they saddled up and rode down the hill to the gate of the walled town.

"So what's the master plan, Lieutenant Peters?" enquired Sean.

Will swallowed hard. "Collier loaded?"

"Yup!"

"Simple, ride down real slow to meet them and hope that they come out soon. That way we won't be too near the town and we're out of musket range. I'll wave the white flag.

If they start shooting, we turn around and ride like hell. If they talk, we tell them that there are millions more of our lot on the way. If they tell us to get stuffed, don't turn your back on them. Let them ride away first."

"That's it?"

"Yeah. I spent all night thinking about that."

"Brilliant; we're going to die."

To Will's enormous relief the gate of the town opened and a group of four men on horseback emerged. As the light gradually improved he could see that they too were carrying a white flag. The white flags hung limp in the morning dew. Far too quickly for Sean and Will, the six men met about a hundred yards from the gate.

The representative of New Ross, a balding man in his fifties, spoke first.

"Are you the official representatives of the Revolutionary Army of France?"

"We are," croaked Will and Sean in unison.

"Grand," replied the man. "I am authorised to hand over the keys of the town to you, on your solemn pledge that no man nor property will be harmed."

"Bloody hell!" murmured Sean, as Will scowled at him.

The reaction to the news from the victorious duo was mixed. Some seemed genuinely disappointed not to have a fight on their hands. They were all heroes, full of tales of their own bravery and what they would have done to their enemies. The General and his wife were delighted.

"A priceless victory? Was that what he said?" asked Will, as they left the general's house.

"A victory without cost," translated Sean. "I think we might get a medal. Never mind breakfast, I need a drink."

"Don't they want us to supervise the taking over of the town?"

"No, it seems they have others more suited to that kind of work. We're more suited to getting killed, only we didn't. For the love of God, where's the fire? He's in a hell of a hurry."

A rider raced up past them and dropped from his horse. Bidding the guard hold the reins he sprinted inside with his satchel over his shoulder.

"Let's hang around a moment and see what's going down," suggested Sean. "The drink can wait a bit."

Within moments the guards called to them and they were ushered back inside and up the stairs to the general's bedchamber. Sean and Will were agog to hear the news. The general was asleep. His wife explained and Sean translated, grim faced.

"It appears that the army has moved up towards Arklow and encountered a major English force. A huge battle is about to take place."

Will's face fell. "Oh dear lord, have our friends gone with them?"

Sean shook his head. "She doesn't know any details, but we are all instructed to abandon New Ross in the hands of the minimum number of men and proceed to reinforce immediately. She plans to move our men by nightfall."

"Nightfall! Christ that's hours away. We'll lose a day. Can't we go ahead?"

Sean turned to Madame Couteaux, who seemed a kindly old lady, and explained their circumstances. She spoke softly in French to Sean, whilst pointing at Will.

Sean smiled. "She asks if you love this Mary?"

Will looked at the old lady and replied, "Oui."

With that she pushed her snoring husband over in the bed and pulled a sheet of paper from under him. Smoothing out the creased document she demanded a quill and ink from the orderly by the door. In minutes she had written and signed it and, blotting it on the pillow, passed it to Sean.

"This is a written order to leave this force behind and proceed ahead to the battlefield. I don't think we will be challenged with this. It is signed by the general himself," said Sean with a wink.

Madame Couteaux beckoned Will, who approached the bed. She kissed him on the forehead and whispered, "bonne chance" in his ear. Will kissed her on the cheek and in moments the two men, with neither drink nor breakfast, were on the road back to Wexford, the precious orders tucked safely in an inside pocket.

Comfortably surrounded by his gang in a bar in Dublin, The Fox welcomed the arrival of a messenger. He confided in few and trusted none, but this news was vital to his plans. He let a couple of his closest supporters stay to hear it. He held up his hand to silence the breathless messenger, until the others had departed.

"Tell me your news," he ordered the young man.

"The army has gone to New Ross…"

"Yes, yes, I now all that. Did the Englishman and his partner go with them?" demanded The Fox.

"I'm pretty sure they did."

"Pretty sure, you'd better be bloody certain. Did they go?"

The messenger nodded his head vigorously.

The Fox turned to his companions, with a smile. "Good, they're out of the way and I can deal with the girl and their friend more easily. I need her alive, as bait, although I'm sure there'll be time for some fun." He turned to address the messenger. "Never mind all that man, what about the main army?"

"Oh, they have taken the field against the English near Arklow, er to, er, coincide with the uprising in Dublin, er, Sir."

The Fox eased back in his chair and grinned broadly. "Oh I do so love it when a plan comes together," he rasped.

Chapter 29

The road from New Ross to Enniscorthy
May 9th 1797

"Oh come on Will, we've no time for distractions. We're probably too…" Sean could have bitten his tongue.

"…too late?" Will finished his sentence for him, as he encouraged his horse to draw level with Sean's mount. "I want to catch up with our friends more than anyone. It's just it's right here. It'll only take ten minutes to check. Scullabogue! Never mind the people killed, never mind the arguments that are still raging two hundred years later, it gave the Victorians such a great excuse to paint the Irish as barbarians, as animals." They had stopped by now, Sean fidgeting with impatience in his saddle.

Will couldn't let it go. "For God's sake Sean, the rebels, our supporters burnt Protestants alive in a barn. Everyone saw Cruickshank's cartoons in the 1840's. They were probably one of the reasons they let them all starve in Ireland in the Famine."

"Alright, alright I don't need another history lesson right now," responded Sean. "I think you do though. All that stuff at Scullabogue blew up in reaction to the bloody defeat at New Ross. Have you forgotten already? We great heroes have just taken the town without a shot fired. It's not going to happen Mr History Man."

"Of course I bloody know that. I'm not stupid you know. It's just you can't be certain."

"Oh we're back to that again are we? We can't be certain Big Al." Sean poured scorn on Will's doubts.

"Right that's fine. You go on and I'll catch you. It'll only take ten minutes. I'll know the place in an instant." Will turned his horse and headed off down a side lane towards a hamlet.

It didn't take ten minutes to find the barn of Cruikshank's cartoons. As Will turned here and there amongst the cottages and old farm buildings he attracted suspicious looks from the locals. It was not there and Will's frustration grew. Gradually it dawned on him that he was looking for a building that didn't exist. The events had been real. The barn was solely in the imagination of a cartoonist nearly forty years after the event.

Nothing of significance was happening in Scullabogue. They had changed history!

A horseman appeared at his side. "Come on Will. Let's go. There's nothing for us here. It's not happening." He smiled, resisting the temptation to say 'I told you so'. "We've still plenty of the day in front of us and it will've given the horses a break."

"Thanks for waiting. You were right and I've wasted precious time. I hope I don't live to regret…"

"Will, it's no good having regrets. We are where we are. If I started regretting the things I've done, I would never get out of bed in the morning. No more talk, let's ride."

They were brave words and for a while they reassured both of them. As the hours passed the doubts crept back in to both men's minds.

They were both tired after little sleep the previous night and the tensions of the encounter before the walls of New Ross. Their route did not take them back to Wexford. Instead they headed direct for Enniscorthy and the crossing of the River Slaney.

Neither man had any desire to stop at Enniscorthy and rekindle the memories of their last visit. Stopping briefly to buy provisions they soon proceeded north towards Gorey and Arklow beyond.

"Will, I've got to stop. Never mind the horse my backside can't take any more. Besides we need to eat this stuff that we've just bought."

Reluctantly Will agreed and they pulled over beside the road to dismount.

"Oh my God my back is killing me," groaned Will, lying full length in the damp grass.

They ate and drank in silence until Will voiced what they knew in their hearts. "We're not going to make it tonight are we?"

Sean shook his head. "No chance. We left too late. It can't be helped."

They tried to smile. Neither man could repress the ominous feeling of foreboding that gripped them. It was almost tangible.

Sean forced the conversation. "Just think Will, when this is all over you can grab yourself some nice house with an estate and settle down with Mary."

"I'm not sure if she'd go for that. She might find it all a bit grand."

"Don't kid yourself. Put her in some fancy mansion with a few servants and I reckon she'll get the hang of it real fast."

"And how am I going to get my hands on somewhere like that?"

Sean took a long look at his companion. "You are joking aren't you? When this lot is finished, you'll just be able to march up the drive of some Protestant palace with a few of my boys and just tell the buggers to clear off. Send them to a hovel in Connaught, like Cromwell's boys did a few generations ago."

Will was up on his feet, fumbling for his Collier. "Stand up and say that again. We're not fighting for that. Say it again and I'll shoot you now."

Sean didn't move.

"You're no better than Cromwell, if that's what you're planning. Is this what it's all about for you?"

Sean put his head in his hands. "Oh Will, sit down I didn't mean it. Not like it sounded, really I didn't. I was just talking to cheer you up a bit. Put that bloody thing away before you have an accident."

Reluctantly Will tucked the weapon out of sight. More calmly he added, "We can't do that sort of thing, Sean, not if we really want to change things for the better."

"No I take your point, but what about the family living in squalor in the West that these guys evicted hundred years or so ago. What about their rights?"

Will brushed his hand across his brow. "It's not easy. You can't sort out hundreds of years of injustices in ten minutes. I don't know all the answers. Right now all I can think about is getting out of this mess. Perhaps you and I should be thinking not about pubs and country estates and more about helping the new government, if we all live to see it."

"Let's plan to play to our strengths. I'll own a string of bars and make myself fabulously wealthy. You can run for President and I'll fund your campaign."

At last a smile fell across Will's face. "I'm not sure that independent Ireland's first president should be an Englishman."

"Oh I don't know. Why change the habits of a lifetime?" grinned Sean. "Come on let's get going. If the battle's today we've missed it. If it's tomorrow it'll probably kick off at dawn and we need to be nearer."

"Sean."

"Yeah."

"I believe you."

Without knowing why they both embraced before they remounted and rode north.

Chapter 30

Between Enniscorthy and Arklow
May 10th 1797

It was the silence that Sean and Will noticed first. It didn't come suddenly; it crept up on them over a couple of hours.

After a miserable night in the open by a campfire that kept going out, they rose and set off before dawn. Having ridden for a couple of hours Sean pulled them up. "Is it me or has everything in the world died? It's like the world is holding its breath."

Will slowed his pace and cocked his head to one side. "You're right. All I can hear is us and the horses."

The only sign of life was their mounts harsh breath in the damp dawn air. A rumble murmured in the north.

"Is that thunder?" Sean asked Will. "It doesn't feel like a storm brewing."

Will halted his mount, always grateful for a break in the rhythm that chafed his legs and made his back stiff. He turned his head to one side and concentrated. He too picked up the rumble in the distance and his face fell with realisation. "That's not thunder; those are guns, big guns.

We're too late Sean, it's started. The battle's started. Come on or we'll be too late." He kicked the sides of his horse and urged it on.

Over the next two hours, as the rumble grew louder, peaked, and then died down, they realised that the battlefield was further away than they had anticipated. They would indeed be too late. They became accustomed to the rumble of the big canon growing louder and more threatening. They heard what they thought was the crash of volley fire. "The French are taking some punishment," commented Will. They even fancied that they could here the sporadic crackle of the skirmishers.

Then, as they strained hard to judge how close they were, the realisation dawned that it had stopped. Silence. Not even the birds were singing. By just after midday it was all over. Whatever the result the two men would play no part in it. They could only guess as to the outcome and that speculation was unbearable. They forced their tired horses on.

The first signs were encouraging. Wagon loads of supplies under the control of French infantry officers being driven forwards, not back. Sean cross-examined a young French subaltern. "He doesn't know much, except he's been told to advance," explained Sean, as he remounted and they continued their progress. "It looks like a French victory, Will, we might have to hurry to catch them before they get to Dublin."

Both men knew that this was not their real concern. The battle, from the prolonged noise had been a major one. What had happened to their friends and loved ones? Maybe they weren't even involved.

Then came the injured, not the trickle they had anticipated, but rounding a bend in the road, a rush. A field hospital came into view and the most appalling chaos. Cartloads of wounded men were being unloaded, faster than anyone could attend to them. They were piled up, waiting the surgeon's knife, the dead, the dying; all wishing that they were dead. Some crippled stragglers, still capable of crawling, were simply looking for somewhere peaceful to die. Piles of bodies were growing. They would have to wait. Stray dogs appeared from nowhere, sensing a free meal.

The injuries appalled the two men. The pathetic cries were worse to endure. It was turning hot and the wounded men called for water.

And then they caught the smell.

No man should know that smell. Sean and Will instinctively knew what it was and they both shuddered. It was the smell of death, death on a scale that neither could truly comprehend. The effect on the two men was similar.

They had both been apprehensive of another conflict. Now they knew that was passed, panic gnawed at their guts. What would they find? What appalling remains of their friends and loved ones would greet them when they topped the rise behind the field hospital? Maybe, just maybe, it would not be so bad as they feared. Both men clung to this foolish self-deception.

In spite of their reluctance to see the grisly truth, they hastened their pace, passing a wrecked canon; the weapon blown from its carriage, before it could be brought to bear.

Topping the brow of the hill the two men looked across the lower plain that led to the sea. Their hearts fell. It was difficult to hold back the tears. The scene of carnage was just too much to bear. Smoke rolled across the fields and it seemed at first that nobody moved. Men, horses, nothing seemed to move. Hell had come to earth. They looked closer. Figures like wraiths moved amongst the bodies. They were tending to the wounded. With a sudden horror it dawned on both men simultaneously. Sean caught Will's eye. They were plundering the dead and those too injured to defend themselves.

Sean was first to recover his senses. "Come on Will, we've got to find them."

He didn't say, 'if they're still alive.'

Will prayed. He prayed like he'd never prayed before, to any god, who would listen. "Just let her be spared. Just let her not be here," he said out loud. He knew she would be. She would have gone with them. She would never have stayed behind.

They forced themselves down amongst the dead and dying. Men cried out for a drink of water, for a prayer to be said for them, to be released from their suffering. With handkerchiefs over their noses they searched about through the smoke, the smell and the misery.

It was hard to resist the pathetic pleas for water. They both relented and abandoned their search long enough to pour the contents of their canteens down powder dried throats. English, French or Irish, it made no difference. By the time their canteens were empty they had worked out the pattern of the battlefield, the areas where the soldiers of each side were piled high, where regiments had stood and fallen. They found where the nationalities lay mixed, entwined in a last embrace of death.

"Jesus, is it worth this? Is anything worth this?" muttered Sean. "Two hundred years later and we're still doing it. Will we never learn?"

And then they found them, the dismembered remains of the people they knew. Both men tried hard not to retch. They had to be strong, just in case, just in case.

"Will, quick, here!" cried Sean. He was on foot now, searching amongst the piles of corpses.

Will slid from the saddle and hurried to where Sean was frantically trying to push an upturned cart away from some object on the ground.

"Will, help me, it's Rikki. I think he's alive."

Will threw all his strength at the cart and suddenly it rolled over with a horrendous groan of timber. The noise seemed frightening, as if it would wake something dreadful amongst this ocean of decay.

It was Rikki and he was alive, but in seconds both men's hopes were dashed. He was dying and even as they pulled the cart away they might be too late.

"Sean, Will, is that you," he cried, blind, blackened eyes seeking about him. "Water, do you have water?"

The two men wept in despair. Both had given up their last water already to the other needy souls.

Will was first to kneel beside the dying man. "You'll be fine," he lied. "We'll soon have you fixed up."

Rikki started to laugh, soon changing to a death rattle. "I love you, Will. You're a fine fellow." He coughed again. "Even you can't save me now."

Before Will could reassure him, Rikki seized his jacket with frightening vigour. "I'm sorry, Will, so sorry. I tried to stop them, to save her."

Will felt a wave of horror sweep over him, so powerful that it left him weak and defeated.

"They took her, Will. I'm so sorry. I couldn't stop them."

It was selfish and callous. As Rikki was dying in his arms, Will felt another wave of emotion; this time a rush of exultation. "They took her. They took her!" Oh God! Thank you God! She was alive! He leaned over close to Rikki's charred face. "Who took her, Rikki? Who took her?"

He listened hard to his seventeenth century Irish friend and heard nothing.

"Will, Will, he's gone." Sean started to sob, as he put his hand on Will's shoulder. "He's dead old son."

Will cried. It all came out. He stood and the two men embraced in their grief.

Will pulled away and shook Sean's shoulders. "Sean, who took her, the English army?"

Sean bent down and pulled back the old coat that covered Rikki's legs. Both knees had been shot at close range. Sean's colour drained from his face. He shook as he said, "That's not English work. I know who did this and he wasn't wearing a red coat. I'll fucking kill him with my bare hands." He stepped away and tried to compose himself.

Will pursued him. "What are you saying? Was it The Fox? Has The Fox taken her?"

Sean turned to face his companion. "He's been knee-capped, twice. That bastard would have crippled him and then taunted him, as he took Mary. He knows that Rikki would have given his life to protect her, to save her for you, Will. He thought the world of you. He admired you and loved you."

"Should we bury him?" asked Will.

"Not here. Let's get him out of here," agreed Sean and they lifted Rikki's broken body onto Sean's horse and walked from the battlefield, heading north for Dublin, for rescue and revenge.

"Do you know, I wasn't going to, but now I think I might?" The Fox pulled Mary towards him and kissed her, despite her efforts to ward him off. "You might not like it at first, but by the time I've finished, you'll be begging me for more!"

His men roared in appreciation and Mary squirmed and fought in vain.

"You would not touch me in my…" Mary's voice trailed off.

Like the head of some great carnivorous dinosaur, The Fox swung slowly back from his men towards Mary. He grinned, "In your what? In your condition? Oh listen boys, the little bitch is over the stick." He pulled her close until their faces were inches apart. "You're not by any chance carrying the Englishman's bastard are you?"

She fought to turn her face away.

The Fox seized her jaw and pulled her face around to meet his. He kissed her on the lips, as she struggled. "Don't worry, darling. Rest easy. Whilst the thought of his child disgusts me," he whispered, "it'll not deter me." He turned to his men and roared, "I think I'll still be able to manage it!"

The men roared back.

The Fox released her and, as she stepped back he spun and caught her across the side of her face with the back of his hand. She screamed and fell to the floor.

"That's what you get for sleeping with the enemy, you little whore!"

Safely a few miles north of the battlefield and to the west of the retreating English army The Fox had halted his men and was enjoying himself. Unusually for him his moments of self-indulgence had dulled his senses and he did not notice the approaching French cavalry.

"Capitaine O'Malley, let zat woman go immediately. This is not the behaviour of a French officer," barked Bapaume from astride his horse.

As The Fox's men reached for their weapons they realised that they were outnumbered by at least three to one.

The Fox collected his thoughts immediately. "Ah, Capitaine Bapaume, what a pleasant surprise. Surely it is the duty of every officer in the Republican Army to entertain the local populace and share with them the pleasures to be found under the new regime?"

Bapaume was not so easily drawn in by the Irishman's charm. "Release her to me right now. I do not permit such behaviour in my army." He drew himself erect in the saddle and smiled down at Mary, who looked up wearily at her supposed rescuer. She had seen it all before. "Madamemoiselle, you have nothing to fear from me. I will take you into my custody." He added, looking at The Fox, "It is for the best, I'm sure you can see that."

"We can take them," whispered a voice in The Fox's ear.

The Fox raised his hand and whispered back, "Steady, Rory, old son, there's a time and a place for everything, not now." In a louder voice he addressed Bapaume. "Of course, Monsieur. It will be my pleasure to hand her to you in the confidence that you will take *very good* care of her."

"Come on, you're not going to let them get away with this are?" encouraged Rory again.

The French brought their weapons to bear. Bapaume had a short cavalry carbine pointing at The Fox's heart.

"Just a little youthful enthusiasm," shrugged The Fox to Bapaume. "I will deal with it later."

"Be sure that you do, Capitaine. In the meantime you are to report to General Bonaparte at his field headquarters to the south. He has secured a great victory over the English, but at some cost. He will want news of the uprising in Dublin."

Bapaume slipped his carbine back into his saddle holster and beckoned Mary to come over. She complied, too tired to argue. With some skill he lifted her to his saddle and, turning his horse, led his men away.

As the French disappeared from view The Fox turned suddenly and struck Rory viciously in the face, knocking him to the ground. "If you ever argue with me again, in front of the French, I'll cut out your stupid heart," he yelled. As if to prove it, he pulled his bayonet knife from his belt and brandished in the prostrate man's face. "Do you understand me?"

Rory muttered, "Aye."

"Good," smiled The Fox, putting away the blade. "Let me do the thinking, you've not the brains for that. Even you must be able to see that fornicating with a treacherous little whore is not worth getting shot by some greasy French piece of shit. There's always another way of doing things, but you have to live long enough to do it."

"But don't you need her to lure the Englishman to Dublin?" braved Rory.

"There you go again, doing the thinking, when you weren't born with the equipment to do it."

Rory stared at The Fox, puzzled.

"They'll come to Dublin, with or without her. They'll come for me. Trust me. Besides when that young fellow sees the shiner on his girl's face, he'll get all emotional and want to fight me. I know these things."

"What about the Frenchman? Will you let him get away with that?" asked Rory.

The Fox scowled and his men feared that Rory would pay the price for his impertinence. In an instant the smile was back on their leader's face.

"Don't worry! It'll be fine. The Frenchman will die a violent death, just like God intended. I have a plan. Don't I always?

The Englishman and Sean can't be far behind. They'll have headed for the battlefield. I want you," he pointed to the youngest looking lad in his band, "to go back and find them. Tell them that you're fed up with me and you've left to go home. Tell them what happened and how that French bastard has taken the girl." He looked around at his men and asked, "And what do you think they'll do then?" Before they could respond he continued, grasping his hands together in a mock-heroic gesture, "they'll have to rescue the damsel in distress. They'll kill the Frenchman for me."

One of the more foolhardy men enquired, "might not the Frenchman kill them?"

The Fox pondered. "That is a possibility and a risk, but on balance I think the Englishman will win. A couple of weeks ago I wouldn't have given a fig for his chances; now, my money's on him. He's wised up a lot. The Frenchman will be full of honour and all that shit. The Englishman will just want to fucking kill him. There's no place for honour in this world."

The Fox laughed. "And now we have more pressing business to attend to. We have an uprising to organise." To himself he added under his breath, "but not as you know it, Napoleon old son."

His men mounted up and he led them back to Dublin.

The news of the defeat of the English Army near Arklow spread like an epidemic through Dublin. By the afternoon of the following day the city had descended into chaos. The trickle had turned to a torrent. Carts laden with the contents of city mansions choked the approaches to the harbour. Members of the Ascendancy bribed and out-bribed the commanders of any sea worthy vessel in the harbour to take them to England. The less wealthy were heading north to Belfast. It might not be any safer, but at least it was further away from the advancing French.

Troops tried to control the crowds of looters and rioters that roamed the streets. Strangely the one event that many feared and predicted had not come to pass; there was no organised uprising.

Most of the city's garrison had gone south with General Lake. Those remaining ran around the city trying to stamp out the little bushfires of rebellion. Some tried to keep order at the port. It might be necessary to organise a full-scale military evacuation. The port must be under military control. The harbour must not be depleted of all suitable vessels.

At this time of full scale alert Dublin Castle's security was stretched woefully thin. It did not go unnoticed by The Fox's spies.

The Viceroy, Lord Camden had called together as many of his team as he could muster in the same room, where the news of de Guilbert's defeat and death had been announced. Some of the same faces were present; others were attending to the security of their families. All except Castlereagh were in a state of extreme agitation.

"Before we make any rash decisions we should remember that our troops inflicted as much damage on the French forces as they did on ours," explained Castlereagh. "Our army may be in retreat, but theirs is a spent force. With the Royal Navy back on patrol, they have received no reinforcements and are unlikely to do so. I say that we can defend the city, when Lake has regrouped his men…"

"Are you mad?" interrupted Beresford. "I am told that we have lost all our artillery, most of our infantry and that no coherent cavalry force remains. If you had heeded my warnings and kept back a force to defend the city…"

"Gentlemen, gentlemen, it will not serve us to argue and apportion blame," Camden took control. "The key issue is that we cannot defend ourselves against an uprising. This is our most serious…Who the devil are you?"

Unannounced a tall longhaired man, clad in a black leather coat had entered the room. He smiled and pulled open his coat to reveal the pair of Colliers at his belt.

Half rising from his seat, Camden spluttered, "Guards, GUARDS!"

There was no response. Two of The Fox's men revealed themselves at the door to show the gathered company that salvation was unlikely from that direction. The

Fox pulled up a vacant seat and sat down, while the gentlemen of Camden's government calmed themselves.

"Be not afraid," the intruder smiled. "If I'd come to kill you I would have done it by now and you'd never have known how it happened. We are all gentlemen here and I am quite sure that there is no need for violence."

"Who the devil are you?" repeated Camden.

"Who I am does not really matter. It is who and what I represent that you should concern yourselves with." There was complete calm in the room, except for a slight fidgeting from Lord Clare.

Without looking away from Camden, The Fox snapped, "If you even think about drawing a pistol on me, my Lord, I will instruct my men to shoot Castlereagh in the head and I will personally wipe his brains off this nice carpet with your face."

The fidgeting stopped.

"Excellent. Let's get on with it." The Fox was smiling again. "I expect that you have been arguing about the state of your forces and what options remain open to you. It is simple you have two options; the one I am about to offer you or watching everyone and everything that you hold dear destroyed before your helpless eyes. Do you want to hear more?"

They nodded in silence.

"Good. To begin with I will answer your question, I represent the French Commanding Officer, General Bonaparte and the Irish Forces here in the city and elsewhere. I assure you that I have the power to make what I am about to offer you happen.

I shall be honest with you. I do not have control of your Castle, not yet. We have, how shall I put it, bypassed your security, which, by the way is atrocious. So the uprising has not yet happened." He turned to Lord Clare, "but if you think that your guards will save you, forget it. We will slaughter you all in this room, before they take us and, if we don't return within the hour, our supporters will burn Dublin to the ground before nightfall. So let us proceed.

Your army is mortally wounded. It will not recover. Your only salvation would be for major reinforcements to arrive in the next twenty-four hours. No longer than this, you have run out of time." He looked around at the ashened faces. "Forget it. It isn't going to happen.

If I give the word, the uprising that you have all feared will happen and I will not be able to control it. Your homes, your possessions will be burned to the ground. There are guillotines hidden, which will appear on the streets. Your heads will be paraded on pikes through the streets. There is nothing you can do to stop this." He paused to judge the effect of his words.

With perfect poise Castlereagh interjected, "Except for this option that you will offer. Get to the point man," Castlereagh smiled back at The Fox, "no pun intended."

"I love a man with a sense of occasion," returned The Fox. "The option is simple, we let you go. We help you to load up whatever you can and give safe passage to all who want to leave. For those who cannot find passage from Dublin, we will give them protection to Belfast and they can sail to Scotland from there."

"What? You'll just turn your backs and let us leave?" blustered Camden.

"That's about the size of it," replied The Fox.

"Damned infernal cheek!" Clare could control himself no longer. "You have the gall to march in here off the street and tell us we can leave our own country. For God's sake don't listen to this scoundrel."

The Fox turned to Clare. "I thought that might be the reaction, from some at least. So let me spell it out to you. Firstly this is not *your* country. That is the point of all this.

Secondly do you think that I could be sitting here now if the whole place wasn't collapsing about your ears? Don't doubt an uprising. Haven't you been expecting it for weeks? Why do you think it hasn't happened? I'll tell you why…because I didn't want it. And why? That's simple too. We're not kicking you lot out just to be ruled by those wine-swilling lunatics from over the Channel.

And that's what will happen if we rise up and get ourselves all killed fighting the remains of the existing regime. Oh, don't doubt we'll do it. Your day is done, but what comes next? Think about it.

If you and your friends trot off nicely back to England, we'll have our uprising, but it won't be against the English. The French army is badly wounded and their chances of reinforcements are slim, now that your jolly jack tars have gone back to work. Their supply lines are stretched from Wexford to just south of Dublin. They are not expecting to fight us. Added to that, Lake's army kindly left us hundreds of muskets and a few artillery teams, who were only too pleased to defect, rather than have their manhood removed."

The Fox's audience listened in stunned silence as he continued. "Just think a little further ahead. Which would suit you better, the Irish ruling Ireland or the French? If we take control, what will we do first? We'll probably get drunk for about a year and then we'll start fighting each other. Is that a threat to Good King George? I don't think so. We'll just be that noisy neighbour next door. You won't like us, but we'll not encroach on your garden.

On the other hand, if the French take over, what then? It doesn't take a great brain to work out that Ireland will only be a stepping-stone. The French won't stop there. The next step will be simultaneous landings in Kent and Scotland. It's not far to sail to Stranraer from Belfast. How will the Scots react? Now isn't that an interesting one to consider? They might just welcome us ashore. It's only just over fifty years since Bonnie Prince Charlie made a similar journey."

The Fox leaned back in his chair and put his hands behind his head. "The French landing in Dover and a combined French-Irish-Scots army at the gates of Carlisle. What a picture!"

The room fell silent again and The Fox stood up and announced. "That's it. I want an answer in an hour to be brought to this address." He handed over a slip of paper. "And don't think of sending the military around. I won't be there, only my envoy and he's expendable. If the answer's yes, you will hand over the castle. If the answer's no, well, God rest your poor souls. If I unleash the rabble, I will not be able to control them. Good day gentlemen."

He swept out of the room.

So confident was The Fox of victory that he was at the address on the note. A carriage pulled up and a bewigged coachman marched up the steps to the inn with a document, sporting the official castle seal. He had to wait patiently, while The Fox finished his beer. Breaking the seal on the document he scanned its contents.

"Friends, call a meeting of the committee. Ireland is ours!"

When the tumult had died down and the runners had been despatched, The Fox turned to one of his most trusted companions. "We have come to the endgame. The committee will decide to slaughter the Frogs, the English will depart and Ireland will be mine. I can't make up my mind if I'll be King or Emperor.

Huh, enough of that, we mustn't let it slip now. I want you and the boys to get the gunpowder to the Castle. I want the first meeting of the provisional government called there. Then, as soon as you've prepared the charges I want those two fucking clowns and the girl allowed through. They're essential for my plan to succeed. We must be ready for them."

Chapter 31

Outskirts of Arklow
May 10th 1797

Will and Sean spent a miserable day trying to find somewhere suitable to bury Rikki and, with hard ground and no tools, they had not anticipated the practical difficulties. There were just too many to bury and too few people interested in doing it. Dead bodies were cheap currency. By nightfall they decide to build a fire, a funeral pyre they told themselves, the only practical option. It was well that neither remained to see how inadequately the fire coped with its task.

Besides they needed to find The Fox and Mary.

For once The Fox's plans did not work out. They did not need to. Bapaume, at the head of a procession of munitions wagons and cavalry, found them; sleeping on open ground. Bapaume's men shook them awake. As they struggled to shade their eyes from the morning sunshine they were subjected to a barrage from the French officer.

"What is the meaning of this? You are deserters. I will have you shot."

Sean was the first to his feet. "No we're not. We have orders. Will. Will show him Couteaux's orders."

Will struggled to pull himself together and rummaged in his coat pocket. "Here, Capitaine Bapaume, we have orders permitting us to be here." Shading his eyes, he presented them to the mounted captain, who had kept the sun behind him.

Bapaume leaned forward in the saddle and snatched them from Will's grasp. He scanned them quickly and sneered. "These are meaningless. It would not surprise me if you wrote these yourselves." He ripped the orders to shreds and scattered them on the ground. Looking down on the two companions, tired dirty and dishevelled, he shouted, "You are a disgrace to the uniforms of our Great Republic. I think I will give you a chance to redeem yourselves, a chance to risk death in the service of France. Hm, perhaps we will need to siege Dublin."

It was too much for Will. "You have the fucking cheek to talk to us like that. We have seen more action in the last couple of weeks than you will see in your life. Look at your bloody uniform, it's immaculate, you haven't done a day's soldiering in your pathetic life. If I were…"

He never finished his sentence. Mary appeared. She was riding with one of Bapaume's men.

She saw him at the same moment. "Will, Will oh thank the Lord, Will you're here." She slipped from the horse and ran towards him.

Bapaume was too quick and, leaping from his horse, seized her, before she could reach Will's outstretched arms. "Oh I don't think so," said Bapaume.

Will snapped.

"Steady, Will," murmured Sean.

Too late, Will swung his fist and caught Bapaume full in the face. The Frenchman staggered back under the force of the blow. A dozen French carbines instantly pointed at Will's chest.

Bapaume recovered quickly. "You filthy English pig." He hesitated and held up his arm to signal his men to lower their weapons. "No, that is too good for you. I will do this myself, here and now." He squared up to Will. "You want the lady? Fight me for her."

Will gaped at him, uncomprehending.

"For Christ's sake, Will, wake up. He wants a duel," Sean's words were in his ear.

Will shook himself, looked at Sean and whispered, "If he kills me, shoot the bastard."

Sean smiled and whispered back, "Much as I'd love to, I'd rather you did that for me. Mind, if you win, be ready for what follows. Take any cover you can find and use the Collier."

Will gave Sean a brief wink to signal his comprehension and turned to Bapaume. "I accept your challenge, but this must be a fight between you and I, man to man."

"Of course, what else?" responded the Frenchman.

"Tell your men to stand off. I must have room to kill you."

"You are very brave with your words. Very well. It will be over quickly." He waved his men away.

Will slowly removed his coat and passed it to Mary. He said nothing and simply held her gaze as he slipped the Collier to her. She stood back, placing the coat over her arm, the weapon concealed in her hand beneath it.

Both men drew their swords and the duel began. They started cautiously, weighing up each other's strengths and weaknesses. After a few minutes of play, Bapaume made his decision and increased the pace. His speed and skill were mesmerising. Will felt the fear rise in his stomach. No time to think, he parried and retreated, losing ground all the time. Still Bapaume increased his speed and drew first blood, whipping the point of his blade across Will's chest. His shirt wet with his own blood, Will felt the shock and then the pain. He wanted to check the wound, but Bapaume was relentless and Will was forced to defend himself from a thrust aimed at his stomach.

Will knew he could not beat this man. As he fought his adversary he also fought the despair and anger, which rose within him. He wanted to look at Mary, if only he could take his eyes off the Frenchman's flashing blade.

He was not sure if it was his fear or just a mistake. Bapaume unexpectedly withdrew and tempted Will to make an attack. Off balance it was child's play to catch Will on the guard of his weapon and flip it from his grasp. The sword, which was once de Guilbert's flew five yards across the field and landed point first on the hard earth, close to where Sean stood. For a moment it quivered and then symbolically fell to the ground.

Will's eyes followed the weapon and then he turned slowly back to find the point of Bapaume's sword inches from his face. The Frenchman grinned and shrugged. Both men knew that there was only one outcome of this conflict.

"Please. This is a duel to the death, not an execution." He lowered his sword. "Go and retrieve it, please."

Will's shoulders dropped. The man was playing with him. He walked towards his fallen weapon. As he bent to pick it up Mary called to him.

"Will, before you do that, answer me one question. You must be honest."

Will left the sword on the ground and turned to her.

"Will, can you win this fight?"

Will opened his mouth to reassure her and saw the look in her eyes. He shook his head.

In a moment Mary drew Will's Collier took a couple of paces forward and shot the unsuspecting Bapaume in the back.

As the Frenchman fell to his knees he turned to see his attacker. His face full of loathing and disgust, he whispered his last words, "There is no honour in that!"

Mary watched him die, her eyes blazing in defiance. "There is no honour in an unmarried woman burying the father of her unborn child!"

Will froze. For a brief moment all was still and her words hung on the heavy air between them. All hell was about to break loose.

Sean typically was the first to give the storm warning. "Will quick! To Mary, I'll cover your back." Snatching up Will's fallen weapon, he rushed to stand between Bapaume's men and his two friends. The French were too distant; the pistol was useless. Glancing to assure himself that Will and Mary were running for the few trees and some cover, he too turned and ran. He prayed that the short-barrelled Cavalry carbines were as inaccurate as Will had told him.

A huge explosion ripped across the field as one of the French wagons flew into the air and showered everything in embers and wood splinters. Horses reared up and musket fire came from all directions. Men screamed and yelled and, as the fleeing trio turned to look, Bapaume's cavalry disappeared in a wall of flame and smoke.

"Christ, someone's started another war!" exclaimed Sean, unaware of the truth of his words.

In a moment the French troop were no longer witnessing a gentleman's duel; they were on the ground wrestling and kicking as a swathe of Irish rebels fell on them.

"Come on, you two, I don't know what's going on and I don't rightly care. Someone is saving us for another day, RUN!"

Through the trees and across another field they ran. Squeezing through a hedge and another copse, they paused for breath.

Mary touched Will's arm. "Are you badly hurt?"

"No, it's only a scratch," he responded heroically.

"Good, it'll wait, I need to pee," she hissed.

"Oh, er sorry, of course. Don't go too far away," instructed Will, a little crestfallen at the lack of sympathy.

She parted for the trees and left Will and Sean looking at each other.

Sean laughed, "You're going to have to get used to this."

Will beamed back, "I can't believe it."

"Well it's hardly a miracle now is it?"

Will reddened, "Well no not really."

Sean brought him back down to earth by returning his sword. "Another silver medal, well done."

"Yeah, he was a bit good wasn't he? To be honest he was better than anyone I've ever seen, never mind fought."

"Difference between a hobby and a living eh?"

Will grinned sheepishly, "I think I'm lucky to be here."

"You are and you're not. You had the faith in that girl of yours to give her the gun. I'd never have done that. And she had the guts to do it. You two deserve each other."

"I haven't thanked her. It must have taken huge courage to do that."

"I think she knows all that, Will. And I'll tell you something else she knows; you knew that French bastard was going to kill you, but you were still willing to pick up that sword and let him, you prat, rather than hand over your sword and her with it. That takes some courage."

"He'd have killed us anyway."

"You're probably right. Doesn't change anything though." He slapped Will on the shoulder. "For once in my life I'm trying to be serious here. You're a better man than I am Will Peters. I've never admired anyone like I do you." He turned away in embarrassment and left Will to check on Mary's safety.

A few yards away three frightened horses had come to rest.

"Our luck is going to run out soon, but not yet, thank the Lord," Sean muttered to himself and strolled towards them as casually as his stretched nerves would permit.

He caught the horses and led them back to where Mary and Will were in each other's arms.

Sean grinned at them. "Ride for ten minutes and then you can do that, while I reload that pistol of yours. I think we're going to need it. We must head for Dublin now. Mary, I don't suppose there is any point in me trying to persuade you to stay behind, is there?"

She shook her head and smiled, "It's probably no safer here with all this going on."

Sean was forced to agree. "In that case keep close and when we do meet The Fox, as I know we will, leave him to me. He's my problem."

They set off, Will and Mary in the lead. The two lovers could not see Sean's chalky pallor. He was looking at Will's back and muttered under his breath. "Dear Lord, I know what I'm about to face. Give me the wisdom to make the right choice and the strength to carry it through."

The Fox left it until the morning after the note had been delivered to approach the castle again. His threats had not been idle; his promises were weak. Dublin was rapidly slipping out of any semblance of order and the departing regime would have to take their chances. Troops loyal to the English had kept control of the harbour and all those wanting to leave by that route just had to run the gauntlet to reach it. Lake's defeated army was drifting back in dribs and drabs to reinforce them.

The arrival of The Fox and his men at the castle went almost unnoticed, so busy were the few remaining staff, boxing up or burning documents. One or two of The Fox's men went to stop them.

"Leave them. Let them destroy the evidence. There's no doubt about their guilt. It'll save us a job. Besides we have more important matters to attend to."

They toured the old ramshackle collection of buildings that was loosely termed a castle and determined that there was no threat to their activities. The Fox then instructed them to bring in the three wagon loads of gunpowder and the barrels were taken up to what had been Camden's office and meeting room.

"I want them out of sight and I want the United Irish Committee on standby. The timing has to be perfect. I want them all in place, when our friends arrive. I gather that the Englishman survived his encounter with that French bastard – I wish I'd seen that."

He had his usual collection of cronies around him and couldn't resist the temptation to gloat at the prospect of his plan coming to pass.

"What a tragedy it will be. The fledgling Irish Republican Government will all be killed in the explosion, a trap set by these two renegade revolutionaries. I will arrive just in time to kill the two lunatics and their whore, but sadly too late to save our heroic United Irishmen. Who will be left to run the country and pull us out of our grief?

I'm not looking to take power, but if I'm called by my people what else can I do?"

Chapter 32

Near Arklow
May 10th 1797

Still clad in their French uniforms, Sean and Will did not fully appreciate the change in the affairs of Ireland, which was happening around them. Neither did they appreciate the danger. First there were questions to be answered and Will's wounds to attend to. They paused by a stream and watered the horses.

"Come here Will, take off your coat and let me look at that wound," said Mary.

Will obediently removed his coat. His shirt was soaked in blood, but, on removing it gingerly, a cut across his chest was revealed to be only skin deep. Mary ripped a piece off her petticoat, dipped it in the stream and wiped the cut. Will winced.

"Oh some hero you are! Don't make a fuss, it's only a scratch," she scolded him. Pausing, she enquired, "Why must we go to Dublin? Would it not be better to return home? You two have burned your bridges with the French army. Surely now they will shoot you as deserters?"

Will and Sean looked at each other to see how they could explain their situation to Mary. Both spoke simultaneously and then immediately stopped.

Sean indicated to Will, "I think you'd better explain."

Will considered for a minute and cleared his throat. "Well I suppose the best thing here is to say that a group of people in England sent us here to try and put things right, to try and change the government of Ireland and make things better than they are. We were meant to stop some of the bloodshed that they thought was going to happen." He looked to Sean, for encouragement.

"Go on," Sean urged.

"Well I'm not sure how successful we've been, given everything that's happened." Will paused again as a wave of emotion swept over him, thinking about all the death and violence he had witnessed over the last few weeks. "Anyway it will all be a waste if we end up with a government worse than the one we had before. Just imagine if the new rulers send troops around the villages whipping and torturing folk, just because they're Catholic or Protestant or they come from Wexford or Galway or something. I suppose what Sean and I are going to do is to talk to the new people in Dublin and try and make them set up a fair government."

As he said the words it all sounded so naïve and simplistic. It sounded as though he was talking down to her, although she had saved his life at least twice. Besides it was her country, her time, not his or Sean's. He felt pathetic and hopeless. How on earth did he imagine that this renegade psychologist from Dublin and an academic from Harrow were going to tame this revolution? He knew too that it would come down to how they would deal with The Fox? Sean kept saying he would deal with him. How? Would he fight him? Would it come down to a fight between him, Will Peters, and this dark demon that scared him? The next sword fight could end with one of The Fox's men shooting him in the back.

With that thought he suddenly felt ashamed of how Bapaume had died. Will was glad there was no mirror for him to look into. The Frenchman had been right. Where was the honour in that? Those words would haunt him. Within a moment his tired mind fluttered full circle as he chided himself for his weakness. He was hardly the ruthless revolutionary. Wouldn't he need to be to see this business through?

Mary must have seen his internal torment. She decided not to pursue it. "I don't really understand what you're doing, Will. I do know that you will do your best and

I will be with you." She smiled at both men. "We've survived so far, we'll do it again."

Sean smiled too. The veneer of confidence was back, polished and presentable. In his head the screams were rising to such a crescendo, Sean could hardly think. He needed to have a plan and to prepare himself. He alone knew what they were going to face. It was his responsibility to resolve this mess. He *must* have a plan. If only this noise in his head would stop he could think of one. Never mind, something would come up, it always did, he told himself. The panic in his gut told him that was a lie. He wanted to run away, away to some beach in France. He wanted to step off the path that was leading him to what he alone would have to face. It was something that he had run away from all his life. Why did his father's words keep ringing in his ears? Why could he not erase that image of his father's face from his mind's eye?

The time for introspection ended suddenly. Both men were dragged back to reality by the sound of musket fire and shouting close by. The horses twitched nervously and they leapt up to calm them. Tethering the beasts more securely they crept along the stream and up the wooded embankment to where they could peer out and see what was happening.

A wagon of injured troops, accompanied by some French infantry was under attack. In an instant it was clear that this was no counter-attack by the English. The French troops' assailants were an assorted mob, none in uniform, armed mostly with pikes. The outcome was obvious. The French, although disciplined and better armed, were massively outnumbered.

Within a few minutes it was over and to the relief of the hidden audience there was no massacre. It was more like the end of a rugby match when both teams shake hands. Clearly there was no malice here and, after disarming their opponents, the victors looked to help the injured men.

They drew back from their vantage points and Will asked, "What's going on, Sean?"

"It seems pretty obvious that our boys have turned on our friends from France. Good time to murder a senior officer," he grinned at Will. "You're a hero all over again and you didn't mean it."

Will didn't laugh. "This isn't your doing is it, Sean? This isn't another of your little schemes that you've forgotten to mention?"

Sean shook his head. "Not me, Will. It may just be a bunch of them acting independently and yet somehow I doubt it. There's too much going on. First the gang that hit Bapaume's men, now this lot, I reckon this has been orchestrated from Dublin. If that's the case we can both guess who's started this."

Will, think about it. Do you remember what you said to me back at Boroughbridge?" Sean glanced at Mary, who was listening to the conversation. "You said that the real problem with a French invasion was kicking the French out again. I can't lie to you; I didn't keep your thoughts to myself. I shared this with the staff at Boroughbridge and they would have passed it on."

Will stared at Sean unable to voice his thoughts.

"There no use for it, we need to find out. I'll talk to them." Sean rose to descend the bank and show himself.

Will rose to go with him.

"No, not you, Will. There's no point in us both going. You stay here and keep an eye on Mary. Besides," he smiled, "I've heard your Irish accent and I think it might be a bit easier for me to explain what's going on without you. Here, take my rifle and cover me, when I go down there."

Will and Mary watched Sean slip off his French uniform coat and creep down the bank to reveal himself to the men below. Muskets were pointed at him and soon lowered. They couldn't hear what he was saying. Whatever it was they could see that it was working. In no time they were all slapping Sean on the back and Will lowered the rifle. He didn't want to undo all Sean's good work by shooting someone in error. Sean looked up and beckoned them down.

"I've explained who we are and how we were forced into the French Army. I've told them how Bapaume used his position to try and kill you and how you heroically defeated him in a duel." Sean turned so that only Will and Mary could see him and pulled a face.

They both went along with his story and Will acted the hero, showing off his injuries to much appreciation. It was a passable excuse for being English.

"So which way are you heading?" enquired a bearded man, with a scythe.

"Dublin," Will responded immediately.

"And why would you be doing that?" continued the man, suspiciously.

Sean butted in quickly. "We were instructed by the Wexford Committee to go to Dublin for instructions."

It was a poor story and there were more questions, but Sean somehow pulled it off. Between the living and the dead, they found clothes to replace the French uniforms and six of them agreed to escort them to the outskirts of Dublin.

They left for Dublin in high spirits. It didn't last. Their new companions were in no hurry and found every excuse to stop. They wanted to stop early for the night at a pub on the road and were drunk within an hour. For once Sean was in no mood for drinking.

In the morning the good weather broke and it started to rain. The roads turned muddy and at every turn they encountered some part of the fallout of the counter-revolution. A skirmish between French and Irish was best avoided and a detour led to more mud and more delays. They ran into a rearguard action between a remnant of Lake's army and a band of Irish militia. Will was thrown from his horse, which bolted.

They spent the next night in the open. At least the rain relented and they managed to dry out by a fire. The escort produced whiskey from nowhere and were drunk again.

Will trusted none of them and caught a few words with Sean. "Do you trust them, Sean?" he whispered when he thought they were all sleeping. "Did The Fox send them? Do you think they are leading us into a trap? Are they helping us or keeping an eye on us?"

"Whoa, hold on, Will. I don't like them either. That doesn't make them spies or enemies. I think you might be a touch paranoid."

"Come on Sean," Will hissed, "no disrespect to you, it's just it was all a bit too easy, a bit too convenient, them offering to escort us."

"Alright, I get the point. Look, we're only a couple of hours from the city in the morning. It might be dangerous on our own, but if you really want to, we'll try and ditch them. They'll be in a hell of a state in the morning. We'll leave early and tell them to catch us up. All we have to do then is make sure that they don't. Are you up for it?"

Will agreed.

"In that case it's your turn to stay awake first, so that we don't oversleep in the morning!"

It worked. They barely stirred, as the three companions left. There seemed no point in rousing them at all to make excuses. Five minutes down the road and they kicked life into their mounts and made the best speed they could for an hour. They were not pursued. It brought short relief to them. In no time they were in the outskirts of the city and becoming ever more apprehensive.

Will wondered if they would even reach the centre. What kind of chaos would Dublin have descended into by now? Would there be mobs roaming the streets? Where were they heading in the city? Again the futility of it all wore him down, tired and hungry as he was.

Sean's mood was no better. He could only think of one thing; what would he do, when faced with The Fox. There was no ducking the issue now; the man would not harm him. Will and Mary were probably riding to their deaths, unless he did something. There just remained those two questions – what should he do and, if he reached that point of realisation, could he do the right thing?

Mary rode on in the early morning damp, watching the sun come up to warm their bones. Whatever they were riding towards, she would face it resolutely, beside the man she loved.

Clattering over cobbled streets, the city was wakening all around them. It was nothing that any of them had anticipated. There was an air of excitement and expectation about the place. Fears of violence and conflict, of looting and riots soon disappeared with the early morning mists. Dublin folk were emerging onto the streets, not to fight; they wanted to party.

Soon it became obvious why. They were greeted on every corner. Green flags and sprigs of every type of green vegetation were going on display. The English had gone. The French threat had receded. A new order was coming in to being. The world would be a better, fairer and more prosperous place. A man would have food on the table, a few coins left in his pocket for beer and he could speak his mind, as much as the drink would let him. Early as it was, some had started the drinking ahead of the speaking their minds.

It was difficult not to become caught up in the carnival atmosphere. They were given drinks, as they rode by. Some children ran up and placed sprigs of shamrock in their hands, as they leaned down from the saddle to speak to them.

From gossip and chat the centre of the celebrations and their ultimate destination became clear, Dublin Castle. The new interim *Irish* Government was to be announced and speeches made to the gathered throng outside the castle. All were convinced that a public holiday was to be called. The new government might just as well, since nobody was working anyway.

The crowds grew thicker and progress became slower. From their early start to avoid their companions the day was running away and they began to panic.

"Sean, we have to get a move on or we'll be too late," called Will over his shoulder as they pushed on through the joyous throng.

"Too late for what? We don't know exactly what is going to happen," responded Sean.

Will pulled a face. Sean knew as well as him that once a government was announced, it would be virtually impossible to change it. What sort of government anyway? If The Fox was behind it, there was no doubt what kind of regime would be set up. Would he involve the United Irish Committee members? How could he not do so, given the number of their supporters?

The panic was rising inside him, worsened by the frustration at their slow progress. He could feel the last vestiges of control slipping away. It was all going terribly wrong. He glanced around at Sean and could tell, despite his words, that he felt the same.

On the banks of the Liffey they abandoned their horses, which seemed to be swept away on the tide of revellers. Sean pulled his rifle from its saddle holder and used it to force a path across the footbridge, Will and Mary close on his heels. It was madness. Their hopes of even reaching the castle seemed to be sucked down into the morass of people.

By some miracle they floated into Castle Green. Sean and Will both looked at each other for direction.

"Which building?" they asked each other.

Sean knew the area like the back of his hand, so close as it was to Trinity College. His Dublin, alas, was two hundred years hence. Will knew it only from old illustrations in books. They opted for a central building and fought up the steps to the main door. They made no plans how to deal with the guards, placed to keep the crowds at bay and in a moment of blinding clarity, they realised that their old torn and bloodied clothes were hardly appropriate to gain entry.

"Have you come for the committee meeting?" enquired the guard.

"Er, yes that's right," replied Sean.

"That's fine. In you come. Not her mind. No women allowed."

"She's been invited specially by The Fox," responded Sean.

"That's fine then. In you go."

They could not believe their luck.

"We'll have to do something about security," whispered Will.

Sean did not seem to hear him. "Committee meeting?" he enquired of a man in a wig. The man indicated up, with his thumb. Sean marched forcefully forward towards the large marble staircase that led to a half landing and then back up to the first floor. There were people everywhere and none took any notice of the trio, who climbed the stairs.

At the top of the staircase large, ceiling high, double doors to the left and right offered them a choice. The doors to the right were ajar and voices could be heard from inside. Sean chose these and Will, holding Mary's hand, followed. Sean peered through the crack between the doors. Two men, finely dressed in britches, silk stockings, waistcoats and long coats disappeared through large double doors on the opposite side of the room. The room, with no furniture, appeared empty.

"Come on," beckoned Sean and pushed open the double doors, which gave way too easily.

The three entered the room. The doors closed behind them and eager hands seized them. Faced with at least a dozen men, struggling was useless. They were caught in The Fox's trap!

In moments they were relieved of their weapons and forced at gunpoint to sit on the floor. Will stared up at the end wall. Above a low wall about a foot high, a huge stained glass window dominated this side of the room. It portrayed traditional scenes of kings and angels and knights slaying dragons. The old regime personified, Will found himself thinking, in spite of his predicament. He was surprised that nobody had put a stone through it.

They sat in shocked silence for some moments, awaiting the grand entrance that they knew was inevitable. Finally the doors to the room beyond opened and the man entered. This time there was no grin of triumph.

"I want you out," was all he said to his men.

Shocked, they hesitated, uncomprehending faces turned to their leader.

"Give her to me," he pointed at Mary, who was pulled to her feet and bundled towards The Fox. He drew his Collier and pointed it at her head, as he seized her and pulled her close. "Who says modern stories don't have a happy ending?" he rasped, licking her ear, like the animal he was.

"I want those two split up. Here and there," he indicated different sides of the room and each position several yards from his own. "The rest of you get out. OUT!" he bellowed.

As his men hastened subserviently for the door, carrying Will's sword, the Colliers and Sean's rifle, The Fox snapped, " No, wait, not that one. Give that back to him."

The man holding Sean's rifle hovered, dull incomprehension clouding his eyes.

"Yes that, you idiot. Give the boy his gun back. He's got a job to do," ordered The Fox.

Confounded the man handed Sean's rifle back to him and followed his colleagues from the room.

In a trance Sean took the weapon and stood, the weapon at his side, like an automaton, whose motor had expired.

Paralysed too, Will watched these events unfold in slow motion, unable to move, incapable of thought. His legs had seized, his breath would not come, his brain was shutting down. He must think, before it was too late. It was too late. Something was so wrong. Way beyond their immediate crisis there was something. He should have foreseen this, should have anticipated it. But what?

With a huge effort Will forced his eyes to look at Sean's down turned face. Great spasms shook Will's tired frame. Sean, the man he had finally trusted, had betrayed him. He knew and yet there was something missing. He could not force his brain to work it out.

The Fox, glowing with self-satisfaction, drew Mary close to him, the pistol pressed against her rounded belly. "I think it's time that we all had a frank little chat, don't you? And you," he nodded to Sean, "had better listen carefully and do as your told, if you want to play a part in all this. You've meddled and played games and it's time to tow the line.

As for you," he pointed to Will, "I think you've outlived your usefulness and yet I might find something for you in my Ireland, if I think you can behave yourself," added The Fox, craftily giving him a glimmer of hope, enough to increase his uncertainty.

"You'll never get away with it," blurted out Will. "They'll send someone to sort you out. We were given a job to do."

"A job to do?" sneered The Fox. "Oh please, grow up. You two were just the clowns. You didn't really think that they'd leave this to you two fools. A couple of little jousts and you think you're heroes. You had no idea what you were doing.

Look at you both, all chums together. Will, how many times are you going to be fooled before you see him for what he is? He conned you right from the start.

The last vestige of doubt slipped from Will's mind, like a glass to the floor, and shattered.

"You neither of you wanted to come. We drugged you both," continued The Fox. "The only difference is that you, Will, had no idea. He did. He knew what they were doing and was quite happy to let them, while he was shagging that Canadian piece, behind your back."

The stab of pain that struck Will was too sharp to conceal from a man as astute as The Fox.

"Ha, I thought not. You had no idea." The Fox turned his vitriol on Sean. "As well as a pathetic liar and cheat, you're as naïve as he is. What did you say to your Dad? Oh don't worry father, I'll run off and do your bidding. Did you really think he'd trust a job like this to the likes of you? You're weak and self-indulgent. You always were."

The words rang round Will's head, deafening him till he was forced to put both hands to his ears.

Still The Fox would not relent. Finally he looked down at Mary. "You're just the interlude, the amusing five minutes, before we return to what's really important. And do you know what? I'm finally tired of you. You just bore me." He cocked the pistol.

"Sean, do something. For Christ's sake shoot him," screamed Will.

Sean hung his head, the rifle slipping through his hand, the stock thumping the floor.

"Will, what's happening? What's the matter with Sean?" Mary was trembling, a fear in her voice that Will had never heard before.

Will took a pace towards Sean and instantly The Fox pressed the barrel of his pistol back at Mary's temple. Will halted.

"Sean, don't lose your nerve now. If you don't help us now it's all over, the struggle, everything we've fought for, even our lives," pleaded Will. He knew he was wasting his breath.

Sean shook, sobbing. He looked up at Will, the tears rolling down his face. "I'm sorry, Will. I'm so sorry. I thought I could deal with this, but I can't. He knows. I, I can't do it." He let the rifle barrel slip to the floor with a clatter.

"Well what do you know?" crowed The Fox, his moment of glory arrived. "At last your mate's finally revealed his true colours and they ain't the ones you wanted to see are they, young Will?" The Fox moved the pistol from Mary's temple back to her belly. "Do you know what I'm going to do? I'm going to remove this abomination, before it comes back to haunt me in my old age. And there's nothing you can do about it. Do you know the really pathetic bit about it all? You've still no idea what this is all about do you, Will Peters?"

Will's mouth moved in silence.

The Fox pressed home his advantage. "For all your Oxford education and fancy book learning, you've no idea what's going on here, do you?" he sneered. "There's just one more tinsy, tiny detail that your old mate Sean has omitted to mention. He's not going to shoot me, not now, not later, not ever, are you Sean? Or shall we call you little Mick? We always used to. You good as murdered one brother, didn't you Mick? You sure as hell, couldn't face all that again could you?"

At last The Fox paused. Will, helpless, waited for him to pronounce sentence.

"Wake up Will, he'll not be shooting me; I'm his brother."

Chapter 33

South Armagh
Long ago in the future

Little Mickey knew it was his fault. He couldn't run fast enough. He was too breathless to call out a warning. He had seen the man with the gun, but thought it was part of the game. He should have called out and then Patrick would have thrown the bomb at him and killed him and they would have won and gone home and everyone would have been proud of them.

It was his fault that he didn't run for help.

"Look at him he's just standing there. You'd have thought he would have bent down to see if his brother was still breathing." He'd heard them say it, when they finally came to tell him that Jesus had taken his brother away. Mickey didn't understand. He hadn't moved and he hadn't seen Jesus come. No man in an old blood stained cloak and a beard had been anywhere near them.

The sun was setting when they came, the police and his aunt and uncle.

"Who did it Mickey? Did you see them?"

All he could say was 'a man with a gun.'

"It'll be the fuckin' UDA - murderin' bastards – they call us the terrorists – he's just a kid but they know the family – we're all targets in this war."

"What's the matter with him? He must have stood like that for hours."

"It's shock poor love. Come here Mickey," his aunt said and held him to her bosom.

He couldn't cry, not for days.

His uncle was appalled at his lack of tears. "Why doesn't he cry? Didn't he love his brother?"

It was nothing compared to the nightmare that awaited him back home in Portadown. His brothers and sisters stared sullenly. Their silence cut him to his soul. He wanted to scream. He dared not show himself up. This was not about him.

His father could not speak to him. His mother held him so tight that it hurt his neck and shoulders. She was punishing him.

He was banished.

Then when he did cry he couldn't stop.

"Not much point in crying now, Mickey me lad. It's too bloody late for all that," admonished his father.

Everyone was angry. It was his fault. They must be angry with him.

Seamus took him out to the back yard a few days later. "How could you let it happen? It's a pity they didn't get you, instead."

He deserved it. He deserved to be sent away. He deserved to be sent to France, where they just thought he was odd and he could hide behind the language, pretending not to understand, even when he eventually could.

"Heh Mickey. Mickey boy," crooned Seamus. "Listen to me now. Just do as I tell you."

Sean listened hard. Did someone say something? There it was again. It was something he could barely remember, barely hear. He struggled to catch the words. His mother and father were arguing. He could only hear a few snatches, through his bedroom door. They were shouting. Why couldn't they stop shouting and let him go to sleep? He was hiding under the bedcovers and he heard his Mother again. She was shrieking. "Enough is enough. Let it stop with you. Don't drag him into it. God knows it's too late with the older ones, but leave Mickey out. Let him find his own way."

That's what he wanted. He wanted to find his own way. He wanted them to leave him alone to do his own thing.

Oh and that smell! Why did it keep coming back? Don't let it come! Sean peered at his brother through his tears. Which brother? He didn't know. He could still smell the moist grass and the late summer flowers. That was a nice smell. He could hear the skylarks overhead. He could see his beloved brother. It was Patrick, with the sticky red marks on his chest and in the corner of his mouth. No not that; please not that again.

"Come on Mickey, pick up the rifle and shoot that Englishman. You know, the one that hurt Patrick," Seamus whispered.

Then it was there.

He shuddered and shook. That terrible smell filled his nostrils, the smell of petrol. And there was something else. He didn't want to see it again. He always saw it, when he woke in the night, shaking and frightening some poor girl from his bed. His brother's hair was burning.

"Let it stop here," he heard his mother beg.

Sean looked up at Will. "I am so sorry I brought you to this."

He picked up the rifle, cocked it and pointed the weapon at Will.

"Forgive me mother. Now I am truly banished."

Dublin Castle
May 13th 1797

In a dream Sean picked up his precious rifle. Swinging the weapon to bear on his brother Seamus, Sean pulled the trigger.

Chapter 34

Dublin Castle
May 13th 1797

In the confined space of the room the noise of the rifle shot was deafening. Sean, dropping the weapon, held his ears and stared at Seamus.

A great dark red patch appeared on his shirt. It reminded Sean of fruit juice.

Mary screamed and threw herself to the floor, released from Seamus' grasp. Seamus lowered the cock on the pistol and stood for a moment gazing in incredulity at his brother. As he slid to the floor his weapon fell from his hand and spun away across the hard surface, coming to rest beneath the huge stained glass window.

"Well I'll be damned. I never thought you'd have the balls to do it, little brother. The boy, Mickey becomes the man, Sean. I'm impressed. Good on yer." He coughed blood and winced in pain. "Oh, all the saints preserve us, it's getting dark. Are you still there, Sean? Come and sit with me."

Sean moved, in a trance across the room to sit beside his older brother. "Seamus, I'm sorry. I had to do it. I couldn't let you, well you know just…"

"Sean, Sean, Sean don't spoil it all now by saying you're sorry." He coughed again, more blood spilling down his chin and onto his chest. "You're meant to say, 'I deserved it and you're on the side of good and all that.' It's up to you now what happens. Mind, you'll have to explain to our father what you've done.

Christ it's getting bloody dark in here! Heh Sean, do one last thing for your brother; take me over to the window nearer the light."

Sean turned and pushed his arm behind Seamus to hoist him up to a standing position.

"Whoa, go easy it hurts," groaned Seamus, as the two men staggered over to the large window. "That'll do. Put me down here. Gently now and step back a bit I need ter breathe."

Riven with grief and guilt Sean was eager to please his dying brother. He left him sitting against the low wall, with his back to the stained glass.

As Sean backed away Seamus let his arm drop casually to one side and slipped his hand around the pistol, where it had come to rest. He slid the weapon behind his leg, hidden from the view of the others and sighed. "That's better. I know I'm going to meet the Good Lord soon. There's just one thing we need to sort out before I go. Come here you three."

Warily Sean and Will, his arm firmly around Mary's waist, approached the dying man.

Seamus sat up suddenly and pulled up his left sleeve. "Look!" His eyes glinted.

"I told you," whispered Mary. "He's got one just like yours and Sean's."

"Not quite bitch," snarled Seamus. "Does yours do this boys?" With a loud click he twisted the bracelet, which instantly lit up, casting a blue glow over his demented face.

Will and Sean gasped in amazement.

"Yes lads," crowed Seamus. "What a conundrum! One working bracelet and two of you. Will you kill each other for it?"

It was difficult to tell if Seamus laughed or coughed at their incredulous faces.

"I'm tempted to take the trip myself. Sadly I think it would kill me. So that just leaves one thing to do before I die."

His breath was coming in short gasps and he seemed to be gathering what little strength he had remaining. "I just want…" He forced himself quickly to a kneeling position, as he raised and cocked the pistol, "…to shoot that traitorous bitch!"

Sean did not follow what happened next. Seamus aimed the Collier. Will gave a scream and leapt past him to seize Seamus' gun arm. Both men pitched backwards through the stained glass window.

The stained glass images of men in gowns and ermine, the images of the old ordered disintegrated in a mighty explosion of glass and light.

Will and Seamus fell. Lights flashed, the sounds of ancient battles were all around them. They fell and fell and disappeared from sight.

END OF PART FOUR

PART FIVE

Once I lay on that sod, it lies over Wolf Tone,
And thought how he perished in prison alone,
His friends unavenged, and his country unfreed,
Oh, bitter, say I, is the patriot's mead.

For in him the heart of a woman combined
With a heroic fate and a governing mind,
A martyr for Ireland, his grave has no stone,
His name seldom mentioned, his virtues unknown.

Extract from Bodenstown Churchyard by Thomas Davis

Chapter 35

Oxford, University College
Thursday June 19th 2003

Will lay in his bed in that state which is part way between sleeping and waking.

He played it all through in his mind for the thousandth time. It was like some fantastic dream. He had felt so alive. All the things he had yearned for were his; a beautiful woman, who loved him, excitement and action, a chance to meet the historical characters he admired and a real purpose to his life. He had tilted at giants and won.

It had to have been real. He would never forget the look on Seamus O'Grady's face as he, the man he'd feared as The Fox, clung to Will and they fell through time. Will had seized the hand with the gun in it with both his own hands, until it fell from them both. Somehow he had seized the bracelet. Had he managed to twist it? All he knew was that it came away in his hands.

Now, as they fell, the struggle changed. No longer Will clinging to Seamus. Seamus clung to Will – for his life. Will tried to shake his adversary off, whilst Seamus hung on, as if to a life raft through space and time. Will was mesmerised with the dial on Seamus' bracelet, which wound back through time.

Will escaped from Seamus grip some time around 1888. He watched him fall into a great city. It looked like the London he had seen on his first 'journey.' It smelt like it. And the year; he was sure of it. 1888, the year of 'The Ripper!' It would explain how that demon had suddenly started his grisly crimes and equally suddenly stopped. Will shuddered. It was all too easy to imagine a deranged Seamus, bitter, his victory snatched away just at the moment of glory. What atrocities was he capable of committing?

It could not be. Such thoughts were the road to madness. Despite the bracelet still on his wrist, Will was convinced that he was mad. Forget the psychiatrists' diagnoses, he could no longer differentiate reality from fantasy. Had he dreamt it? If he hadn't dreamt it, how in hell's name could he go back? If he had dreamt it, he was mad to even ask that question. If this was reality…this was no good, going over it time and time again. He had to escape this damn room.

Escape? Out there people laughed at him. To make it all worse, the world to which he had returned was subtly different. Things he 'knew' were changed. History had changed. His knowledge was flawed. He never knew when he would make some foolish blunder and prompt mirth and scorn from colleagues and acquaintances.

He could not lie there any longer.

Will hauled himself out of bed, dragged on yesterdays clothes, seized his wallet and headed down the corridors of University College towards the main gate by the Porter's Lodge. He glanced towards the mailroom. Don't go in there, he muttered, too loud. A couple of undergraduates gave him knowing looks. 'Mad Will', they're saying, thought Will. He forced himself to walk out of the main gate and onto High Street.

Standing on the pavement, looking at the traffic, he fiddled nervously for the millionth time with the damned metal bracelet on his wrist. It was a fake and still he couldn't bring himself to cut it off. Oh the bracelet, it must have been true, he murmured.

A cyclist rode against the traffic causing other cyclists to shout and jeer. Something stirred in Will's brain. The coffee shop was still there, the one he'd taken Inge into all that time ago. Or was it yesterday. Will didn't know. He remembered the boy on the bicycle. The boy on the bike! In his mind's eye he could see him just like it had been yesterday. He looked like… Will turned cold with the sudden realisation…he looked like Owen!

The street swayed and the spires of Oxford spun around his head.

The boy, who fell off his bike, the wallet he threw, the photo of the church with the date on the back, what was it? Suddenly it came back, June 20th 2003. He tried to make the world stop spinning. Dear God, that was tomorrow! Will steadied himself against a lamppost.

"Are you alright mate?" enquired a concerned passer by.

Will waved his hand to show that he was. He wasn't.

Sudden exhilaration at this revelation was just as suddenly replaced by fear, panic. Tomorrow was significant, vital and there was no time to find out why. "Think, Will, think!" he muttered. The clue was that church. "Right come on boy, do something," he said and did not care who heard. "Got to find it and now!"

All other thoughts forgotten Will crossed the road and headed for the Bodleian Library. It might be easier to use old technology and search their vast collection of books. So many places to look, he started to run and only just checked his pace, so as not to cause dismay at the security barriers, entering the vast old library. They had him marked as an odd one as it was. Now was not the time to be barred. He smiled at the security guards. Without a bag to search they let him pass unhindered. Will headed for the section, where he knew they had a collection of books on ecclesiastical buildings.

He scanned the shelves; 'Cathedrals of England,' no too grand, 'English Parish Churches,' much more likely. After an hour, he had found nothing, even after bribing a young female undergraduate to let him look at the book she was using. He headed down to the workstations, where he could research online; no stations free. He could have screamed. He paced up and down impatiently and attracted the attention of a librarian. He had fallen foul of her as well and left, before she had him evicted.

Without knowing how, he ended up in an old pub, just a few hundred yards from the Bodleian. A pint in his hand he could feel the anger and frustration welling up inside him. "Damn it, how fucking hard can it be to find a bloody church?" he blurted out.

An elderly man looked up from his newspaper, gave Will a withering stare, finished his drink and walked out. As he left he tossed his paper down in disgust onto the wet bar top. Will glanced across, as the beer soaked slowly into it and turned the sheet a sombre grey. 'Gerry Adams to give the memorial lecture at Bodenstown,' it said. Will shuddered. The day of the lecture was tomorrow.

"Bodenstown, oh my God!" he exclaimed aloud. "How could I have been so bloody stupid? The burial place of Wolf Tone, I was sure I'd seen it before. It can't be coincidence."

Snatching up the beer soaked paper, Will left the remains of his pint on the bar and ran to the Bodleian. A workstation was free and in an instant he had images on the screen of Bodenstown church and cemetery. It was the same as the photo! Will could hardly control his fingers on the keys, as he tried to print it.

He paid his fee to the librarian for the print and laughed. It had to be this. It had to be right. He must go to Bodenstown.

Back at the computer he searched for flights. Birmingham to Dublin, leaving 9 a.m. His heart pounding, he waited for what seemed an age until the screen confirmed that there was a seat. He booked. It would be cutting it fine to arrive for the afternoon lecture, yet it was possible. In an instant he decided to go to Birmingham that night and not risk missing the flight. Before leaving he booked a car from Dublin airport. How long will you want it? The screen asked. Will could not answer. How long? What am I hoping to do? He asked himself. He could not answer that either. A little flicker of doubt entered his mind. "Two days," he replied.

Those doubts returned later that night as he tried to sleep in the chain motel at the airport. The wait was intolerable. Perhaps he should have driven to the ferry. He would be half way there by now. The people in the next room were noisy, laughing, lovemaking.

At 2 a.m. he was convinced. It was ridiculous. What *did* he expect to find? He was just indulging his fantasies.

At 4 a.m. he rose, showered, dressed and headed for the terminal. He must not miss that flight. Never mind, once through security, it would be plain sailing.

The flight was delayed, grounded at its previous destination. Then it was cancelled. Did he want to take the bus to East Midlands and connect with a later flight? Or would he go via Glasgow?

He landed in Dublin just before 1 p.m. There was still time, if everything ran smoothly. It was only a few miles to the exit for the N7.

The traffic on the Dublin ring road was static. Local radio told him about the accident. At 3.30 p.m., just short of his exit, Will switched off the engine and beat his head on the steering wheel.

When the road finally opened up and Will was approaching Bodenstown, he noticed the weight of traffic in the opposite direction. They were leaving. He was too late. He was calm now. It was fate. It was meant to be.

Will parked the car. He walked slowly into the graveyard. To match his mood a soft, gentle rain started to fall. Will sheltered under a tree from the drops falling slowly from the sky. He looked at the ruined side of the church, the graves, the flowerbeds. The boy's photo; it must have been taken from exactly this spot.

Glancing around he noticed a burial in progress. Family gathered around the grave, the priest was saying a few words. He closed his prayer book and the party of mourners began to disperse. Comforting arms slipped around distraught shoulders. I wonder who has died? Will aimlessly asked himself.

A young redheaded boy, about twelve years old, dressed in a dark suit, remained by the graveside as the others drifted away towards the car park. Watching the familiar form from his sheltered position under the trees, Will felt his mouth go dry. Bent over the grave, the boy was shaking, as if sobbing with grief. He turned and looked up. Will could see he was not crying. He was laughing!

Will froze. It was Owen. No, that was ridiculous. The boy took a few steps towards Will and beckoned him. The warmth and affection in the child's eyes filled Will with emotion. He tried to run, but his legs did not respond.

"Come on Will," the boy encouraged him. The voice left him with no doubts. It *was* Owen.

Will's legs stumbled and his breath came short as he ran towards the young lad. The boy smiled and suddenly, as Will was just a few metres short of embracing the child he had thought dead, Owen turned, took two or three strides, jumped into the grave and disappeared.

There was a crunch of gravel and he looked up to see some passers by nodding sympathetically at him. It deepened Will's despair further. They clearly thought that he was mourning the departure of a loved one. Had they known the truth, they would probably be disgusted or, at the very least, have him locked up. He stayed on his knees, letting the damp from the soil creep through his trousers and listening to the soft patter of rain on leaves. He wanted to roll into the grave and be buried with this stranger below him.

Will gazed into the grave. Six feet down the freshly varnished wood caused the rain to form into droplets. Gradually the handfuls of dirt, thrown by the mourners were forming muddy slurry, which was beginning to obscure the brass nameplate on the coffin.

Will Peters R.I.P.
1979 – 1850

Suddenly there was no damp at his knees, no sounds of rain or mourners. Will stared. He shook his head and wiped the tears and rain from his eyes. The inscription had not changed, but as the mud spread, it was becoming more difficult to read. The little crack in time was closing fast. Will threw himself forwards into the grave and fell.

Chapter 36

Location - undetermined
1900

Lights flashed passed him and he roared with fear, pleasure and relief. Noise, wars, horses, people; it was all a blur at first and then it cleared. He was lying on the floor of a lift and it was silent except for the faint whirring of machinery. Surprised and unsure, Will stood up. The lift was of the cage type, ornate, probably 1930's, art deco. It was moving very fast between floors, which whizzed past in a blur, unseen. He was descending.

The old fashioned metal dial above the door caught his attention. Instead of floors it was marked with dates. At one end was 2003. At the other was 1797. For a moment Will stared, mesmerised as the dial steadily wound down. Passing through the 1920's it slowed and at 1900, halfway on its journey through time, it halted.

The doors opened.

Will looked out on an empty corridor. A time worn red carpet led into the darkness, closed doors on either side gave no clue as to his whereabouts. Just visible at the far end was another door, slightly ajar. As Will's eyes became accustomed to the gloom, he fancied he could see a light flickering from within the room beyond. Cautiously Will left the lift and tiptoed along the carpet, acutely aware of the unknown menace from the side doors and fearful that the lift might depart leaving him stranded in 1900.

As he reached the end of the corridor, he could see that a soft light emanated from the room. There was a fire and maybe a gas lamp burning inside. Slowly Will reached for the handle to ease the door open further and reveal the secrets beyond. A familiar voice called out and startled him.

"Come in, Will. You've nothing to fear."

Will pushed the door wide and looked in. Eyes now adjusted to the low light, he could see a Victorian study. Two gas lamps hung above a coal fire, which had died to a glow. Rows of leather bound books filled shelves on every wall, except one, where dark velvet drapes concealed a door or window beyond. Two high winged leather chairs, their backs to Will, stood, one either side of the fire. An elbow on the arm of one revealed it to be occupied by the owner of the voice.

"Take a seat, Will." A hand indicated the chair opposite.

It had to be Owen, thought Will, even if the voice sounded odd. Cautiously he peered around the back of the chair, as he backed into the seat offered. He froze.

"I know, I know. I look a little older now. It's not how you remember me. Time does that to a man," smiled Owen. He leaned forward and added, "Believe me, I've had a lot of time, one way and another."

"It, it is you, isn't it Owen?" Will asked self-consciously. He knew it was a stupid question and yet he had to be sure.

"**Of course it is.** Make yourself comfortable, I'm sure you've a lot of questions and I'll do my best to answer them. Mind, you might not understand the answers. Here, let me pour you a drink." Owen turned to a crystal decanter, sitting with two glasses on a silver tray on the table beside him. "You'll enjoy this, vintage port, a hundred years old, or I think it is. Even I get a bit confused these days. Never mind, it's excellent." He handed Will the glass.

In a dream, Will sipped the deep red liquid. "Where are we?"

"That's a good question and really difficult to explain. Let me see. We're in a time corridor. It's like a road through time. The trouble is that they don't stay open for ever, but they're always there." Owen looked at Will, who was staring into his glass, mouth partly open. "Alright, let me try again. Can you imagine a road that is only passable at low tide? If you try to cross it at high tide it has simply disappeared under the sea. Why can't you cross it at midday every day?"

Will made no response.

"Will, why can't you cross a road like that at the same time every day?" Owen shook Will's arm.

"Uh, oh, um, because the tide is at a different time every day, I suppose."

"Precisely, but if you look at your tide tables, you know exactly when it will be open, don't you? So it's the same with these time tunnels, only a wee bit more complicated. Just the same we know where they are and can predict when they open and for how long. You have to be careful that you get through them, before the tide comes in, so to speak. Is that clear?"

Will nodded. "Who's 'we'? You said 'we know where they are'. Who are you Owen? What are you?"

"Don't look so worried, Will, I won't turn into a two-headed monster. We're basically the same as you. We just evolved a bit more and we don't have the same emotions as you do. All that loving and hating, murder and mayhem, I don't know how you cope with it." Owen laughed at Will. "Come on, get that drink down you and snap out of it. I know this is a bit much to handle. This tunnel will not stay open forever and you will have questions and you have a big decision to make shortly. So what's the next question?"

Will downed the port in one and tried to kick-start his brain. He was not mad. He had not dreamt about Owen and Mary and all of it. Or maybe he was mad and this was a particularly bad fit, he was having.

"You died. I saw you. How did you survive? I cried over you. Why did you do that?"

"I am sorry. I didn't intend it quite like that. I had to leave and there was no time for explanations.

Will's addled brain tried to grasp this.

"Yes, yes, how did they make us travel through time, at Boroughbridge? That did all happen, didn't it? And why did the bracelet only work at the end, in Dublin Castle?"

"Boroughbridge? Those fools! It happened alright, Will, but not like you thought. Those clowns knew nothing. The bracelets were never more than a prop, I'm afraid. Your so-called experts couldn't have timed an egg without my help."

"But I was there and I travelled in time, and so did Sean, and what about The Fox, you know, Seamus?"

"Will, this is difficult, so listen carefully. Boroughbridge was a good location, like the grave you just used. I'm not even going to bother with why. Just take my word for it. That is all. Their activities attracted our attention and I was sent to see what they were doing. We were worried. There was no need. A few folk had had psychotic experiences and that was it. They did not have a clue and I was about to leave, when a pattern of time tunnels appeared and I couldn't resist it. I thought I'd see what you all did with it."

"You mean all that stuff about the drugs and the lectures and everything was rubbish?"

"Afraid so. They believed in it. They really thought they'd cracked it, if that helps."

"So what really happened and what was all that stuff in Oxford with the bike? That was you wasn't it?"

"It was me Will. I set up this little escape plan for you, if you were smart enough to find it and if you had grown confident enough in yourself to believe it. You were and you had. Before you ask, I knew what would happen, because I had been there and travelled back." Owen noted the expression on Will's face. "Never mind all that. Do you want me to try and explain how the time travel works?"

"Yes, well no, just hold on a minute." Will, still confounded by all this new information, was relieved at first to discover that he was not mad, nor had he dreamt it. Suddenly these emotions were overtaken by anger and resentment. "Are you telling me that you set all this up for your amusement? What the hell gives you the right, whoever or whatever you are, to manipulate people or to decide who lives and dies? You lied and deceived me. You're as bad as Sean and all the rest. Who do you think you are?"

Owen smiled, unphased at Will's outburst. "I wondered when we'd get around to that. Let's just take a look at it then. Did I make you sleep with that Suki girl or chase after the German blonde? Did I make you go to Boroughbridge or make you become infatuated with the Canadian girl? There's a bit of a pattern here, don't you think. I reckon you have a bit of a problem with the ladies, Will. Or you did until you met Mary. I do claim some responsibility for that. I put you in the right place at the right time."

Will opened his mouth to interrupt and caught Owen's stern look.

"Whoa, I haven't finished yet, young Will," continued Owen. "Before you start accusing me, who decided to end the life of de Guilbert or start the life of Mary's child? Let's look at Mary for a moment. She loves you without question and chooses to have your child. Have you been honest with her so that she can make the right decisions? I don't think so. Finally there is the little matter of manipulating history and deciding the fate of entire countries. Any of this ring true, Will?"

"Well yes," acknowledged Will, "but I couldn't have done that, if you hadn't done what you did."

"I placed you in that situation. You didn't need to do anything, Will. Everything came from your own actions and decisions." Owen folded his arms and considered. "I'll tell you what I am going to do, Will Peters. I am going to give you a chance to choose. I intended to let you decide between the past and your old future, but I can drop you a little ahead of your old future." He scratched his head and leaned forward. "You can go back to Ireland in 1797, just three days after you left it or you can go back Oxford, the day before you met Suki. You choose, but I warn you, if it's Oxford you choose and you don't change your actions on that first day back, you will lose your free will. You'll find yourself on the same path unable to step off. The only difference will be that I won't be there in Bantry to meet you.

You decide, 1797 or 2003 and a chance to change your life if you make the latter choice. Is that restoring enough freewill for you?"

"I don't know. That's not fair," hesitated Will.

"Not fair! No, you're probably right. I'd say it was more than fair and more chances than most men have in three lifetimes. While you ponder that one, let me explain a little bit about how it all works."

Owen rose and walked over to a desk. Opening a drawer, he pulled out a pad of paper and a pencil. "Nothing like a bit of old technology," he laughed. He drew a circle with a large dot in the middle, adding lines from the centre to the edges. "Imagine a bicycle wheel. This point," he made a cross on the rim, "is your present day, when I saw you that first time in Oxford. Are you with me so far?"

"Yeh."

"Right, this is you travelling back to 1797," he moved his pencil down one of the spokes to the hub of his wheel. He laughed again. "That was the only thing that they got right at Boroughbridge. Once you stop at this point," he tapped the hub, "that's it. You can't go back any further. Let's face it, it would be a nonsense wouldn't it, if you could."

Will nodded in agreement, but he had no idea why that would be more impossible than travelling in time at all.

Owen looked at him. "If you went further along this line," his pencil move from the hub to the rim, on the opposite side from where he had started, "you'd end up back in the present, but right over here on the other side. That would be the same time but in an opposing dimension." He could see that Will was not following his explanation

"Look Will, you went back to Oxford to what was your present, but was it the same?"

Will shook his head. "It was mostly the same except some stuff was different. Bits of history had changed. Some of the people were different. I thought I was going mad. I didn't know what I could be sure of and what I couldn't."

"Exactly. This is what happened to you. You came down one spoke from the rim and then, because of the changes you made to *your history*, you came back up one next to it." He made a cross on the rim of the wheel a few millimetres from the first cross. "You see, back in the present, just a different place. You were lucky, if you'd gone over the opposite side, it would have been totally different. You'd never have coped with that. Most men turn into lunatics. Da Vinci was the only one I know, who survived."

Will started. "Wait a minute, how did I come back at all, if the bracelets didn't work? Why didn't they work before?"

"I did it. I saved you. If I'm honest, it was only luck that I spotted you and I only just did it. I didn't want to move you at all and if there hadn't been a tunnel handy, well…I couldn't let you die."

"What happened to The Fox, I mean Seamus? Did he die?"

"Not there and then. It happened later, not much later. What else do you want to know?"

Will brushed his hand through his hair. "There's so much and I don't know where to start. This is stupid. Am I going to see you again?"

"I don't know, Will. I do not have as much control over these things as you may think. So don't go jumping off buildings again, I might not be there."

"Are you saying that I can I go back?"

"Back where, Will? When do you want to be? You have to decide."

"I don't know. The twenty first century is where I belong; TV, hot showers, cars, rock and roll."

Owen eyed Will. "Sure?"

Will shook his head. "Not really. I belong and yet there's nothing there for me. I was something back in Ireland. It was weird. I didn't care if I lived or died in Oxford. In Ireland I had every reason to live, yet I would have died for, for, well for those people and…" he blushed, "…for Mary. If I do go back to her, will it really be, you know, just the way it was?"

Owen smiled. "Is that what you want? Are you sure?"

"I don't know. It's all so confusing."

Owen rose and walked to the window. He drew back the curtain. Outside there was only darkness and then Will noticed a strange blue light.

"I hate to say this. Time is running out. You are going to have to make up your mind. Heh, look on the bright side, Will, you're in good company. Few people in history have had this privilege, Newton, Napoleon…"

"Napoleon! You're kidding me! Aren't you?"

Owen shook his head. "No time for that tale now, Will. This tunnel will be gone soon. That's fine for me. Not for you. It's time to decide. Back to your Oxford, before Suki's death or back to the Ireland you helped create, to Sean and to Mary? You decide, but you must do it now. Look." Owen pointed to the corridor through the door, where Will had entered. It was becoming foggy. "It's breaking up. Go now. Go. Go."

With surprising agility, Owen leapt up and pulled Will to his feet.

"Owen, there's so much I need to know."

"Another time, Will."

"I'll see you again?"

"We'll see. We'll see. NOW GO."

Owen propelled Will out of the room and into the corridor. "RUN, WILL!"

The lift was lost in a thick fog that consumed the corridor. Will ran into oblivion. The floor seemed to be crumbling beneath him, as he threw himself through the open doors of the lift. The doors shut behind him and everything was secure again. Will collapsed on the floor and sighed with relief.

He looked at the dial, frozen on 1900. There were two buttons from which to choose. Up or down? 2003 or 1797? Oxford or Ireland? TV or Mary?

The fog started to creep under the lift doors.

He pictured himself sitting outside her cottage, with their children playing at their feet, an idyllic scene in a new peaceful Ireland, which they had helped create.

Will hit the down button.

END OF PART FIVE

EPILOGUE

Oh, croppies ye'd better be quiet and still,
Ye shan't have your liberty, do what ye will;
As long as salt water is formed in the deep
A foot on the neck of the croppies we'll keep.
And drink, as in bumpers past troubles we drown,
A health to the lads that made croppies lie down.
Down, down, croppies lie down.

Extract from Croppies, Lie Down! (Traditional Irish Song)

London, Whitehall
December 1798

A storm had blown into Bantry Bay from the Atlantic. The first of the winter, it was the worst in living memory. An anguished westerly wailed and thrashed and forced angry water into the beautiful bay. It seemed the bay's sides would split and its islands be sucked back into the black ocean. The cliffs moaned in despair as the planet tried to rearrange itself and restore the natural order.

The Gods were displeased.

In London the weather was little better. Sir Edmund Pettigrew ducked in from the windswept street and shook the rain from his cloak. He was too old for all this. It was late, he was tired and his rheumatism was sending stabbing pains through his knees and lower back.

The War Office building was almost in darkness so late was the hour. An orderly took his cloak and silently indicated the staircase to the upper rooms. Pettigrew groaned inwardly at the thought of all those stairs. He climbed the carpeted stairway slowly and thought back on his career. He had been happy to take retirement after a long life of service to his master Lord Appleby. How easy to disappear into the shadows created on the fringes of that shining light, which was William Pitt. Then Ireland had fallen and Pitt with it.

Henry Addington had been asked to form a new administration. Your country needs you again, he was told, but he couldn't really believe that England would collapse without the help of a seventy-two year-old man. Nonetheless he would do his duty, as long as the Good Lord spared him. His thoughts were interrupted by the need to present his credentials to the guard at the ornately decorated door at the top of the stairs. His identity confirmed for the fifth time that week by the same guard, he knocked and entered.

Even with the heavy full-length curtains drawn, Pettigrew could sense the storm outside. The crystal chandelier was not in use. Only three candles burnt, two on the large mahogany table in the centre of the room and one fluttered on the War Minister's desk. A fire was glowing low in the grate. Pettigrew ran his hand over the smooth surface of the table as he approached the desk. A hint of polish remained on his wizened fingers.

"Damned infernal weather," chimed the Minister, without looking up. He was even older than his aide, bent over with arthritis and plagued with gout. "At least it will keep the French tucked up in harbour. I've been obliged to withdraw the Mediterranean Fleet to home waters to pacify the fools that think they will try an invasion. Poor bastards, out in this lot."

Pettigrew assumed that the 'poor bastards, out in this lot' were the sailors of the fleet and not those, who were expecting an invasion. "Yes, my Lord."

"I had hoped to go down to the country and spend Christmas with Beatrice. Not in this weather. Besides, they won't let me leave here."

"Of course not, my Lord."

"I want you to find him and bring him here. Get a message to him. It is essential that we make our plans now, in readiness for the Spring and I want the best. For me, he is the best."

Pettigrew decided to sit uninvited, before his knees gave way completely. He withdrew a notebook and a pencil from his leather satchel, which dripped rainwater onto the Minister's worn silk carpet. He had no idea what his master was talking about, but what did it matter? His supper was ruined and he had nobody to go home to. It was warm and dry in the office and he was resting his knees.

"And what about Moore? Is he recovered from his fever? Not Yellow Jack, I trust? Where is he? I want them *both* here!" His Majesty's Minster for War, Lord Appleby finally looked up from his papers and caught the bemused look on Pettigrew's face. "The Duke of York wants his brevet rank of Brigadier General reinstated. *I* want a naval man, who can work with him, bring land and sea forces together. Nelson! They proved that they could work together in Corsica! That was a sideshow. Now I've a real job for them!"

Pettigrew quietly recalled that Nelson had lost an eye during this 'sideshow'. He was about to caution the Minister. Instead he quietly made a note and tried to refocus his tired eyes on his master's face.

"Don't look so bemused. I want them here to make plans for the Spring invasion."

Pettigrew's mouth opened but no sound came out. Eventually he managed to stammer, "You, you're planning to invade France?"

"Good God, no man! Do you think I've lost my wits? Ireland you fool, Ireland!"

The Shan Bhean Bhoct

Oh the French are on the sea, says the Shan Bhean Bhoct,
Oh the French are on the sea, says the Shan Bhean Bhoct,
Oh the French are on the bay, they'll be here without delay,
And the orange will decay, says the Shan Bhean Bhoct.
Oh the French are on the bay, they'll be here without delay,
And the orange will decay, says the Shan Bhean Bhoct.

And where will they have their camp, says the Shan Bhean
Bhoct,
And where will they have their camp, says the Shan
Bhean Bhoct,
On the Curragh of Kildare, and the boys will all be there
With their pikes in good repair, says the Shan Bhean Bhoct.
On the Curragh of Kildare, and the boys will all be there
With their pikes in good repair, says the Shan Bhean Bhoct.

And what colours will they wear, says the Shan Bhean
Bhoct,
And what colours will they wear, says the Shan Bhean
Bhoct,
Oh, what colours will be seen, where their fathers' homes
have been
But their own immortal green, says the Shan Bhean Bhoct.
Oh, what colours will be seen, where their fathers' homes
have been
But their own immortal green, says the Shan Bhean Bhoct.

And what will the yeomen do, says the Shan Bhean Boct,
And what will the yeomen do, says the Shan Bhean Boct,
Oh, what will the yeomen do, but throw off the red and blue
And swear that they'll be true to the Shan Bhean Bhoct.
Oh, what will the yeomen do, but throw off the red and blue
And swear that they'll be true to the Shan Bhean Bhoct.

Oh, will Ireland then be free, says the Shan Bhean Bhoct,
Oh, will Ireland then be free, says the Shan Bhean
Bhoct,
Yes! Then Ireland will be free, from the centre to the sea,
So hurrah! For Liberty, says the Shan Bhean Bhoct.
Yes! Then Ireland will be free, from the centre to the sea,
So hurrah! For Liberty, says the Shan Bhean Bhoct.

'The Shan Bhean Bhoct' (The Poor Old Woman – Ireland)
Traditional Song, 1798

23168759R00280

Printed in Poland
by Amazon Fulfillment
Poland Sp. z o.o., Wrocław